知識工場
Knowledge is everything！

知識工場
Knowledge is everything！

100% 隨手貼+替換句

隨書附贈
E-mail 範本 + 替換句
資料光碟

英文E-mail
萬用貼大全

張翔 / 編著

Copy & Paste! Let's Write A
Perfect E-mail in English.

E-mail 上手，用「貼」的就行！

E-mail 1分鐘
速成必殺技

E-MAIL
簡單複製
輕鬆貼

4 大特點

化繁為簡，立即破除E-mail恐懼症！

1 核心破解E-mail 概念

3 絕對簡單的速成密技

2 究極精選 5 大實用主題

4 實力躍進的全方位補充

隨手貼 ＋ 替換句，英文 E-mail，一分鐘就搞定！

Point

1 E-mail 架構一次就通

於第一章破解 **E-mail 基本架構**，除了介紹 E-mail 各欄位的重點之外，還另外提供例子，幫助讀者迅速跨越編寫 E-mail 時會遇到的初期關卡。

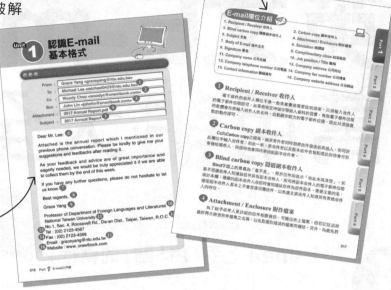

Point

2 實用主題的究極精選

首度融合**日常生活＆商務交易**兩大範疇，並依使用情境分成 5 大章，不管是提升人際關係的信函、還是商務往來的公事交流，這一本都能解決。

Point

3 內文框架一貼到位

選定主題，善用 **Ctrl ＋ c（複製）** 和 **Ctrl ＋ v（貼上）**，幾秒鐘就貼出一篇 E-mail，提升效率的超捷徑就從這裡開始！

Point 4 重點單字一目了然

於 E-mail 範本下方補充**核心字彙充電站**，列出範本內的重點單字，就算只是複製＋貼上，也要同步提升單字力。

Point 5 替換句打造百變 E-mail

範本下面補充**替換好用句**，供讀者依需求自行替換，就算發信的主題相近，也要讓你的 E-mail 封封充滿新意。

Point 6 全方位實力無死角

每篇最後的**進階補充站**分為三種類型：**單字／片語 Focus**、**文法／句型 Focus**、以及**實用資訊 Focus**，視學習需求補充，全面提升英語力。

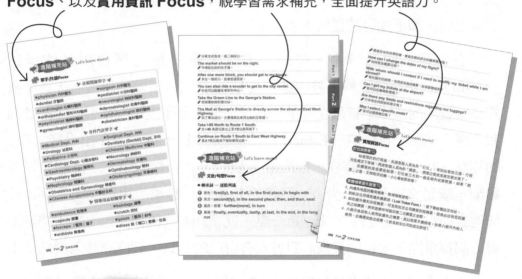

Point 7 不藏私的超值資料片

隨書附贈包含 **E-mail 範本**及**替換好用句**的資料片，內文以 word 檔呈現，好用易編輯，隨手就能貼。

E-mail 交流，
一鍵就能輕鬆上手！

在華人學習英語的過程中，英文作文多半不是被強調的對象。大多數老師們在教學時，所採用的方式也大同小異。面對平常較著重於單字、片語背誦的學生，會在行文間鼓勵他們交錯使用較為困難的詞彙；若是單字、片語較弱的學生，就先講求文章的流暢度。長久下來，這種不怎麼強調「寫」的教學法，會產生一個問題，「明明平常不覺得寫很困難，但真的需要時，卻不知道該從何下手。」

在「寫」的範疇中，有一項現代人幾乎每天都會用到的型態—E-mail。出乎我意料之外的是，在 E-mail 吃足苦頭的學習者，竟比我想像中要來的多！不管是在校生、亦或是出社會好幾年的學習者，都曾向我反應「老師，我很怕寫 E-mail。」本質上，E-mail 跳脫不出「寫文章」的範疇，但卻帶有其特性，E-mail 重視的，並非你的單字、片語用得多艱澀，或是文字量有多少，一篇好的 E-mail，必須「用精簡的文字，確切地表達自己的意思」，光是這一點，就讓許多人困擾不已，寫太詳細怕對方漏掉重點，太精簡又擔心對方誤會自己的語氣，到底應該怎麼寫？！

因為有不少學生與讀者向我反應這個困擾，所以，我才有了編寫本書的想法。寫中文時，有起承轉合的說法，英文 E-mail 其實也有類似的架構，分為開頭（Introduction）、內文（Development）、以及結尾（Conclusion）三大部分，掌握了基本架構，剩下的就是將文字填入而已。

　　理論上是這樣沒錯，但對多數人而言，最大的困難就在「將文字填入」這點上，為了一封短短的信而困擾了好幾十分鐘的人不在少數，因此，在編寫本書時，我採用了「複製 & 貼上」的這個想法，希望能幫助讀者在幾個步驟內，輕鬆貼出一封文詞達意的 E-mail。除此之外，為了因應每位學習者不同的需求，因此衍生出「替換好用句」的想法，讀者可依不同情境，去替換範本裡面的句子，這種設計是為了幫助大家活用，而不僅是死板地複製同樣的說法。

　　於編寫本書的期間，我也產生了另外一個想法。雖然複製 & 貼上的內容足以成為學習者的龐大資料庫，但一直以來投身於教育事業的我，還是希望能更進一步地幫助學習者，想讓讀者在「速效性」之外，更紮實地提升自己的英語實力。因此有了「進階補充站」的構想，分為單字 / 片語 Focus、文法 / 句型 Focus、以及實用資訊 Focus 三大類，每篇 E-mail 都會視需求作補充，也希望各位讀者在使用資料庫之餘，持續充實自我，相信這樣所得到的收穫會更大。

　　在編寫初期，我也參考了許多學習者的意見，因為坊間工具書多半注重「商務 E-mail」的寫法，忽略日常生活的信函，但其實學生在這一範疇的需求並不亞於公司的商務來往，所以，我也花了一點時間，挑選出日常生活 & 商務交易最常用到的主題，力求完整、實用，也希望這樣的一本書，能解決讀者編寫 E-mail 時的困擾，減低對 E-mail 的恐懼感；也期盼各位在熟悉了英文 E-mail 的結構後，自己完成一封獨一無二的信函。

張翔

目錄 Contents

Part 1 E-mail 入門篇
～書寫前的必備基礎

Part 2 日常生活篇
～人際往來這樣貼

Unit 1 關於人際交往

目錄
Contents

Part 3 校園求學篇
～必備對話這樣貼

Unit 1 入學申請事宜

Unit 2 住宿事宜詢問

Unit **3** 銀行業務相關

Part **4** 商場求職篇
～脫穎而出這樣貼

Unit **1** 徵才與求職

目錄
Contents

Unit 2 產品詢問與回覆

Unit 3 報價與議價

目錄
Contents

Part 6 工作職場篇

～提升表現這樣貼

Unit 1 公司內部通知

目錄
Contents

Unit 2 公司對外的通知函

Unit 3 祝賀函與邀請函

Part 1

入門篇～書寫前的必備基礎

Unit 1 認識 E-mail 基本格式

Unit 2 表達到位的書寫妙招

動 動詞	名 名詞
副 副詞	形 形容詞
介 介系詞	片 片語

Point

　　工欲善其事，必先利其器。寫 E-mail 之前，當然必須先了解 E-mail 的架構。各個欄位代表的是什麼，填寫欄位時又有哪些注意事項，掌握關鍵，讓你從一開始就事半功倍。

From :	Grace Yang <graceyang@ntu.edu.tw>
To :	Michael Lee <michael0423@ntu.edu.tw> 1
Cc :	Woody Chou <woodyc@onextbook.com> 2
Bcc :	John Lin <johnlin@onextbook.com> 3
Attachment :	2017 Annual Report.pdf 4
Subject :	2017 Annual Report 5

Dear Mr. Lee: 6

Attached is the annual report which I mentioned in our previous phone conversation. Please be kindly to give me your suggestions and feedbacks after reading it.

As your feedback and advice are of great importance and eagerly needed, we would be truly appreciated it if we are able to collect them by the end of this week.

If you have any further questions, please do not hesitate to let us know. 7

Best regards, 8

Grace Yang 9

Professor of Department of Foreign Languages and Literatures 10
National Taiwan University 11
No.1, Sec. 4, Roosevelt Rd., Da-an Dist., Taipei, Taiwan, R.O.C. 12
13 Tel : (02) 2123-4567
14 Fax : (02) 2123-4568
Email : graceyang@ntu.edu.tw 15
16 Website : www. onextbook.com

Part 1

Part 2

Part 3

Part 4

Part 5

Part 6

E-mail欄位介紹

1. Recipient / Receiver 收件人
2. Carbon copy 副本收件人
3. Blind carbon copy 隱匿副本收件人
4. Attachment / Enclosure 附件檔案
5. Subject 主旨
6. Salutation 稱謂語
7. Body of E-mail 信件主文
8. Complimentary close 結尾敬語
9. Signature 署名
10. Job position / Title 職稱
11. Company name 公司名稱
12. Company address 公司地址
13. Company telephone number 公司電話
14. Company fax number 公司傳真
15. Contact information 聯絡資料
16. Company website address 公司網站

❶ Recipient / Receiver 收件人

電子郵件的收件人欄位不像一般商業書信需要註明頭銜，只須輸入收件人的電子郵件信箱即可。如果你有定時儲存聯絡人資料的習慣，有些電子郵件信箱的軟體會在你輸入收件人姓名時，自動顯示對方的電子郵件信箱，因此只須做選取的動作即可。

❷ Carbon copy 副本收件人

Cc為Carbon copy之縮寫。如果寄件者同時想將信件發送給其他人，則可於此欄位中輸入收件者；如此一來，原收件者以及副本收件者皆知道此封信會分別寄發給哪些人，回信時也會同時寄回給副本收件者。

❸ Blind carbon copy 隱匿副本收件人

Blind字面上的意義為「看不見」，用於信件則表示「地址未寫清楚」。如果不想讓收件人知道該信件另有副本收件人，則可將副本收件人的電子郵件信箱填於本欄；隱藏的副本收件人收信時會知道該信件為密件副本。需要注意的是，隱匿副本收件人基本上不會直接回覆信件，以免讓主要收件人知道另有其他收件人的存在。

❹ Attachment / Enclosure 附件檔案

為了給予收件人更詳細的信件相關資訊，可隨信附上檔案。但切記送出前最好再次檢查附件檔案之名稱，以免點選到錯誤的檔案而傳送。另外，為避免對

方電腦中毒，最好先替檔案做病毒掃描。如果收到的信件中有附加檔案，也建議下載前先進行病毒掃描，以減低網路傳送或讀取檔案時對電腦造成的損害。

⑤ Subject 主旨

信件主旨是為了幫助收件人對於信件內容一目了然而落的標題，功能如同作文題目和報紙頭條。試想，若收件人每天必須處理上百封電子郵件，信件主旨就必須提綱挈領、簡明扼要，以節省收件人的處理時間。

✎ 商務類主旨書寫範例

❶ Price List 價目表

❷ Making An Appointment 安排會議

❸ Request for Catalogs 目錄索取

❹ Agenda for The Meeting 會議的議程

❺ Costumer Mailing List 顧客郵件地址清單

❻ Conflict of Interest 利益衝突

❼ Sales Policy 銷售政策

❽ Medical Leave 醫療休假

❾ Vacation Request 休假請求

❿ London International Business Show 倫敦商展

✎ 生活類主旨書寫範例

❶ Re: Lunch on Friday 回覆：週五的午餐約會（主旨欄中時常出現的Re：為 reply，即回覆的意思；而 FW：則為 forward，表示轉寄之意。）

❷ Can we meet this Saturday? 是否可於週六會面？

❸ Thank you for your email 感謝您的來信

❹ Thanks for your hospitality 謝謝您的款待

❺ We will arrive at Taiwan on Sep. 9th 我們將於九月九日抵達台灣

❻ Hope you feel better now 希望您的身體已康復

❼ Employment Notification 工作錄取通知

8 Letter of Recommendation 推薦函
9 Sales Manager Position 業務經理求職信
10 The Xmas Party 聖誕派對

6 Salutation 稱謂語

　　稱謂語通常位於信件主文的開頭，用來稱呼收件者。稱謂語後可不接標點符號，或是接冒號（：）或逗號（，），如：Dear Mr. Lee, / Dear Mr. Lee: / Dear Mr. Lee。

✑ 稱謂語書寫範例

1 **Dear Sir or Madam,** 親愛的先生及女士，指稱公司全體。
2 **Dear Sir,** 親愛的先生，不知道男士的姓名時使用。
3 **Dear Madam,** 親愛的女士，不知道女士的姓名時使用。
4 **Dear Mr. Chou,** 親愛的周先生，指稱已婚／未婚男士。
5 **Dear Ms. Chou,** 親愛的周女士，指稱已婚／未婚女士。
6 **Dear Mrs. Chou,** 親愛的周夫人，指稱已婚女士。
7 **Dear Miss Chou,** 親愛的周小姐，指稱未婚小姐。
8 **Dear Peggy,** 親愛的佩姬，指稱熟識的朋友。
9 **Dear Product Managers,** 親愛的產品經理，指稱對象不只一人。
10 **Ladies and Gentlemen,** 敬啟者，不確定指稱之對象及其性別。
11 **To Whom It May Concern,** 敬啟者，不確定指稱之對象。

7 Body of E-mail 信件主文（將於 Unit 2 詳細介紹）

8 Complimentary close 結尾敬語

　　撰寫英文E-mail時，通常會在信件的結尾留下問候語或祝福語，以表示禮貌。結尾後可接逗號（，）或不接，如：Yours sincerely, / Yours sincerely。

✍ 正式的結尾敬語

指稱Dear Sir or Madam, Dear Managers, Ladies and Gentlemen, 以及To Whom It May Concern, 等信件時，可於結尾敬語使用：

1. Very truly yours,   2. Truly yours,
3. Yours truly,   4. Very sincerely yours,
5. Sincerely yours,   6. Yours sincerely,
7. Faithfully yours,   8. Yours faithfully,
9. Respectfully,   10. Respectfully yours,
11. Yours respectfully,   12. Very respectfully,

✍ 一般性結尾敬語

指稱Dear Mr. Chou, Dear Ms. Chou, Dear Mrs. Chou, 以及Dear Miss Chou, 等信件時，可使用：

1. Sincerely yours,   2. Sincerely,
3. Cordially yours,   4. Cordially,
5. Regards,   6. Best regards,
7. Kind regards,   8. Best wishes,

✍ 熟識性結尾敬語

指稱熟識朋友如Dear Peggy, 等信件時，可使用：

1. Best regards,   2. Best wishes,
3. Take care!   4. All the best!
5. Continuous success!   6. Be good!
7. Love,   8. With love,
9. Cheers,   10. Good luck!
11. Your devoted friend,   12. Warmest regards,

13. As always!   14. Ciao! / Bye for now!
15. Have a nice / good / wonderful day!

⑨ ~ ⑯ Signature 簽名檔

　　簽名檔用以標示撰寫該信件之撰信者，分為正式署名及簡易署名。正式署名涵蓋寄件人的完整資訊（請參閱第16頁之E-mail架構範例）；然而，並不是每一封英文E-mail都必須包含完整的署名資訊，因為收件者已經可以從信件中得知您的E-mail，過多的資訊反而顯得累贅，因此，可使用簡易署名的方式：

Grace Yang → **Signature** 署名
Professor of Department of Foreign Languages → **Job title** 職稱
National Taiwan University → **Company name** 公司名稱

Grace Yang → **Signature** 署名
No.1, Sec. 4, Roosevelt Rd., Da-an Dist.
Taipei, Taiwan, R.O.C. → **Company address** 公司地址
Tel：(02) 2123-4567 → **Company telephone number** 公司電話
Fax：(02) 2123-4568 → **Company fax number** 公司傳真

Grace Yang → **Signature** 署名
Email：graceyang@ntu.edu.tw → **Contact information** 聯絡資訊

Grace Yang → **Signature** 署名

Part 1
Part 2
Part 3
Part 4
Part 5
Part 6

Unit 2 表達到位的書寫妙招

　　英文E-mail的主文（Body of E-mail）是信件的主體，所有欲讓收件者知曉的訊息，都會包含在主體內容中。英文E-mail寫作的普遍原則如下：

1 一段落一主題。如需提及另一主題，最好能夠另起一段。

2 每個段落的主題皆應緊扣信件主旨。

3 簡潔、明瞭為最高指導原則。冗長、繁瑣的文章會使溝通失去效率，浪費收信者以及撰信者彼此的時間。

4 撰寫句子時，避免用同一個單字表達不同的意思。

5 多使用語氣肯定的字彙，避免使用如seem, probably, maybe等含有不確定意味之詞彙。

6 避免文章句型過於單調，可使用長短句交叉、主被動式結合的行文方式。如同中文寫作一般，英文E-mail的撰寫也適用起承轉合的原則；然而英文寫作較常使用的架構為所謂的「三大段落」：Introduction（介紹）、Development（發展）、以及Conclusion（結論）。首先介紹 Introduction開頭語的部分：

1 寫信給對方常用的開頭句型（To begin a message）

1 **We are writing to enquire about...** 我們來信詢問有關…的事情。

2 **We are writing in connection with...** 我們來信是與…有關。

3 **We are interested in...** 我們對…感興趣。

4 **And we would like to know...** 而且，我們想要知道…。

替換好用句 Copy & Paste

We are writing to enquire about the price of your refrigerators.
✎ 我們來信詢問冰箱的價格。

We are writing in connection with your advertisement in the

newspaper yesterday.
🖋 我們寫信來是為了你們昨天在報上刊登的廣告。

We are writing to enquire if you are able to send us the latest catalog.
🖋 我們來信詢問您是否能寄最新的目錄給我們。

② 常用的回覆句型（To reply a message）

🖊 回覆對方的詢問

1 **Thank you for your email (of date) asking...** 謝謝您來信詢問…。

2 **Thank you for your fax enquiring about...** 謝謝您的傳真，詢問…。

3 **I have received your email...** 我收到您的電子郵件…。

替換好用句 Copy & Paste

Thank you for your email asking if we would be interested in the new product.
🖋 感謝您來信詢問我們是否對新產品感興趣。

I received your email today and I hastened to write to thank you for it.
🖋 我今天收到了您的電子信件，趕緊寫信向您致謝。

I was so happy that you got in touch with me again.
🖋 很高興您再度與我聯繫。

As I read your email, I am happy to know that you are doing well.
🖋 在讀你寄來的電子郵件時，我很高興得知你過得很好。

I was so surprised to hear from you after such a long time.
🖋 我很驚訝過了這麼久還能收到你的來信。

It is so delightful to received your letter!
🖋 收到你的來信真令人感到愉快！

It is good to hear from you.
🖋 收到你的信真好。

I am glad to hear of your good news.
🖋 很高興聽到你的好消息。

Thank you for your email / reply.
🖊 謝謝你的來信／回覆。

Many thanks for your kind letter.
🖊 非常感謝你貼心的來信。

🖊 回覆熟悉的對象（於開頭加上簡單的問候）

1 How have you been doing recently? 最近過得如何？

2 How are things going? 近來可好？

3 How are you feeling today? 今天覺得如何？

4 Are you doing well? 你過得好嗎？

5 How is the weather there? 那裡的天氣如何？

6 Greetings from Taipei! 我從台北向你問候喔！

🖊 回覆對方問候的句型

1 I am same as usual. 我和往常一樣。

2 Nothing special. / Nothing new. 沒什麼特別的。

3 Things are going well for me. 一切都很好。

4 Busy as always, I guess! 和往常一樣忙碌囉！

③ 常用的結尾句型（To end a message）

1 I look forward to... 期盼⋯。

2 I hope that... 希望⋯。

3 Please contact me if you... 如果你⋯，請與我連絡。

4 Please let me know if you... 如果你⋯，請告知我。

5 Thank you for... 感謝您的⋯。

替換好用句 *Copy & Paste*

I look forward to hearing from you.
✍ 期盼收到您的來信。

I look forward to receiving your reply soon.
✍ 期盼儘快收到您的回信。

I look forward to receiving your order.
✍ 期盼接到您的訂單。

I hope this information will be useful for you.
✍ 希望這份資訊對您有用。

Please contact me if you need any further information.
✍ 如果您需要更多資料，請與我連絡。

Please let me know if you have any problems.
✍ 若有任何問題，請告知我。

I will be in touch with you again.
✍ 我會再次與您聯繫。

We look forward to working together through the years.
✍ 我們期盼能與您長期合作。

Thank you again for your interest / enquiry.
✍ 再次感謝您的關注／詢問。

Thank you for your cooperation.
✍ 謝謝您的合作。

Drop me a line!
✍ 有空寫封信給我吧！

Hope to see you soon.
✍ 希望能儘早與您相見。

④ 日期書寫方式（The Date）

　　日期非常重要。我們買東西時，會注意它的品嚐期限；在學校，會注意教授規定的報告繳交日期；職場上，我們更會特別注意出貨或繳款日期。因此，日

Part 1

Part 2

Part 3

Part 4

Part 5

Part 6

期的正確性以及表示方法必須更加留意。

　　日期的表現方式，主要分為美式以及英式。英式英文中，日期（date）會寫在月份前面；而美式用法則是將月份（month）寫在前面、日期寫在後面。所以，12-06-2020，在英國表示2020年6月12日，在美國則表示2020年12月6日。

　　最好的書寫方式為以英文表示月份、數字表示日期，如此一來就很清楚：

> 12 June, 2020（英式寫法），或是 June 12, 2020（美式寫法）

常見的日期呈現方式：

1 We will send your order on Jun. 12, 2016.

2 We will send your order on June 12th, 2016.

3 We will send your order on Tuesday, Jun. 12, 2016.

4 We will send your order on the 12th of June, 2016.

5 We will send your order on June of 12, 2016.

5 縮寫式（Abbreviation）

　　縮寫式，例如Mr.表示Mister，BTW表示by the way。以下列出一些常用的縮寫式，但建議要在通信雙方都非常了解英語用法的狀態下使用。如果不確定對方是否了解縮寫法的運用，建議將全文打出，讓信件更具專業性，避免造成收件人的困擾。

月份

1. Jan. = January 一月
2. Feb. = February 二月
3. Mar. = March 三月
4. Apr. = April 四月
5. May = May 五月
6. Jun. = June 六月
7. Jul. = July 七月
8. Aug. = August 八月
9. Sep. = September 九月
10. Oct. = October 十月
11. Nov. = November 十一月
12. Dec. = December 十二月

✎ 星期

1. Mon. = Monday 星期一
2. Tue. = Tuesday 星期二
3. Wed. = Wednesday 星期三
4. Thu. = Thursday 星期四
5. Fri. = Friday 星期五
6. Sat. = Saturday 星期六
7. Sun. = Sunday 星期日

✎ 其他常見縮寫（記得每個字都要大寫）

1. 1CE = once 曾經；一度
2. 2DAY = today 今天
3. 2MOR = tomorrow 明天
4. 2NITE = tonight 今晚
5. EZ = easy 簡單
6. BE4 = before 之前
7. COZ = because 因為
8. CU = see you 再見
9. BFN = bye for now 再見
10. BCNU = be seeing you 再會
11. BTW = by the way 順便一提
12. BRB = be right back 馬上回來
13. F2F = face to face 面對面
14. OIC = oh, I see 我了解了
15. POV = point of view 觀點
16. PLS = please 請；拜託
17. OTP = on the phone 電話中
18. POC = piece of cake 小事一樁
19. CUL8er = see you later 等會兒見
20. ASAP = as soon as possible 儘快
21. OMG = oh, my God 我的天啊！
22. IOW = in other words 換言之
23. TTYL = talk to you later 晚點聊
24. THX / TKS / TNX = thanks 謝謝
25. OBO = our best offer 最優惠價格
26. HTH = hope this helps 希望有幫助
27. FYI = for your information 供您參考
28. FWIW = for what it's worth 不管值不值得
29. IMHO = in my humble opinion 依我之愚見

Part 1

Part 2

Part 3

Part 4

Part 5

Part 6

30. FAQ = frequently asked questions 常見問答集
31. OTOH = on the other hand 另一方面來說
32. ROTFL = rolling on the floor laughing 笑到在地上滾
33. LOL = laughing out loud 大聲笑出來／**loads of love** 大量的愛

⑥ 表情符號（Smiley）

　　編寫電子郵件不比直接面對面溝通，看不見對方的肢體語言或表情，因此，電子書信就發展出用線條讓人得知情緒反應的表情符號，最常見的例子如用 : -) 表示微笑。

📝 常見的表情符號

1 :) 或 : -) 或 (^_^) 微笑

2 : > 或 (^v^) 開心、愉快

3 ;) 或 ; -) 開心地眨眼

4 B-) 戴著眼鏡微笑

5 : D 或 :-D 開心大笑

6 :-o 表示「Oh, no-!」或訝異

7 :-(難過，不開心或生氣

8 :-P 表吐舌開心狀

9 :-# 保守秘密

10 (>0<) 糟糕！

11 (@ @) 或 (?_?) 疑惑、疑問

12 :-| 無任何反應的表情

13 (^^)// 鼓掌

14 :-@ 尖叫

15 -_- 瞇著眼看

16 (^_*) 眨眼

　　在非正式的英文E-mail中，用表情符號來表達情緒是允許的；然而，一般職場中的英文E-mail有一定的格式和須遵循的禮節，應儘量避免使用表情符號。另外要提醒的是，在電子郵件往來傳送的過程中，通信者無法面對面得知對方的表情、口氣與現場的情境狀態；因此，電子郵件的書寫方式及文字使用必須格外適當、得體。

Part 2
日常生活篇~人際往來這樣貼

Unit 1 關於人際交往
Unit 2 旅遊細節安排
Unit 3 交通問題詢問
Unit 4 醫療相關事宜

動 動詞　　名 名詞
副 副詞　　形 形容詞
介 介系詞　　片 片語

Point

日常生活常用的信件往來，往往是重要的第一步。E-mail 不比面對面的交談，全得靠文字表達，客氣地詢問、誠摯地感謝，這些說法其實都不難，翻開本章，立即通關交際表達。

·1-01· 邀約與回覆

Subject	**Want to See You Again!**

Dear Jane:

I hope it will not **appear**[1] **impertinent**[2] to write you this email after we've met on the **orientation**[3] day last Friday for the first time. The fact is, I would like to make a friend with you and want to know you better. May I ask you out for a date on Sunday evening, September 10th?

As you know, our school will hold a **gorgeous**[4] outdoor **concert**[5] on that day. I would like to bring a partner. As you are the only girl I'd like to go to the concert with, won't you kindly give a **nod**[6] to say yes?

I will wait for your reply and I hope we both can have a wonderful Sunday night.

Best wishes,
Neil Kuo

親愛的珍：

在新生訓練見過一次面後就寫電子郵件給你，希望不會讓你感到太唐突。因為我很想和你交朋友，也想多了解你。不知道九月十日（週日）那天晚上你方不方便出來見個面呢？

如你所知，當天學校會舉辦一場很棒的戶外音樂會，我想攜伴參加。因為你是我唯一想約去聽音樂會的女孩，所以能否請你發發慈悲，點頭答應呢？

我會等你的回覆，希望我倆都能有個美好的週日夜晚。

郭尼爾 敬上

Send ▶

Part 1

Part 2

Part 3

Part 4

Part 5

Part 6

Subject Re: Want to See You Again!

Dear Neil:

It is most **charming**[7] of you to write and ask me to be with you to the concert together. I am glad to **accept**[8] your **invitation**[9].

Please let me know when you are going to **pick me up**[10], and I shall be ready.

Best,
Jane Brown

Send

親愛的尼爾：

很高興收到你來信邀請我一同參加音樂會。我很樂意接受你的邀請。

請你告知何時會來接我，我會準備好等你。

珍·布朗 謹上

核心字彙充電站 *Key Words*

1. **appear [+ to]** 片 似乎
2. **impertinent** 形 不恰當的
3. **orientation** 名 新生導覽
4. **gorgeous** 形 極好的；豪華的
5. **concert** 名 音樂會
6. **nod** 名 點頭
7. **charming** 形 令人高興的
8. **accept** 動 接受；答應
9. **invitation** 名 邀請
10. **pick sb. up** 片 接某人

 *Copy & Paste*

 進一步邀約

I couldn't help but notice your beautiful eyes.
🖉 我無法不注意到你美麗的雙眼。

Do you think we could meet sometimes?
🖉 我們可以找個時間見面嗎？

As you know, our school is having its annual dinner dance on that day.

🖊 如你所知，學校當天將舉行年度舞會。

Each of the students attending the dance is bringing a partner.
🖊 每位到場的同學都會攜伴參加。

How about dinner and a movie?
🖊 要不要一起吃頓飯、看場電影呢？

I think we will hit it off. Will you go out with me tonight?
🖊 我覺得我們會很合得來，你願意今晚和我一起出去嗎？

I'm glad we met. Let's get to know each other better!
🖊 很高興能認識你，讓我們更認識彼此一些吧！

Would you like to grab a cup of coffee with me next Wednesday?
🖊 你下週三願意和我一起去喝咖啡嗎？

I would love to see you again.
🖊 我很想再見到你。

Will you consider going out with me?
🖊 你願意和我一起出去嗎？

I am so surprised that we have so much in common.
🖊 我很驚訝我們有這麼多的共通點。

Perhaps we could catch a movie next weekend.
🖊 或許下個週末我們可以去看場電影。

I've got one more ticket for the concert. Would you like to come with me?
🖊 我有多一張音樂會的票，你想和我一起去嗎？

I heard that the show has discounts for students. Let's go this weekend!
🖊 聽說那場表演學生買票有優待，我們這個週末一起去吧！

I really want to go watch "You Are The Apple Of My Eye". Do you want to come?
🖊 我很想去看《那些年，我們一起追的女孩》，你想一起去嗎？

I can't wait to meet you on Sunday.
🖊 我等不及要在這週日與你碰面。

I have feelings for you.
🖊 我對你有好感。

You are really my type.
🖉 你是我喜歡的類型。

 回覆對方的邀約

I really appreciate your email.
🖉 謝謝你的來信。

I am delighted to receive your letter.
🖉 我很開心能收到你的來信。

Thank you so much for your email. I'm sorry I didn't write to you sooner.
🖉 謝謝你的來信，很抱歉這麼晚才回信給你。

I haven't expected to receive an email from you.
🖉 我沒想到會收到你的來信。

It was very kind of you to write me a letter / an email.
🖉 謝謝你寫信給我。

Please forgive me for the delay in sending my reply to you.
🖉 請原諒我這麼晚才回信給你。

I have been thinking of writing to you, but I am sorry that I've missed a chance to do so.
🖉 我一直很想寫信給你，但很抱歉一直都沒有機會。

I have been quite busy with my exams, so it's been late to write to you.
🖉 最近忙著準備考試，所以這麼晚才寫信給你。

It is so exciting to receive an email from a sweet friend like you.
🖉 收到一封像你這樣貼心好友的來信真令人興奮。

I really appreciate our friendship.
🖉 我真的很珍惜我們的友誼。

I hope you will write me a letter soon.
🖉 希望你可以儘快寫信給我。

Part 1
Part 2
Part 3
Part 4
Part 5
Part 6

進階補充站 Let's learn more!

文法/句型Focus

✱ 接受告白

❶ **So, I think I like you, too.** 我想我也喜歡你。

❷ **Yeah, I'm kind of interested, too.** 其實我也對你有意思。

❸ **To be honest, I have feelings for you, too.** 老實說，我對你也有感覺。

✱ 迴避告白

❶ **So, why are you telling me this?** 為什麼要跟我說這個呢？

❷ **I don't know how to respond.** 我不知道怎麼回答你。

❸ **Could we talk about this next time?** 我們可以下次再聊這個話題嗎？

❹ **It's bad timing for me to talk about this.** 對我來說，現在不是談這個的好時機。

✱ 直接拒絕告白

❶ **Well, I already have a boyfriend / girlfriend.**
我已經有男 / 女朋友了。

❷ **I'm not really looking for a relationship right now.**
我現在沒打算交男 / 女朋友。

Part 1

Part 2

Part 3

Part 4

Part 5

Part 6

1-02 與友人談天

Subject Buy You Dinner

Dear Lulu:

I'm terribly sorry for not making it to your birthday party. My manager suddenly asked us to finish a project at work, and we ended up working till 11:00 p.m. Let's get together next week! I'd like to buy you dinner to make up for it.

Best,
Owen Lee

親愛的露露：

我很抱歉沒能趕上你的生日派對。我的經理突然要我們完成一份工作報告，結束的時候都已經晚上十一點了。下星期一起出去吧！作為補償，我想請你吃頓晚餐。

李歐文 敬上

Send

Subject FYI: What a Day!

Dear Jack:

What a day! I was planning to play soccer with some friends after work today. However, it started raining pretty hard, so we had to call it off. Instead, I went to the bookstore to pick up some magazines, and I met a nice woman named Rose Lee. She's an author, too! I'm planning to meet her tomorrow for dinner. I can't wait!

Love,
Carol White

親愛的傑克：

今天真是特別的一天！我原本計劃下班後和朋友一起去踢足球，但是後來下了一場好大的雨，只好打消念頭。之後我去書店買雜誌，遇到了一位叫李蘿絲的女士，她也是一位作家喔！我明天要和她共進晚餐，真令人期待不已！

卡蘿‧懷特 謹上

Send

Subject: House-Sitting

Dear Sam:

Thanks for house-sitting for me. Just remember to set the **security**[1] alarm when you go out **during the day**[2]. You'll find the **keypad**[3] next to the front door. Just punch in 3456, listen for the **beep**[4], and press the * key. Then you'll hear a series of fast beeps, which means you have thirty seconds to get out and lock the door. You can use the same code to get in when you come back. See you next Monday! Thanks a lot.

Best,
Paula Mann

Send

親愛的山姆：

謝謝你幫我看家。你要外出前，記得幫我設定安全警報器。你會在大門旁邊看到一個小型鍵盤，按下3456，聽到嗶嗶聲後，再按＊鍵。之後你會聽到一連串短暫的嗶嗶聲，代表你有三十秒可以離開並鎖上大門。回來的時候，用同一組密碼即可解除設定。下週一見，謝謝。

寶拉・曼恩 敬上

Subject: FYI: A Great Language Learning Site

Dear Grace:

I found this great website that offers a lot of English-learning resources: www.bbc.co.uk. Please take a look. I think you will like it.

Cheers,
Winnie Kao

Send

親愛的葛蕾絲：

我發現一個提供很多英文學習資源的網站：www.bbc.co.uk。參考看看吧，我相信你會喜歡。

高溫妮 敬上

Part 1

Part 2

Part 3

Part 4

Part 5

Part 6

核心字彙充電站 Key Words

1. security 名 安全
2. during the day 片 白天時
3. keypad 名 小型鍵盤
4. beep 名 嗶嗶聲

替換好用句 Copy & Paste

I found this great magazine that offers the plot summaries of some latest movies. Please take a look. You might like it.
🖋 我發現一本提供最新電影大綱的雜誌，請翻翻內容，你也許會喜歡。

Let's look at this website which offers some information you may need for traveling in Italy.
🖋 來看看這個網站吧！上面會提供在義大利旅行所需的資訊。

You have to read this book- X1 Paradise. It is interesting! It talks about certain places in Canada.
🖋 你一定要讀《X1天堂》這本書，很有趣！裡面介紹加拿大的某些地方。

How about the movie, Batman 3? It seems to be exciting and awesome.
🖋 看電影《蝙蝠俠3》怎麼樣？似乎很刺激又精彩。

Our teacher suggests us to buy this dictionary. It contains lots of English-learning resources and details of definitions and examples.
🖋 老師建議我們買這本字典，它介紹許多英文學習的資訊、單字解釋和例句。

We can both use some help with our stress, can't we?
🖋 我們可以一起解決我們的壓力問題，好嗎？

Here's the good news. I read this great article on BBC News on stress management.
🖋 有個好消息，我在BBC新聞上讀到一篇關於紓解壓力的好文章。

I have the article and left it on your desk. I hope you find it as useful as I did.
🖋 我留了這篇文章在你桌上，希望你跟我一樣覺得有幫助。

What about going for a drink to relax after the final exam? I found a good place.
🖋 期末考後放鬆一下，來喝一杯吧！我知道一個不錯的地點。

You are interested in some new food to keep in shape. I have some great recipes.

🖉 你對保持身材的新飲食有興趣對吧？我這裡有些不錯的食譜。

We can take a walk to improve our health, can't we? I found a great place to walk around.

🖉 散步可以讓我們更健康，不是嗎？我發現一個很棒的散步地點。

 進階補充站　Let's learn more!

 文法/句型Focus

✱ 朋友之間保持聯絡的結尾用語

❶ **Let's keep in touch!** 我們保持聯絡吧！

❷ **Please send me an email sometime.** 有空寄封電子郵件給我。

❸ **I'll give you a call sometime.** 我會再找時間打電話給你。

❹ **Let me know how you're doing once in a while.**
　偶爾讓我知道你的近況。

 實用資訊Focus

什麼是FYI？(What's FYI?) 🔍

　　For-your-information（FYI）信件，有時是轉寄文章或是附帶檔案，甚至也可能只是轉寄網址。一方面是為了提供資訊，二方面是想和對方分享趣事。若是一天寄上好幾封FYI信件，我們就得想想，收件者是否真的需要此信件？簡單明瞭又有趣的FYI信件，可以讓你和朋友保持友好關係，但過多的FYI信件也可能弄巧成拙，讓人感到不悅喔！

·1-03· 向人表達感謝

Subject Thanks for Your Congratulations

Dear Amelia:

Thank you very much for your warm greetings and the lovely flowers for my birthday, which was delivered this morning.

Please do come to see us together with your husband when you are in Taichung.

My husband asked me to give our best wishes to you and your family.

Best regards,
Julie

Send

親愛的艾美莉雅：

謝謝您給我的生日祝賀，還有今早送達的漂亮花束。

如果您來台中，請務必和您先生來拜訪我們。

外子要我向您與家人問好。

茱莉 敬上

Subject Thank You for Your Present

Dear Mr. Smith:

I wanted to write to you right away for the lovely painting you sent to my office. Everyone here **appreciate**[1] your **excellent**[2] taste in **selecting**[3] a picture which perfectly matches our office decor. You really **have a good eye for**[4] art.

We are so touched by your thoughtfulness. I hope you will have the opportunity to visit our office in the near future. We look

史密斯先生您好：

我想立即寫封信給您，感謝您送畫給我。辦公室裡的每個人看到畫，都覺得您很會選，那幅畫與我們公司的裝潢很搭，您對藝術真是獨具慧眼。

我們感謝您的貼心，希望您有機會拜訪我們。期待近日能夠在台灣見到您。

039

forward to seeing you soon in Taiwan.

Regards,
Richard

理查 敬上

Send

Subject Thanks for Help

Dear Helen:

I am writing this to express my **gratitude**[5] with all my heart.

Because of your suggestion and **support**[6], I have **established**[7] my own company successfully. I do not know how to thank you enough. You are my **benefactor**[8]!

With warm regards,
Polly

親愛的海倫：

寫此信是想表達對您真誠的感謝之意。

因為您的建議和支持，我成功創立了自己的公司。我不知道要怎麼感謝您才夠，您是我的恩人！

誠摯地祝福您。

波莉 敬上

Send

核心字彙充電站 *Key Words*

1. **appreciate** 動 感謝；感激
2. **excellent** 形 出色的；傑出的
3. **select** 動 挑選；選擇
4. **have a good eye for** 片 有…的眼光
5. **gratitude** 名 感激之情
6. **support** 名 支持；扶持
7. **establish** 動 建立；創辦
8. **benefactor** 名 恩人

 替換好用句 *Copy & Paste*

 感謝祝賀

Thank you so much for your warm wishes for my birthday.
🖊 謝謝您貼心地給我的生日祝賀。

Thank you for those good wishes.
🖊 謝謝您的美好祝福。

Thank you so much for your email congratulating me.
🖊 謝謝您的電子祝賀郵件。

Your email of congratulations gave us a great deal of pleasure.
🖊 您的電子祝賀郵件帶給我們莫大的歡樂。

Your email of congratulations is deeply appreciated.
🖊 感謝您的電子祝賀郵件。

Thank you for your congratulations and the lovely gift.
🖊 謝謝您的祝賀與可愛的禮物。

 感謝贈禮

I would like to thank you for the beautiful present you sent to us.
🖊 謝謝您寄給我們這麼漂亮的禮物。

I can never thank you enough for the thoughtful gift you sent to my son for his wedding.
🖊 真的很感激您送給我兒子的結婚禮物。

I cannot find the words to thank you for sending me such a wonderful gift.
🖊 送給我這麼好的禮物，不知如何言謝。

Thank you very much for the gift; it was just what I wanted!
🖊 謝謝您的禮物；這正是我想要的！

The present looks beautiful in my living room! It is a lovely reminder of the generosity of my friends and colleagues at Adidas Company.
🖊 禮物擺放在我的客廳裡看起來真棒！同時也讓我想起在愛迪達公司裡的朋友和同事們

有多麼貼心。

Your gift brightened my day.
🖊 您的禮物讓我開心了一整天。

Your thoughtfulness means a lot to me.
🖊 您的貼心對我而言意義重大。

It would be the most beautiful gift in the office.
🖊 這將會是辦公室裡最美的禮物。

Where did you find this present?
🖊 您是在哪裡找到這個禮物的呢？

I can't wait to show off the gift to my colleagues.
🖊 我等不及要拿禮物給同事看了。

I cannot find enough words to express my gratitude to you.
🖊 我找不出適當的言語來表達對您的感謝。

It was something that I have always wanted.
🖊 這是我夢寐以求的東西。

Thank you for thinking of me.
🖊 謝謝您想到我。

 感謝協助

I am writing this letter to thank you for your timely support during the time of crisis where I was helpless.
🖊 寫這封信是要感謝您在我無助時，及時幫了我的忙。

Please accept my sincere thanks for the trouble you have taken.
🖊 麻煩之處，請接受我誠摯的感謝。

Allow me to thank you for your kind help.
🖊 感謝您的盛情相助。

Also, this isn't the first time you helped me.
🖊 這已不是您第一次幫助我了。

You have always shown your compassion and care towards me.
🖊 您總是對我付出關懷。

I would not have noticed it if you didn't remind me.

✐ 如果您沒有提醒我，我不會注意到的。

Without your reminder, I would not solve the problem.
✐ 沒有您的提醒，我就無法解決此問題。

How can I repay you for such a great support?
✐ 我該怎麼報答您的支持呢？

I am grateful for all your help.
✐ 我很感激您的幫助。

I am so lucky to have such a good friend like you.
✐ 我很幸運擁有您這樣的好朋友。

Please accept my sincerest thanks.
✐ 請接受我最誠摯的感謝。

Without your assistance, I would not have finished it.
✐ 沒有您的協助，我就無法完成。

Thanks again for your assistance over the years.
✐ 再次感謝您這幾年的協助。

I appreciate your support and guidance, which was really needed.
✐ 感謝您給予我所需的支持以及指導。

 Let's learn more!

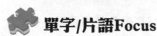 單字/片語Focus

❧ 表達感謝 ❧	
✱gratitude 感激之情	**✱affection** 情感；愛
✱appreciation 感謝；感激	**✱grateful** 感激的；感謝的
✱thank for sth. 感謝（某事）	**✱thank to sb.** 感謝（某人）

Part 1

Part 2

Part 3

Part 4

Part 5

Part 6

·1-04· 生日祝福

生日對於一個人來說，是一年中最特別的一天。給予生日的祝福或關心往往能增進彼此的關係，千萬別忽略了。若受邀參加生日宴會，卻不克前往參加時，也別忘了在委婉告知的同時，給予誠摯的祝福。

Subject | **Happy Birthday!**

Dear Charlotte:

I recall that your birthday is just **around the corner**[1]. I am sure you must have lots of plans for it – a big **rocking**[2] dances party or something. Did you know "growing old is **mandatory**[3], growing up is **optional**[4]"? I feel this holds true for you. Each time I meet you, I see a child somewhere in you always alive and full of life. I really need to learn so much from you.

I pray to God for a long, healthy and rocking life for you. May He shower all His grace on you and your family!

Enjoy yourself on your birthday and every day of the year, too.

Take care!

Love,
Polly

親愛的夏洛蒂：

我想起您的生日快到了，相信您一定有很多計畫，像是舉辦一場絕佳的舞會之類的。「變老是一定的，但是成長是可以選擇的。」我覺得這句話很適合您。每次見到您，您總是生氣勃勃、充滿活力，我需要向您學習。

希望上帝賜予您健康精彩的人生，希望祂保佑您與您的家人。

好好享受您的生日及往後的每一天。

保重！

愛您的波莉 敬上

Send ▶

核心字彙充電站 Key Words

1. **around the corner** 片 即將到來
2. **rocking** 形 (俚)極好的
3. **mandatory** 形 強制的
4. **optional** 形 非必需的

替換好用句 Copy & Paste

It is your 30th birthday.
✎ 您三十歲的生日到了。

Happy to congratulate you to your 30th birthday.
✎ 祝賀您三十歲生日。

I wish you happy birthday in quite advance.
✎ 讓我預先祝您生日快樂。

Hope this would be a special birthday for you!
✎ 希望您這次的生日特別不一樣！

May you enjoy good health and a long life!
✎ 祝您健康長壽！

I am really sorry to inform you that it will be highly impossible for me to attend your birthday party.
✎ 很抱歉，我無法參加您的生日宴會。

I cannot stretch my hand to shake with you.
✎ 我無法當面祝賀您。

I send this mail to offer you my heartiest congratulations.
✎ 在此寄一封電子郵件給您，並給予我衷心的祝福。

May your future be attended with prosperity and happiness!
✎ 希望您未來充滿成就和快樂！

Wish you have a great birthday and a year filled with happiness!
✎ 希望您有個很棒的生日，一整年都快樂！

I will soon come to meet you.
✎ 我近期會拜訪您。

Part 1
Part 2
Part 3
Part 4
Part 5
Part 6

1-05 新婚祝福

Subject Congratulations on The Marriage!

Dear Marvin:

I was really full of joy to hear of your decision. Last Sunday was your **engagement**[1] and you are going to **get married**[2] next month! I am giving my best wishes to you for both **occasions**[3].

I am feeling very happy that you and your fiancee are going to step in your new life. My best wishes are always with you. May God give you all the happiness in the world! However, I am really sorry to tell you that I cannot come for your wedding. I am going to Europe for an office meeting next month. It is such an important meeting that cannot be **avoided**[4]. I tried a lot to come, but it is not possible for me.

Still, my wishes are with you.

Best regards,
George

親愛的馬文：

很高興聽到您的決定。上週日您才訂婚，下個月就將步入禮堂了！我由衷地祝福這二件人生大事。

很開心您與未婚妻將要邁入人生的下個階段，我由衷祝福您，願主賜予您快樂！但很抱歉的是，我無法參加您的婚禮。我下個月必須到歐洲參加會議，而且是場極為重要、非去不可的會議。我試圖想參加您的婚禮，但實在是不克前往。

無論如何，您仍擁有我最衷心的祝福。

喬治 敬上

Send ▶

核心字彙充電站 *Key Words*

1. engagement 名 訂婚；婚約   **2. get married** 片 結婚

3. occasion 名 場合；重大活動   **4. avoid** 動 避開；避免

替換好用句 *Copy & Paste*

Hi! How have all of you been?
🖊 嗨！您們最近好嗎？

The news has made me truly happy for you.
🖊 知道此消息後，我真是為你感到開心。

Please accept my heartiest congratulations on the happiest event of your marriage.
🖊 請接受我對您的婚禮祝福。

Congratulations on your crystal wedding anniversary!
🖊 祝賀您十五周年結婚紀念日快樂！

Congratulations on your marriage!
🖊 恭喜你結婚！

What a great news!
🖊 真是令人高興的消息！

I am so happy that you have finally decided to settle down.
🖊 很高興你終於決定要安定下來了。

Please convey my heartiest congratulations to Rita and to your family as well.
🖊 請接受我對芮塔和您家人的誠心祝福。

Needless to say, you can always count on me for any help during the wedding time.
🖊 不用說，婚禮需要幫忙時，你隨時都可以找我。

Please accept my heartfelt congratulations.
🖊 請接受我衷心的祝福。

To the Bride and Groom, I wish you love and happiness!
🖊 祝新娘新郎永浴愛河！

Please accept my congratulations and my best wishes to you for a marriage filled with all good things in life.
🖊 請接受我的祝賀，祝您婚後事事如意。

You two have my earnest and warmest congratulations on this event.

Part 1

Part 2

Part 3

Part 4

Part 5

Part 6

🖊 獻上我對此盛事最衷心的祝福。

You two make a perfect couple.
🖊 你們是天生一對。

Good wishes for a long and happy life!
🖊 祝你們白頭偕老！

Best wishes for many years of happiness for you two.
🖊 祝百年好合。

Mr. Martin joins me in sending the kindest regards and best wishes to you all.
🖊 馬丁先生和我一起問候各位，並致以美好的祝福。

 Let's learn more!

 單字/片語Focus

❧ 常用的西方婚齡稱謂 ❧

✱**Paper wedding** 紙婚(1周年)	✱**Calico wedding** 棉布婚(2周年)
✱**Muslin wedding** 羊皮婚(3周年)	✱**Silk wedding** 絲婚(4周年)
✱**Wood wedding** 木婚(5周年)	✱**Tin wedding** 錫婚(10周年)
✱**Crystal wedding** 水晶婚(15周年)	✱**China wedding** 搪瓷婚(20周年)
✱**Silver wedding** 銀婚(25周年)	✱**Pearl wedding** 珍珠婚(30周年)
✱**Coral wedding** 珊瑚婚(35周年)	✱**Ruby wedding** 紅寶石婚(40周年)

✱**Sapphire wedding** 藍寶石婚(45周年)

✱**Golden wedding** 金婚(50周年)

✱**Emerald wedding** 翠玉婚(55周年)

✱**Diamond wedding** 鑽石婚(60～75周年)

Part 1

Part 2

Part 3

Part 4

Part 5

Part 6

·1-06· 邀請參加派對

Subject **Party Ideas**

Dear Peter:

As you know, we are **approaching**[1] the end of the **semester**[2], so it's time to think about the end of the year party. Please let me know if you have any **suggestions**[3].

Last year, we had a great **karaoke**[4] evening, but perhaps we could do something different this time. Please reply and give me your ideas.

Best,
Ian Trueman

親愛的彼得：

學期即將結束，是該好好規劃年末聚會了，如果你有什麼建議，請告訴我。

我們去年舉辦一場很棒的卡拉OK晚會，但今年讓我們來點不同的吧，請回信告訴我你的想法。

伊恩・楚門 謹上

Send

核心字彙充電站 *Key Words*

1. **approach** 動 接近；靠近
2. **semester** 名 學期
3. **suggestion** 名 建議；提議
4. **karaoke** 名 卡拉OK

替換好用句 *Copy & Paste*

We're going to have potluck party and barbecue this Sunday at Central Park.
🖊 我們週日將於中央公園舉辦餐會及烤肉活動。

All of your friends and families are invited to join us.
🖊 歡迎邀請您的朋友和家人一同共襄盛舉。

If you need a map, please send me an email.
🖊 如果各位需要地圖，請寄信到我的信箱。

Everyone is invited to bring something to eat at our potluck party tonight.
🖊 每個人都可以準備一道菜，來參加我們今晚的餐會。

Let's have a housewarming to celebrate moving into our new house!
🖊 慶祝新居落成，我們來舉辦新家派對吧！

Let's have a bachelor party for Tommy before his wedding!
🖊 讓我們在婚禮前為湯姆舉辦單身派對吧！

It will be the most exciting party this year.
🖊 這會是今年最令人興奮的派對。

I am just wondering how you would feel about joining our party this Friday night.
🖊 週五晚上來參加我們的派對，不知道你覺得如何？

Please come and see us. You will have a great time.
🖊 請來參加派對，你會玩得很開心。

Your presence is sincerely requested.
🖊 期待你的參與。

We look forward to having the pleasure of your company.
🖊 期待你的蒞臨。

We would be much obliged if you could honor us with your company.
🖊 若你能蒞臨，我們將感到非常榮幸。

I will extend my warmest hospitality to you.
🖊 我會給你最熱忱的款待。

You can bring whatever you want.
🖊 你可以帶任何你想帶的食物與會。

I will tell them the location, the date and the time.
🖊 我會告訴他們地點、日期和時間。

Let's gather around to celebrate our victory.
🖊 讓我們一起慶祝勝利。

Eat whatever you want.
🖊 美食隨你吃。

 進階補充站 Let's learn more!

 單字/片語Focus

各式派對名稱

* **farewell party** 歡送會
* **holiday party** 假期派對
* **Christmas party** 聖誕派對
* **Halloween party** 萬聖節派對
* **theme party** 主題派對
* **surprise party** 驚喜派對
* **welcome party** 歡迎會
* **luncheon party** 午餐會
* **cocktail party** 雞尾酒會
* **tea party** 茶會
* **year-end dinner party** 尾牙晚宴
* **baby shower** （即將出生的）新生兒派對
* **bachelor / bachelorette party** 單身派對

 文法/句型Focus

✽ 轉承詞 — 對比

❶ 但是：**but**

❷ 然而：**however, while, whereas, but, yet**

❸ 相對地：**in contrast (to / with), by contrast**

❹ 並非；而不是：**instead of, rather than**

❺ 否則：**or, otherwise**

·1-07· 生病慰問信函

寫一封慰問信函給正在生病的人，能讓對方感受到溫暖和關懷。然而，倘若病情嚴重到可能有不治之虞，就千萬不可以使用「早日康復」之類較不切實際的語句。

Subject Get Well Soon

Dear Joan:

I hope you don't mind that Jason told me about your **illness**[1]. Please know that you are in my heart and prayers. I'll give you a call soon. I'm hoping you'll **feel up to**[2] having me **drop by**[3] for a visit.

Also know that if, at any time when I call, you don't feel up to talking or a visit, I hope you'll tell me so. I won't be **offended**[4]. I'll understand your **situation**[5]. I only want what's best for you.

I'm **looking forward to**[6] seeing you as soon as you're up to it.

Best regards,
Helen

親愛的瓊安：

希望您不會介意傑森告訴我您生病的事，請知道我會掛念您，並為您禱告。我近日會致電給您，希望您感覺好一點時，能讓我去探望您。

如果您覺得尚未復原，不希望被打擾，也請告訴我，我不會見怪的。我可以理解您的狀況，只希望您好，那就最好了。

期待見到您早日康復。

海倫 敬上

Send ▶

核心字彙充電站 *Key Words*

1. illness 名 患病（狀態）
2. feel up to 片 （口）感覺能擔當
3. drop by 片 順道拜訪
4. offend 動 冒犯；引起不舒服
5. situation 名 處境；境遇
6. look forward to 片 期待

Part 1
Part 2
Part 3
Part 4
Part 5
Part 6

替換好用句 Copy & Paste

I have learned with deepest regret that you are in bed.
🖉 獲知您臥病在床，我深感難過。

I have heard from a friend of mine that you are ill in bed.
🖉 我從友人口中得知您臥病在床。

When your secretary told me that you would not be able keep our appointment due to a sudden illness, I was deeply concerned.
🖉 當您的秘書通知我，您因為突然感到不適而無法赴約時，我十分擔心。

The business matter which we were going to discuss can wait until you are back.
🖉 我們要討論的事宜，可以等您回來之後再說。

We are very sorry to hear that your recent illness has taken a bad turn.
🖉 獲知您的病情惡化，我們很難過。

I am relieved to hear that his heart attack was a small one.
🖉 聽到他的心臟病不是那麼嚴重，讓我鬆了一口氣。

We are relieved to hear that you were not badly injured in the accident.
🖉 聽到您受傷不重，我們才放心。

I was distressed to learn of your recent illness and hope that you are resting comfortably now.
🖉 得知您最近身體不適，希望您現在已經覺得好多了。

I was shocked to hear that your mother had been hospitalized with a cancer.
🖉 我很驚訝令堂因為癌症住院。

We are very happy to hear that you are making good progress in recovering.
🖉 很開心得知您順利康復的消息。

I am sorry to hear that you have been hospitalized.
🖉 很遺憾聽到您住院的消息。

I am deeply concerned.

🖉 我深表關切。

I am sure that the medical attention you have received is quite successful.
🖉 我相信您所接受的治療非常成功。

I am sure you will have the best treatment that you need at the hospital, and hope this will lead to a speedy recovery.
🖉 我相信您在醫院裡會得到最好的治療，希望您迅速康復。

We hope your stay in the hospital is as comfortable as possible in a pleasant environment.
🖉 希望您在住院期間，周遭環境能讓您感到舒適。

If you are feeling up to see visitors, I will drop in to see you.
🖉 如果您的身體好一點，感覺能見訪客了，我會去看您的。

We are happy to hear that he will be out in a few weeks.
🖉 我們很開心知道，他幾週後就可以出院了。

I will drop by and visit you as soon as you are allowed to have visitors.
🖉 您可以會客時，我就會去看您。

I trust that you are feeling better, and send you my best wishes for a speedy recovery.
🖉 我相信您已經好多了，祝您迅速康復。

Everyone at the Taipei office joins me in wishing you a speedy recovery.
🖉 台北分公司的同仁和我祝您早日康復。

Please let me know if there is anything you need.
🖉 如果您需要任何東西，請告知我。

Take it easy and have a good rest!
🖉 放鬆心情，好好休養吧！

Please know that you are in our thoughts and prayers.
🖉 請記得我們掛念著您，並為您祈禱。

Part 1

Part 2

Part 3

Part 4

Part 5

Part 6

·1-08· 親友過世慰問

　　在哀悼信中，盡量不要刻意提及他人的痛楚或是疾病，最好在信中多給予安慰以及鼓勵。

Subject | **My Sincere Condolences**

Dear Paul:

My **associates**[1] and I were deeply **saddened**[2] to learn about the death of your father. We all know that he will be greatly missed by everyone in your family. We wish to **convey**[3] our sincere **sympathy**[4] to members of your family.

Sincerely yours,
Ella

親愛的保羅：

我的同僚與我對於令尊的過世感到非常哀痛，我們知道您所有的家人都會想念他，我們謹向您的家人致上哀悼之情。

艾拉 敬上

Send ►

核心字彙充電站 Key Words

1. **associate** 名 夥伴；同事
2. **sadden** 動 使悲傷；使難過
3. **convey** 動 傳達；傳遞
4. **sympathy** 名 同情；慰問

替換好用句 Copy & Paste

I was deeply saddened to hear of the sudden death of your mother.
🖉 聽到令堂驟逝的消息，令人深感哀痛。

I was shocked to hear of your mother's passing.
🖉 令堂辭世的消息讓我感到非常震驚。

We wish to extend our condolences to you and your family.
🖉 謹向您與家人致上哀悼之意。.

I have just heard of the loss of your father, and I hasten to send you my sincere condolences.
🖊 剛得知令尊過世的消息，在此致上我最誠摯的哀悼之意。

I recently heard that you had a tremendous loss.
🖊 我剛聽聞您遭受重大損失。

I know that words are not much comfort at a time like this.
🖊 我知道在此刻，任何言語也無法安慰您。

Your mother, Mary, was such a kind and gentle soul.
🖊 令堂瑪莉，有一顆善良溫柔的心。

His kindness, courtesy and experience were rare qualities that we shall remember.
🖊 他寬厚仁慈、有禮、閱歷豐富等高尚品格，我們都將銘記在心。

Your father was so considerate whenever I visited your house.
🖊 每次我到您家裡拜訪時，令尊總是非常細心。

I shall always remember your mother with fondness and gratitude for all of the kindness she showed me.
🖊 我會懷念令堂，並感謝她的仁慈對待。

May the love of those around you help you go through your difficult time.
🖊 希望您摯愛的親友們能幫助您渡過難關。

I just want you to know that you have my deepest and heartfelt sympathy.
🖊 希望您知道我對此深感難過。

You are in my thoughts and prayers.
🖊 我會掛念您，並為您祈禱。

May God bless you and your family during this time and always!
🖊 願上帝保佑您與家人渡過此刻，並長久庇佑。

I want to offer my deepest condolences.
🖊 我願致上我最深的哀悼之意。

I'm truly sorry for your loss.
🖊 對於您失去家人的這件事，我深感遺憾。

I am writing to extend my deepest sympathy to you and your family.
🖊 謹以此信向您及家人致上我最深的哀悼之意。

Our staff joins me in conveying our sincere sympathy to members of your family.
🖊 本公司的同仁與我，希望向您的家人致上由衷的哀悼。

Please let me know if there is anything I can do to help during this difficult time.
🖊 在這樣艱難的時刻，如果有任何需要幫忙的地方，請讓我知道。

 Let's learn more!

文法/句型Focus

✳ 表哀悼及回應

① **grieve + at / for N** 或是 **+ to V** 悲傷；哀悼

② **remember sb. with fondness / affection**
緬懷某人（適用於書信）

③ **gratitude for sth.(N)** 對⋯表示感激（後面接事件，而非人）

實用資訊Focus

表哀痛的方式 🔍

　　對失去親人的人而言，其他人無論如何表達慰問之意，都無法真的減輕其內心的悲痛，因此，外國人在這種場合，並不會多說什麼，以免言語淪於空泛，反而達不到原本的慰問之意。

　　若是參加他人的喪禮，可以藉由肢體動作（例如輕拍肩膀、擁抱、或者握手）來表達，這時候母語人士最常說的英文就是I am really sorry. 以此句表達「遺憾之情」。要記得此時語調宜放慢，誠懇地慢慢說。

　　相反地，若非當面慰問，而是以E-mail表達時，最好將情緒明白地寫出來，例如：感到震驚、難過⋯等等，用這些具體的文字讓對方感受到你的心意。

Part 1
Part 2
Part 3
Part 4
Part 5
Part 6

• 2-01 • 旅遊廣告宣傳

Subject Bali Island Trip

Dear Customers:

The ezTravel is offering a 5-day tour of Bali. It's a chance to visit the most beautiful **island**[1] of **Indonesia**[2]. There you will enjoy a **cruise**[3] around the **harbor**[4], which is famed for its **magnificent**[5] beach. At night, you'll be able to experience the **excitement**[6] of streets and **alleyways**[7].

At all of the beaches, you'll be able to enjoy a **myriad**[8] of water sports such as **snorkeling**[9], scuba-diving, **windsurfing**[10], and water-skiing.

Paradise is only a phone call away, so call ezTravel today at 999-7777 for a vacation you won't forget!

Best,
Helen Balton

親愛的客戶：

易遊網現正提供峇里島五日遊行程，這是個造訪印尼最美麗島嶼的機會。您可以搭船漫遊海港，一覽著名的海灘。夜晚，您可以體驗當地大街小巷精彩的夜生活。

您可以在當地海灘從事各式各樣的水上活動，包括浮潛、潛水、風帆、滑水等。

只要一通電話，便能前往海灘天堂！馬上撥打999-7777到易遊網，給自己一個難忘的假期！

海倫・巴爾頓 敬上

Send ▸

核心字彙充電站 Key Words

1. **island** 名 島嶼
2. **Indonesia** 名 印尼
3. **cruise** 名 (坐船)旅行
4. **harbor** 名 港灣;海港
5. **magnificent** 形 極美的
6. **excitement** 名 興奮
7. **alleyway** 名 (建築間的)小巷
8. **myriad** 名 無數;大量
9. **snorkel** 動 浮潛
10. **windsurf** 動 做風帆衝浪運動

替換好用句 Copy & Paste

Here are the three pages of the London brochure that you needed.
🖉 附上三頁您需要的倫敦手冊。

I tried scanning them to you, but it didn't work.
🖉 我試著要把資料掃描給你,但沒有成功。

I will send two or three full brochures to you ASAP.
🖉 我會盡快寄兩、三份完整的手冊給您。

There aren't many beaches on the island. The coastline is rocky with steep cliffs.
🖉 這個島上沒有很多沙灘,海岸線滿是岩石漫佈的懸崖峭壁。

The Netherlands has a temperate climate, with mild winters and cool summers.
🖉 荷蘭的氣候溫和,冬暖夏涼。

This beautiful old church is one of our national heritages.
🖉 這座美麗的古老教堂是我們的國家遺產之一。

New Zealand lies in the South Pacific Ocean.
🖉 紐西蘭位在南太平洋上。

It consists of two islands.
🖉 它由兩個島嶼組成。

It is located 1,600 km south-east of Australia.
🖉 它位在澳大利亞東南方一千六百公里處。

The climate is generally temperate and damp.

✎ 天氣大多溫和且潮濕。

The extreme north has got a subtropical climate.
✎ 最北端屬於亞熱帶氣候。

The landscape is largely unspoiled and very varied.
✎ 大部分的景觀都未受汙染，而且景致變化多端。

There are mountains, lakes, and glaciers.
✎ 有高山、湖泊、與冰河景緻。

Floating on the Pacific Ocean, Guan offers the perfect location for an exciting holiday.
✎ 位於太平洋的關島提供了最完美的地點，讓你擁有一個刺激的假期。

The island lies between Spain and the North African coast.
✎ 這座島嶼位於西班牙和北非沿岸的中間。

We offer the 10-day tour of Scotland visiting historic castles.
✎ 我們提供蘇格蘭的古堡十日遊。

Are you interested in mountain climbing?
✎ 你對登山有興趣嗎？

How about windsurfing?
✎ 風帆衝浪運動如何？

We also provide the tour of cycling in the mountains and deserts in Mongolia.
✎ 我們也提供蒙古高山和沙漠的單車之旅。

Our agency also provides a four-week trip to Canada for students to learn English.
✎ 我們旅行社也提供為期四週的加拿大英語學習旅行團。

I would appreciate it if you could fax me more information.
✎ 我希望你可以傳真其他資料給我。

 進階補充站 *Let's learn more!*

 單字/片語Focus

❧ 一般旅遊景點 ❧

✽castle 城堡	✽palace 皇宮
✽cathedral 大教堂	✽temple 寺廟
✽theme park 主題樂園	✽historic monument 歷史紀念館
✽duty-free shops 免稅商店	✽natural wonder 天然景觀
✽beautiful coast area 美麗的海岸風景	
✽magnificent coral beach 極美的珊瑚海灘	
✽natural geographic feature 自然地理景觀	

❧ 假期活動 ❧

✽sailing 坐帆船	✽windsurfing 風帆活動
✽snorkeling 浮潛	✽scuba-diving 潛水
✽massage 按摩	✽jet skiing 水上摩托車
✽parasailing 帆傘活動	

 文法/句型Focus

✽ 各種各樣的、各類的

❶ a myriad of 各式各樣的
❷ a (wide) variety / diversity of 多樣的
❸ all sorts / kinds of 各式各樣的
❹ a series / sequence of 一系列的

·2-02· 旅遊行程詢問

　　準備旅遊時，常會寫信到旅行社索取有關機票、住宿、旅遊或度假等相關資料。索取資料的信件中除了提出問題之外，還可以寫上預定抵達日期、參加人數、兒童年齡以及喜好，方便對方估價。

| Subject | About Helicopter Flight Services |

Dear Sir:

I read your **advertisement**[1] with interest. From the **concierge**[2] at my hotel, I found the tickets are available here, but they couldn't provide the details. Would you mind answering a few questions to help me join the **helicopter**[3] tour?

Your **brochure**[4] says flight routing and conditions can **vary**[5]. We won't consider flying too long. Is the tour safe? Also, we are bringing our son along with us. So we are wondering if there is any discount for the school age passengers? We also have one **handicapped**[6] person with us. Does the helicopter have any handicapped seating? Finally, are we allowed to take pictures in the air?

Thanks for your help with this matter.

Best regards,
Carl Jason

先生您好：

看完貴公司的旅遊服務廣告後，我很有興趣。從旅館櫃檯人員口中得知可以在旅館購票，但櫃檯無法提供詳細資訊。可否勞煩您回答一些問題，好讓我參加直升機之旅？

簡介手冊上說飛行路徑和狀況會隨之改變。我們不考慮坐太久飛機，那搭直升機旅遊安全嗎？另外，我們的兒子將會同行，想了解學齡乘客是否享有折扣？同時，我們還會有一位殘障人士同行，請問直升機上是否有殘障人士專用的座位？最後，我們可否在空中照相呢？

感謝您的幫忙。

卡爾・傑森 敬上

Send

1. **advertisement** 名 廣告
2. **concierge** 名 （法）門房
3. **helicopter** 名 直升機
4. **brochure** 名 小冊子
5. **vary** 動 使多樣化
6. **handicapped** 形 有生理缺陷的

替換好用句 Copy & Paste

My husband, my two-year-old daughter and I are planning a vacation to Hong Kong this coming July.
✎ 我老公、我和我兩歲的女兒計劃在七月份到香港旅行。

We would like to visit the Disneyland.
✎ 我們想要到迪士尼樂園玩。

I'm planning to visit New York next month on a business trip.
✎ 我計劃下個月到紐約出差。

Please send us the information you have on tours, special packages, and other events that may be scheduled during July.
✎ 請寄給我們關於七月份的旅遊行程、特惠方案及其他活動資訊。

Also, we would like a map of the area and a list of moderately priced hotels.
✎ 此外，我們還想索取地圖以及中價位飯店的資訊。

As I explained on the telephone this morning, we will go on your September 4th tour of Macau.
✎ 就像我今天早上在電話裡說的，我們打算參加你們九月四日出發的澳門之旅。

I would like to know if you offer a city tour for three days from July 1st.
✎ 我想知道你們是否有提供從七月一日開始，長達三天的市區觀光旅行。

I am interested in visiting London. Could you please send the following information to me?
✎ 我對到倫敦旅行很感興趣，可否請你寄給我以下資訊？

What's the length of the tour?
✎ 旅遊的天數為？

Do you have any tours which depart for the end of July or the beginning of August?
🖊 有沒有任何行程是於七月底或八月初出發的呢？

What type of accommodation will you have?
🖊 你們有什麼樣的住宿方案呢？

How much will the tour cost for one person using a single room?
🖊 若是一個人住單人房的話，旅費是多少呢？

What's the basic price of the tour?
🖊 旅行團的基本費用是多少？

Does the cost of the tour include all food and meals?
🖊 旅費包括食物餐點嗎？

Does the cost of the tour include the entry costs to those monuments?
🖊 旅費包括紀念館的入場門票嗎？

Is the cost per person, or per room?
🖊 價格是以人數計算、還是以房間計算？

Does the cost of the tour include the arrival and departure transfers?
🖊 旅費包括機場來回的接送服務嗎？

Will there be a guide on the tour?
🖊 旅行中會有導遊嗎？

Could you please help with visa and passport applications?
🖊 你們是否能提供簽證和護照申請的服務呢？

Can you help buy airline tickets for us?
🖊 你們能協助我們購買機票嗎？

Do you offer the coach tours in Hong Kong?
🖊 你們有提供搭觀光巴士遊香港的行程嗎？

How safe are these destinations?
🖊 觀光景點的治安好嗎？

What do I need to bring?
🖊 我需要帶什麼物品呢？

What if I'm a vegetarian?
🖊 如果我吃素怎麼辦？

What is the weather like?
✏️ 當地的天氣如何？

 Let's learn more!

 實用資訊Focus

旅行必備物品 🔍

1. long sleeved shirts, pants and socks to protect from mosquito bites
   能避免被蚊蟲叮咬的長袖衣物、長褲和襪子

2. adapter plugs and convertors for electrical devices
   電子產品的轉接插頭和變壓器

3. anti malaria medication and basic medical kit
   瘧疾藥品和基本的醫藥箱

4. a small flashlight and its batteries
   小型手電筒和電池

5. sun glasses, sun hat and sun screen
   太陽眼鏡、帽子和防曬乳

6. long skirts, T-shirts, sweaters, pants, and flip-flops
   長裙、襯衫、毛衣、長褲、平底人字拖鞋

7. good walking shoes
   方便走路的鞋子

8. a good camera, batteries and a charger
   照相機、電池、充電器

9. insect repellent
   驅蟲劑

10. warm clothes for the morning and evening
    早晚天涼時可穿的保暖衣物

Part 1
Part 2
Part 3
Part 4
Part 5
Part 6

Subject Flight Details From Taipei to Los Angeles

Dear Ms. Chou:

Following your instructions in our telephone conversation this morning, I have made **enquiries**[1] about the details of your flights, which are listed below:

Outward[2] journey (Saturday, January 4, 2018)
AA123 (American Airlines)
Dep[3]: Taipei (TPE) 17:15
Arr[4]: Los Angeles (LAX) 11:20

Return journey (Tuesday, January 12, 2018)
AA678
Dep: Los Angeles (LAX) 00:15
Arr: Taipei (TPE) 14:20

I have reserved a seat in your name, but I need to confirm this within forty-eight hours. To make a **confirmation**[5], I will need your full name and your passport number.

I also need to know if you are happy with an **electronic ticket**[6], or if you want me to issue a paper ticket.

Please reply me ASAP. Thanks.

親愛的周小姐：

根據您早上在電話中的請求，以下是我調查過關於您班機的詳細資料：

出發行程：2018.1.4（六）
美國航空：123航班
起飛時間：17:15（台灣桃園國際機場）
抵達時間：11:20（美國洛杉磯機場）

回程：2018.1.12（二）
美國航空：678航班
起飛時間：00:15（美國洛杉磯機場）
抵達時間：14:20（台灣桃園國際機場）

我已訂好機位，需要您在四十八小時內確認，確認時請提供您的全名和護照號碼。

此外，你想要電子機票還是一般紙本機票呢？

Sincerely yours,
Fay Black

請盡快回信給我，謝謝。

菲‧布雷克 敬上

Send ►

Part 1
Part 2
Part 3
Part 4
Part 5
Part 6

 核心字彙充電站 *Key Words*

1. **enquiry** 名 調查；詢問
2. **outward** 形 往外去的
3. **Dep = Departure** 名 出發
4. **Arr = Arrival** 名 到達
5. **confirmation** 名 確定
6. **electronic ticket** 片 電子機票

 替換好用句 *Copy & Paste*

This flight would bet you back to Tokyo early the next day. The flight details are:
🖊 這班機保證讓你可以於隔天一早回到東京。班機詳情如下：

I am sorry that I made a mistake with the dates for a flight you booked for me.
🖊 很抱歉，關於您之前幫我訂的機票，我搞錯日期了。

How can I be sure that my reservation has been completed successfully?
🖊 我該如何確認是否已成功預約機位了呢？

What can I do if I don't remember the number of my reservation?
🖊 如果我忘了預約的號碼怎麼辦？

Will I be asked to give you more information, such as passport number or copy of the credit card after the payment?
🖊 付款後，需要提供護照號碼或信用卡影本等資料嗎？

How can I cancel or modify my air ticket?
🖊 如何取消或更改我的機票？

Is there any kind of full or partial refund for a ticket that I will not finally use?

🖊 最後若沒有搭乘班機，會退全額或部分的機票費用嗎？

How can I change the dates of my flight?
🖊 如何更改機票日期？

With whom should I contact if I need to modify my ticket while I am abroad?
🖊 我在國外的期間，若想更改我的機票，該與誰聯絡呢？

Can I get my tickets at the airport?
🖊 我可以在機場取票嗎？

Are there any limits and restrictions regarding our luggage?
🖊 行李有任何限制和要求嗎？

May I select specific seats?
🖊 我可以選擇機位嗎？

進階補充站　Let's learn more!

實用資訊Focus

訂位與開票 🔍

　　知道預計的行程後，先請客服人員為你「訂位」，等到出發前三週，行程完全確定下來後，再請客服人員為你「開票」，開票之後就是確定要出發了。

　　若購買的是低價促銷票，訂位後三天到一個星期內就要開票。如果「開票」之後，又想取消班機，小心會被罰款喔！

實體機票遺失處理 🔍

1. 向遺失地區的警局報案，取得報案證明。
2. 到航空公司填寫遺失機票表（Lost Ticket Form），留下聯絡電話及地址。
3. 如在國外遺失回程機票，可至原航空公司購買回程機票，但務必註明是因遺失之故購買，將來退費時可退回第二次購票之金額。
4. 六個月後若無人使用該遺失之機票，就以退票手續辦理。如果六個月內被人使用，此機票就無法退費。（依各航空公司的規定辦理）

Part 1

Part 2

Part 3

Part 4

Part 5

Part 6

·2-04· 詢問飯店訂房

　　越早訂房就越有機會訂到想要的房型和房價。在信件中提出想要的房間、停留的天數、房價或特惠；如果需要特殊的安排或要求，記得要在信件中提出來。雖然只是一封電子郵件，但可以做為日後的參考憑據，在對方未達成你對房間的要求時，也可能依此憑據獲得賠償。

Subject **Accommodation for Doctor Luo**

Dear Emma: I have just got the phone call from our hotel in Hokkaido, and I am sorry to tell you that they are fully booked on the first two nights of Doctor Luo's stay in Japan. I know that Doctor Luo is an important **client**[1], so I am not very sure what to do next. Do we have an **alternative**[2] hotel in the city to **lodge**[3] Dr. Lou? Your **prompt**[4] reply will be appreciated. Best regards, Tina Smith	親愛的艾瑪： 今早我接到北海道飯店打來的電話。很抱歉，飯店那邊說羅醫師停留在日本的前兩個晚上，他們那裡沒有任何空房。由於羅醫師是我們重要的顧客，所以目前我實在不知道該如何處理。 我們是否還有其他可以選擇的飯店讓羅醫師居住呢？ 感謝你的迅速回覆。 蒂娜・史密斯 敬上

Send ▶

核心字彙充電站 Key Words

1. **client** 名 顧客；客戶
2. **alternative** 形 供選擇的
3. **lodge** 動 提供臨時住處
4. **prompt** 形 迅速的；及時的

Thank you for the information on your resort that you sent us.
🖊 謝謝你寄來貴渡假中心的相關資料。

We would like to reserve a room for one week beginning from Friday, October 10, and ending on Saturday, October 16.
🖊 我們想要預約訂房，十月十日（五）到十月十六日（六），為期一週的住宿。

We would like one room with two double beds.
🖊 我們需要一間有兩張雙人床的房間。

I understand your daily rate for such a room is $150.
🖊 我知道你們這種房型平日的房價是一百五十元。

Please send me a confirmation of our reservation and a receipt for the deposit.
🖊 請寄給我訂房的確認信和訂金的發票。

We'll arrive in the afternoon on Friday, October 10.
🖊 我們會在十月十日（週五）的下午抵達。

We probably will not get there before 8 p.m.
🖊 我們可能無法趕在晚上八點前抵達飯店。

The hotel is fully booked right now, so I'm looking for an alternative.
🖊 飯店房間已經客滿，所以我在找其他替代方案。

Would you prefer me to book Professor Chou to the alternative hotel for the whole of her stay, or just for those first two nights?
🖊 你要我幫周教授更改所有停留天數的下榻飯店，還是只更改前二晚的飯店？

I recommend the five-star King Plaza Hotel.
🖊 我推薦五星級的國王皇宮飯店。

It's an old building in British colonial style.
🖊 它是一棟英國殖民地式的老建築。

There are also deluxe rooms and suites.
🖊 也有豪華房間和套房。

The deluxe rooms are $155/night, and the suites $165/night.
🖊 豪華房間每晚一百五十五元，而套房每晚一百六十五元。

Part 1

Part 2

Part 3

Part 4

Part 5

Part 6

·2-05· 客訴服務品質

Subject | **Your Service Concerns**

Dear Sir:

Despite[1] the fact that this was not my first stay at your hotel, I was quite **disappointed**[2] with this visit.

Firstly, the staff didn't keep their promise to provide us with a lake-view room rather than a courtyard-view room on my second day. I was informed a lake-view room was not available when I **checked in**[3], but I was **assured**[4] that a lake-view room would be available. However, the front desk staff was unwilling to change my room the next day. Secondly, despite a brightly-lit sign **indicating**[5] a **sauna**[6] in the basement, I found it was not in service.

I would like to consider staying at your hotel again, so could you please handle these questions ASAP?

Sincerely,
Tony Walter

敬啟者:

雖然我不是第一次在你們飯店住宿,但這次令我十分失望。

首先,服務人員未依約在住宿第二天給我面湖的景觀房,反而給我面向中庭的房間。我入住的時候就被告知面湖景觀房沒有空房,但他們向我保證之後會有空房。然而,櫃台人員隔天卻不願意幫我換成面湖景觀房。其次,我看到有個閃亮的指示牌,寫著地下室有三溫暖,結果發現它根本沒開。

我考慮下回再到你們飯店住宿,所以可否請您儘速處理這些問題呢?

東尼·沃爾特 謹上

 Send

1. despite 介 不管；儘管
2. disappointed 形 令人失望的
3. check in 片 登記入住
4. assure 動 向…保證
5. indicate 動 指出；指示
6. sauna 名 桑拿浴

替換好用句 *Copy & Paste*

I'm afraid that your staff sometimes does not record the special needs of the patrons.
✎ 很遺憾，你們的服務人員有時會漏記房客的特別需求。

Your staff members should concern the customers' special requests.
✎ 你們的服務人員應該考慮到顧客的特別需求。

Was the operation of your sauna suspended?
✎ 三溫暖暫時關閉了嗎？

Is that because of an electrical problem?
✎ 是因為電力方面的問題嗎？

My key doesn't work.
✎ 我房門的鑰匙無法使用。

You did not show an explanatory sign.
✎ 你們並沒有另立告示牌說明。

I am in Room 701. The air-conditioner / heater / TV / toilet is broken.
✎ 我住701號房，房間裡的冷氣／暖氣／電視／廁所壞掉了。

The toilet / sink / shower is leaking.
✎ 馬桶／水槽／淋浴間在漏水。

There is a weird smell in my room.
✎ 房間裡有股異味。

The guests next door were very noisy.
✎ 隔壁房的客人很吵。

We waited for fifteen minutes just for a pitcher of water.
✎ 我們光是等一壺水就等了十五分鐘。

Part 1

Part 2

Part 3

Part 4

Part 5

Part 6

We were very disappointed with your restaurant and staff.

✎ 貴餐廳與服務人員令我我感到十分失望。

On the evening of Sep. 1, my wife and I arrived at your hotel with reservation for a double room.

✎ 我太太和我於九月一日傍晚抵達你們飯店，預約了一間雙人房。

Even though we had reserved our room one month ago, we were told that no rooms were vacant in the entire hotel.

✎ 我們已經在一個月前訂好房間，但事後竟然告知我們整間飯店都沒有空房。

We spent the night in your hotel lobby, sleeping on one of the couches.

✎ 我們整晚都待在你們的飯店大廳，睡在沙發上。

We felt disgusted when we received our monthly credit card statement and discovered we had been charged extra fees.

✎ 我們在收到信用卡帳單後發現，我們竟然被要求支付額外費用。

In fact, your hotel accepted our reservation and failed to provide the room.

✎ 實際上，你們飯店接受了我們的預約，但並沒有提供房間給我們。

 進階補充站 Let's learn more!

 文法/句型Focus

✱ 可用於客訴的例句

❶ I'm sorry to bother you, but I wanted a muffin, not fries. 抱歉打擾了，但我點的是鬆餅，不是炸薯條。

❷ Excuse me, my coat came back from the laundry missing buttons.

不好意思，我的衣服送洗後掉了幾顆鈕子。

❸ I understand it's not your fault, but the airline promised they would change the seat for me.

我了解錯不在你，但航空公司承諾要幫我換位子。

2-06 機場遺失行李

　　旅行過程中，難免會遺失重要物品，不論是在旅館或機場，都要向對方提出申請，幸運的話，就能找到遺失或遺留在那裡的物件。申請時除了通知對方郵寄的地址之外，別忘了寄一張支票支付該物件的郵資，或要求貨到付款，並感謝對方的協助。

Subject | Luggage Loss

Dear Sir:

I am writing to report to the nearest Lost and Found Center about my **baggage**[1] loss. One of my bags got lost on July 8 at the **airport**[2], and I would like to know what I can do to get it back. I am wondering how China Airline **handles**[3] this situation and how I can follow the general **procedure**[4].

I will appreciate your help.

Best regards,
Fred Chapman

先生您好：

我寫信來提報附近的失物招領中心有關我行李遺失的事宜。我的一件行李在七月八日時遺失，我想了解如何才能找回我的行李。請問中華航空會如何處理這樣的問題，以及我該如何依循一般程序呢？

非常感謝您的幫忙！

弗瑞德‧查普曼 謹上

Send ▶

核心字彙充電站 Key Words

1. **baggage** 名 行李
2. **airport** 名 機場
3. **handle** 動 處理
4. **procedure** 名 程序

 替換好用句 *Copy & Paste*

 行李遺失通報

I can't find my baggage.
✎ 我找不到我的行李。

I was on China Airline 68 from Taiwan.
✎ 我從台灣搭乘中華航空68號班機。

A large blue suitcase and a medium black duffel bag.
✎ 一個大型藍色皮箱，還有中型黑色圓筒旅行袋。

I'm staying at the W Hotel. My cell phone number is 0912-333-222.
✎ 我住在W飯店，手機號碼是：0912-333-222。

Please contact me and deliver it to my hotel.
✎ 請聯絡我，並將行李送到我的下榻飯店。

When will I get my luggage?
✎ 我何時可以拿到我的行李？

 航空公司回應

First, you need to report it to the appropriate airline office.
✎ 首先，請向你的航空公司申報此事。

The lost luggage form will ask you to provide a description of the luggage, some personal information and other contact details.
✎ 遺失行李表上會要求你描述行李外觀，並填寫個人資料和其他聯絡細節。

You have more than a 90 percent chance of recovering your luggage within twenty-four hours.
✎ 你有超過百分之九十的機率可以在二十四小時內找回自己的行李。

The airline will deliver it to your hotel or place of stay.
✎ 航空公司會將它送到你下榻的飯店或住處。

After twenty-four hours, if you still haven't recovered your luggage, you may apply to be compensated.
✎ 若二十四小時後仍未找回您的行李，您可以申請賠償。

Part 1
Part 2
Part 3
Part 4
Part 5
Part 6

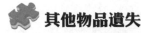 **其他物品遺失**

By the way, I think I left my backpack at your place yesterday.
🖊 順帶一提，我昨天在您府上掉了一個登山包。

Could you please look around and see if it's there?
🖊 可否請您幫我找看看，是否在那裡？

It is dark blue, has two zippers and red shoulder straps.
🖊 它是深藍色的，有二個拉鍊及紅色背帶。

Thank you for telling us about our travel packet and keys in your hotel room.
🖊 謝謝您通知我們領取遺留在貴飯店的旅行包和鑰匙。

As I promised on the phone, I'm enclosing a check to reimburse you for the cost of mailing the travel bags and keys back to us.
🖊 如同電話裡談過的，我會附上支票來補償您郵寄旅行包和鑰匙給我們的費用。

Please send the package to the following address:
🖊 請將包裹寄到以下住址：

 **進階補充站** *Let's learn more!*

 實用資訊Focus

行李延誤的處理 🔍
1. 正常情況下，轉機約需一個半小時以上，若轉機時間不足，就很容易發生行李延誤的情形。
2. 普通因轉機時間而發生的行李狀況，通常是延誤，而非遺失，此時若發覺行李失蹤，可先至櫃台詢問，出示行李的「條碼收據」，並留下資料，請對方待行李抵達後，替你送往指定地點。

行李遺失該怎麼辦？ 🔍
1. 被誤拿的情況經常發生，所以可先當場查看四周是否有相似的行李箱。
2. 確定找不到時，請拿著行李牌與機票至失物招領處（Lost & Found）登記。
3. 登記時請盡量提供詳細的描述，例如行李的特殊標記等，以利找尋。

3 交通問題詢問

Part 1

Part 2

Part 3

Part 4

Part 5

Part 6

• 3-01 • 如何到…地點？

Subject Directions to Emily's Birthday Party

You are invited to Emily's Birthday Party
Saturday, October 23, 2019
From 3 to 9 o'clock
At La Casa Restaurant
Please respond by October 10.
The Chou's Family: 912-111-222

Directions[1] to La Casa Restaurant from Hope School:

Turn right on David Street from the parking lot of the school. Stay on David Street until the first traffic light. Then turn right again on Windy Boulevard. Stay on Windy Boulevard for about four blocks. Next, turn left at the corner of Windy Boulevard and Main Street. Main Street is a long street with many turns. Stay on it for a mile. At that point, you should turn left and then quickly turn right. Be careful here. This **intersection**[2] sometimes is very busy. You should stay on Brook Street for four or five more **blocks**[3]. Finally, stop when you get to Central Park. La Casa is at 366 Brook Street before Central Park.

Your **devoted**[4] friend,

歡迎來參加愛蜜莉的生日派對
二〇一九年十月二十三日
星期六下午三點到九點
地點：義家歐式餐館
請於十月十日前回覆。
周家電話：912-111-222

從希望學校到義家歐式餐館的路線圖：

從學校停車場右轉到大衛街上，沿著大衛街直走至第一個紅綠燈，然後再右轉接溫蒂大道，直走過四個街口左右，在溫蒂大道和主街的交匯口左轉。主街很長，有許多轉彎路口，沿著主街直走約一英里。此時，你要左轉，然後立刻再右轉。在這個地方要小心，這個十字路口有時候十分危險。接著，在布魯克街上過四到五個街口。最後，在中央公園前停下來，義家歐式餐館

Tanaka

就在中央公園前的布魯克街366號。

田中 敬上

Send ▶

核心字彙充電站 *Key Words*

1. **direction** 名 方向；方位
2. **intersection** 名 十字路口
3. **block** 名 (美)街區
4. **devoted** 形 忠實的；摯愛的

替換好用句 *Copy & Paste*

Here are the directions from school to Carol's Café.
🖊 這是從學校到卡蘿咖啡廳的路線圖。

Follow this map, and you will get to the Science Museum.
🖊 照這張地圖走,你就能抵達科學博物館。

Turn left onto SanMin Road, stay on it for three blocks.
🖊 左轉三民路,直走三個街口。

Turn right at Ming's Market. There is no street sign, but you should see a fruit shop outside and a sign that says Ming's.
🖊 在明記市場右轉,這條路沒有路標,但你可以看到有家水果攤在外面,有個招牌寫著:明記。

Turn left at the corner of Lee Boulevard and Henry Street.
🖊 在李大道和亨利街的交匯處左轉。

You have to cross a very busy intersection.
🖊 你會經過一個非常繁忙的十字路口。

You can walk or drive to my house from our school.
🖊 你可以從我們學校走路或開車到我家。

Stay on Main Street for two blocks.

🖊 沿著主街直走，過二個街口。

The market should be on the right.
🖊 市場就在你的右手邊。

After one more block, you should get to my house.
🖊 多走一個街口，就會抵達我家。

You can also ride a scooter to get to the city center.
🖊 你也可以騎摩托車到市中心。

Take the Green Line to the George's Station.
🖊 搭捷運綠線到喬治站。

The Mall at George's Station is directly across the street on East West Highway.
🖊 出了喬治站口，大賣場就在東西公路的正對面。

Take I-95 North to Route 1 South.
🖊 走 I-95 高速公路北上至1號公路再南下。

Continue on Route 1 South to East West Highway.
🖊 直走1號公路南下接到東西公路。

 進階補充站 Let's learn more!

 文法/句型Focus

＊ 轉承詞 — 逐點列述

❶ 首先：**first(ly), first of all, in the first place, to begin with**

❷ 其次：**second(ly), in the second place, then, and then, next**

❸ 進而；接著：**further(more), in turn**

❹ 最後：**finally, eventually, lastly, at last, in the end, in the long run**

·3-02· 了解國外駕照規定

到美國短期旅遊時，可以使用在台灣申請的國際駕照，但若要長期居住（留學或工作），可向美國州政府當地申請駕照。各州取得駕照的方式稍有不同。例如：在賓州，國際駕照可以使用一年，但在其他州僅能使用三十到九十天不等。除了筆試和路考外，有的地方也需要做視力測驗。到各州的 Department of Motor Vehicles（DMV，像台灣的監理站）就能諮詢相關問題。

Subject｜Pennsylvania Driver's License

Dear Sir:

I am writing to enquire about obtaining a Pennsylvania Driver's License. I would like to know the requirements and fees about the written driving test and the road test.

I have a driver's license from my home country along with an international license. However, I am planning to stay here for more than one year, so I think I will need a Pennsylvania Driver's License. I will appreciate it if you could tell me how I can take the tests, where I should go to, and how much they cost.

Yours truly,
Melinda Willow

Send

先生您好：

我寫信來詢問有關取得賓州駕照的相關事宜。我想要了解關於筆試和路考的條件和費用。

我有本國駕照和國際駕照。但是我計劃待在賓州超過一年以上，所以，我想我會需要正式的當地駕照。若您可以告訴我如何參加考試、在哪裡考試、以及相關費用的資訊，我將十分感激。

梅琳達・威洛 敬上

 **替換好用句** *Copy & Paste*

I am writing to know about how I can apply for a driver's license.
🖊 我寫信來問關於申請駕照的方式。

If I already have a valid driver's license in my home country, how do I get a driver's license here?
🖊 我有我們國家的有效駕照，請問我應該如何在這裡申請駕照呢？

I want to take a driving test. Please send me a copy of the driver's manual.
🖊 我要考駕照，請寄給我一份駕駛手冊。

Do you have a driver's manual in Chinese?
🖊 你們有中文版的駕駛手冊嗎？

Is my international driver's license valid in every state?
🖊 我的國際駕照在美國各州都通用嗎？

If I get a ticket in another state, will it affect my driver's license?
🖊 如果我在其他州被開罰單，會影響我的駕照嗎？

When can my driver's license be suspended?
🖊 我的駕照在什麼情形下會被吊銷？

If you pass the test, you can have a Temporary Instruction Permit (TIP).
🖊 通過筆試後，你會拿到一張臨時駕駛證。

You have to wait for thirty days to take a road test.
🖊 你必須要等三十天後才可以參加路考。

Practice driving as much as you can.
🖊 盡可能在路上練習駕駛。

Have a person with a driver's license to accompany you when you practice driving.
🖊 當你在路上練習駕駛時，請一位有駕照的朋友陪伴你。

Make an appointment with a driving school to take the road test.
🖊 和汽車駕駛訓練班預約，參加路考。

If you pass the road test, a certificate will be issued to you.
🖊 假如你通過了路考，就會發證照給你。

Part 1
Part 2
Part 3
Part 4
Part 5
Part 6

Your official driver's license will arrive in mail in two weeks.
🖊 你的正式駕駛職照會在兩個星期後郵寄給你。

If you make a move to another state, you will have to go to the local Department of Motor Vehicles (DMV) to apply for a new license.
🖊 如果你搬到另一個州,就必須到當地的監理站申請新駕照。

Usually, you must do this within thirty days after moving to the new state.
🖊 一般情況下,你必須在遷入三十天內申請新駕照。

 **進階補充站** Let's learn more!

 實用資訊Focus

在台辦理國際駕照 🔍

　　憑中華民國駕照申請換發國際駕照,請攜帶下列證件到當地監理處辦理:身分證明文件正本或影本,中華民國駕照正本,最近六個月內拍攝之半身黑白或彩色照片兩張(二吋),汽車駕駛人審驗暨各項異動登記書,並至監理服務站索取空白書表,填與護照相同之英文姓名,規費新台幣二百五十元。

駕駛違規事項 🔍

1. 酒後駕車 driving under the influence of alcohol
2. 拒絕酒測 refusing to take a blood-alcohol test
3. 未投保汽機車駕駛責任險 driving without liability insurance
4. 超速行駛 speeding
5. 魯莽駕駛 reckless driving
6. 肇事逃逸 leaving the scene of an injury accident
7. 未繳納罰單 failing to pay a driving-related fine
8. 拒絕交通違規的傳訊 failing to answer a traffic summons
9. 拒絕做車禍筆錄 failing to file an accident report

·3-03· 購買二手車

　　選購二手車幾乎是每位留學生在美國生活必須面對的問題之一，其重要性不亞於找房子和找指導教授。包括：購買二手車的管道、車型或廠牌、看車和試車、了解車主賣車的動機、保養修理紀錄、購買前先送廠檢修或殺價問題等。美國的新車有較完善的售後服務和三年的品質保證，價格也比在台灣的同級車便宜一半，如果打算在美國待五、六年以上，或者畢業後想把車子運回台灣的同學，不妨考慮買新車。但是，不管是新車或是二手車都有其優缺點，必須衡量經濟能力、交通狀況以及使用頻率來選擇適合自己的車子。

| Subject | Buy A Used Car |

Dear Mr. Lin:

I am an international student from Taiwan and studying at Ann Arbor. I just got the driver's license here and saw some used car information on your website. I am writing in connection with purchasing a used car.

I'll drive my car to school and will take long road trips during the weekends. I enjoy driving a car and I need one to keep me warm in 6-month long winter time. Could you please suggest some used cars to me? I would like to buy a second-hand car which was driven by someone with a good driving record. Thank you.

I look forward to hearing from you.

Best wishes,
Darren Ho

林先生您好：

我是在安娜堡市求學的國際學生，來自台灣。我剛取得本地駕照，看到貴網站上的二手車資訊，所以寫信來詢問相關問題。

我會開車上學，而且週末會開著車去旅遊。我很喜歡開車，需要一輛可以讓我在長達六個月的寒冬下保暖的車。可否請您推薦一些二手車給我？我想要買前車主駕駛紀錄優良的車子。

期待您的回音。

何戴倫 敬上

Send ▶

替換好用句 Copy & Paste

I am interested in buying a used car, so I am writing to ask some questions.
🖉 我想買輛二手車，所以寫信來詢問一些問題。

I drive home on the weekends and take long road trips sometimes.
🖉 我每週末都開車回家，而且有時會開車做長途旅行。

How many miles does this used car have?
🖉 這輛二手車跑了多少英里？

What kind of optional equipment does this car have?
🖉 這輛車有什麼樣的配備可以選擇？

What year is this used car?
🖉 這輛二手車是幾年出廠的？

Do you have the maintenance records?
🖉 你們有維修紀錄嗎？

I drive twenty miles a day as I live several hours away from my office, so I need a car more reliable.
🖉 因為我住的地方離公司距離好幾個小時的車程，所以我每天要開二十英里路，需要一輛較可靠的車。

Do you know any one who is looking to unload a used car in decent condition?
🖉 你有認識的人要脫手車況不錯的二手車嗎？

Do you know any one of the sellers who is likely to take decent care of their automobiles?
🖉 你知道有任何優良維修的汽車賣家嗎？

What is the best type of make and model, or its mileage?
🖉 哪一款車型、或多少行駛總哩數是最好的呢？

Are there any previous damages occurred to this car?
🖉 這輛車有往年的事故紀錄嗎？

Is there a warranty if I purchase this used car?
🖉 如果購買這台二手車的話，有含保固嗎？

I would like to make sure what exactly the warranty will cover.
🖋 我想要知道它的確切保固項目。

If I purchase the car, what remaining costs will I have to pay?
🖋 如果我購買這輛車的話,還需要付什麼額外的費用嗎?

I'd like to do a thorough inspection of the vehicle, both inside and outside.
🖋 我想要做一次完整的汽車檢查,包括內部和外部。

I would like to have a mechanic look at this car.
🖋 我想找位技師來看車。

I would like to make an appointment with you to test-drive the car.
🖋 我想要和你們預約試車。

I am on a tight budget, so I would purchase the car with my student auto loan.
🖋 我的預算有限,所以要用我的學生汽車貸款購車。

What type of financing do you have?
🖋 你們有什麼付款方案?

What type of used car will fit into my price range?
🖋 哪一款二手車的價格符合我的預算範圍呢?

 進階補充站　Let's learn more!

 文法/句型Focus

✳ 轉承詞 — 話題轉換

① 與…有關:in connection with, have to do with

② 關於:with regard to, in regard to, with respect to, concerning, regarding, in reference to, in relation to

③ 就…而言;至於…:for..., as for..., as to..., so far as...

④ 提及:when it comes to N. / V-ing, speaking of...

Part 1
Part 2
Part 3
Part 4
Part 5
Part 6

• 3-04 • 詢問汽車保險

Subject | Car Rental and Travel Expense

Dear Sir:

I am writing to enquire about the **automobile**[1] **insurance**[2]. I will have **a business trip**[3] next month and need to travel from San Francisco to New York. I would like to ask if you offer any of the insurances covering some of the **rental**[4] **charges**[5]. For instance, I rent a car while my car cannot be driven because of an accident or loss.

Please contact me if you have any of this **coverage**[6]. Thanks a lot.

Regards,
Fiona Tripson

先生您好：

我想詢問汽車保險事宜。下個月我將從舊金山至紐約出差，我想了解貴公司是否有與租車費用相關的保險。例如，萬一我因車禍或是車輛遺失而必須租車時，保險會支付多少額度的租車費？

如果您有任何這類型的保險，請與我聯絡，謝謝。

費歐娜・崔普森 敬上

Send

核心字彙充電站 *Key Words*

1. **automobile** 名 (美)汽車
2. **insurance** 名 保險
3. **a business trip** 片 公差
4. **rental** 名 租賃；出租
5. **charge** 名 費用；價錢
6. **coverage** 名 保險項目(或範圍)

替換好用句 Copy & Paste

詢問保險的問題

I'm an international student and have already got a driver's license. Is it possible for me to buy a car and get an auto insurance?
🖊 我是國際學生，已取得駕照。請問我是否可以買車及購買汽車保險？

Please explain the coverage of the auto insurance policy.
🖊 請說明汽車保險之保障範圍。

I want to know about mandatory coverage and optional coverage.
🖊 我想了解強制險和選擇險的相關內容。

What types of car insurance do you offer?
🖊 你們提供何種類型的汽車保險？

Is it possible to purchase insurance before obtaining a driver's license?
🖊 有可能在取得駕照前先行投保嗎？

When I have a flat tire in the remote area, can I be compensated for the cost?
🖊 當我在偏遠地區爆胎時，可以取得補助嗎？

When I damage a rental car, do you pay the total cost of repairs?
🖊 當我租的車損毀時，你們是否會負擔全額的維修費用？

租賃方的回應

There are two different types of car insurance: Basic Coverage vs. Full Coverage.
🖊 有二種不同的汽車保險類型：基本險和全險。

Liability Coverage protects for damages to others if you are at fault in an accident.
🖊 若車禍責任歸屬於您時，責任險保障他人的損失。

Collision Coverage helps pay to repair your car after an accident.
🖊 車禍發生時，碰撞險可以給付您車輛的維修費用。

Part 1
Part 2
Part 3
Part 4
Part 5
Part 6

Comprehensive Coverage helps pay for your car resulting from a peril, such as theft or an earthquake.

🖋 綜合險可以賠償如竊盜、地震等危險因素所造成的損失。

Many companies will insist on a minimum of three years of US driving experience in order to qualify for lower rates and higher coverage.

🖋 許多公司會堅持要有三年以上的美國駕駛經驗，才能享有較低的保費和較多的保障。

Since the majority of international students have little or no experience driving in the States, they will end up paying more for less coverage.

🖋 由於大多數的國際學生都沒有什麼美國駕駛經驗，所以保費都較高，保障亦較少。

進階補充站 Let's learn more!

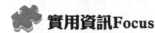

實用資訊Focus

汽車保險介紹 🔍

　　購買汽車保險須貨比三家。如果是購買新車，通常有與車商配合的保險公司；若是購買二手車，則須事先詢問清楚，在汽車過戶當天取得保單號碼，保險即可從過戶當天生效。每家保險公司的政策跟價格不同，車主買車條件也不同，所以要多方比較。例如：你可以在台灣申請無肇事證明，詢問保險員是否有折扣。有的保險公司完全不承認美國以外的紀錄，有的可享有折扣，有的則是購車第二年才可使用。

　　保險費的多寡涉及很多因素，如車況、居住地區（治安越好的地方保費越低）、汽車使用方式（每週使用天數等）、駕駛年紀及婚姻狀況等。此外，一旦接到罰單或發生事故，下一期的保費就會隨之增加。

常見的汽車保險 🔍

1. 責任險（Liability）：需強制投保。若車禍責任歸屬於你，責任險可賠償對方的損失，但不賠償你的損失。

2. 碰撞險（Collision）：可以賠償保險人的車輛。

3. 綜合險（Comprehensive）：賠償竊盜、地震等非車禍因素所造成的損失。

Unit 4 醫療相關事宜

·4-01· 掛號看診

Subject **Register With A Doctor**

Dear Sir or Madam:

I just moved to this town in the U.K. last month and would like to **register**[1] with a doctor and access your health services. I am wondering when is **available**[2] to see your doctor and to ask some questions.

Although there are many doctors' surgeries in Coventry, one of my friends **recommended**[3] me to visit your surgery near where I live and he explained that the services you offer may suit my family's needs.

I will appreciate it if you can reply me by telephone or email to let me know when I can **access**[4] your surgery.

Sincerely yours,
Tony Payton

Send ▸

敬啟者：

我上個月剛搬到英國這個城鎮，想要預約看診，並了解貴診療室的醫療服務。我想知道什麼時候方便與醫師見面，詢問一些問題。

雖然考文垂鎮上有許多診療室，但一位朋友建議我到住家附近的貴診療室。他說您提供的服務或許能符合我家人的需求。

如果您可以回電，或寄電子郵件給我，告訴我方便至貴診療室就診的時間，將不勝感激。

東尼‧佩頓 敬上

1. register 動 登記；註冊　　2. available 形 有空的
3. recommend 動 推薦　　4. access 動 進入；接近

替換好用句 Copy & Paste

I'd like to make an appointment to see a doctor.
🖋 我想要與醫師預約看診。

Can you recommend a good pediatrician near here?
🖋 您可以推薦附近好的小兒科醫生嗎？

Is Dr. Lee available on Thursday morning?
🖋 李醫師週四上午有空嗎？

Do you take morning appointments?
🖋 你們接受上午的預約嗎？

Do I need to register at the front desk when I arrive?
🖋 我到的時候，需不需要先到櫃檯掛號呢？

If I have insurance, should I bring my insurance card?
🖋 如果我有保險，需要帶保險卡去嗎？

Should I bring any medical records, x-rays or related documents?
🖋 我需要攜帶病歷或X光片等相關資料嗎？

I am wiring to enquire about what treatments are covered in my insurance.
🖋 我來信詢問有關我的醫療保險所支付的就診項目。

What is this medication effective for?
🖋 這種藥物的功效是什麼？

I am allergic to some drugs.
🖋 我對某些藥物過敏。

How long does each treatment last?
🖋 每次治療要多久時間？

How long is the entire course of therapy?

✏️ 整個療程有多長？

How often will I be treated a month?
✏️ 我一個月會做幾次療程？

Can someone accompany me to my treatment?
✏️ 我在進行治療時是否能有人陪同？

Can I have someone stay with me after my treatment?
✏️ 做完治療後，有人陪在身邊可以嗎？

Are there any foods, medications or activities that I should avoid after the treatment?
✏️ 做完治療後，我應避免食用哪些食品、藥物或避開哪些活動呢？

How soon can I go back to work after the treatment?
✏️ 做完治療後多久我才能回去工作？

Will the treatment fees be covered by my insurance?
✏️ 治療費用可以列入保險支付的範圍嗎？

Could you please explain the names and purposes of this test?
✏️ 可否請你解釋一下這項檢驗的名稱及用途？

When should I return for the next examination?
✏️ 下一次的回診檢查是什麼時候？

How often should I get an examination?
✏️ 我多久要做一次檢查？

When should I expect the results of these tests?
✏️ 何時能得知檢查結果？

I would like to get the copies of my records, scans, and X-rays.
✏️ 我需要就診紀錄、掃描圖以及X光片的影本。

Do these tests have any side effects?
✏️ 做這些檢查有任何副作用嗎？

What is the total number of sprays an allergy sufferer is recommended to take at one time?
✏️ 建議過敏性患者一回噴幾下？

What is the recommended minimum dose of tablets per day for an infant?
✏️ 建議嬰兒每日的最小服用量是幾錠？

Part 1
Part 2
Part 3
Part 4
Part 5
Part 6

進階補充站 Let's learn more!

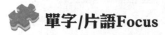
單字/片語Focus

❧ **各類醫師單字** ❧

* **physician** 內科醫生
* **surgeon** 外科醫生
* **dentist** 牙醫師
* **pediatrist** 小兒科醫師
* **cardiologist** 心臟科醫師
* **neurologist** 神經科醫師
* **orthopaedist** 整形外科醫師
* **dermatologist** 皮膚科醫師
* **psychiatrist** 精神科醫師
* **ophthalmologist** 眼科醫師
* **gynecologist** 婦科醫師
* **obstetrician** 產科醫師

❧ **各科門診單字** ❧

* **Medical Dept.** 內科
* **Surgical Dept.** 外科
* **Urology** 泌尿科
* **Dentistry (Dental) Dept.** 牙科
* **Pediatrics** 小兒科
* **Chinese Medicine** 中醫科
* **Cardiology Dept.** 心臟血管科
* **Neurology** 神經科
* **Gastroenterology** 腸胃科
* **Dermatology** 皮膚科
* **Psychiatry** 精神科
* **Ophthalmology** 眼科
* **Nephrology** 腎臟科
* **Otolaryngology** 耳鼻喉科
* **Obstetrics and Gynecology** 婦產科
* **Chinese Acupuncture** 中醫針灸科

❧ **醫藥用品相關單字** ❧

* **ambulance** 救護車
* **bandage** 繃帶
* **capsule** 膠囊
* **crutch** 拐杖
* **forceps** （醫用）鑷子
* **gauze** （醫用）紗布
* **antidote** 解毒劑
* **dress** 給（傷口）敷藥、包紮

✱oxygen mask 氧氣罩	✱penicillin 盤尼西林
✱plaster cast 石膏	✱sedative 鎮靜劑
✱stretcher 擔架	✱ultrasound 超音波
✱vaccination 接種（疫苗）	✱wheelchair 輪椅

❧ 診斷相關用語 ❧

✱waiting room 候診室	✱symptom 症狀
✱diagnosis 診斷	✱family history 家族病史
✱blood pressure 血壓	✱genetic 遺傳的
✱immune system 免疫系統	✱infection 感染
✱prescription 處方	✱pharmacy 藥房
✱side effects 副作用	✱vein 血管
✱chemotherapy 化學治療	✱deficiency 缺乏（營養）
✱emergency room (ER) 急診室	✱operating room (OR) 手術室

 實用資訊Focus

英文單字辨別 🔍

1. Hospital: 通常指一般的大型醫院，例如：長庚紀念醫院 Chang Gung Memorial Hospital；榮民總醫院 Veterans General Hospital 或 Veterans Hospital。
2. Clinic: 指私人診所，例如：吳醫師牙醫診所 Dr. Wu Dental Clinic；全德診所 Chan Der Clinic。
3. Surgery: 指的是診療室或診療地點，為英式用法。

在國外看診 🔍

　　國外看診的習慣不比國內，在台灣，大部分的診所或醫院皆為**walk-in service**，走進診所即可看病，但國外並非如此，除非緊急狀況，否則國外看診皆須事先預約，有時一等就要等好幾週，因此建議讀者，如果實在痛得受不了，可以先到藥房買止痛藥。

Part 1
Part 2
Part 3
Part 4
Part 5
Part 6

· 4-02 · 感謝醫師協助

Dear Doctor and Nurses:

Our family wishes to express our sincere appreciation for your kindness and excellent care during our mother, Mary Chen's hospitalization. We realized that she received the best care and support from your fine staff. You all helped us go through a difficult time, and we will never forget your kindness. Please express our appreciation to everyone who worked with our mom.

Very sincerely yours,
Jerry Chen

親愛的醫師及護理人員：

我們全家由衷地獻上感謝，謝謝你們對家母陳瑪麗於住院期間無微不至的照顧。我們了解貴醫院的醫療人員提供了最完善的照顧和支援，幫助我們一家渡過艱難的時刻，我們永遠都不會忘記你們的協助。請代我們向每一位照顧過家母的同仁致上我們的感謝。

陳傑瑞 敬上

Send ▶

替換好用句 Copy & Paste

All of us wish to thank you, Dr. Lee, for your kindness and wisdom during our father's bout of meningitis.
✐ 我們想要感謝李醫師，謝謝您在家父腦膜炎發作時所表達的關切和明智的處理。

Competent and sensitive physicians like you are the prize of the medical profession.
✐ 像您們這樣能幹又敏銳的醫師，不愧是醫界的杏林子。

The sensitivity and support we received from your fine staff helped us go through a very difficult time.
✐ 您們護理人員的細心照顧，幫助我們渡過難關。

I wish to express my gratitude to those who aided my recovery at the hospital.
🖋 我要獻上感謝給協助我的醫療人員。

Now that Father is gone, our family wishes to thank you for making his final months as comfortable and meaningful as possible.
🖋 如今父親雖已過世，我們還是要感謝您們讓他在人生最後的幾個月，得以活得自在、充滿意義。

Without your quick diagnosis and skilled hands, our daughter would not be celebrating her tenth birthday.
🖋 若是沒有您敏銳的診斷和技術，我們的女兒可能就無法迎接她的十歲生日了。

Your patience, sensitivity, and genuine concern enabled our mother to pass from this life with her pride.
🖋 您的耐心、敏銳與真誠的考量，使家母得以驕傲地離開人世。

You gave me the courage to believe in myself and try to walk again.
🖋 您的鼓勵使我相信自己，再次試著站起來走路。

Thanks to your skill, we are confident that Carol will recover quickly.
🖋 謝謝您的高超技術，我們有信心卡蘿很快就會復原。

 *Let's learn more!*

 單字/片語Focus

💊 一般病情描述 💊	
✱**headache** 頭痛	✱**nausea** 噁心
✱**vomiting** 嘔吐	✱**loss of appetite** 沒有食欲
✱**weight loss** 體重減輕	✱**fatigue** 疲倦；勞累
✱**fever** 發燒；發熱	✱**chills** 發冷；打顫
✱**drowsy** 昏昏欲睡	✱**dizzy** 頭暈目眩
💊 感冒症狀 💊	
✱**influenza** 流行性感冒	✱**cough** 咳嗽

Part 1
Part 2
Part 3
Part 4
Part 5
Part 6

✱thick spit 濃痰	✱persistent cough 不停咳嗽
✱yellow phlegm 黃色的痰	✱feel itchy 發癢
✱sneeze 打噴嚏	✱aching muscles 肌肉酸痛
✱sore throat 喉嚨痛	✱scratchy throat 喉嚨沙啞
✱stuffy nose 鼻塞	✱runny nose 流鼻水

🦴 腸胃毛病 🦴

✱indigestion 消化不良	✱abdominal pain 腹痛
✱bloated after eating 脹氣	✱constipation 便秘
✱diarrhea 拉肚子	

🦴 其他疾病 🦴

✱anemia 貧血（症）	✱anorexia 厭食
✱arrhythmia 心律不整	✱asthma 氣喘
✱diabetes 糖尿病	✱hemorrhoid 痔瘡
✱hypertension 高血壓	✱insomnia 失眠

 文法/句型Focus

✱ **感謝／感恩句型**

① **appreciate all you did** 感謝您所做的

② **for supporting us through** 支持我們渡過…

③ **for your patience** 因您的耐心

④ **have gratitude in our hearts** 真心感謝

⑤ **may God bless you** 願神祝福您

⑥ **thanks to your expertise and skills** 感謝您的專業和技術

Part 1

Part 2

Part 3

Part 4

Part 5

Part 6

· 4-03 · 懷孕問題與回覆

Subject | **Am I Pregnant?**

Dear Sir:

I have missed a **period**[1] for two months; however, I continue to have light periods for these days. Am I **pregnant**[2]? Should I see a doctor? Also, I would like to ask what the common pregnancy **symptoms**[3] are. Thanks for your reply.

Best regards,
Ella Lee

醫生您好：

我的經期已經有二個月沒來了，但這幾天都有微量的經血出現。我懷孕了嗎？需要看醫生嗎？我同時也想詢問懷孕常見的症狀，謝謝您的回覆。

李艾拉 敬上

Send

Subject | **Re: Am I Pregnant?**

Dear Ms. Lee:

Thanks for your message. If you have missed a period or **suspected**[4] you may be pregnant, we suggest you perform a Home Pregnancy Test or have your doctor perform a test to confirm pregnancy. The symptoms below are some of those **frequently**[5] reported signs by pregnant women. You can take a look.

1. Missed period. This is a common sign of pregnancy but is not an absolute one. Be sure to **consult**[6] your doctor.
2. Morning sickness. It is possible to begin feeling nauseated as early as a few days

親愛的李小姐：

謝謝您的來信。如果您發現經期沒來，或懷疑自己可能懷孕，我們建議您買驗孕棒測試，或請醫師檢查，確定是否懷孕。以下徵狀是大多數孕婦的常見現象，您可以參考看看。

1. 月經停止：這是懷孕常見的徵兆，但並非絕對的判斷依據。可以請教您的醫師。
2. 孕吐：受孕後幾天可能

after **conception**[7]. It doesn't just occur in the morning. It can occur any time of the day.

3. **Swollen**[8] breasts. Tender and swollen breasts are a common sign of pregnancy.

4. Changed appearance of breasts. The skin around your nipples usually darkens in color when you are pregnant.

5. **Extreme**[9] tiredness and frequent **urination**[10].

6. Food cravings. You may feel an **overwhelming**[11] **urge**[12] to eat certain foods.

7. Changed tastes or strange tastes.

Of course, everybody is different, and people suspect they are pregnant based on all sorts of symptoms. Don't forget to see your doctor first, and tell us if you are pregnant. We look forward to hearing from your good news.

Best regards,
Dr. Gerald

會開始感覺噁心、想吐。這種感覺不一定只出現在早晨，任何時候都有可能。

3. 乳房腫脹：乳房腫脹、輕觸就會疼痛是常見的懷孕現象。

4．乳房顏色變化：懷孕時，乳暈顏色通常會變深。

5. 容易疲倦和頻尿。

6. 食慾大增，會突然想吃某種食物。

7．對飲食的偏好有所改變。

當然，每個人的症狀不同，人們會因各式各樣的徵狀懷疑自己懷孕。所以，別忘了先去請教醫師，再告訴我們您是否懷孕。我們期盼聽到您的好消息。

傑洛德醫生 謹上

Send

核心字彙充電站 *Key Words*

1. **period** 名 月經
2. **pregnant** 形 懷孕的
3. **symptom** 名 症狀
4. **suspect** 動 疑有
5. **frequently** 副 經常
6. **consult** 動 請教
7. **conception** 名 胚胎；懷孕
8. **swollen** 形 膨脹的

Part 1

Part 2

Part 3

Part 4

Part 5

Part 6

9. extreme 形 極端的　　　**10. urination** 名 撒尿
11. overwhelming 形 壓倒的　　**12. urge** 名 衝動

 **替換好用句** Copy & Paste

 懷孕的相關問題

Is there any way I can tell if it is a girl or a boy?
🖊 如何得知寶寶是女孩還是男孩？

How long will the morning sickness last?
🖊 孕吐會持續多久？

How much weight will I gain?
🖊 體重會增加多少呢？

When will I feel the baby kick?
🖊 何時會開始感覺到胎動？

In what month does the baby start to see or hear?
🖊 寶寶從幾個月開始看得到、聽得到？

What can I do about my fatigue?
🖊 如何可以減輕疲勞？

How can I help my labor along?
🖊 如何可以幫助順產？

How do I calculate my due date?
🖊 如何計算我的預產期？

What dangers should I watch out for?
🖊 我需要注意什麼？

Is there anything unsafe in my house?
🖊 居家生活有何不安全之處？

 醫師回覆

Ultrasounds are pretty accurate (surprisingly not 100%).
🖊 超音波十分精準（但並非百分之百正確）。

Morning sickness should occur less and less by four months.

🖊 孕吐在四個月時，發生的次數就會越來越少。

The ideal weight zone you should gain is around 12-16 kg.

🖊 最理想的體重範圍應該是增加十二到十六公斤左右。

Be sure to ask your doctor how many calories you should be consuming.

🖊 請向你的醫師詢問卡路里攝取量的問題。

Between sixteen weeks to twenty weeks, you should feel the first noticeable kick.

🖊 十六週到二十週之間，你會首次感覺到明顯的胎動。

The baby should be able to hear the mother's voice at twenty weeks.

🖊 寶寶應該會在二十週時聽到母親的聲音。

You can play music for your baby, talk to your baby and have hubby talk to your baby.

🖊 你可以放音樂給寶寶聽，和你的寶寶說話，並讓爸爸和寶寶說話。

Avoid rough exercise.

🖊 避免劇烈運動。

Avoid drugs and alcohol, or secondhand smoke.

🖊 避免接觸藥物、酒類、及二手菸。

Always check with your doctor before taking any kind of medication.

🖊 須經醫師許可，才能服用藥物。

Avoid eating raw fish, unpasteurized milk, undercooked meat, and junk foods.

🖊 避免食用生魚、未經高溫消毒的牛奶、未煮熟的肉類、及垃圾食物。

進階補充站 Let's learn more!

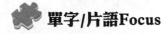

單字/片語Focus

🎀 懷孕期單字 🎀	
＊pregnancy 懷孕	**＊ovary** 卵巢

* ovulation 排卵
* fetal 胎兒的
* uterus 子宮
* fetal movement 胎動
* edema 水腫
* ultrasound 超音波
* miscarriage 流產
* premature birth 早產
* morning sickness 害喜（晨吐）
* striations of pregnancy 妊娠紋
* obstetrician visit (OB visit) 產檢

🔖 生產過程單字 🔖

* birth canal 產道
* cervix 子宮頸
* umbilical cord 臍帶
* placenta 胎盤
* labor pain 陣痛
* contraction 子宮收縮
* delivery 分娩
* natural labor 自然產
* epidural anesthesia 無痛分娩
* Caesarean section (C Section) 剖腹產
* date of delivery / due date 預產期

🔖 新生兒相關單字 🔖

* bib 圍兜
* burp 打嗝
* car seat 汽車安全座椅
* crib 嬰兒床
* cradle 嬰兒搖籃
* cuddle 擁抱
* diaper 尿布
* diaper bag 育嬰袋
* formula 奶粉
* high chair 兒童用高腳餐椅
* pacifier 奶嘴
* receiving blanket 嬰兒包巾
* stroller 嬰兒推車
* walker 學步車

Part 1
Part 2
Part 3
Part 4
Part 5
Part 6

Part 3

校園求學篇~必備對話這樣貼

Unit 1 入學申請事宜
Unit 2 住宿事宜詢問
Unit 3 銀行業務相關

動 動詞	名 名詞
副 副詞	形 形容詞
介 介系詞	片 片語

Point

校園信函的使用度其實相當高,舉凡註冊、課程、獎學金,甚至是住宿及申辦學生信用卡,這些全都用得上。這樣高頻的實用 E-mail,當然也能輕鬆「貼」,現在就來看看留學生活的話題有哪些。

•1-01• 詢問入學資訊

寫信到想就讀的大專院校，索取申請表或是詢問相關問題，不僅能獲得較詳細的資訊，也能藉此讓校方更認識你，錄取機率可能會更大呢！

Subject | **Request for Application**

Dear Sir or Madam:

My name is Abby Chou and **currently**[1] a student at National Taiwan University in Taiwan. I am planning to study English at your school next summer and would like to know more about the **application**[2] **details**[3]. I would appreciate it if you could send the information to the following mailing address:

Attn: Abby, Chou
No.9, Lane 29, San Min Road,
Taipei City 105,
Taiwan, R.O.C.

Thank you very much for your **assistance**[4] and I look forward to hearing from you.

Sincerely,
Abby Chou

Send ▶

敬啟者：

我的名字叫周艾比，目前是台灣大學的學生。我打算明年暑假到貴校進修英語，所以想請問學校可否先寄入學申請的相關資料給我，麻煩將資料寄至以下住址：

105台北市三民路29巷9號，周艾比收。

謝謝您的協助，期望收到您的回覆。

周艾比 謹上

Part 1

Part 2

Part 3

Part 4

Part 5

Part 6

核心字彙充電站 *Key Words*

1. **currently** 副 目前
2. **application** 名 申請；請求
3. **detail** 名 細節；詳情
4. **assistance** 名 援助；幫助

替換好用句 *Copy & Paste*

 簡述自己

I will graduate in the coming summer, and I am now beginning to gather information about the universities in America.

🖊 我將於今年暑假畢業，目前正開始蒐集美國大學的相關資料。

I was enrolled to study chemistry in National Taipei University in September, 2012.

🖊 我於二〇一二年九月入學，就讀國立台北大學化學系。

I had been studying at THU for four years and graduated in June, 2015.

🖊 我在東海大學就讀四年，於二〇一五年六月畢業。

I wish to enter University of Cambridge for a master degree in physics.

🖊 我想進入劍橋大學攻讀物理學碩士。

I am applying for admission to your graduate school of Education program for the spring term of 2016.

🖊 我目前正在申請貴校二〇一六年教育研究所的春季班。

Deeply interested in your graduate school of your MBA program, I plan to apply for the fall term of 2017.

🖊 我對貴校商管研究所的課程感興趣，欲申請於二〇一七年秋季班入學。

I would like to study history in your college and hope for a place for the next semester.

🖊 我想在貴學院攻讀歷史，希望下學期可以入學。

I am particularly interested in and good at engineering.

🖊 我對工程科系特別感興趣，也很擅長這個領域。

My GPA in the university was 3.5.

✐ 我大學的畢業成績是3.5。

I have achieved a score of 600+ on the GMAT.
✐ 我的GMAT分數有600分以上。

I have finished my bachelor's degree in Taiwan.
✐ 我在台灣完成學士學位。

I could be an ideal candidate for your program.
✐ 我會是貴系所要錄取的理想人選。

 ## 入學相關資料

I will certainly have my documents prepared as soon as I can.
✐ 我會盡快將資料備齊。

I enclose my qualifications herewith.
✐ 隨信附上我的學位證書。

Are there any other departmental requirements to be fulfilled?
✐ 貴系是否需要我附上其他相關文件呢？

I am very grateful for the information about entry to your college.
✐ 我很高興得到貴校的申請就讀資訊。

I will appreciate it if you send me the necessary application forms.
✐ 若您能寄來申請表，我將非常感激。

Please send the application forms to the following email address:123cjl@net.com.
✐ 請將申請表寄至以下電子信箱：123cjl@net.com。

 ## 其他相關問題

Is there a personal interview?
✐ 需要進行個人面談嗎？

How can I request a fee waiver?
✐ 我該如何申請學費減免？

Can I get a receipt for my application fee?
✐ 可以給我申請費的收據嗎？

What kind of admissions criteria does your university use?
🖋 貴校申請入學的標準為何？

How important are extracurricular activities in admissions decisions?
🖋 課外活動的表現對於決定入學有多重要？

Could you kindly suggest which of the program would be most likely suitable for me?
🖋 您可以推薦適合我的課程嗎？

I have no idea which courses I should apply for.
🖋 我不知道該申請哪一門課程。

 Let's learn more!

 單字/片語Focus

🏷 申請與註冊課程 🏷

✱**course** 課程	✱**semester** 學期
✱**credit** 學分	✱**enroll in** 登記
✱**add** 加選	✱**drop** 退選
✱**selection** 選擇	✱**professor** 教授

 實用資訊Focus

篩選學校的考量 🔍

蒐集學校資料是件手續浩繁的工程，閱讀學校網頁上的資訊也很花時間。一般在篩選學校的過程中，有幾點主要考量：

1. 符合自己需求的主修類別（Major）
2. 符合自己的入學門檻（Requirements）
3. 選擇自己喜歡的學校地點（Location）
4. 對學校排名的重視（Ranking）
5. 預期範圍內的費用（包含學費Tuition與生活費Expenses）

Part 1
Part 2
Part 3
Part 4
Part 5
Part 6

·1-02· 申請入學信函

Dear Mr. Smith:

I am writing to apply for **admission**[1] to your MA program this coming **academic**[2] year. I am sending you with my application form and **transcript**[3] of record. I am also **submitting**[4] my **resume**[5], personal statement, and two letters of **recommendation**[6] from my department director and one of my teachers for your reference.

I hope that I will be admitted to your department which is the outstanding academic program among the top schools in the country. I know that I will be able to get a good education at your department which will help me in **pursuing**[7] a career in computer science. I believe that my good **scholastic**[8] records make me a good **candidate**[9] to become a graduate student at your college. I am an **industrious**[10] student and I take my studies seriously. I hope you will give me this opportunity to become part of your **distinguished**[11] program.

Thank you for your kind **consideration**[12].

Respectfully yours,
Margaret Cole

Send

史密斯先生您好：

我來信申請下學年的碩士班課程。隨信附上申請表和成績單，以及我的履歷表、讀書計畫、及兩封分別由系主任和老師撰寫之推薦信，供您參考。

希望我能被貴系錄取。貴系在全國學術的表現上名列前茅。在貴校接受與電腦資訊有關的良好知識，將裨益我的職涯。以敝人在學術上優秀的表現，應該能成為貴系的研究生。我勤於學習、專於研究，盼望您可以給我就讀貴校的機會。

謝謝您的考慮。

瑪格麗特·柯爾 謹上

Part 1

Part 2

Part 3

Part 4

Part 5

Part 6

核心字彙充電站 Key Words

1. **admission** 名 進入許可
2. **academic** 形 學術的
3. **transcript** 名 學生成績單
4. **submit** 動 提交；呈遞
5. **resume** 名 履歷
6. **recommendation** 名 推薦
7. **pursue** 動 從事；繼續
8. **scholastic** 形 學校的
9. **candidate** 名 候選人；應試者
10. **industrious** 形 勤勉的
11. **distinguished** 形 卓越的
12. **consideration** 名 考慮

替換好用句 Copy & Paste

I have learned from my professor that your university is one of the best in the field of Teaching.
🖉 教授曾提及貴校在教學領域中十分有名。

I would like to apply for admission to your university next academic year.
🖉 我欲於下學年申請貴校。

I found out the Graduate School program on your website.
🖉 我在網站上看到貴校的研究所課程。

I am very interested in applying for admission to your Graduate School.
🖉 我對申請貴校的碩士班課程深感興趣。

I am sending you my application form and other requirements as stated on your website.
🖉 隨信附上申請表及網站上提到的相關資料。

I have attached the duly signed application form with this letter.
🖉 附上已簽名的申請表。

I have also attached a copy of my undergraduate transcript and two recommendation letters.
🖉 隨信附上我的大學成績單和兩封推薦信。

I graduated last year as one of the top students in my class.
🖉 去年我以優異的成績畢業。

I was recognized for my excellent performance in engineering.
🖉 我在工程學的優異表現有目共睹。

I took up my undergraduate degree in Biology from a distinguished school in Taiwan.
🖉 我在台灣一所卓越的大學就讀生物系。

I graduated with honors and received a special award for excellence in science subjects.
🖉 我以優秀的成績畢業，並榮獲科學領域的特別獎。

I have represented my school in several English speech contests and won the awards.
🖉 我數度代表學校參加英語演講比賽得獎。

I have been interested in the field of science since I was a child.
🖉 我從小就對自然科學感興趣。

I was an active member of the History Society in school and was the vice director for a year before I graduated.
🖉 我參加學校的歷史社時，表現很活躍，曾於畢業前擔任一年的副社長。

I want to pursue higher studies because I believe that learning does not stop after receiving a bachelor's degree.
🖉 我相信學無止境，因此大學畢業後想繼續深造。

I am looking forward to joining your program.
🖉 我期盼能夠加入您的課程。

The Warwick MBA is ranked among the world's best business schools.
🖉 華威大學的企業管理碩士是世界排名領先的商管學程。

Having a chance to spend another year in your lively campus is my dream.
🖉 能再於貴校就讀一年，融入學校活躍的氣氛是我的夢想。

Your university will be providing me with knowledge and development opportunities for life.
🖉 貴校能提供我所需學習的知識以及未來發展的機會。

Your college also offers exciting and interactive talks, discussions, workshops and entertainment.
🖉 貴校也提供有趣的互動式演講、討論、研討會和娛樂活動。

Your university is one of the most famous universities in the U.S.

✒ 貴校是全美最有名氣的大學之一。

Your university has a long history of over one hundred years and enjoys worldwide reputation.
✒ 貴校擁有百年歷史，且聲譽享遍全球。

The climate in San Francisco is favorable and suits me a lot.
✒ 舊金山氣候宜人，非常適合我。

I am looking for a university where living expenses are not as high as in big cities.
✒ 我正在尋找一所生活費用沒有大城市那麼貴的大學就讀。

All these might be the reasons why I select USC as the ideal university where I would like to have my further studies.
✒ 這些是我選擇到加州州立大學進修的原因。

I hope you would give me an opportunity to pursue this dream.
✒ 盼望您能給予我追求夢想的機會。

I hope I will be considered for admission to your program.
✒ 盼望我可以被貴系錄取。

 Let's learn more!

 實用資訊Focus

申請表格 🔍

　　申請表格（Application Form / Enrollment Form）為提供申請者填寫基本資料的表格。除了填寫姓名、地址、欲申請之課程等基本資料外，可能會要求你附上其他資料。比較常見的要求如下：

1. 畢業英文成績單，含 GPA （Transcripts）
2. 托福／雅思／研究生入學考試等成績（TOEFL, IELTS, GRE）
3. 財力證明（Financial Statement）
4. 推薦信（Recommendation Letter）
5. 履歷表（Resume）
6. 自傳（Autobiography）

Part 1
Part 2
Part 3
Part 4
Part 5
Part 6

7. 個人陳述（Personal Statement）

8. 讀書計劃（Statement of Purpose）

9. 英文寫作（Writing Samples）

10. 工作經驗與研究經驗 （Work & Research Experiences）

11. 曾得過的獎項或發表過的作品 （Awards & Achievements）

　　目前，很多學校採取網路填寫表格的方式，不僅省下郵寄費用，更省下魚雁往返的時間。此外，關於申請入學的手續費，儘可能在送出申請資料的同時匯款給校方，讓申請程序得以順利進行。若申請人在申請時沒有繳交手續費，將無法進行申請程序。申請費用通常不會因校方拒絕申請者的申請、或是申請者決定取消入學而退還。

申請美國學校需準備的考試

　　越來越多人選擇赴美深造，但是對於要準備的考試類型卻不甚清楚，因此以下將介紹幾種常見的考試類型：

1. 托福（TOFEL, Test of English as a Foreign Language）：語言類考試。由美國教育考試服務處舉辦，為申請去美國或加拿大等國家就學之非英語系國家學生所提供的一種英語水準考試。考試成績的有效期為兩年。

2. SAT（Scholastic Assessment Test）：為「美國高中生進入大學」所必須參加的考試，也是世界各國高中生申請美國大學、及能否得到獎學金的重要參考。SAT成績的有效期為兩年。

3. GRE（Graduate Record Examination）：為攻讀碩士、博士學位的大學生幾乎都必須參加的考試。GRE成績也是各大學決定是否提供獎學金的重要參考依據。考題由語文、數學和邏輯三個部分組成，成績有效期為五年。

4. GMAT（Graduate Management Admission Test）：為美國商科和管理類研究生的入學考試。滿分800分，一般大學都要求在600分以上。

5. LAST（Law School Admission Test）：測試赴美加地區留學學生的英語能力，其成績只是作為申請進入法學院的評估條件之一。成績有效期為五年。

Part 1
Part 2
Part 3
Part 4
Part 5
Part 6

·1-03· 詢問獎助學金

Subject Request for Scholarship

Dear Sir:

Having graduated from Department of Sociology at TungHai University in June, 2016, I would like to apply for admission and a scholarship at your university for the full semester of 2017. I would appreciate it if you could send me the necessary application forms and details of financial assistance.

I will forward my supporting documents to you as soon as I receive your reply. I look forward to hearing from you.

Respectfully yours,
Jenny Fang

Send

先生您好：

二〇一六年六月我畢業於東海大學社會系，目前計劃申請貴校二〇一七年秋季入學的招生及獎學金。如果您能寄給我貴系的入學申請表及獎助學金詳情，將深表感謝。

收到您的回覆後，我會盡快把所有相關證明文件寄給您。期待您的消息。

方珍妮 敬上

替換好用句 *Copy & Paste*

I would like to know more details about the scholarships that offer to students from other countries.
🖊 我想了解關於提供給國際學生的獎學金詳情。

- - - - - - - - - - - - - - - - - - - -

I would appreciate it if you could send me the information about financial assistance for Master's Degree.
🖊 如能寄給我關於碩士班獎助學金方案之資訊，將不勝感激。

- - - - - - - - - - - - - - - - - - - -

I want to apply for the scholarship at your university during the 2017-2018 academic years.

✐ 我想申請貴校二〇一七到二〇一八學年的獎學金。

Dr. Chou advised me to contact you for information about the scholarship opportunities.
✐ 周教授建議我與您聯繫，詢問關於獎學金的資訊。

I want to apply for the scholarship, and I should be grateful to know the conditions under which your committee is prepared for the applicants.
✐ 我要申請獎學金，想知道申請者需要具備什麼條件？

I was wondering if you would kindly grant me an assistantship with an annual stipend of US$5,000.
✐ 不知道您是否願意提供我一年五千美元的助理獎學金？

In order to reduce the financial responsibility of my parents, I earnestly hope to obtain some financial aid.
✐ 為了減輕雙親的經濟負擔，我極為盼望能獲得獎學金補助。

Would you kindly consider this request and advise me as to the possibilities?
✐ 可否勞駕您考慮我的請求，並告知我錄取的機率？

Should further information be required, please let me know at your earliest convenience.
✐ 如需進一步資料，您若方便請儘早告知我。

進階補充站　*Let's learn more!*

文法/句型Focus

❶ 完成式分詞構句：**having + V-p.p.** 已經…（表時間相對較早之事件）

Having graduated from the university, I would like to apply for the master's degree.
我已大學畢業，想申請碩士學位。

❷ 副詞子句（附屬連接詞所引導的子句）：**as soon as / the instant / the moment / the minute / immediately / instantly** 一…，就…

As soon as I get spam emails, I delete them without reading them.

我一收到垃圾郵件，讀也不讀就刪除了。

 實用資訊Focus

美國獎學金之種類 🔍

美國大學可供國際學生申請的獎學金有以下六種：

1. 助學金（Fellowship）：免學雜費、住宿費、保險費、生活費，還會補貼學生的個人消費。
2. 獎學金（Scholarship）：按規定金額數量頒發給學生，金額比Fellowship要少一些，是一種榮譽性的獎勵。
3. 學費減免（Tuition-Waiver）：分為州內學費、州外學費、國際學生學費。
4. 研究助理和教學助理獎學金（Research Assistantship & Teaching Assistantship）：屬服務性資金，學生必須協助教授研究和教學達一定程度才能獲准申請。
5. 校內和校外住宿減免（On or Off-Campus Housing Credit or Saving）：校內是學校提供免費住宿；校外則是透過學校安排校外相對便宜的住宿。
6. 校內工作（On-Campus Job）：學生藉由校內打工獲得收入。

申請國外學校須知 🔍

1. 申請人須在校成績優秀。
2. 申請人的英文程度須達考試標準（須提供托福或雅思成績證明）。
3. 詢問學校是否提供獎學金給國際學生（半額或全額獎學金）。
4. 詢問本國國內提供獎學金的機構，如公費留學考試。

國外獎學金申請要求概略（以MBA商業管理碩士為例）🔍

1. GMAT（Graduate Management Admission Test）認證考試：630分以上
2. 畢業成績（GPA）：3.0以上（換算成台灣標準要達80分以上）
3. 工作經驗：三年以上（兼職或實習經歷皆可）
4. 英語能力：電腦托福100分以上；紙本托福580以上；雅思6.5分以上

·1-04· 申請獎助學金

Dear Sir or Madam:

I am an international student from Taiwan and my name is Hen-ni Lee. I am **recently**[1] qualified for the MA program in the Applied **Linguistics**[2] in your **esteemed**[3] university this autumn. I am writing to request you to kindly consider my application for a half or full **scholarship**[4].

I finished my **undergraduate**[5] degree from National Taipei University and was among the top 3 students in my department. I also took part in the World English Project 2014 held in London and won an award for our country.

It has always been my dream to study in your university and a scholarship will be of great help to me because of my **feeble**[6] **financial**[7] condition. I am **enclosing**[8] copies of my academic and nonacademic **certificates**[9] and mark sheets for your **reference**[10]. I will be very grateful if you accept my application.

I hope to hear from you soon.

Yours truly,
Hen-ni Lee

Send

敬啟者：

我是來自台灣的國際學生，名叫李涵妮。我將於今年秋季就讀貴校應用語言學的碩士課程。我來信是想請您考慮我的半額或全額獎學金申請。

我在國立台北大學完成學士學位，系上成績排名是在前三名。也曾於倫敦參加二〇一四年世界英語計劃，還因此贏得獎項，為國爭光。

就讀貴校一直是我的夢想，獎學金的取得將給予我經濟上極大的幫助。隨信附上在學時的校內成績單和校外各項表現記錄，供您參考。若能被錄取，將感激不盡。

盼望佳音。

李涵妮 謹上

Part 1

Part 2

Part 3

Part 4

Part 5

Part 6

核心字彙充電站 Key Words

1. recently 副 最近	2. linguistics 名 語言學
3. esteem 動 尊重;尊敬	4. scholarship 名 獎學金
5. undergraduate 形 大學的	6. feeble 形 微弱的;薄弱的
7. financial 形 財務的	8. enclose 動 把(公文等)封入
9. certificate 名 證明書;執照	10. reference 名 參考;參照

替換好用句 Copy & Paste

One of my friends, an alumnus of your university, introduced me to your scholarship program.
🖉 我有一位朋友是貴校校友,向我介紹貴校的獎學金計畫。

I am extremely interested in this scholarship program and would like to apply for it.
🖉 我對於本獎學金計畫深感興趣,並欲申請。

I am extremely interested in pursuing a higher degree in education program and would be indebted if your prestigious college selects me as an ideal candidate for a scholarship.
🖉 我對於深造教育課程深感興趣,若貴校能提供獎學金給我,將感激不盡。

I am writing to request for a scholarship to support my studies as I belong to a very poor family.
🖉 我來信詢問獎學金事宜,希望能藉此減輕家庭經濟負擔。

The International Student Scholarship is a great match to my interests and personal background.
🖉 國際學生獎學金的申請條件和我的興趣及背景相符合。

I look forward to hearing from you to complete the process.
🖉 期待您們的來信,使我得以完成申請手續。

In the meantime, I would like to attach my resume with this letter.
🖉 同時,隨信附上我的履歷表。

I would like to take this opportunity to thank you and the Scholarship Committee for supporting students with an opportunity for financial assistance.

✐ 藉此感謝您及獎學金委員會，提供學生財務上的支持。

You will also find my application form, high school transcript, letters of recommendation, and other pertinent information enclosed herewith.
✐ 附件為我的申請表、高中成績單、推薦信及其他相關文件。

Together with the application letter, I enclose the completed scholarship application form.
✐ 寄上這封申請信的同時，我也附上填寫完畢的獎學金申請表。

I will be pleased to receive a scholarship offered by your esteemed institution to pursue my Master's Degree in International Relations.
✐ 盼能收到貴校的獎學金錄取通知，並順利就讀國際關係碩士課程。

Thank you for taking time to read this letter of my application for the scholarship.
✐ 感謝您撥冗閱讀我的獎學金申請信函。

I will be very grateful if you accept my application as it will immensely help me financially.
✐ 若您能發給獎學金，給予我經濟上的大力幫助，我將感激不盡。

Your kind consideration is highly appreciated and I look forward to hearing from you soon.
✐ 請予以考慮，我在此靜候佳音。

I request you to kindly accept my application for the scholarship.
✐ 請求您考慮我的獎學金申請。

I believe I would be an ideal candidate for the scholarship.
✐ 我相信我會是這個獎學金的適合人選。

 進階補充站 Let's learn more!

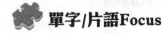 單字/片語Focus

❦ 科系與學院 ❦	
＊Anthropology 人類學	**＊Art** 美術
＊History 歷史	**＊Theater Arts** 戲劇藝術

* **Geography** 地理
* **Biology** 生物
* **Physics** 物理
* **Chemistry** 化學
* **Psychology** 心理
* **Sociology** 社會學
* **Humanities** 人文學科
* **Nursing** 護理
* **Economics** 經濟學
* **Political Science** 政治學
* **Communications** 傳播
* **English Literature** 英國文學
* **Special Education** 特殊教育
* **Clinical Science** 臨床科學
* **Social Work** 社會工作
* **Computer Science** 電腦科學
* **Public Administration** 公共行政
* **MBA** 商業管理研究
* **College of Education** 教育學院
* **College of Public Policy** 公共政策學院
* **College of Liberal Arts** 人文藝術學院
* **College of Business Administration** 企業管理學院
* **College of Health and Human Services** 健康與人類服務學院

❧ 學級與學制 ❧

* **day nursery** 托兒所
* **kindergarten** 幼稚園
* **elementary school** 小學
* **junior high school** 中學
* **senior high school** 高中
* **technical high school** 高工
* **commercial high school** 高商
* **junior college** 專科學校
* **university** 綜合大學
* **community college** 社區大學
* **private** 私立的
* **public** 公立的
* **bachelor** 學士
* **master** 碩士
* **PhD** 博士
* **Certificate Course** 證照課程

Part 1
Part 2
Part 3
Part 4
Part 5
Part 6

1-05 請求撰寫推薦信

應該請誰幫你寫推薦信最恰當？教過你的老師、班導師、系主任、指導教授、上司都是不錯的人選。由於推薦信不得對外公開，所以要記得請求推薦人寫完推薦信後，將信件放入你為他準備好的信封內，彌封後簽名，接著申請人就可把推薦信寄到欲申請的學校單位。最後，別忘了謝謝費心幫你寫推薦信的人喔！

Subject Recommendation Letter

Dear Dr. Zheng:

I am Emma, a junior in your music department. I am applying for a summer **session**[1] program in Music this summer, and my **contact**[2] to you today is regarding a recommendation I am seeking for you to write **on my behalf**[3]. I would appreciate it if you could do this for me since you know the quality of my work and my **potential**[4] for studying in this field.

The course I took from you last semester, music performance, has helped me develop self-confidence and growth of my **passion**[5] for music performance. I got an A in your class. And I believe that you will support my decision to this summer session program. What's more, since the program is held by the University of Pennsylvania, and I know that you've studied there and have been in a good relationship with some **professors**[6], I do believe that you are in the best position to write a recommendation letter for me. They have put a deadline

鄭教授您好：

我是艾瑪，音樂系三年級的學生。今天寫信給您，是想請您幫我寫推薦信。我正計劃於今年暑假申請一個音樂系的暑期課程，而您了解我課業上的表現以及在這個領域的發展潛力，所以，如果您能幫助我，將深深感謝。

上學期我修習您開設的音樂表演課程，幫助我建立自信心，也增加了我對音樂表演的熱忱。我在您的課堂上取得A的好成績，相信您會支持我參加暑期音樂課程。此外，該課程是由美國賓州大學所舉辦，我知道您曾於此求學，與校內教授互動良好，所以我相信您是幫我撰寫推薦信的最佳人選。

of June 30, so, should you decide to recommend me, I would send you a **draft**[7] of my statement of purpose, copies of my transcripts, my resume, a writing sample, and some other **materials**[8] to help you in the recommendation process.

Your **aid**[9] in this request would greatly be appreciated. If you have any questions or concerns, you can **contact**[10] me by phone: 0912-115115 or through email at emmalin@net.com.

Thank you for your time and consideration. I'm looking forward to hearing from you!

Yours sincerely,
Emma Lin

學校收推薦信的最後期限是六月三十日，若您決定幫我寫推薦信，我會將我的讀書計畫、成績單影本、履歷表、寫作範例，以及其他能夠用得上的文件附給您。

十分感謝您的協助。若您有任何疑問，請用手機或電子郵件和我聯絡。

謝謝您撥出寶貴的時間考慮，期盼回音！

林艾瑪 敬上

核心字彙充電站 Key Words

1. session 名 （大學的）學期
2. contact 名 聯繫；聯絡
3. on one's behalf 片 代表
4. potential 名 潛力
5. passion 名 熱情
6. professor 名 教授
7. draft 名 草稿
8. material 名 資料；材料
9. aid 名 幫助；援助
10. contact 動 聯絡

替換好用句 Copy & Paste

I am writing to ask whether it would be possible for you to provide a reference for me.

🖉 我寫信是想詢問您是否能幫我寫推薦信？

Part 1
Part 2
Part 3
Part 4
Part 5
Part 6

My contact to you today is regarding a recommendation I am seeking for you to write on my behalf.
🖋 我想請您替我撰寫推薦信。

I am hoping you will agree to serve as one of my references.
🖋 希望您能夠同意幫我撰寫推薦信。

Enclose my autobiography and studying plan as follows.
🖋 以下附上我的自傳以及讀書計畫。

I appreciate you for taking the time to write this letter of recommendation.
🖋 非常感謝您撥冗幫我寫推薦信。

Please let me know if you need any other information from me.
🖋 若您需要更多資訊,煩請告知。

Please use the attached envelope to mail the letter directly to the college.
🖋 煩請直接把信件寄到學校。

 進階補充站 Let's learn more!

 文法/句型Focus

✱ 句型結構剖析

① 現在完成式:**have + V-p.p.** 已經⋯
They have put a deadline of June 30.
他們已將截止期限設在六月三十日。

② 被動態:**be + V-p.p.** 被⋯
The program is held by the University of Pennsylvania.
課程於賓州大學舉辦。

③ 倒裝句-假設語氣中的**if**省略後
If anyone should ring, please take a message.
→ **Should anyone ring, please take a message.**
若有人來電,煩請幫忙留言。

Part 1

Part 2

Part 3

Part 4

Part 5

Part 6

·1–06· 推薦信範例

Subject Recommendation for Emma Lin

Dear Sir and Madam:

It is with much pleasure that I recommend Ms. Emma Lin as a **worthwhile**[1] applicant for admission to your university in the field of Music, **commencing**[2] this summer of 2016.

Emma was an outstanding student. As the **Chairman**[3] of the Department of Music from 2011 to 2014, I have known her since 2012 when she **participated in**[4] several music **competitions**[5], and won the awards for her best performances. I was **impressed**[6] by her excellence in music performance when she took my courses in her **sophomore**[7] year. On account of her hard work, her grades were ranked on the top 5% of her class. She was really a student I know, who was **enthusiastic**[8] over her work.

Emma was a student with great potentialities and made some musical **achievements**[9] in our department. In addition to her **superiority**[10] in violin, she was also interested in **symphony**[11] **orchestra**[12]. She has been participated in Taiwan Symphony Orchestra for three years. She showed herself to have a better potentiality. If guided and trained well, she will be

敬啟者：

能夠推薦林艾瑪小姐為合格的申請者是我極大的榮幸，她將申請於二〇一六年暑假到貴校音樂系就讀。

艾瑪是位傑出的學生。在我二〇一一年至二〇一四年擔任音樂系的系主任期間，她曾於二〇一二年參加數場音樂競賽，皆表現優異而獲獎。當她二年級上我的課時，我對她的傑出表現印象深刻。因為她在學業上的認真表現，因此學期成績在班上排名前百分之五。就我對她的認識，她對音樂充滿了熱忱。

艾瑪擁有無限潛力且在系上創下不少音樂成就。除了在小提琴方面的優勢外，她也對交響樂團感興趣。她加入台灣交響樂團已有三年的時間，展現出優越的潛力。若經由良好的指導和訓練，她就會在

successful in this field.

音樂領域上發光發熱。

Ms. Emma Lin is an **ambitious**[13] and **promising**[14] young girl. If given an opportunity, she will be a credit to your university. Your favorable consideration for the admission will be appreciated.

林艾瑪小姐是位野心勃勃、前途無量的年輕女孩。如果能給她一個機會，她將會是為貴校增光的優秀人才。在此感謝您的贊同及考慮入學許可。

Truly yours,
Zheng Ching-Yi

鄭景益 謹上

Send

核心字彙充電站 *Key Words*

1. **worthwhile** 形 又真實價值的
2. **commence** 動 開始；著手
3. **chairman** 名（大學的）系主任
4. **participate in** 片 參與
5. **competition** 名 競賽
6. **impress** 動 使人印象深刻
7. **sophomore** 名 大二生
8. **enthusiastic** 形 熱情的；熱心的
9. **achievement** 名 成就；成績
10. **superiority** 名 優勢；上等
11. **symphony** 名 交響樂
12. **orchestra** 名 管弦樂團
13. **ambitious** 形 野心勃勃的
14. **promising** 形 有前途的

替換好用句 *Copy & Paste*

At the request of Emma, a former student of mine, I am writing this letter in support of her application.
🖊 我之前的學生艾瑪請我為她寫這封信，以表示支持她的申請。

She comes with my highest recommendation.
🖊 我非常推薦她。

I am glad to have this opportunity to recommend Emma.

✏ 我很高興有這個機會推薦艾瑪。

During her time as a student here, her academic performance was excellent.
✏ 在本校求學期間，她的課業表現優良。

She always listened attentively, and participated actively in class.
✏ 她總是專心聽講，並積極參與課程。

Emma is not only quick at learning and good at solving problems, but also with a logical mind that enables her to effectively analyze all kinds of data.
✏ 艾瑪不僅學習能力強、善於解決難題，且邏輯能力佳，能有效分析各種資訊。

I will do my best to persuade you: She is exactly the student who you want.
✏ 我願竭盡所能說服您：她的確是您們想要的學生。

Actually, she is so reliable that I assign her with heavy responsibilities.
✏ 實際上，她是個可靠的學生，我讓她擔負重大責任。

I have faith in her abilities.
✏ 我對她的能力深具信心。

Based on her previous performance, I am certain that she will be a very successful student at your university.
✏ 根據她先前的表現，我深信她在貴校會是一位成功的學生。

I feel confident that she will continue to succeed in her studies.
✏ 我深信她在課業上將持續有傑出表現。

I am thus pleased to give my full support and recommendation to Emma's application for admission to your school.
✏ 我全力支持並推薦艾瑪申請貴校。

I know that the good chance is only offered to outstanding students.
✏ 我知道好機會只提供給優秀的學生。

Throughout the years, he was consistently involved with extracurricular activities.
✏ 這些年來，他都參與課外活動。

I am pleased to have this opportunity to commend on his contributions.
✏ 很高興有機會讚賞他的貢獻。

Part 1
Part 2
Part 3
Part 4
Part 5
Part 6

I truly believe that you will find him to be an excellent student.
🖊 相信您會發現他是一位優秀的學生。

If any further information is required, please feel free to contact me.
🖊 如果有任何疑問，歡迎你們聯絡我。

 進階補充站　*Let's learn more!*

文法/句型Focus

❶ 稱謂語**Gentlemen**可以用**To Whom It May Concern**代替（完全不知道收信者相關資訊時可用）。

❷ **On account of + N.**（因為…；由於…）後接名詞，與**due to**的概念相同。

It is due to / on account of all his hard work over the winter months that he has passed the exam with such a good grade.
由於寒假期間的努力，他取得好成績。

That was on account of lack of exercise.
那是由於缺乏運動。

All transportation services have been suspended on account of typhoon.
所有的運輸服務皆因颱風而暫停行駛。

實用資訊Focus

推薦信的重要性 🔍

　　推薦信是現實生活中推銷自己的一種廣告。找到有利於自己的推薦者極為重要。推薦信數量依學校要求而有所不同，通常有工作經驗之申請者，最好準備學術（學校教授）及工作（工作長官）的推薦信各一份，以證明學術及專業上的平衡。推薦信的重要性不僅影響到能否出國留學，也關係到獎學金的申請喔！

Part 1

Part 2

Part 3

Part 4

Part 5

Part 6

•1-07• 詢問如何撰寫讀書計畫

Subject How to Write An SOP

Dear Professor:

I am an international student in your English class on Monday morning. My name is Jessie Chou. I am planning to apply for Oxford University this summer; therefore, I would like to make an **appointment**[1] with you this Thursday to **discuss**[2] how to write a good statement of purpose (SOP).

Your assistance will be appreciated.

Sincerely yours,
Jessie Chou

教授您好：

我叫周潔西，是一名國際學生，就讀您每週一上午的英文課程。我正計劃於今年暑假申請牛津大學，因此，想跟您預約本週四向您討教如何寫好一篇讀書計畫。

感謝您的協助。

周潔西 敬上

Send

Subject Re: How to Write an SOP

Dear Jessie:

I am glad to hear your good news. Please come during my office hours on Thursday morning. We can talk about your statement of purpose (SOP). Before we discuss, please think about the following issue:

A story of your "future". In other words, the story of your SOP should link your past to your future. Paint a personal future while **weaving**[3] your **relevant**[4] past **experience**[5]

親愛的潔西：

我很開心聽到你的好消息，請在週四上午我的辦公時間前來，我們可以討論你的讀書計畫。在我們討論之前，請先思考以下主題：

一篇關於你「未來」的故事。換言之，讀書計畫須提及你過去和未來的故

would make a SOP more interesting and **memorable**[6].

Cheers,
Rita Katz

事。你在計劃未來的同時，也編織著過去的經驗，這樣的讀書計畫會更有趣，也更令人印象深刻。

瑞塔・卡茲 謹上

Send ►

核心字彙充電站 *Key Words*

1. **appointment** 名（會面的）約定
2. **discuss** 動 討論；商談
3. **weave** 動 編排；編製
4. **relevant** 形 相關的
5. **experience** 名 經驗
6. **memorable** 形 難忘的

進階補充站 *Let's learn more!*

實用資訊Focus

個人陳述與讀書計畫 🔍

　　一般人很容易將personal statement（個人陳述）和statement of purpose（讀書計畫）搞混。前者敘述較簡單，如同寫故事般具體呈現過去的生活經驗（包括家庭、教育、學業、參與活動、個人特質），主要是關於自己的背景資料。後者（讀書計畫）則較正式且直接切入重點，特別強調學習領域、學習動機，以及目標或生涯規劃的敘述。

　　每間學校的要求不同，因此在撰寫前務必先詳讀學校的寫作說明，了解問題的重點，並注意要求的字數。寫作內容應具體、簡潔、清楚、明確、態度誠懇，完成後可以請專業人士或老師幫忙修改。

Subject　Admission Letter

3 **January**[1] 2016
Mr. Woody Chou
8F, No.8, Lane 29, San Min Road,
Song Shan **District**[2], Taipei City 105,
Taiwan, R.O.C.

Dear Mr. Chou:

I am **delighted**[3] to be able to tell you that your application to study at University of London has been successful, and I am pleased to make you an offer of a place. My **colleagues**[4] and I look forward to welcoming you to the College and **ensuring**[5] that your studies and life in London would be **enjoyable**[6] and **fulfilling**[7].

The terms and conditions of your offer are set out on the enclosed sheet. Please read these carefully. The sheet also gives the name and contact details of the person in the Admissions Office who is **dealing with**[8] your application if you have any questions.

Also enclosed with this letter is a form to be returned if you would like to accept our offer of a place. Please complete and return the form within one month of its **receipt**[9] or email to admissions@london.ac.uk. On receipt of your acceptance, I will send you information about **accommodation**[10] at the

二〇一六年一月三日
周伍迪先生
105台灣台北市松山區
三民路29巷8號8樓

周先生您好：

很高興通知您，您已成功錄取倫敦大學。我們期待並歡迎您加入敝學院，並相信你在倫敦的求學生活將會十分多采多姿。

附件表格為入學條件及相關細則，煩請詳讀。信件中包含註冊組聯絡人的姓名以及資料，如有任何問題，可與該聯絡人討論。

另外附上一張「接受入學回函表」，如您決定接受入學許可，煩請於一個月內將表格填寫完畢並寄至 admissions@london.ac.uk。收到您的回函後，我會將住宿資訊寄給您。

再次歡迎並期待您來到倫敦，祝福您在英國的留學生活充實美好。

College.

維克多‧懷特 謹上

Once again, we look forward to welcoming you to London and hope that you will enjoy your time at the College and in UK.

Yours sincerely,
Victor White

Send ▶

核心字彙充電站 *Key Words*

1. **January** 名 一月份
2. **district** 名 行政區
3. **delighted** 形 高興地；快樂的
4. **colleague** 名 同事
5. **ensure** 動 保證；擔保
6. **enjoyable** 形 有樂趣的
7. **fulfilling** 形 能實現抱負的
8. **deal with** 片 處理
9. **receipt** 名 收到；接到
10. **accommodation** 名 住處

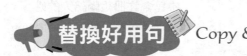
替換好用句 *Copy & Paste*

校方通知

I am pleased to confirm below the full details of the degree program to which Mr. Jung (Date of birth: 20 / 05 / 1985) has now been admitted.
🖊 很高興在此向您確認鍾先生（生於一九八五年五月二十日）的入學申請已經獲准，隨後說明本學位的課程細節。

This is to certify that Chin-tsai Chou has been offered admission to University of Warwick.
🖊 這份文件證明周瑾才已錄取華威大學。

Mr. Chou is expected to take up the place on September 21st, 2016.
🖊 周先生應於二〇一六年九月二十一日起就讀本校。

The period of study for a Master's program is one year full time or

two years part time.
🖊 碩士學程的期間是一年全職，或二年兼職。

Full-time students are expected to allocate around 60 hours per week to study, of which a minimum of 12 hours per week would be within a structured classroom environment.
🖊 一般生每週的學習時數平均應為六十個小時左右，其中至少有十二個小時安排在教室上課。

Please kindly see the attached file for the bank detailed information.
🖊 麻煩請查看附件檔關於銀行之詳細資料。

The deadline for paying the tuition fee is June 19, 2017.
🖊 學費付款的截止日為二〇一七年六月十九日。

Don't forget to write the name and home address and quote "English Language Program" on the check.
🖊 別忘了在支票上填寫姓名和住址，並註明「英語語言課程」。

The deposit will be refunded if you fail to meet any conditions we have set, and we have to withdraw the place.
🖊 若您無法達到我們的要求，導致未能順利入學，將退還訂金。

Please return the Acceptance of Offer Form, the Financial Guarantee Form, the $500 deposit and 4 passport-sized photographs direct to the address as soon as possible.
🖊 請儘快將入學同意書、財力證明、五百元訂金、以及四張護照大小的大頭照寄回。

 申請方回應

I hereby accept the place offered to me on the Master of Business Administration Program in October 2017.
🖊 我在此接受二〇一七年十月份商業管理碩士班課程的入學許可。

I have read and agree to any special conditions as set out in the offer letter.
🖊 我已閱讀並同意入學許可中的所有條件。

I understand that the full-time fee is $18,000 for US.
🖊 我了解日間部學生的學費是一萬八千美元。

To secure my place on the program, I enclose a deposit of $500 and four passport-sized photographs.
🖊 為確認接受入學，在此附上五百元訂金及四張護照大小的大頭照。

Part 1
Part 2
Part 3
Part 4
Part 5
Part 6

·1-09· 邀請參加新生訓練

Subject | Orientation Letter to Incoming Students

Dear **Incoming**[1] Student:

My name is Elizabeth and, as the Student Organization vice president and orientation chairperson, I would like to **congratulate**[2] you on making the decision to **attend**[3] our college. I would also like to take this opportunity to welcome you to this big family!

I believe that making the **transition**[4] from high school to college is quite difficult. It can be **intimidating**[5] while entering a new **environment**[6] and **adjusting to**[7] the changes. I can honestly say that the first week of school was a **struggle**[8]. The orientation team and I are **dedicated to**[9] making your experiences positive and enjoyable, and our hope is that you will form friendship that can last a lifetime.

Your school life begins on Orientation Day on September 6. Orientation Day will be filled with activities that will provide you with the opportunity to become **familiar with**[10] the campus, **obtain**[11] important information, learn about student life and meet your fellow classmates. On this day, you will also meet some of the **upperclassmen**[12] who have **volunteered**[13] their time to serve as your orientation leaders. We encourage you

親愛的新生：

我是學生會副主席暨新生訓練總召集人伊莉莎白。恭喜您決定就讀本校，也歡迎您加入這個大家庭！

我相信從高中到大學的轉變過程是很艱辛的過渡期。進入一個新的環境與適應新的變化，可能讓人感到害怕。老實說，開學的第一週會比較難過。新生訓練團隊和我致力於幫助您有個積極且美好的經驗，我們希望您可以在校園裡建立畢生難忘的友誼。

您的大學生活從九月六日的新生訓練開始。訓練期間將提供您不同的活動，幫助您熟悉校園、取得重要資訊、認識學校和你的同學。當天，你也會遇到一些學長姐，他們義務擔任新生訓練的領隊。我們鼓勵您放鬆心情享受，並融入校園生活。

to relax and enjoy here and **get involved in**[14] campus life.

Your orientation experience continues a week with many exciting events. Here are some of the activities planned for the week:

September 7: Back-to-School BBQ
September 8: Club Fair
September 9: Movie: "Harry Potter 7"
September 10: Concert
September 11-12: Trip to Yosemite National Park
September 13: Broadway show: "Mamma mia!"

If you have any questions, comments or concerns during the summer, I encourage you to contact the Office of Student Organization at 713-000-5555, or you can contact me at elizabeth@student.usa.edu. Take a look at the Orientation 2016 website and be sure to join our Facebook page.

Enjoy the rest of your summer. Truly look forward to meeting you on September 6.

Sincerely,
Elizabeth Chen
Chair, Orientation 2016

為期一週的新生訓練將提供許多有趣的活動。以下為活動時間表：

9/7 重返校園BBQ烤肉
9/8 社團博覽會
9/9 電影欣賞：《哈利波特7》
9/10 音樂會
9/11-12 優勝美地國家公園二日遊
9/13 百老匯秀：《媽媽咪呀！》

若您暑假期間有任何問題或想法，建議您可撥電話與學生會聯絡：713-000-5555，或寫電子郵件給我：elizabeth@student.usa.edu。看看我們今年的新生訓練網頁，並加入我們的臉書。

祝暑假愉快！真心期盼在九月六日與您相見。

二〇一六年新生訓練總召集人
陳伊莉莎白 敬上

1. **incoming** 形 進來的
2. **congratulate** 動 恭喜
3. **attend** 動 上（大學等）
4. **transition** 名 轉變；過渡
5. **intimidating** 形 令人生畏的
6. **environment** 名 環境
7. **adjust to** 片 適應
8. **struggle** 名 難事
9. **dedicate to** 片 奉獻給
10. **be familiar with** 片 熟悉
11. **obtain** 動 得到；獲得
12. **upperclassman** 名 大三、大四生
13. **volunteer** 動 自願做
14. **be/get involved in** 片 參加；關心

替換好用句 *Copy & Paste*

We will help you learn new skills, or just enhance your own professional and personal life.
✎ 我們會協助你學習新的技能，提升專業能力及個人生活品質。

We'll be hosting activities for our younger guests such as tours of the campus and creative activities.
✎ 我們將舉辦校園導覽和有趣的活動來歡迎我們的新生。

Your family, friends and children are always welcome to our campus.
✎ 我們也歡迎你的家人、朋友或小孩來到我們學校。

It's going to be fun and informative and will be free to attend.
✎ 這場活動具趣味性及教育性質，歡迎免費入場。

You can book the activity online today and join our campus tour.
✎ 你可以今天就上網預約，參加我們的校園導覽。

You can book your place on the website.
✎ 你可以在網站上預約。

You can get the latest updates by joining our Facebook page.
✎ 你可以加入我們的臉書，得知最新消息。

If you'd like to find out more, email us or join us on Twitter or Facebook.
✎ 如果你想得知更多資訊，請寄電子郵件給我們，或加入我們的推特或臉書。

進階補充站 Let's learn more!

 文法/句型Focus

✱ 句型結構剖析

❶ 同位語：**S, N,...** 後面的名詞用來説明前面的主詞。

My name is Grace, your teacher. I would like to...
我的名字叫做葛蕾絲，是你們的老師，我想要…

❷ 動名詞**V-ing**當名詞用 → 當主詞（視為單數）

Making the transition from high school to college is quite difficult.
高中生上大學的轉換期相當艱難。

 實用資訊Focus

🔍 **以E-mail聯繫注意事項**

1. E-mail 主旨（subject）要簡短、清楚，且不能空著不填。沒有主旨，給人的印象不好。

2. 稱呼上，建議直接使用該聯繫人姓名，如：Dear Mr. Brown代替 Dear Sir or Madam。若不知對方姓名，則使用Dear Sir or Madam，或To Whom It May Concern。

3. 正文部分的編寫要簡練，事情陳述清楚，一封 E-mail 不要超過三個問題。

4. 收到學校的回覆信件後，無論是否有得到幫助，都要回信表示感謝。

5. 結尾部分除了寫上 Best regards 之外，遇到逢年過節或週末，加上幾句 Happy New Year或Have a nice weekend，會讓對方覺得心情愉快。

Part 1
Part 2
Part 3
Part 4
Part 5
Part 6

Unit 2 住宿事宜詢問

•2-01• 申請學校住宿

　　大多數新生會選擇住校，出國前就要向學校住宿組（Housing Office）申請入住。各個學校的住宿費用不同，但住校費用通常會高於校外住宿，因此也有不少學生會選擇在校外租公寓。

Subject　Ask for An Apartment

Dear Sir:

I am an international student at Eastern Michigan University. My sister and I have been looking for accommodation for the following **semester**[1] for some time. We are interested in the university housing on **campus**[2].

I have some questions. When will the rental next be available? We hope to move in this summer soon. And, since we have a car, is there a parking space for the **resident**[3]? Could you please give us some detailed information? We are also willing to come and see the place.

I will be appreciated it if you can email me back, so we can **schedule**[4] an appointment to meet with you.

Best regards,
Linda Du

先生您好：

我是在東密西根大學就讀的國際學生。我和妹妹花了好一陣子尋找下學期的住處，我們對學校的宿舍相當感興趣。

我有一些問題：宿舍何時可開放承租？我們希望能於這個暑假搬進去。另外，我們有輛汽車，請問有提供停車位給住戶嗎？能否給我們詳細資訊呢？我們希望能去參觀宿舍。

若您能回信，以便我們安排時間與您約談，我會十分感激。

杜琳達 敬上

Send ▸

核心字彙充電站 Key Words

1. semester 名 學期
2. campus 名 學校；校園
3. resident 名 居民
4. schedule 動 安排；預定

替換好用句 Copy & Paste

 住宿選擇

A sleeping room is the least expensive option, but provides little privacy.
✎ 通鋪是最便宜的選擇，但較沒有隱私。

I am wondering if the kitchen provides a stove, refrigerator, sink, and cabinet space.
✎ 我在想廚房是否附有烤箱、冰箱、洗碗槽和櫥櫃。

A furnished apartment will cost you an extra $50-100 per month.
✎ 附傢俱的公寓每個月的費用會多出五十元到一百元。

Sharing a house with several students is relatively cheap.
✎ 和幾個學生合租獨棟房子相對之下較為便宜。

You only have a small room to yourself.
✎ 你自己只有一間小房間可用。

You have to share the kitchen and living room with other students.
✎ 你必須和其他學生共用廚房和客廳。

Renting an apartment from housing agency at school is safer.
✎ 向學校住宿單位申請公寓住宿比較安全。

The rent includes meal passes and your room will be cleaned by staffs regularly if you live in the university dorms.
✎ 如果你住學校宿舍，餐券包含在房租內，且有專人定期打掃房間。

You have the choice of one-bedroom versus two-bedroom, furnished room versus unfurnished room if you live in university housing.
✎ 如果住學校提供的一般宿舍，可以選擇單人房或雙人房、附傢俱或不附傢俱。

The rent is cheaper, but you have to cook and clean the room by yourself.

Part 1
Part 2
Part 3
Part 4
Part 5
Part 6

✏ 房租比較便宜，但是你需要自己下廚和打掃房間。

There are several types of apartments in our school, such as sleeping room, single room, and double room.
✏ 我們學校提供不同類型的公寓，如通鋪、單人房、以及雙人房。

 ## 住宿規條

Do not destroy public facilities.
✏ 請勿破壞公物。

Do not bother others.
✏ 請勿打擾其他人。

Please keep the public places clean.
✏ 請保持公共區域的整潔。

Our students who apply for accommodation should make an application within the specified time period.
✏ 本校學生申請住宿，應於規定期間內提出申請。

New applicants should complete the application form and submit it directly to the housing office.
✏ 新申請者須填寫申請書，直接向學校住宿組申請。

When you move out, you need to clean up the bedroom and finish the check-out procedure.
✏ 搬離宿舍時，必須清理寢室，並辦理退宿手續。

Dangerous or prohibited items cannot be stored in the room (such as drugs, alcohol, gambling devices, etc.)
✏ 寢室內不得留有危險或違禁物品（例如毒品、酒類、賭博用具等）。

You're not allowed to gamble, drink, and make noise or trouble in the dormitory.
✏ 不得在宿舍內賭博、飲酒、喧嘩或滋事。

Books and magazines in the drawing room or fellowship hall should not be taken out.
✏ 會客室或交誼廳內之書報雜誌不得攜帶外出。

You shall not keep animals in the dormitory.
✏ 宿舍內禁止飼養動物。

The equipment in the bedroom should be used carefully.
🖊 寢室的設備請愛惜使用。

Please swipe the student card when you get into the dorm.
🖊 進入宿舍請刷卡。

If you lose the room key, you can report to the office, and be required to pay costs and expenses $100.
🖊 若遺失寢室鑰匙，可向住宿組報備補配，須繳交工本費一百元。

 Let's learn more!

單字/片語Focus

❦ 學校生活範圍 ❦

*dormitory 宿舍	*laboratory 實驗室
*library 圖書館	*auditorium 禮堂
*stadium 體育場	*natatorium 室內游泳池
*Administration Building 行政大樓	

文法/句型Focus

＊可數名詞之單數形：

❶ 使用不定冠詞 **a / an** 表單數：

I am an international student.
我是一名國際學生。

❷ 定冠詞 **the** 後若接可數單數名詞，表「特指」：

We are also willing to come see the place.
我們也想要去看看那個地方。

·2-02· 校外找公寓

各學校的宿舍房間數量不一，有時宿舍房間會供不應求。如果你首選的宿舍已經排滿，要申請另外一種住宿方式時，須馬上和學校聯絡告知你的第二選擇，並索取新的住宿資料，否則就只剩下校外住宿可供選擇。

Subject | **Apartment Near NTU Area?**

Dear Sir:

I am interested in your apartment posted on the advertisement in the school newspaper yesterday. I saw there's an apartment with one bedroom and one living room near NTU. It is near the Gongguan marketplace, isn't it?

I would like to know if it is still available and how much the rent is for the place? I am wondering if I can go see the apartment this weekend.

Your reply will be appreciated.

Regards,
Ken Batson

Send

先生您好：

我對於您昨天刊登在校刊上的租屋廣告感興趣。廣告上寫的是靠近台大，一房一廳的公寓，請問是位於公館市集附近嗎？

我想知道是否仍有機會承租，以及房租是多少？我也想知道這個週末我是否可以去看房子？

謝謝您的回信。

肯·貝森 敬上

替換好用句　Copy & Paste

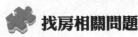 找房相關問題

I am writing about an ad I saw for an apartment in the newspaper.
✏️ 我來信詢問關於我在報上看到的一則公寓廣告。

I would like to know if it is still available, and how much is the rent for the place.
🖊 我想知道是否仍有機會承租，以及房租是多少？

I am looking for a two-bedroom apartment.
🖊 我在找一間兩房的公寓。

I am looking for a single room, furnished with a shared bathroom and a kitchen.
🖊 我正在找一間附傢俱、公共衛浴和廚房的單人房。

I am looking for a single room with a private bathroom.
🖊 我正在找附有個人衛浴設備的單人套房。

I am interested in an apartment which has a separate kitchen and eating area.
🖊 我對附有獨立廚房和餐廳的公寓感興趣。

I'd prefer an apartment near a supermarket, and not too far from a bus stop.
🖊 我比較喜歡附近有超市，且不會離公車站太遠的公寓。

What exactly does the rent include?
🖊 房租包含哪些費用呢？

Are utilities included in the price?
🖊 房租包含水電和瓦斯費嗎？

Is there a maintenance fee?
🖊 須付管理費嗎？

Is parking included in the apartment rental, or is there an additional charge?
🖊 停車費包含在房租裡，還是須另外付費呢？

When and how do I pay for the rent?
🖊 我何時及如何繳納房租呢？

I would like to know how long the lease will last.
🖊 我想知道合約的租期多長。

How much is the security deposit, and how many months I have to pay in advance?
🖊 押金是多少，而我必須先付幾個月的押金呢？

How can I lose the deposit and how soon after I move out would the deposit be returned?

Part 1

Part 2

Part 3

Part 4

Part 5

Part 6

✏ 何種情形下押金會遭扣押，且搬出後多久可以拿回押金呢？

And I need to know who to contact if I would like to see the apartment.
✏ 如果我想要參觀公寓的話，我應該跟誰聯絡呢？

What time can I come to see the house?
✏ 我什麼時候可以去看房子？

Can I have roommates and what is the policy on adding someone to the lease?
✏ 我是否能另外增加室友呢？請問這樣做的相關規定為何？

Are there any additional charges for the use of the gym or meeting room?
✏ 使用健身房或會議室需要另外付費嗎？

Who should I contact if something happens and repairs need to be made?
✏ 如果發生需要維修的狀況，該與誰聯繫呢？

Are there any charges for repairs not covered in the lease?
✏ 是否有任何維修費用是不包含在租約裡的？

 回應問題

I will tell our landlord to answer your questions about the payments, fees, and contract details.
✏ 我會請房東回答你關於費用及合約的細節。

The rent is $550 a month.
✏ 一個月的房租為五百五十元美金。

The utilities are not included.
✏ 水電及瓦斯費不包含在內。

The contract states that the renter is responsible for all utility payments.
✏ 合約規定，房客須支付所有公共設施的費用。

Parking is free.
✏ 停車免費。

The rent is due on the first day of the month.
✏ 房租於每個月的一號付款。

進階補充站 *Let's learn more!*

實用資訊Focus

常見的租屋條件 🔍

找房子是件非常令人頭痛的事。首先要決定你的租屋條件，包括：

1. Location 地點
2. Flat, house, studio, room 住宅型態
3. Length of tenancy period 租期時間
4. Furnished or unfurnished 有無附設傢俱
5. Number of bedrooms, bathrooms, reception rooms 房間數
6. Off-street parking 停車位
7. Garden 庭院

簽約注意事項 🔍

學生在校外租屋，要特別注意房客與房東各自擁有的法律權利與義務。不論是退租、轉租、中途解約、押金取回等問題，都應好好了解，萬一發生個人無法解決的問題時，可以請求學校支援及協助處理。校外住宿要特別注意簽約的部分。一般來說，合約內容分為以下幾項：

1. Lease term 租約期限
2. Monthly rent amount 每月租金
3. When the rent is due 每月租金付款日
4. Security deposit amount 訂金費用
5. Utilities / Services provided by the... 水電 / 服務費的歸屬
6. What the tenant is responsible for 房客須負擔的責任
7. Building rules and special clauses 房屋條款及特別注意事項

·2-03· 請求延遲支付房租

房租須按時繳納。若沒有按時繳款，可能得支付罰金。若還是不付房租的話，房東可能會開始催繳或請你搬走，甚至採取法律行動，不可不慎。

Subject | **Pay The Rent Late?**

Dear Mr. Chang:

I am Andrew Lee. I've been living in your apartment near the Gongguan area for about six months. It has been really enjoyable and **comfortable**[1]. **Unfortunately**[2], it now appears to have some family issues for me to pay the rent on time.

Do you think it is possible for me to pay the rent late next week? Since I will pay the rent later than the due date, will I be charged the extra NT$500 a day? I would appreciate your kindest **understanding**[3] in this matter and hope to be able to hear from your **response**[4].

Best regards,
Andrew Lee

張先生您好：

我是李安竹，承租您在公館附近的公寓將近六個月。住在這裡真的很棒，很舒服。不過最近由於家庭因素，我無法準時繳交房租。

我可以下個星期再繳房租嗎？我沒有準時付款的話，是否會被罰以每日五百元台幣的罰金呢？在此懇請您的諒解，並希望能得到您的回應。

李安竹 敬上

Send

核心字彙充電站 *Key Words*

1. **comfortable** 形 舒適的
2. **unfortunately** 副 遺憾地
3. **understanding** 名 理解
4. **response** 名 回覆；回答

If you pay your bills after the due date, you will be charged a late fee.
✐ 如果在期限後才繳納租金，你就要付滯納金。

We have experienced with a late fee.
✐ 我們曾有因為延後繳交租金而要付滯納金的經驗。

Is it possible for me to pay my rent late?
✐ 我可以晚一點付租金嗎？

I am thinking if I could pay my rent late.
✐ 我在想是否可以晚點付租金。

Am I allowed to pay my electricity bill late?
✐ 我可以晚一點付電費嗎？

Our landlord will charge $25 for a late fee a day.
✐ 我們房東會收我們一天二十五元的滯納金。

Late fee is more flexible in the universities.
✐ 大學校園裡的滯納金通常比較彈性。

There are some reasons for paying the rent late.
✐ 我會延後繳款是有原因的。

You are lucky enough to get your late fee waived.
✐ 你很幸運，無須繳交罰金。

It's much better to keep track of your bills.
✐ 最好能夠記錄你的每筆帳單。

You should pay it on time rather than go through the hassle.
✐ 最好能夠按時繳款，總比引起爭論好。

·2-04· 申請停車證

若要在學校停車，需要向行政單位申請停車證，但並不是每所學校都提供停車位給學生。住在校外的學生，也可以詢問房東是否提供免費或需付費的停車位。

Subject | **Apply for A Parking Permit**

Dear Sir:

I am an international student from Taiwan, studying in the Language and International Trade Program. I am writing to **inquire**[1] about how to apply for the parking **permit**[2] on campus.

I bought a new car last month, so I am quite worried about where I can park in school. Since the upperclassmen told me to contact you for the process of getting, renewing and **withdrawing**[3] a parking permit, I would like to know if I am **eligible**[4] for a permit, what the permit allows me to do and how to apply for one.

Your reply will be appreciated.

Sincerely,
Kelly Chang

先生您好：

我是來自台灣的國際學生，就讀語言及國際貿易，來信詢問有關申請校園停車證的問題。

我上個月買了一輛新車，所以有點擔心在校園停車的問題。有學長建議我和您聯絡，向您請教關於申請停車證、換證或退證程序的問題。我想知道我是否能申請停車證，也想請教停車證的功用為何，以及申請方式。

謝謝您的回覆。

張凱莉 敬上

Send

核心字彙充電站 *Key Words*

1. **inquire** 動 詢問；調查
2. **permit** 名 許可證
3. **withdraw** 動 撤回；撤銷
4. **eligible** 形 法律上合格的

 替換好用句 *Copy & Paste*

 詢問停車事宜

I am writing to inquire about the parking permit on campus.
✎ 我來信詢問有關校園停車證的事情。

Could you let me know if there are any pay parking lots available?
✎ 我想知道是否有收費停車場呢?

Could you send me some information about parking on our campus?
✎ 可否寄給我校園停車的相關資訊呢?

Please let me know how I pay for the parking.
✎ 請告訴我該如何支付停車費。

Is there a limit to how long I can park?
✎ 有限制停車的時間嗎?

Are there designated car parking spaces for the dorm residents?
✎ 住宿生有專用的車位嗎?

Are there any bike racks on campus?
✎ 校園裡有腳踏車停車架嗎?

Is it free to park at the apartment on campus?
✎ 在學校宿舍停車是免費的嗎?

How many permits can I apply for?
✎ 我可以申請幾張停車證呢?

How do I apply for a permit?
✎ 我要如何申請停車證呢?

What is the fee for the permit?
✎ 停車證的費用是多少?

What time does the campus parking lot close?
✎ 校園停車場何時關閉呢?

Is the parking lot open on weekends?
✎ 週末是否開放停車?

Part 1
Part 2
Part 3
Part 4
Part 5
Part 6

What if I need to park overnight on campus while I am preparing my paperwork?

🖊 如果我要準備作業，需要將車子停在校園內過夜，該怎麼做呢？

Could you please let me know where I can get information about the temporary parking permits?

🖊 請告訴我哪裡可以取得關於臨時停車證的資訊。

What if I change my vehicle or license plate after I have purchased the permit for the whole year?

🖊 假如在購買了一年份的停車證後，發生了換車或是牌照的情況，應該怎麼做呢？

 ## 校方規定

Our university doesn't give parking permits to students.

🖊 我們大學不提供停車證給學生。

You are allowed to apply for a parking permit.

🖊 你可以申請停車證。

All of our students are charged $60 for a parking permit for one semester.

🖊 學生的停車證費用是一學期六十美金。

You can also buy a summer time parking permit for $45.

🖊 你也可以購買四十五元的暑期停車證。

The parking lot opens at 6 a.m. and closes at 11 p.m.

🖊 停車場早上六點開，晚上十一點關。

It has a security guard on duty from 6 a.m. to 11 p.m.

🖊 從早上六點鐘到晚上十一點鐘，都有警衛值班。

I suggest you register your car with the University Campus Security Office.

🖊 我建議你向大學校園安全室申請汽車註冊。

 Let's learn more!

 文法/句型Focus

✱ **形容詞子句 — 關係副詞**

❶ where 地點

My apartment, where I study and sleep, is my favorite retreat.
我的公寓是我最喜愛的休憩場所，也是我學習和睡覺的地方。

❷ when 時間

The night, when my husband proposed to me, has been on my mind.
我一直忘不了丈夫向我求婚的那一晚。

❸ why 原因

We didn't understand the reason why she didn't qualify for the program.
我們無法理解她沒取得那門課程資格的原因。

❹ how 方法

People were impressed with how he faced his difficulty.
大家對他正視困難的作法印象深刻。

Unit 3 銀行業務相關

·3-01· 銀行開戶

　　在國外銀行開戶需花費較長時間，不像在台灣可以隨辦隨用。無論是美國或英國，都需花費數週、甚至長達一個月的時間。因此，務必儘早辦理，最好能夠在抵達當地不久後就進行申辦，並且耐心等待。

Subject　Open An Account

Dear Sir:

I am writing in connection with opening an account. I would like to ask what types of accounts do you offer and where I can obtain an application form. Also, I'd like to sign up for online banking.

Your reply will be appreciated.

Regards,
Jack Fox

先生您好：

我來信詢問關於開立帳戶的事宜。我想請教貴行提供何種帳戶，以及我可以在哪裡取得申請表。另外，我想要申請網路銀行。

謝謝您的回信。

傑克·福克斯 敬上

Send ▶

 替換好用句 Copy & Paste

We offer two types of accounts: checking account and savings account.
🖊 我們提供兩種帳戶：支票帳戶和儲蓄帳戶。

Where can I obtain an application form?
🖊 哪裡可以取得申請書呢？

What documents should I bring?
🖊 要攜帶哪些文件呢？

Is there a transaction fee every time I withdraw?
🖊 每次提領是否要扣除手續費？

Could you please set up online banking for me?
🖊 可以麻煩你幫我申請網路銀行嗎？

We do have free online banking.
🖊 我們有免費的網路銀行服務。

Would you like to sign up for online banking?
🖊 您要申請登入網路銀行嗎？

You can pay all your bills and manage your accounts over the Internet.
🖊 您可以直接透過網路支付所有帳單以及管理您的帳戶。

How do I open a bank account?
🖊 我要如何開戶？

Just fill out the application form and sign on the sheet.
🖊 只要填好申請表格，並在單子上簽名。

What do I need to do to open a bank account?
🖊 開戶須辦理哪些手續？

A minimum deposit for the savings account is $1,000.
🖊 儲蓄帳戶最低需要一千元的存款。

Please bring your bankbook when making transactions.
🖊 交易時請攜帶存摺。

You can change your password through the ATM.
🖊 您可以藉由自動櫃員提款機更改密碼。

I would like to make a withdrawal from my savings account.
🖊 我想從我的儲蓄存款帳戶提款。

I need your bankbook and the withdrawal slip.
🖊 我需要您的存摺和提款單。

Also, I would like to cash the check.
🖊 還有，我想要兌現支票。

I would like to deposit my paycheck into my savings account.
🖊 我想把薪資支票存到我的儲蓄存款帳戶。

Part 1
Part 2
Part 3
Part 4
Part 5
Part 6

Please endorse the back of the check.
🖊 麻煩您在支票背面簽名。

I need to wire money overseas.
🖊 我要電匯一筆錢到國外。

Do you have the recipient's bank account information?
🖊 您有收款人的銀行帳戶資料嗎？

 Let's learn more!

 單字/片語Focus

🐾 銀行業務 🐾	
✳**deposit** 存款；押金	✳**withdrawal** 提款；收回
✳**check** 支票；帳單	✳**bankbook** 存摺
✳**savings account** 儲蓄存款帳戶	✳**checking account** 活期存款帳戶

 文法/句型Focus

✳ **在銀行詢問業務**

① **I want to transfer money from my savings account to...**
我想把錢從儲蓄存款帳戶轉到⋯。

② **I would like to make a withdrawal from...**
我想從⋯提款。

③ **Which counter should I go to if I want to...**
如果我要辦理⋯的話，要去哪個櫃台？

④ **Please tell me the interest rate for...**
請告訴我⋯的利率是多少？

3-02 申請信用卡

Subject Credit Card

Dear Sir:

I am writing in connection with issuing a credit card. I would like to ask what types of credit cards do you offer and where I can obtain an application form. Also, I'd like to apply for one with no credit limit.

Look forward to hearing from you soon.

Regards,
Jonathon Hsu

先生您好：

我寫信來詢問申請信用卡的事宜。我想請教貴銀行提供何種信用卡，以及我可以在哪裡取得申請表。另外，我想要申請一張無額度上限的信用卡。

期待您的回信。

徐強納森 敬上

 Send

Subject ATT Trustee Savings Bank Credit Card

Dear Mr. Hsu:

First of all, thank you for your recent application for an ATT Trustee Savings Bank platinum credit card. We have reviewed your application and have done a credit check in your name, and now approved the issuance of a platinum credit card to you with no credit limit.

However, in order to process your account and issue your card, we must confirm your home and work telephone numbers, which were not written on the application form.

徐先生您好：

首先，感謝您申請ATT信託儲蓄銀行白金卡。我們已審閱過您的申請資料，並針對您名下作了信用調查。您已通過審核，我們將發給您一張無額度上限的白金信用卡。

不過，申請書上並未填寫您的住家及公司電話，為處理帳戶及發卡作業需

Thank you again for your application and we look forward to issuing your platinum card soon.

Sincerely yours,
Carl Walters

要，我們必須向您確認這兩項資料。

再次感謝您的申請，我們期待能盡快將白金卡核發給您。

卡爾・渥特斯 敬上

Send ▶

 替換好用句 *Copy & Paste*

Our credit card can be used all over the world.
🖊 我們的信用卡可於全球使用。

The annual fee of fifty dollars for the card will be waived for your first year of membership.
🖊 第一年免繳本行信用卡之年費五十元。

You will be reimbursed for the annual fee if you make purchases totaling five thousand dollars or more.
🖊 持信用卡每年消費滿五千元或以上者，免繳年費。

Gift points can be used towards the items listed in the quarterly gift catalog and on our website.
🖊 紅利點數可折抵禮品季刊和網站上之商品。

We request that you make your payments before the 30th of each month after you have been billed.
🖊 請您在收到帳單後，於每月三十日前付款。

We have increased your credit rating.
🖊 我們增加了您的信用等級。

The payment day changed from the 1st to the 30th of the month.
🖊 付款日從每個月一日更改為三十日。

Thank you for your continued patronage.
🖊 感謝您的繼續支持。

進階補充站　Let's learn more!

單字/片語Focus

❧ 信用卡的核發與撤銷 ❧

＊**issuance** 發行	＊**waive** 撤銷；放棄
＊**reimburse** 償還；歸還	＊**patronage** 光顧；資助
＊**Trustee Savings Bank** 信託儲蓄銀行	

文法/句型Focus

＊**六大常用時態**

1. 進行式：**be + V-ing** （正）在…
2. 被動態：**be + V-p.p.** 被…
3. 進行被動態：**be + being + V-p.p.** 正被…
4. 完成式：**have + V-p.p.** 已經…
5. 完成進行式：**have + been + V-ing** 一直在…
6. 完成被動態：**have + been + V-p.p.** 已經被…

Part 1
Part 2
Part 3
Part 4
Part 5
Part 6

·3-03· 開立支票

Dear Ms. Lai:

Thank you for your fax of July 18, concerning how to **issue**[1] a check. Here are the ways to write a check.

First, please use a pen when writing a personal check - never a pencil. You should write in correct date on the "Date Line". And on the "Pay To The Order Of Line", fill in the name of the person or company to whom the check is being written. And then, in the "Dollar Box", write the dollar amount on this blank. Be careful, here you should **confirm**[2] the amount of your check. Finally, on the "Signature[3] Line", sign your name and get the **spelling**[4] right.

Meanwhile[5], please let me know if you have any **further**[6] questions.

Best regards,
Larry Tian

賴小姐您好：

謝謝您七月十八日發出的傳真，以下為開立支票的方法。

首先，開立支票時，請用原子筆書寫，勿用鉛筆。您必須在「日期欄」寫上正確的日期。然後，於「收款者欄」寫上對方或公司收款人的姓名。之後，在「金額欄」用數字填上金額，請再次確認支票上的金額。最後於「簽名欄」寫上你的姓名，並確認無誤。

在這期間，如果你有進一步的問題，請告知我。

田賴瑞 敬上

Send

核心字彙充電站 Key Words

1. **issue** 動 發行；核發
2. **confirm** 動 確認
3. **signature** 名 簽名
4. **spelling** 名 拼字；拼寫
5. **meanwhile** 副 同時
6. **further** 形 進一步的

替換好用句 Copy & Paste

Enter the date in the blank in upper right corner.
✎ 在右上角空白欄填上日期。

The date should include the month, the date, and the year.
✎ 日期需包括月份、日期和年份。

You should confirm the amount of the check.
✎ 您必須確認支票上的金額。

Make sure that your handwriting is easy to read on the dollar-sign blank.
✎ 確認金額欄的字體清楚易懂。

If you have any room left on the blank, draw a line to the end of the blank.
✎ 如果空白欄後面尚有空白處,請劃一條線到底。

Just in case no one can add anything to what you've written on that blank.
✎ 以防他人在金額欄上加入任何數字。

The Memo Line in the lower left corner is a reminder line.
✎ 「備註欄」在左下角,供記錄提醒用。

You can write "Rent" on this line which helps you identify the check paid for the rent.
✎ 你可以在備註欄寫上「租金」,以表示用這張支票支付了房租。

The line in the lower right corner of the check is the signature line.
✎ 簽名欄在支票的右下角。

Your bank will keep your signature on file to verify your signature on checks.
✎ 你的銀行會記錄你的簽名,以確保支票上的簽名無誤。

Part 4

商場求職篇～脫穎而出這樣貼

Unit 1 徵才與求職

Unit 2 面談通知與結果通知

Unit 3 接受與拒絕工作信函

動 動詞　　名 名詞

副 副詞　　形 形容詞

介 介系詞　　片 片語

Point

　　求職信函的寫法，往往是許多人的罩門。該如何求職才能令人印象深刻，接受或拒絕工作的時候要怎麼寫才明確又不失禮，不要再花幾個小時琢磨一封信，現在就教你最合乎禮儀的用字遣詞。

徵才與求才

1-01 徵才公告與求職信

各大專院校每年會與企業合作舉辦求職博覽會。對於感興趣的工作,可以利用英文求職信增加機會。如果能寫出一封內容完善、表達清楚合宜的求職信,就能讓雇主了解你的能力與資格,且留下深刻的印象,有助於取得職位。

Subject | **Collegiate Job Fair**

Dear Everybody:

If you are looking for a job, you will want to be at this event!

Collegiate[1] Job Fair
Friday, March 25, 2017
9 a.m. - 3 p.m.
Over 100 companies with jobs!
Register at http://www.twjf.org
$100 NTD fee

This is your job fair, made available to you. Please **take advantage of**[2] this opportunity! If you have any questions, please call me at 02-1111-1041.

I look forward to seeing you at the event.

Best wishes,
Linda Ho

各位同學:

如果你正在找工作,這個活動正適合你!

大學就業博覽會
二〇一七年三月二十五日,星期五上午九點至下午三點
超過一百家企業蒞臨現場徵才!
請上網站預約:h t t p : / /www.twjf.org
入場費:新台幣一百元

難得一見的就業博覽會,請把握機會。若有任何問題,請洽詢:02-1111-1041。

期待與你們相見。

何琳達 謹上

Send ▶

Dear Madam:

I joined the National Career Fair on March 25 and saw the post of **Executive**[3] **Secretary**[4]. I am quite interested in the job you have offered in your company.

I have pleasure in enclosing my personal resume. As you will be able to see, I have been working as a **private**[5] secretary to Mr. Chou, the sales director at HannStar Corp. Ltd., for the past five years. Therefore, I feel that I have the experience to carry out the **duties**[6] of an executive secretary **satisfactorily**[7]. If you decide to **appoint**[8] me, I will give the company my complete loyalty.

I will be able to attend an interview any time at your convenience, and I can be reached by telephone at 02-3088-8855.

Best regards,
Abby Chou

親愛的女士：

三月二十五日我參加就業博覽會時，看到貴公司有關執行秘書的職缺，感到十分有興趣。

我很樂意附上我的個人履歷。如您所見，我曾在瀚宇彩晶公司擔任業務處長周先生的私人秘書長達五年。我相信我的經驗足以勝任執行秘書。如果您願意聘請我，我必會忠心奉獻自己的能力給貴公司。

只要你們方便，我隨時能前去參加面試。可以用電話與我聯繫：02-3088-8855。

周艾比 敬上

Send

核心字彙充電站 *Key Words*

1. **collegiate** 形 大學的
2. **take advantage of** 片 利用
3. **executive** 形 行政上的
4. **secretary** 名 秘書
5. **private** 形 私人的
6. **duty** 名 職責；職務
7. **satisfactorily** 副 令人滿意地
8. **appoint** 動 任命；指派

一般求職信（Application Letter）是用來申請特定職務，吸引雇主給予面試的機會。內容包括：描述資格、工作經驗、能力等。最好能打字以避免拼字錯誤。若不知道收信者的大名，別忘了以「Dear Sir or Madam」來稱呼。信件一定要引人注意，把重心放在如何能符合公司的需求。

Subject Web Designer Position

Dear Ms. Gill:

I am applying for the web **designer**[1] **position**[2] which was advertised this week.

Your position requires skills in programming and software. I have experience in designing webpage for a **previous**[3] company where I gained knowledge of **various**[4] web systems and **operations**[5]. My enclosed resume provides more details on my **qualifications**[6].

Could you please consider my request for a personal interview to discuss my qualifications and to learn more about this opportunity? I shall call you next week to see if a meeting can be arranged. If you need to reach me, please feel free to contact me at 1234-5678 or woodychou@mail.net.

Thank you for your consideration. I look forward to talking with you.

Sincerely yours,
Woody Chou

吉爾女士您好：

我想要應徵本週有關網頁設計的職缺。

貴公司要求程式設計和軟體技術的技能。我在之前的公司學到各種網頁設計系統和操作的技能。隨信附上個人履歷，提供您更多詳細的資格證照。

可否提供我面試的機會，以便進一步討論我的資格與機會？我下週會來電詢問面試機會。如果需要與我聯繫，歡迎隨時來電：1 2 3 4 - 5 6 7 8，或來信：woodychou@mail.net.

謝謝您的考慮，期盼與您會面。

周伍迪 敬上

Send ▶

Part 1

Part 2

Part 3

Part 4

Part 5

Part 6

 核心字彙充電站 Key Words

1. **designer** 名 設計師
2. **position** 名 職位；職缺
3. **previous** 形 以前的
4. **various** 形 各種的
5. **operation** 名 工作；操作
6. **qualification** 名 資格；能力

 替換好用句 Copy & Paste

敘述個人能力

My former employer has praised me for my ability to meet strict deadlines.

🖉 我的前雇主對我準時完成工作的能力讚賞有加。

I managed a regional marketing campaign that increased interest in our products and services by 20%.

🖉 我掌管一項區域性的行銷活動，提高了顧客對我們產品及服務的興趣達百分之二十。

As a result of my experience at HannStar Corp., I am sure I can meet the aggressive sales objectives your company has set.

🖉 彩晶公司的工作經驗使我確信自己能夠達到貴公司訂出的銷售目標。

During one year at HannStar Corp., I saved the company over $500,000 through various cost-cutting strategies.

🖉 在彩晶公司服務的這一年間，我透過各種降低成本的策略為公司省下的花費超過五十萬美金。

As the enclosed resume indicates, I've had more than ten years' experience in all phases of sales.

🖉 從附檔的履歷表可知，我擁有十年各種業務的工作經驗。

For the past five years, I've supervised a group of ten employees.

🖉 過去五年來，我監管包含十位員工的團隊。

其他技能與特色

During my time as a counselor, I developed my communicative and interpersonal skills.

🖉 我在擔任顧問期間，培養出溝通與人際相處的技巧。

I am willing to relocate in North America or other countries.
✐ 我很樂於外派到北美或其他國家。

I spent two years in Germany as an exchange student, and still speak and write German very well.
✐ 我在德國當了一年的交換學生，德文說寫流利。

My language skills in English and French will prove invaluable in your goals to expand into the European countries.
✐ 您目標進軍歐洲市場，而我的英文與法文能力能將貴公司帶來無法估量的效益。

 ## 請求面試與感謝

I'd appreciate the chance to talk to you and to get your opinion on whether I would be suitable for the job you offer.
✐ 若能有機會與您會面，了解是否有機會取得公司所提供的職缺，將不勝感激。

I would welcome the opportunity to meet you in person to discuss how I could contribute to your company.
✐ 企盼能有機會與您見面，討論我如何在貴公司貢獻所長。

I am delighted to meet you to discuss how I could fill your marketing needs.
✐ 我很樂意與您見面，討論我如何滿足貴公司的行銷需求。

I would be pleased to come by your school to go over my resume and teaching methods.
✐ 若能前往貴校，就我的履歷和教學方法進行討論，我會很高興。

I hope you will give my application due consideration.
✐ 希望您能慎重考慮我的申請。

If I can supply you with any other needed information about myself, please don't hesitate to let me know.
✐ 若您需要我提供更多個人資訊，請隨時通知我。

I will be happy to tell more about my experience in an interview.
✐ 我很樂意在面談中詳述我的工作經驗。

Part 1

Part 2

Part 3

Part 4

Part 5

Part 6

·1-03· 應徵職缺II

Subject | Retail Management Position

Dear Mr. Network:

I read your company's description in US Job Career Magazine and would like to inquire about employment opportunities in your management training program. I would like to work in **retail**[1] **management**[2] in Detroit after graduation.

I shall receive my B.S. degree this June in Economics. My interest in business started in high school and developed a variety of retail positions during college. And I found you provide the kind of **professional**[3] environment I **seek**[4].

My resume is enclosed for your consideration. My education and experience match the qualifications you seek and I have the **interpersonal**[5] skills and **motivation**[6] to build a successful career in retail management.

I know how busy you must be during this time of year, but I would appreciate a few minutes of your time. I shall call you during this week to discuss the employment possibilities. In the meantime, you can also contact me at 1234-5678 or gracelin@mail.net.

奈特沃克先生您好：

我看到貴公司在《US求職雜誌》中的刊登說明，藉此想詢問有關管理訓練部門的工作機會。畢業後，我想要在底特律從事零售管理的工作。

今年六月我將於經濟系畢業。我對商業的興趣源自於高中，大學時期則從事各式各樣的零售工作，而貴公司正好提供我所追求的專業環境。

附上我的履歷供您參考。我的學歷和經驗都符合貴公司要求，我很積極、也善於處理人際關係，這能讓我在零售管理的領域中有好發展。

我想您此時必定十分忙碌，但若能給我面試的機會，將不勝感激。我本週會致電貴公司討論工作機會。您也可以透過電話或電子郵件聯絡我：1234-5678，

Thank you very much for considering my request. I look forward to talking to you.

Sincerely,
Grace Lin

gracelin@mail.net。

謝謝您的考量，我期待與您會面。

林葛蕾絲 敬上

Send

核心字彙充電站 *Key Words*

1. **retail** 名 零售
2. **management** 名 管理
3. **professional** 形 專業的
4. **seek** 動 尋找；追求
5. **interpersonal** 形 人與人之間的
6. **motivation** 名 積極性；幹勁

替換好用句 *Copy & Paste*

開頭：說明看到求職公告

I am writing in response to your advertisement in the Career Journal for a Product Manager.
✎ 我來信回應貴公司在《職涯月刊》所刊登的產品經理徵才廣告。

Your advertisement for an Engineer posted in the Career Journal is of great interest to me.
✎ 我對貴公司在《職涯月刊》上徵求工程師的廣告十分感興趣。

I've seen your advertisement in China Times of July 27, asking for a clerk in a warehouse in Hsin Chu, and I wish to offer myself for the post.
✎ 我在七月二十七日的中國時報看到您刊登的廣告，想要申請新竹批發店的店員職缺。

The sales position which you described in your advertisement at the Career Fair on March 25 is one for which I think I can show you some excellent qualifications.
✎ 三月二十五日的求職博覽會中，我的一些資格條件非常符合貴公司所要求的業務資格。

自我介紹：年齡和經驗

I am twenty-four years of age, female and have had one year of sales experience in (name of the company).
🖊 我今年二十四歲，女性。曾在（公司名）擔任一年業務。

I am twenty-five years of age, have had five years' experience in my present position, and can give you the references for the past eight years.
🖊 我今年二十五歲，在目前的工作崗位有五年的工作經驗，且可提供過去八年間的推薦信，供您參考。

I am twenty years old and have been employed for two years by the England Furniture Co., as an assistant in the marketing department.
🖊 我今年二十歲，曾於大英國家俱公司服務二年，於行銷部門擔任助理。

I am twenty-three years old, and a graduate of Soochow University where I majored in English Literature.
🖊 我今年二十三歲，畢業於東吳大學英國文學系。

For these three years, I have been working in the office of the Konomi Food Company, where I have been and still am an accountant.
🖊 本人在相撲手食品公司當了三年的會計，現仍在職。

Since graduating in 2013, I have held a job as a secretary in a trade company.
🖊 自從二〇一三年畢業後，我一直在貿易公司擔任秘書的職位。

Over the years, I have become quite experienced as a departmental coordinator.
🖊 這幾年，我對跨部門的溝通協調很有經驗。

I have a thorough working knowledge of marketing and know the various products or its marketing strategies.
🖊 我對於行銷知識有全面的了解，且通曉各樣商品及行銷策略。

My working experience has given me the attitudes and the understanding that would enable me to learn the details of the position you've advertised.
🖊 過去的工作經驗讓我具備更專業的態度和認知，使我能夠在貴公司提供的職位學習到更多細節經驗。

Part 1
Part 2
Part 3
Part 4
Part 5
Part 6

1-04 主動詢問職缺

在求職信的中間段落可以說明自己的優勢。內容要簡短有力，並強調和這個職缺有直接關聯的教育背景和工作經驗。

求職信最後一段要告訴雇主你即將採取什麼行動，請求雇主給予面試的機會，讓對方認可你，藉此取得工作機會。

Subject | **Summer Job Opportunities**

Dear Sir:

I am writing to enquire if you have any opportunities for children's **entertainers**[1] and **nannies**[2] at your school this summer.

I am twenty years old and I currently studying for a **diploma**[3] in **Tourism**[4] at the College of Travel and Tourism in Singapore. I have also worked as a part-time assistant at a local kindergarten. I am fully experienced in looking after babies and young children up to the age of six. I am able to help with **babysitting**[5], preparing children's meals, and organizing **activities**[6]. I enjoy looking after children and I like working as part of a team.

My mother tongue is Chinese and I have a good spoken level of English. I also speak a little Italian.

I would be grateful if you could send me the details of any available positions, including the application forms.

Sincerely yours,
Grace Lin

先生您好：

我寫信來詢問貴校今年暑假是否提供關於兒童指導員或保姆的工作？

我今年二十歲，目前在新加坡旅遊及觀光學院就讀旅遊學程。我曾在當地的幼稚園兼任助理，對照顧幼兒和六歲以下的孩童很有經驗。我能夠擔負保姆的工作，也很會準備餐點和規劃活動。我喜愛照顧小孩，也很喜歡在團體裡面工作。

我的母語是中文，英文口說也很流利，我還會說一點義大利文。

若您可以寄其他詳細的工作職缺或申請表給我，將感激不盡。

林葛蕾絲 敬上

Send

核心字彙充電站 Key Words

1. **entertainer** 名 表演者
2. **nanny** 名 （主英）保姆
3. **diploma** 名 學位證書
4. **tourism** 名 旅遊；觀光
5. **babysit** 動 照料（小孩）
6. **activity** 名 活動

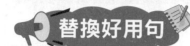

替換好用句 Copy & Paste

 開頭：自薦方式

I am looking for a position as an assistant salesman.
🖊 我正在尋找業務助理的工作。

Perhaps there is a position in your organization for an experienced and conscientious secretary.
🖊 請問貴公司是否需要一名有經驗、負責任的秘書？

Shall you need an experienced receptionist for your hotel next summer?
🖊 貴飯店明年暑期是否需要一名有經驗的櫃台人員？

Like many other young men, I am looking for a position. I want to get started, at the bottom, perhaps, but started.
🖊 我和許多年輕人一樣正在找工作。想要先有個開始，也可以從基層做起。

Because I am desirous of receiving some accounting experience during July and August, I am writing to inquire whether you will need a young man like me.
🖊 我渴望能在七、八月期間獲得會計相關的工作經驗，特別寫信來詢問你們是否需要像我這樣的年輕人？

I am thirty years of age, and have worked for two years in a similar position for ABC Company.
🖊 我今年三十歲，曾於ABC公司任職兩年，工作內容與此類似。

For the last four years, I have been teaching English at ABC High School.
🖊 我過去四年都在ABC高中教英文。

Part 1
Part 2
Part 3
Part 4
Part 5
Part 6

　　若要麻煩別人為你寫推薦信，記得要把下列內容寫入信中：一、想要應徵的職務；二、為什麼要請他當推薦人；三、附上完整的回郵信封，並感謝對方協助。

Subject	Request for The Recommendation

Dear Mr. Lin:

I am applying for the position of the sales assistant at Costco Company in Chicago, Illinois.

Since I received my sales training and management experience in your business office, I feel that you know my work **attitude**[1] and business **strengths**[2] better than anyone.

Would you be willing to write a letter of recommendation on my behalf to Ms. Kristin Chou, the Vice President at Costco? I have enclosed a **stamped**[3] **envelope**[4] for your reply.

Yours sincerely,
Julie Chen

林先生您好：

我欲申請芝加哥伊利諾州，好事多公司的業務助理一職。

因為我曾在您的公司受過業務訓練，也有過管理經驗，我想比起其他人，您更了解我的工作態度及辦事能力。

您是否願意幫我寫一封推薦信給好事多公司的副總周克莉絲小姐？我已附上回郵信封請求您回覆。

陳茱莉 敬上

Send

核心字彙充電站 *Key Words*

1. **attitude** 名 態度；意見
2. **strength** 名 長處
3. **stamp** 動 貼郵票於
4. **envelope** 名 信封

 替換好用句 *Copy & Paste*

I am writing to ask if you would be willing to write a letter of recommendation for me for my application to ABC Company.
🖉 我來信是想請問您是否願意幫我寫推薦信給ABC公司。

I am writing to ask whether it would be possible for you to provide a reference for me.
🖉 我寫信是想詢問您是否能幫我寫推薦信。

I'm applying for a marketing position with ABC Ltd. and I was hoping you would consider writing a letter of recommendation for me.
🖉 我欲申請ABC有限公司行銷主管的職位，希望您可以幫我寫推薦信。

I am writing in the hope of your assistance to write a reference letter for me.
🖉 我希望您能協助我寫推薦信。

Please let me know if you will be able to draft a letter on my behalf.
🖉 若您能夠代表我寫推薦信的話，請讓我知道。

Please let me know if you will be able to assist with this aspect of my search for employment.
🖉 若您能協助我尋找這方面的工作，請讓我知道。

My contact to you today is regarding a recommendation I am seeking for you to write on my behalf. Since we worked together for one year, I feel you are the person best qualified to offer this information.
🖉 我想請您代表我寫推薦信，因為我們曾共事一年，相信您最有資格提供我的個人資訊。

If you would be willing to do so, please briefly describe any qualities which you feel would make me a good candidate in the position.
🖉 若您願意幫我寫推薦函的話，麻煩請在信上簡短描述我有什麼得以勝任這份工作的特點。

Thank you for your kind attention to these requests. Should you have any questions, please do not hesitate to contact me.
🖉 謝謝您重視這個請求，如果您有任何問題，請不用客氣與我聯絡。

Part 1
Part 2
Part 3
Part 4
Part 5
Part 6

·1-06· 工作推薦信函

推薦信（Recommendation Letter）的內容包括：一、推薦人與被推薦人認識時間的長短；二、推薦人（老闆、朋友、同事、教授等）與被推薦人彼此之間的交情或認識的經過；三、推薦人對於被推薦人的個性、資格及工作能力的評價等。

Subject | **Recommendation Letter**

To Whom It May Concern:

Mr. Charles Wang has been in our **employ**[1] for the past three years as an **accountant**[2] in our office.

His work has been satisfactory in every way. He is a careful and **conscientious**[3] worker, and I know nothing against his **character**[4].

Mr. Wang left us because he has the **intention**[5] to enter a **broader**[6] field. We have no **hesitation**[7] in recommending him as an **exceptionally**[8] capable accountant well fitted for a big business company house like yours.

Yours sincerely,
Henry Black

敬啟者：

王查理先生擔任本公司會計已有三年的時間。

他在各方面都表現優秀。他是一位小心謹慎且負責任的員工，個性也很好。

王先生離開公司是因為有心往更廣的領域發展。我們毫不猶豫的向您推薦這位合適的會計人選到貴公司。

亨利・布雷克 謹上

Send ▸

核心字彙充電站 *Key Words*

1. employ 名 雇用
2. accountant 名 會計師
3. conscientious 形 謹慎的
4. character 名 （人的）性格

5. intention 名 意圖；意向　　6. broad 形 遼闊的；廣泛的
7. hesitation 名 猶豫　　8. exceptionally 副 特殊地

 Copy & Paste

第一段 — 開門見山的推薦

It is a pleasure for me to recommend Miss Mei-ing Wang for working in your company.
🖊 推薦王美鶯小姐到貴公司工作是我的榮幸。

I am privileged to write in support of my dear friend and student, Dan Peel.
🖊 我有幸能推薦我最親愛的朋友，同時也是我最親愛的學生丹‧皮爾。

I would like to take this opportunity to recommend Rita to your company.
🖊 我想藉此機會向您推薦芮塔到貴公司。

I am pleased to comply with his request, for I think he is well qualified for being a secretary in your company.
🖊 我很樂意推薦他，他非常適任貴公司的秘書一職。

I am proud to recommend a beloved secretary, Kaya Stone, for your fellowship partner.
🖊 非常驕傲能推薦我鍾愛的秘書卡雅‧史東，作為您的合夥員工。

This reference letter is provided at the written request of Jenny, who has asked me to serve as a reference on her behalf.
🖊 這封推薦信是珍妮請我幫她寫的，希望我能推薦她。

第二段 — 描述表現及能力

It has been a great pleasure for me to work with Ms. Chang, who has been a marketing officer with our company between the year 2010 and 2014.
🖊 我非常榮幸能與張小姐在二○一○年到二○一四年間於公司的行銷部門共事。

She has been working at our company for nearly two years, and she clearly stood out among her co-workers.

Part 1
Part 2
Part 3
Part 4
Part 5
Part 6

✎ 她在我們公司工作近兩年，一向都比其他同事還要來得出類拔萃。

She is sincere and positive. Furthermore, she maintains a positive attitude towards life.
✎ 她為人誠懇、積極，而且對生活很有抱負。

Her work ethic and attitude reflects that she has capabilities of managing and directing.
✎ 工作態度能證明她是一位有管理才能的熱心員工。

She has been able to maintain with good rapport with her colleagues.
✎ 她生性樂觀，與公司同事的互動良好。

In work, she has proven to be a take-charge person who is able to successfully develop the plans and implement them.
✎ 她在工作上能夠成功展開計畫並付諸實行，證明她是位認真負責的人。

She has successfully demonstrated leadership ability by counseling new and prospective employees.
✎ 輔導新進員工時，她充分展現她的領導才能。

As her English Professor, I have seen many examples of her talent and have long been impressed by her diligence and work ethic.
✎ 身為她的英文教授，我一直都有注意到她在這領域的天份，也對她的勤奮不懈與工作態度印象深刻。

She has consistently demonstrated an ability to rise to any challenges that she must face.
✎ 她絕對能夠面對任何挑戰。

Kaya is a highly intelligent, perceptive young woman.
✎ 卡雅是一位非常聰明、領悟力高的年輕人。

He has a confident personality and is able to handle any demands placed upon him with maturity and enthusiasm.
✎ 他相當有自信，能夠以成熟的態度與熱忱處理任何事情。

Cheri has outstanding organizational skills.
✎ 嘉麗擁有傑出的組織能力。

If your company is seeking superior candidates with a record of achievement, Cheri is an excellent choice.
✎ 如果貴公司正在找一位傑出人材，嘉麗會是最棒的人選。

第三段 — 收尾，再次推薦

I feel confident that she will continue to succeed in her work.
🖊 我深信她在工作上一直都會有傑出的表現。

I have every faith in her abilities.
🖊 我對她的能力非常有信心。

I feel confident that he will continue to succeed in his studies.
🖊 我相信他會繼續在他的研究上發光發熱。

It is for these reasons that I offer high recommendations for Hannah without reservation.
🖊 這正是我毫無保留、極力推薦漢娜的原因。

I recommend Danny Chou to your company with absolute confidence.
🖊 我有絕對的信心推薦周丹尼到貴公司。

Thank you once again for the opportunity to recommend such a special and impressive young man.
再次感謝您給我機會推薦這位特別又令人印象深刻的年輕人。

 感謝及提供聯絡方式

If you need more information about Miss Wang, please do not hesitate to contact me.
🖊 如果您需要王小姐進一步的資料，請與我聯絡。

If there are inquiries about her performance and character, I would be more than happy to provide further information.
🖊 只要是關於她的工作表現及品格查詢，本人定當樂意回覆。

I would be happy to offer you more materials about Mr. Lee if you have further inquiries.
🖊 若您對李先生還有任何疑問，我很樂意提供更多資訊給您。

If you face any questions, please contact me at sandyliu@mail.net.
🖊 若您有其他問題，請以email與我聯繫：sandyliu@mail.net。

Part 1
Part 2
Part 3
Part 4
Part 5
Part 6

Unit 2　面談通知與結果通知

·2-01· 通知面談時間

　　面談時間通知信（Interview Notice）的內容通常會以「您的資料已經通過本公司之審核，特此通知您面試相關資訊」為首發展；具體通知內容則包括面試的時間、地點以及聯絡人的資料。

Subject | **MIT Interview Notice**

Dear MIT Applicant:

We have now had the opportunity to review your application to our company and would like to interview you in person in the following location:

Address: 26th floor, No. 1, Songzhi Road, Xinyi District, Taipei City 110, Taiwan, R.O.C.

We would appreciate hearing from you about your availability at the earliest opportunity. Our decision will be communicated to you online through our company website by 5:00 p.m., Monday, April 5, 2016.

Please call 02-2588-5434 between 10:00 a.m. and 4:00 p.m. to schedule your thirty-minute interview.

We look forward to hearing from you about your availability.

親愛的MIT應徵者：

我們審核了你應徵本公司的資料，想要通知你面談，地點如下：

地址：110 台北市信義區松智路1號26樓

我們感謝你與我們聯絡並安排面試時間。最後的錄取結果將會在二〇一六年四月五日（星期一）前，發佈於本公司的網站上。

請於上午十點至下午四點間來電與我們確認三十分鐘的面試時間。

我們期待你的來電。

羅德・格西亞 謹上

Best wishes,
Rod Garcia

Send ↖

 **Copy & Paste**

It is notified for the information of all concerned that:
✎ 這是通知所有面試者的訊息：

- -

The interview of the candidates who have applied for the post shall be conducted on July 4, 2016 at Camp Office of the Company from 8:00 a.m. onwards.
✎ 申請職缺的應徵者將在本公司Camp辦公室，於二〇一六年七月四日上午八點開始舉行面談。

- -

We have reviewed your resume, and would like to discuss your qualifications in person.
✎ 我們已收到您的履歷，希望與您當面討論您的資歷。

- -

Your qualifications appear to be a good fit for this position. Please contact me to arrange for an interview.
✎ 從您的資歷看來，您似乎能勝任此職位。請與我聯絡以安排面試。

- -

We are evaluating the applications and will invite candidates to interview on April 10, 2016. Our interview preparation guide is available on the website.
✎ 我們正在審核應徵者的資料，且將邀請候選人參加二〇一六年四月十日的面試。我們的面試準備將公告在網頁上。

- -

It is notified for the information of the candidates that our Staff Selection Commission will conduct the interviews for the following posts as per schedule given below:
✎ 這是通知應徵者的訊息，我們的員工遴選委員會將舉行面談，面試時間表如下：

- -

As a reminder, please provide an official copy of your resume for your interviewer.
✎ 提醒各位，請準備一份履歷表影本給面試官。

- -

It is also made clear that our Staff Selection Commission will not be responsible for any delay.

Part 1
Part 2
Part 3
Part 4
Part 5
Part 6

✎ 也請注意，我們的員工遴選委員會對應徵者自身的延誤不負任何責任。

When you arrive for your interview, please check in with the receptionist. And you will be told where you can find Mrs. Smith.
✎ 當你抵達面試會場，請向櫃檯人員報到，他會告訴你與史密斯女士的面試地點。

Before leaving for your interview, please check your email for urgent messages from the MIT Company, such as delays or cancellation due to the weather or emergencies.
✎ 前往面試會場前，請確認電子信箱是否有來自本公司的緊急通告，例如：因天氣不佳或意外造成面試延期或取消面試。

Attire is business.
✎ 請穿著正式服裝面試。

進階補充站　Let's learn more!

單字/片語Focus

❧ 工作面試 ❧	
*interview 面試	*interviewer 面試官
*interviewee 應徵者	*intern 實習生
*vacancy 職位空缺	*recruit 應徵
*probation 試用期	*first impression 第一印象

實用資訊Focus

十大面試常見問題 🔍

1. Tell us about yourself and what you have done so far in your career.
闡述自己的教育背景和之前的工作經驗。

2. What do you know about our organization and the industry?
對應徵公司及該產業的了解。

3. Why have you applied for this job?
敘述選擇此份工作的原因。

4. Why should we select you?

應該錄取你的原因。（可提及你的能力、貢獻、專長與技能）

5. What are your career goals and where do you see yourself five years from now?

談談你的職涯目標以及五年目標。

6. Why did you leave your last job?

說明你離開上一份工作的原因。

7. What are your strengths and weaknesses?

闡述你的優點、略提缺點。

8. What is your salary expectation?

說明你的薪資要求。

9. How do you handle a situation such as a conflict or management situation?

談談你處理衝突以及面對困難的方法。

10. Do you have any questions?

求職者對應徵公司的提問。

面試前的準備 🔍

1. 做好功課：預先了解對方公司的產品、服務、管理、文化等。

2. 做好練習：在朋友、家人或是鏡子面前做面試演練。

3. 提早十分鐘抵達面試現場，並攜帶備份的履歷表、推薦信、面試問題及個人作品。

面試過程注意事項 🔍

1. 因為第一印象很重要，所以服裝需適宜，並堅定地與對方握手。

2. 與面試官對談時儘量讓雙方能自在溝通，而非質問式的一問一答。

3. 過程中須充分展現出熱忱，讓面試官了解你對這份工作的興趣和執著。

面試結束的後續 🔍

1. 索取面試官的個人名片，並於面試後立即發送感謝信函給對方。

2. 記錄面試所有人員的姓名職位，並記錄此份工作的重要內容或資料。

3. 最後仔細評估此份工作是否合適。

Part 1
Part 2
Part 3
Part 4
Part 5
Part 6

2-02 錄取通知信函

錄取通知信（Employment Notification）為通知應徵者面試過關之信函，內容包括恭喜應徵者、通知報到時間以及薪資確認。

Subject Joining Letter from YTT

Dear Mr. Yi Lin Tseng:

It is my pleasure to **announce**[1] that you have been **recruited**[2] in our Yen Tai **Textile**[3] Company as a Sales Manager. Firstly, we would like to congratulate you on securing this job. November 6th, 2016 would be your joining date if you are willing to step in to our company.

Our whole team will be welcoming you to work as a sales manager. We believe that you would perfectly suit this job profile with eight and half years of experience. All your previous years of experience would count here as it will certainly help our company's **targets**[4] and in coming up with the new **strategies**[5].

Finally, I just want to conclude by fixing your pay scale. We would like to pay you $80,000 per **annum**[6] which would be quite **reasonable**[7]. For any other **queries**[8], you can reach me at the office contact number.

Best wishes,
Terry Jackson

Send

曾奕麟先生您好：

很榮幸我們將提供您元泰紡織公司業務經理一職。首先，我們要恭喜您錄取本公司，並於二〇一六年十一月六日開始就職。

我們全體同仁非常歡迎您擔任本公司的業務經理。我們相信您是這職位的最佳人選，您長達八年半的工作經驗對公司來說意義非凡，將帶領我們公司朝新目標及新策略邁進。

最後，本公司將調整您的薪資，調升至一年八萬元美金，相信這是相當合理的薪資。若您有任何疑問，歡迎來電詢問。

泰瑞・傑克森 謹上

Part 1

Part 2

Part 3

Part 4

Part 5

Part 6

核心字彙充電站 Key Words

1. **announce** 動 宣布；發布
2. **recruit** 動 雇用；聘用
3. **textile** 名 紡織品
4. **target** 名 目標；指標
5. **strategy** 名 策略
6. **annum** 名 （拉丁文）年
7. **reasonable** 形 合理的
8. **query** 名 疑問；詢問

替換好用句 Copy & Paste

It is with great pleasure that we offer you the position of Product Manager.
很榮幸我們將提供您產品經理一職。

Congratulations! We look forward to having you join our company.
恭喜！期待您加入我們公司。

We look forward to having you start as the Executive Secretary on September 1st.
我們期待您自九月一日開始接任本公司的執行秘書。

This is a formal job offer for the position of Deputy Director, starting from September 1st for a period of one year.
正式通知您獲聘副處長一職，自九月一日起為期一年。

On behalf of the department, I would like to inform you that you are being accepted as one of our members.
謹代表我們部門，在此通知您成為本公司的一份子。

You will be working with fifteen other officers in the Vice President Office.
您將在副總經理辦公室與十五名專員一起工作。

We have carefully screened all the applicants and we deemed your application to be worthy for acceptance.
我們已謹慎審核所有應徵者的資料，認為您是值得我們錄取的一位。

Your application immediately caught our attention as you have exceptional grades and were the president of the student association.
您的申請資料引起我們的注意，您不僅擁有優秀的成績，還曾擔任學生會主席。

Please attend the formal induction of new members on January 31st, 2016 at the organization office. Welcome to our company!
🖊 請於二〇一六年一月三十一日參加新員工的正式就職儀式。歡迎加入本公司！

Your salary shall be $ 58,000 NTD per month.
🖊 你的月薪為新台幣五萬八千元。

For the first year, annual leave shall be prorated, so you will be entitled to five days for this year.
🖊 第一年的年假將按比例分配，所以這一年你會分配到五天假期。

 Let's learn more!

 單字/片語Focus

🐌 工作經歷 🐌

＊responsibility 職責	**＊achievement** 業績
＊accomplish 完成	**＊appoint** 任命；指派
＊control 控制	**＊conduct** 經營；管理
＊work experience 工作經歷	**＊specific experience** 具體經驗

 實用資訊Focus

錄取通知書 🔍

在一些制度完善的公司裡，人事聘僱會有一定的程序。由人事室初步篩選過後，求職者才得以到公司進行面試。若是較重要的職務，可能會再由高階主管進行面試。在公司決定聘用後，將由人事室發出正式的「錄取通知書」給求職者，這種「錄取通知書」基本上會包含：

1. 通知求職者得到這份工作，並告知就職日
2. 工作內容與職掌
3. 公司所提供的福利
4. 期待這位求職者的加入

2-03 不錄取通知信

不錄取通知信（Job Position Filled Letter）主要目的為通知應徵者面試未通過，因此通常會以「感謝您前來參與面試」為起頭，接著描述不錄取之原因。信末通常會加上如「未來若有機會，仍有合作空間」之字樣。

Subject | **Position Filled Letter**

Dear Mr. Lai:

Thanks for the recent **submittal**[1] of your resume and **cover letter**[2] in response to the advertised opening at PCP Company. We **regret**[3] to inform you that the position has already been filled. We will **retain**[4] your information to consider for future **openings**[5] when this or other positions become available in the future. We **encourage**[6] you to follow up with us as well.

Thank you for **expressing**[7] your interest in PCP Company. We will hope to offer another position in the future that matches your personal qualifications and **objectives**[8]. PCP Company wishes you the best of luck in your job search.

Sincerely,
Jack Brown

賴先生您好：

感謝您日前寄來應徵本公司職缺的履歷和求職信。我們很遺憾通知您，您並未錄取該工作職缺。我們將保留您的資料，以便為日後職缺的優先考慮人選，也希望您與我們保持聯絡。

謝謝您對本公司的愛護，希望將來能提供符合您條件與目標的職缺，本公司祝福您求職順利。

傑克・布朗 謹上

Send ►

核心字彙充電站 *Key Words*

1. **submittal** 名 提交
2. **a cover letter** 名 附函
3. **regret** 動 遺憾；為…抱歉
4. **retain** 動 保留；保持

Part 1
Part 2
Part 3
Part 4
Part 5
Part 6

5. opening 名 （職位的）空缺　　**6. encourage** 動 鼓勵

7. express 動 表達；陳述　　**8. objective** 名 目標

替換好用句　Copy & Paste

We appreciate your time, attentiveness and patience throughout the interview process.

✎ 我們感謝您於本次面試過程所投入的時間、專注和耐心。

We did have several highly qualified candidates for the position and it has been a difficult decision, but we have chosen to pursue another candidate for this position who we feel is best qualified.

✎ 有好幾位合適的人選令我們難以抉擇，但我們最終還是選擇了另一位我們認為更合適的人選。

We feel that you are better qualified for another position, and we would like to forward your application to the other departments within the company for evaluation as well. Please let us know if you do not agree with this procedure.

✎ 我們認為您更適合其他職缺，所以想要將您的申請資料送到本公司的其他單位審核。若您不同意，請告知我們。

We will contact you if anything suitable becomes available.

✎ 若有合適的職缺，我們會再與您聯絡。

At this time, we are unable to grant your request for an interview.

✎ 我們目前無法滿足您面試的要求。

The position you applied for has already been filled. We will keep your resume on file for six months.

✎ 您所應徵的職缺已找到人選，我們會將您的履歷保留六個月。

We do thank you for your interest in our company and we wish you good luck in your future endeavors.

✎ 感謝您對本公司的愛護，我們祝您未來努力能成功。

Part 1

Part 2

Part 3

Part 4

Part 5

Part 6

Unit 3 接受或拒絕工作信函

3-01 感謝提供面試

經歷完面試這一關後，你就成了這個職位的候選人之一。面試後寫一封感謝信（Thank-You Letter）會對你有所幫助：一、感謝面試官提供的面試機會；二、讓對方知道你對這份工作的熱忱；三、提醒面試官你具有的資格及將為公司帶來的利益；四、提供對方要求的其他資料。

Subject  Thank-You Letter

Dear Dr. Brown:

I want to thank you for interviewing me yesterday for the retail management position. I enjoyed meeting you and learning more about your company and work.

My **enthusiasm**[1] for the position and my interest in working for Philips were **strengthened**[2] after the interview. I think my education and experiences match nicely with the job **requirements**[3], and I am sure that I could make a **significant**[4] **contribution**[5] to the company over time.

I want to **reiterate**[6] my strong interest in this position and in working with you and your staff. You provide the kind of opportunity I seek. Please feel free to contact me at 2345-6789 or andywang@mail.net if I can provide you with any further information.

親愛的布朗博士：

我想感謝您昨天提供我零售管理職位的面談機會。與您談話很愉快，也很高興學到貴公司的運作和工作內容。

這次面試加深了我對該職位的熱忱，也更想為飛利浦公司效力。我想我的教育背景與經歷十分符合您所要求的條件，我確信自己未來能對公司有很大的貢獻。

我想再次重申我對這份工作以及與你們共事的高度意願。很感激您提供我想要的工作機會。若有其他需要，請隨時撥打2345-6789或來函至

Again, thank you for the interview and your consideration.

Sincerely,
Andy Wang

andywang@mail.net與我聯絡。

再次謝謝您的面談與考慮。

王安迪 敬上

Send

核心字彙充電站 *Key Words*

1. **enthusiasm** 名 熱心；熱忱
2. **strengthen** 動 加強；增強
3. **requirement** 名 要求；條件
4. **significant** 形 重大的
5. **contribution** 名 貢獻
6. **reiterate** 動 重申；重做

替換好用句 *Copy & Paste*

It was a pleasure to meet you and your staff at the company.
🖉 能在公司與您和您的員工會面是我的榮幸。

I enjoyed our meeting this morning.
🖉 我們今天早上的面談十分愉快。

I was very impressed by your working environment and equipment.
🖉 我對貴公司的環境和設備感到印象深刻。

I am more interested in this job since I had a chance to see your operations and learn what your goals for the division are.
🖉 在有機會見識到貴公司的運作及了解公司目標後，我對這份工作更感興趣了。

I am particularly interested in your plans for expanding markets to the European countries.
🖉 我對您的歐洲市場開發計畫特別感興趣。

It is challenging to solve your marketing problems, but I am willing to

take the chance.
🖊 解決貴公司的行銷問題很具挑戰性，但我非常樂意接受挑戰。

- -

I am enclosing my job description which you requested, and have asked my references to write letters of recommendation directly to you.
🖊 在此附上您要求的工作說明，此外，我已請求推薦人直接寄信給您。

- -

I am looking forward to returning for a second interview with the hope that we can further discuss how my skills can be used to push the company forward.
🖊 期盼能有第二次面談的機會，進一步討論如何運用我的專長，來幫助公司成長。

- -

I hope that my qualifications meet your criteria for Sales Manager at your company.
🖊 希望我的條件符合貴公司對業務經理的要求。

- -

Thank you for taking time out of your busy schedule to talk to me about the market analysis after my interview last Tuesday.
🖊 感謝您撥冗於上週二安排的面試機會，並於會後與我分析市場面向。

- -

I appreciate your valuable time and consideration for reviewing my profile and interviewing me for this challenging position.
🖊 感謝您撥出寶貴時間及慎重的考慮，讓我有機會參與這份有挑戰性的面試。

- -

 進階補充站 Let's learn more!

 文法/句型Focus

✱ 感謝對方給予機會

1 **Thank you for your time.** 謝謝您撥空。

2 **I am truly grateful to you for...** 我真心為了…感謝您。

3 **Thank you for giving me this opportunity to...**
謝謝您給我…的機會。

4 **Please accept my sincere appreciation for...**
請接受我對…的誠摯謝意。

3-02 接受工作信函

如果決定接受這份工作，接受工作信函（Acceptance Letter）的內容就必須提及形式上的契約協定，內容包括：一、表示接受工作的聲明；二、簡短說明你接受主管的決定與公司目標；三、你將開始工作的日期。

Subject Acceptance Letter by Audra Well

Dear Sir:

I am writing to confirm my **acceptance**[1] of your **employment**[2] offer of July 4th and to tell you how delighted I am to be joining your company, Philips Inc. The work is exactly what I have prepared to **perform**[3] and hoped to do. I feel **confident**[4] that I can make a significant contribution to the **corporation**[5], and I am **grateful**[6] for the opportunity you have given me.

As we discussed before, I will work at 8:00 a.m. on July 15th for the **orientation**[7]. And I shall complete all employment and **insurance**[8] forms then.

I look forward to working with you and your fine team. I appreciate your confidence in me and I am very happy to be joining your staff.

Sincerely,
Audra Well

Send

先生您好：

我寫信來確認接受您於七月四日提供的工作機會。能加入飛利浦公司，真的令我感到滿心喜悅。這份工作正是我期待的，我有信心可以為公司獻上一己之力，同時也很感謝您給我這個機會。

如我們先前討論過的，我會在七月十五日上午八點到公司參加員工訓練，並完成員工資料表和保險資料。

我期待與您和團隊一起工作。感謝您對我的支持，也很高興成為公司的一份子。

歐卓拉・威爾 敬上

核心字彙充電站 Key Words

1. **acceptance** 名 接受
2. **employment** 名 雇用
3. **perform** 動 履行；執行
4. **confident** 形 有信心的
5. **corporation** 名 股份（有限）公司
6. **grateful** 形 感謝的
7. **orientation** 名 情況介紹
8. **insurance** 名 保險

替換好用句 Copy & Paste

I am pleased to accept your offer of an editor position at Wonderful Books.
🖊 我很高興接受萬德出版社提供的編輯一職。

Firstly, I would like to thank you for giving me this opportunity.
🖊 首先，我要謝謝您提供我這個機會。

I am extremely happy to take up the position of Assistant Manager. I will try my best to implement new plans and schemes which can really enhance our business scope.
🖊 我十分高興可以取得助理經理的職位，我會盡最大的努力來執行新計畫和提升公司的目標。

I would like to go ahead with this employment acceptance letter and I am also satisfied regarding the contract period and salary.
🖊 我願意接受這份工作，同時也十分滿意它所提供的相關聘期和薪資約定。

This would be the time for me to prove my capability, and I won't let you down.
🖊 這是讓我證明自己能力的時候，我不會讓您們失望。

You can be sure I will bring all my experience to bear on this job.
🖊 我將投注過去的經驗，努力完成這份工作，您大可放心。

I will be able to start on Monday, September 1st, as we discussed on the phone.
🖊 如同我們在電話裡討論的那樣，我將於九月一日（星期一）開始工作。

I will report to the personnel office at 8:30 a.m. and to your office at 9 a.m.
🖊 我會在八點半至人事室報告，並於九點鐘抵達辦公室。

Part 1
Part 2
Part 3
Part 4
Part 5
Part 6

Thank you for this opportunity. I look forward to working with you and the rest of staff soon.

✏️ 謝謝您所給予的機會，我期待與您和其他同仁一同工作。

 進階補充站 Let's learn more!

 單字/片語Focus

🔖 能力與性格優勢 🔖

✱**adaptable** 適應能力強的	✱**ambitious** 有企圖心的
✱**capable** 能幹的	✱**communicative** 善於溝通的
✱**creative** 具創意的	✱**consistent** 表現穩定的
✱**dedicated** 敬業的	✱**dynamic** 有活力的
✱**efficient** 有效率的	✱**open-minded** 作風開明的
✱**optimistic** 樂觀的	✱**prudent** 處事謹慎的
✱**rational** 理性的	✱**responsive** 反應敏捷的
✱**trustworthy** 值得信賴的	✱**unbiased** 公正的

 實用資訊Focus

🔍 接受工作信函

　　此信件用來確認你對這份工作的認同，包括薪資、開始工作日、醫療檢查等。通常在接到公司的錄取通知後，就能以信件回覆，接受工作信函通常會包含三段內容：

1. 第一段：確認、接受，並再次確認你進入公司的決定。

2. 第二段：確認錄取工作之相關內容。

3. 第三段：表達感謝之意。

Part 1

Part 2

Part 3

Part 4

Part 5

Part 6

·3-03· 婉拒工作機會

一封能維持好關係的拒絕工作信函很重要，因為日後還是可能會再向該公司應徵。先表示感謝對方提供這個工作機會，再提出拒絕的原因，切記要委婉表達。

Subject | Withdrawal Letter

Dear Mr. Wang:

I am writing to **inform**[1] you that I am **withdrawing**[2] my application for the retail management position in your company. As I **indicated**[3] in my interview with you, I have been **exploring**[4] several employment possibilities. This week, I was offered an executive management position in Chicago and, after careful consideration, I decided to accept it. The position provides a good match for my interests at this point in my **career**[5].

I would like to thank you for interviewing and considering me for your position. I enjoyed meeting you and learning about the projects from your company. You have a fine company and I wish you and your staff well.

Sincerely,
Jason Scott

Send ▶

王先生您好：

我寫信來是要告知您，我無法接受貴公司提供的零售管理職缺。如同我在面試中曾提及的，我同時也申請了其他工作機會。我這週收到來自芝加哥提供的行政管理職位。經過慎重考慮之後，我決定接受芝加哥的這份工作。目前來說，它比較符合我個人的職涯規劃及興趣發展。

我很感激您提供我面試及工作機會。很高興能與您會面，也因此學習到貴公司的發展計畫。你們是很棒的公司，也祝福您與所有同仁一切順心。

傑森·史考特 謹上

Subject: Rejection Letter

Dear Mr. Ferguson:

Thank you so much for offering me the position of retail management in your company. I appreciate your time for discussing the details of the position with me. And also thank you for giving me time to consider your offer.

You have a fine **organization**[6] and there are many **aspects**[7] of the position that are very **appealing**[8] to me. However, I believe it is in our **mutual**[9] best interests that I decline your kind offer. This has been a difficult decision for me, but I believe it is the appropriate one for my career.

I want to thank you for the consideration and **courtesy**[10] given to me. It was a pleasure meeting you and your fine staff.

Sincerely,
Mark Gerard

Send

佛格森先生您好：

謝謝您提供我貴公司零售管理的職位。我很感謝您對這份工作的解說，也很感謝您給我時間考慮。

你們是一家很好的機構，這份工作的許多層面也都很吸引我。然而，我相信拒絕接受這份工作對我們雙方來說都是件好事。這真是非常難以抉擇，但我相信這個決定對我的職涯規劃較為恰當。

我要感謝您們的考慮及好意。能與您和您的職員見面是件開心的事。

馬克・傑拉德 敬上

核心字彙充電站 Key Words

1. **inform** 動 通知；告知
2. **withdraw** 動 取消；撤回
3. **indicate** 動 指示；指出
4. **explore** 動 探索
5. **career** 名 （終身的）職業
6. **organization** 名 機構
7. **aspect** 名 方面；觀點
8. **appealing** 形 有魅力的
9. **mutual** 形 相互的
10. **courtesy** 名 禮貌

替換好用句 Copy & Paste

I appreciate the offer of secretary position at your company.
🖉 感謝貴公司提供我秘書一職。

I have received your letter of appointment for the post of Account Manager and I am much obliged.
🖉 我已收到您寄來關於客戶服務經理職位的信函，十分感激。

I had attended the interview in your company with much anticipation and eagerness to be able to work for a renowned firm like your company.
🖉 我滿懷期望到貴公司面試，渴望能在像你們一樣享負盛名的公司工作。

However, as we discussed, the job would force me to drive two hours a day back and forth.
🖉 然而，如我們討論過的，這份工作迫使我每天開車來回通勤二個小時。

However, I am really sorry to say that I will not be able to join your company for now.
🖉 然而，我真的很抱歉無法到貴公司上班。

I am sorry, but I just accepted another offer that I feel is more suitable to my needs.
🖉 很抱歉，我剛接受了另一份感覺較為符合我需求的工作。

I really appreciate your offer, but I must decline it.
🖉 非常感謝貴公司願意錄用我，但我不得不回絕。

Frankly speaking, I have been thinking that this position may not right for me after the interview.
🖉 坦白說，在面試過後，我覺得這份職位可能沒這麼適合我。

After careful thought, I decided to take a position as a secretary in another company.
🖉 經慎重考慮後，我決定到其他公司擔任秘書。

Although this job is less attractive than the one with your firm, it's much closer to my home and family.
🖉 雖然這份工作無法與您提供的工作相比，但它離我家人較近。

I hope you will understand my situation and accept my apology.
🖉 希望您能了解我的處境，接受我的道歉。

Part 1
Part 2
Part 3
Part 4
Part 5
Part 6

I appreciate the time you spent with me.
🖊 感謝您撥出時間給我。

Thank you once again for considering me for this post in your well-established office.
🖊 再次謝謝您這般信譽卓著的公司提供給我的職位。

I know there are many good candidates who can fill your position.
🖊 我相信有許多優秀的應徵者適合這份工作。

Hope I will have your blessings with me.
🖊 希望您可以祝福我。

 進階補充站　Let's learn more!

 實用資訊Focus

拒絕工作信函的類別 🔍

　　Rejection Letter與Withdrawal Letter的不同之處在於，Withdrawal Letter是指當你已經先接受某公司所提供的職缺，同時又接到其他公司予以更適合的職位時，所回覆的拒絕工作信函。withdrawal有撤銷、撤回的意思；而rejection則表示拒絕。

婉拒工作信函的寫法 🔍

1. 第一段：感謝公司錄取。
2. 第二段：提出深思熟慮後之婉拒原因。
3. 第三段：感謝對方給予的肯定和機會。

Part 5

公司商務篇～交易往來這樣貼

動 動詞　　名 名詞

副 副詞　　形 形容詞

介 介系詞　片 片語

Point

公司商務的往來信件不僅能左右交易結果，還能成為聯繫商務關係的工具，因此，本章特別從頭教起，從尋找合作對象，到各種交易時的突發狀況，現在用 E-mail 都能說。

Unit 1 初步建立商務關係

1-01 推薦新產品

　　「推銷信」的主要目的在於提供產品資訊，以引發客戶對產品的興趣為重點。下列範例屬於簡易版的推銷信，代表撰信者與客戶的往來頻繁；反之，若收信者為新開發之客戶，則一定要在信件開頭簡短且清楚地介紹自己的公司以及產品（如下一頁的範例）。

Subject	Recommend New Products

Dear Sirs:

We have recently designed a new product, which is selling very well in our market in Taiwan, and we are sure you will be interested in it.

We are confident that there is a **potential**[1] sales **prospect**[2] in your market as well; therefore, we are pleased to provide you with some samples as well as the price list.

We very much look forward to hearing from you.

Yours sincerely,
Sally Wang
Sales Director, Imodel Corp.
+886-2-3344-6688

敬啟者：

我們最近設計了一項新產品，在台灣市場的銷售表現十分亮眼，相信您會對它有興趣。

對於本產品在您們市場的銷售潛力，我們深具信心；因此，我們非常樂意提供樣品及價目表給您。

我們期望能夠得到您的回覆。

王莎莉 謹上
愛模股份有限公司
業務處長
+886-2-3344-6688

Send ▸

| Part 1 |
| Part 2 |
| Part 3 |
| Part 4 |
| Part 5 |
| Part 6 |

Subject: Taiwan Bank Credit Card

Dear Sir:

If you are looking for a credit card, Taiwan Bank's Credit Card may just be the right one for you!

Our bank always has our customers in mind and you can see this as we have **extremely**[3] low interest rates, especially for first-time card owners like you!

Moreover, you can apply for our credit card online, and you'll also be **automatically**[4] **enrolled**[5] in our online banking system, ridding yourself of unnecessary paperwork.

You'll enjoy 5% quarterly bonus in **categories**[6] with cards such as **grocery stores**[7], dining, department stores and even home improvement stores. It's free and easy to **activate**[8] your bonus each quarter!

You can also call our customer service line at 2257-3133 to get more information now!

We can't wait to hear from you!

Sincerely yours,
Helen Chen

先生您好：

若您正在尋找信用卡，台灣銀行信用卡將會是您的首選！

敝行一向秉持客戶至上的原則，如您可見，我們的利息很低，尤其是對於像您這樣第一次申辦的客戶而言。

此外，您可以線上申請我們的信用卡，並自動被加入我們的網路銀行，這樣可免去不必要的書面作業。

您可每季免費享有百分之五的紅利回饋，可使用紅利之範圍包含雜貨超商、餐廳、百貨及家用品商店等。使用每季的紅利點數相當容易！

您也可以來電：2257 - 3133，以便得到更多資訊！

希望能夠得到您的回覆！

陳海倫 敬上

Send

核心字彙充電站 Key Words

1. **potential** 形 潛在的；可能的
2. **prospect** 名 預期；可能性
3. **extremely** 副 極端地；非常
4. **automatically** 副 自動地
5. **enroll** 動 登記
6. **category** 名 種類；類型
7. **grocery store** 名 雜貨店
8. **activate** 動 使活動起來

替換好用句 Copy & Paste

🧩 提到新產品

We are pleased to inform you about our latest product.
🖋 我們很樂意向您介紹我們的新產品。

We take the advantage of this opportunity to bring your notice.
🖋 我們趁此機會通知您。

Please allow us to call your attention to attend our new product conference.
🖋 請容許我們告知您新品發表會的消息。

In reply to your letter of the 5th of April, I have to inform you that our new product has been out on the market.
🖋 回覆您四月五日的來信，我想要通知您：我們的新產品已經上市了。

As you have received the information, the Lux Motor Show will take place in May.
🖋 如同您收到的資訊，麗勢車展將於五月舉辦。

We expect that you will be going to have a look at the latest vehicle.
🖋 希望您能前來鑑賞最新車款。

We have heard that your company is seeking for all kinds of kitchenware.
🖋 我們聽聞貴公司正在尋找各類廚房用品。

We are happy to inform you that we have just marketed our new product.
🖋 我們很開心地通知您：我們剛推出新產品。

It's our pleasure to offer you our best service.
🖊 為您提供最好的服務是我們的榮幸。

 介紹公司特色與產品優勢

Our new products are more competitive in both the quality and price.
🖊 我們的新產品在價格以及品質上皆更有競爭力。

One of our main strengths is its fashionable design.
🖊 我們主要的優勢之一在於產品的時尚設計感。

We have enjoyed an excellent reputation for quality products for over thirty years.
🖊 我們的產品享有超過三十年的優良信譽。

We believe that our products are certain to satisfy your customers.
🖊 我們相信您的客戶會滿意我方的產品。

 提供價格優惠

We are pleased to offer you the lowest possible price.
🖊 我們很開心能提供您最優惠的價格。

You may be able to get 10% discount on your initial order.
🖊 初次訂購可享九折優惠。

The special discount now offered can be allowed only on orders placed by the end of May.
🖊 本次優惠僅提供給五月底前下單的訂購者。

You will receive a special discount of 15% which can be maintained until September 30.
🖊 您可享有八五折優惠至九月三十日。

 提供額外資訊

We would like to send you one sample and the manual.
🖊 我們會寄發樣品以及說明書給您。

We look forward to receiving your trial order soon.

Part 1
Part 2
Part 3
Part 4
Part 5
Part 6

🖊 希望能儘快收到您的試用訂單。

The products are now available in stock.
🖊 目前產品皆有現貨。

Delivery can be made within one week after receiving your order.
🖊 可於收到訂單後一週內出貨。

Please see the attached price list, and let us know your requirement by return.
🖊 請參考附件的價目表，並回信告知您的需求。

 結尾可用

If you are interested in our products, please let us know.
🖊 如果您對我們的產品有興趣，請告訴我們。

Please contact us if you are satisfied with our samples.
🖊 如果您滿意我們的樣品，請與我們聯絡。

We would be pleased if we have an opportunity to cooperate with you.
🖊 若有機會與您合作，我們將會很高興。

We are glad to get in touch with you soon.
🖊 希望能夠儘快與您聯絡。

You can contact us whenever you want.
🖊 您隨時都可以聯絡我們。

We await good news with patience.
🖊 我們靜候佳音。

We thank you in advance for the anticipated favor.
🖊 我們感謝您的支持。

We solicit the continuance of your confidence and support.
🖊 懇請您持續的信賴與支持。

We hope to receive the continuance of your kind patronage.
🖊 期待您的持續惠顧。

1-02 網路購物廣告

| Subject | Discount to Die for |

Dear Customers:

Our entire **inventory**[1] items are on sale now! Items like European furniture, closets, dressers, **stools**[2], **armchairs**[3], lamps, coffee tables, end tables, collections, tools, **antiques**[4], and more are included. Everything for your home is all at **fabulous**[5] discounts. Please check it out at www.fabulousitems.com. Just enter the promotion code below when the checkout screen appears and we'll **deduct**[6] the 50 percent off the purchase. All major credit cards are accepted.

Promotion code: 158BX

This offer may not be combined with any other offers or applied to the purchase of a gift card. This offer expires on December 28.

We look forward to seeing your online shopping.

Sincerely yours,
Peter Kao

Send

親愛的顧客：

我們現正舉辦清倉拍賣會！拍賣商品包括：歐洲傢俱、衣櫥、梳妝台、凳子、扶手椅、燈座、茶几、收藏品、工具、古董等，居家用品一應俱全，通通給您滿意折扣，請上：www.fabulousitems.com網站洽詢。買家只要在結帳畫面輸入下方代碼，即可享有五折優待。所有一般信用卡均受理。

優惠代碼：158BX

本活動不與其他優惠活動併用，也不適用於購買禮物卡。活動期間只到十二月二十八日。

我們期待您上網購物。

高彼得 敬上

Part 1 / Part 2 / Part 3 / Part 4 / Part 5 / Part 6

核心字彙充電站 Key Words

1. inventory 名 詳細目錄
2. stool 名 凳子
3. armchair 名 扶手椅
4. antique 名 古董
5. fabulous 形 極好的
6. deduct 動 扣除

替換好用句 Copy & Paste

We offer more options and lower prices for everything online.
🖉 我們線上提供的選擇更多，價格也更優惠。

If it's electronic, they've got it on sale.
🖉 電子商品都有特價。

Find all of your electronic needs at onSale.com.
🖉 可以在onsale.com網站上，尋找您所需的電子商品。

You only need to click on our onsale.com links to access an on sale coupon.
🖉 您只需要在onsale.com網站上，點選優惠折價券即可。

When there is an on sale coupon code or promotion code, you'll need to enter it at the on sale site to get your discount.
🖉 您需要輸入折價券上的號碼，才能得到線上購物的折價優惠。

We frequently update and reduce sale prices even more, so make sure to come back to patronize often.
🖉 我們經常推出新品及折扣優惠，所以請常回來光顧。

Our online specials give you the best prices on all your favorite products.
🖉 線上特惠活動提供您所有喜愛商品最優惠的價格。

If you don't like the item, you may return it within two weeks.
🖉 如果您不喜歡該商品，可以在兩週內退貨。

To return an item, you must present a receipt.
🖉 退貨時，請出示您的購物發票。

We will not accept any return without the receipt.
🖉 沒有發票，我們就不接受任何退貨。

Part 1

Part 2

Part 3

Part 4

Part 5

Part 6

1-03 出口商／賣方建立合作關係

　　尋求買方建立合作關係時，可簡短介紹如何得知買方訊息，並說明希望與買方往來的理由以及好處；最好另外提供目錄、價目表以及公司聯絡資訊，以便進一步的業務往來。

Subject **Establish Business Relations**

Dear Sir or Madam:

We are a **manufacturer**[1] and **exporter**[2] of raw chemical materials from Taiwan. We want to introduce our company to you. If you are interested, please visit us on the website: http://www.chemicaltw.com.tw.

We are **expanding**[3] our market this year and desire to find a partner. Please feel free to let us know your company background and how we can assist and support you in order for you to make more profit by selling the raw chemical materials.

We enclose a copy of our illustrated catalog covering the main items available at present. Please let us know if you are willing to **cooperate**[4] with us.

Yours sincerely,
Paul Chen
Sales Manager

敬啟者：

我們是台灣化學原料出口暨製造商。我們想要向您推薦敝公司，如您有興趣，可參考敝公司網頁：http://www.chemicaltw.com.tw。

我們正在擴大市場，並尋找合作夥伴。請告知我們貴公司的背景資訊，以及我們可以提供的任何支援，以讓您在販售化學原料時獲得更多利潤。

附上包含目前主要商品的目錄，敬請告知貴公司的合作意願。

陳保羅 敬上

業務經理

Send ▶

1. **manufacturer** 名 製造業者　　2. **exporter** 名 出口商
3. **expand** 動 擴大；擴充　　4. **cooperate** 動 合作

替換好用句 *Copy & Paste*

 如何得知對方資訊

Your company was introduced to us by Dr. Liao.
🖉 經由廖博士的介紹得知貴公司。

Your company was highly recommended to us by the Trade Center.
🖉 貿易中心向我們強烈推薦貴公司。

We learned from the Internet that your company is specializing in jewelry.
🖉 我們從網路上得知貴公司從事珠寶業。

We received your information from the British Trade and Cultural Office.
🖉 我們從英國經貿文化辦事處得知您的資訊。

 提出商務合作關係

We are writing in the hope of opening an account with your firm.
🖉 我們特寫此信，尋求與貴公司的商務合作關係。

Our company is seeking the cooperation opportunities.
🖉 敝公司正在尋找合作機會。

Please allow me to introduce our company to you.
🖉 請容許我向您介紹敝公司。

Our company is specialized in electric fans.
🖉 敝公司主要生產電風扇。

We are one of the leading exporters of perfume.
🖉 我們為知名的香水出口商。

We are a newly established company, based in Kaohsiung, offering travel bags.

✎ 我們是一家新成立、位於高雄的公司，主要供應旅行袋。

We have earned a good reputation both in Asia and Europe.

✎ 我們在亞洲及歐洲都擁有良好的聲譽。

Our products are very popular both at home and abroad.

✎ 我們的產品在本地以及國外都非常受歡迎。

Now we are exporting our goods to many countries in Europe and are willing to increase some Asian buyers.

✎ 我們目前主要將貨品出口到歐洲國家，也正積極尋找亞洲買家。

We are looking for partners in order to open the market in China.

✎ 我們正在尋找開發中國市場的合作夥伴。

We are desirous of extending our service in Asia.

✎ 我們渴望在亞洲擴展我們的服務市場。

We are desirous of enlarging our trade in Japan.

✎ 我們想要在日本擴展業務。

We will give you our lowest quotations and try our best to comply with your requirements.

✎ 我們可以因應您的需求，給您最低報價。

You are warmly welcomed to visit our factory and negotiate business with us.

✎ 我們熱情歡迎您到我們的工廠參觀，並一同商討貿易關係。

We hope that our products will be added to the categories of your sample.

✎ 希望我們的產品可以增加到您的樣品目錄上。

We would like to be your supplier in Taiwan.

✎ 我們希望能成為您在台灣的供應商。

If you are interested in the cooperation, please feel free to contact us.

✎ 如果您對此合作關係有興趣，請隨時聯絡我們。

If you have further queries, please feel free to contact me at 0800-112233.

✎ 如果您還有任何疑問，請致電給我，號碼為0800-112233。

Part 1
Part 2
Part 3
Part 4
Part 5
Part 6

1-04 進口商／買方建立合作關係

尋求賣方建立合作關係時，要簡短說明如何得知賣方之產品訊息以及其產品優勢，並清楚告知我方行銷能力以及能夠提供給賣方的服務，以尋求進一步合作。

Subject Establish Business Relations

Dear Sirs:

A few days ago, we had the opportunity to see a **display**[1] of your **products**[2] at the New York **Fashion**[3] Show. We were very impressed by the **quality**[4] and your low prices.

We would like to offer our services as a trading **firm**[5]. We have excellent references and connections in the trade, and are fully experienced with the **import**[6] business for this type of products.

We are sure that we can sell large quantities of your products if you would allow us to promote sales throughout Taiwan.

Please advise us.

Respectfully,
Sandra Wang

Send

敬啟者：

幾天前，我們在紐約時尚展看到貴公司的產品，我們對於產品的質感以及價位印象非常深刻。

我們想要提供敝公司的貿易服務。在此產品業界，我們擁有完整的進口經驗、相關推薦客戶及往來公司。

我們相信，如果您讓我們在台灣促銷，我們將能大量銷售貴公司的產品。

煩請給我方建議回函。

王珊卓　敬上

核心字彙充電站 Key Words

1. display 名 展覽；陳列
2. product 名 產品
3. fashion 名 流行
4. quality 名 品質
5. firm 名 公司；商號
6. import 名 進口

替換好用句 Copy & Paste

Your company was referred to me as a potential supplier.
✎ 您的公司被推薦為潛在供應商。

Your company was indicated by Taiwan Trade Center in France.
✎ 您的公司為駐法台灣貿易中心所推薦。

We take the liberty of writing to you to introduce our company.
✎ 我們冒昧向您介紹敝公司。

We are very interested in knowing more about your products.
✎ 我們想要進一步了解您的產品。

Our company is a leading importer of quality men's wear.
✎ 我們是知名的男性服飾進口商。

Our company is operating as an importer of children's shoes.
✎ 本公司的主要業務為進口童鞋。

We have many shops in Taiwan.
✎ 我們在台灣有許多經銷據點。

We are seeking for new suppliers for good quality and low price of women's apparels.
✎ 我們正在尋找品質良好且價位合理的女性服飾供應商。

We are looking for a partner to supply us with such products.
✎ 我們正在尋求提供此產品的供應商。

There is a large demand for various cosmetics in Taiwan.
✎ 多樣化的化妝品在台灣的需求量非常大。

We have considerable experience in this field.
✎ 我們對這方面的業務有豐富經驗。

Part 1
Part 2
Part 3
Part 4
Part 5
Part 6

Please send us your brochure and catalog of all your men's wear.
🖉 請寄貴公司的男性服飾型錄給我們。

Please also include the price list.
🖉 也請附上價目表。

Please indicate your requirements on the terms of payment, delivery, and minimum order.
🖉 請告知您的付款條件、貨運以及最低訂單量。

If samples are available, we would like to see samples of your goods.
🖉 若能夠提供樣品，我們希望能夠參考一下。

If we are satisfied with the products, we would place an order soon.
🖉 如果我們對產品有興趣，就會下單。

We are sure we can sell large quantities of your products.
🖉 我們確信可以大量銷售您的產品。

We can assure you of increasing your turnover considerably.
🖉 我們向您保證：您的產品會有相當的營業額。

Would you please inform us if you have any partners in Taiwan?
🖉 若您方便，請告知您在台灣是否有其他合作的公司。

We hope we can cooperate with each other in the near future.
🖉 我們希望在不久的將來能與您合作。

We would appreciate your quick response.
🖉 我們會非常感謝您的即時回覆。

 進階補充站　Let's learn more!

 單字/片語Focus

🏷 訂單與項目 🏷

✱**turnover** 營業額；成交量	✱**apparel** 服裝；衣服
✱**quantity** 量；數量	✱**quality** 品質；質
✱**place an order** 下訂單	✱**be connected with** 與…有關聯

Part 1

Part 2

Part 3

Part 4

Part 5

Part 6

·1-05· 尋找代理服務

徵求代理商服務時，可概略說明如何得知此公司，並簡短有力地分析自家產品在對方市場之銷售潛力，並於隨後交待與對方代理商的結算方式，以供對方是否成為代理方之考量依據。

Subject Exclusive Agent in China

Dear Sir or Madam:

We are a manufacturer of keyboards, and we are seeking for a firm to **represent**[1] us in China. We are writing to you as you are one of the leading and potential sales **agents**[2] in your country. We would like to know if you are interested in acting as our **sole agent**[3] in China.

As you will see from the enclosed catalog, our products have been sold well in many countries. With **competitive**[4] price and quality, we decided to promote our market in China. We will offer a 10% **commission**[5] on the list prices.

If you are interested in **developing**[6] this market, please write to us as soon as possible.

Yours sincerely,
Fiona Luis

敬啟者：

我們是電腦鍵盤製造商，正在尋找中國區的代理商。因為您在貴國為極有潛力的代理商，因此我們來函詢問，想了解貴公司是否願意成為我方在中國的總代理商。

附件為產品目錄，我們的產品已在多國銷售，銷售成績良好。我們決定以高品質、且有競爭性的價位打開中國市場。我們將會提供百分之十的佣金。

若您有興趣開發此市場，請儘速來信告知。

費歐娜·路易斯 敬上

1. **represent** 動 作為⋯的代表　　2. **agent** 名 代理商
3. **sole agent** 名 總代理商　　4. **competitive** 形 競爭的
5. **commission** 名 佣金　　6. **develop** 動 開發

替換好用句 *Copy & Paste*

We are writing to you because we are told by the Taipei Chamber Commerce.
✎ 我們從台北商會那裡得知貴公司，特此來函。

We are one of the main producers of scanners.
✎ 我們是掃描機的主要製造商之一。

We are the leading exporter of computer supplies.
✎ 我們為電腦週邊產品的知名出口商。

We can offer a wide range of products.
✎ 我們能提供各式產品。

Our products have attractive design, hard wearing and fully guaranteed for one year.
✎ 我們的產品設計具吸引力、功能實用且有一年保固期。

We have already exported our products to many countries in Europe.
✎ 我們已出口到歐洲各國。

We believe that there is an enormous potential market to be opened in China.
✎ 我們相信中國是個極具開發潛力的市場。

This would be a unique opportunity for your company to start an expanding market.
✎ 這對貴公司而言，將會是一個拓展市場的好機會。

It's an excellent opportunity to establish a wide range of customers.
✎ 這是一個拓展客戶群的絕佳機會。

We are prepared to offer 10% commission to our agent, plus advertising support.

🖉 我們準備提供百分之十的佣金給代理商，並提供廣告支援。

We would supply you with our prices at 10% below the export price list.
🖉 我們願意提供低於出口報價百分之十的佣金。

We are sure this is a golden opportunity for investing.
🖉 我們確信這是一個很好的投資機會。

If you are interested in our proposal, please let us know the terms for commission and other charges on which you would like to represent us.
🖉 若您對本公司的提案有興趣，請告知我們您的佣金條件以及其他費用。

The contract will be from Jan. 1 for one year.
🖉 合約將自一月一日起生效，為期一年。

If both companies agree, the contract will be renewed for a further year.
🖉 如雙方皆同意，合約可再延長一年。

We hope to hear favorably from you soon.
🖉 我們希望能夠儘早得到您善意的回應。

進階補充站　Let's learn more!

 單字/片語Focus

🏷 從製作到銷售 🏷

✳**manufacturer** 製造商	✳**factory** 工廠
✳**sole agent** 總代理商	✳**exclusive agent** 獨家代理商
✳**chief dealer** 總經銷商	✳**distributor** 經銷商
✳**wholesaler** 批發商	✳**retailer** 零售商
✳**consumer** 消費者	✳**customer** 顧客

Part 1
Part 2
Part 3
Part 4
Part 5
Part 6

·1-06· 申請代理服務

申請成為代理商時，記得要強調自己公司的實力以及優勢，以引起對方的注意，進而產生與你洽談代理合作之意願。

Subject | **Import Electric Watches**

Dear Sirs:

Watch Tech is a **reliable**[1] company with wide and varied experience in the line in Japan. We believe there is a potential sales **prospect**[2] of your watch in Taiwan's market. We have experienced staffs of sales **representatives**[3], and we recommend ourselves to act as your sole agent for your **electric**[4] watches in Taiwan.

Enclosed is our Agency Contract **in detail**[5].

Thank you for your time, and we are looking forward to hearing your reply **as soon as possible**[6].

Very truly yours,
Victor

敬啟者：

錶德為一家在日本信譽卓著的公司，在此行業擁有豐富的經驗。我們相信貴公司的錶品在台灣市場具有銷售潛力。我們有經驗豐富的銷售人員，現自我推薦，作為貴公司電子錶在台灣的獨家代理商。

詳見附件的代理權合約明細。

感謝您撥冗閱讀，我方期待能儘快得到您的回覆。

維克多 敬上

Send ▶

核心字彙充電站 *Key Words*

1. reliable 形 可信賴的
2. prospect 名 預期；可能性
3. representative 名 代表；代理人
4. electric 形 電的；用電的
5. in detail 片 詳細地
6. as soon as possible 片 盡快

替換好用句 Copy & Paste

We have been informed that you are presently seeking for an agent.
✎ 我們得知您正在尋找代理商。

We are very interested in your advertisement of March 13 looking for an agent in Japan.
✎ 我們對您在三月十三號刊登尋找日本當地代理商的廣告非常有興趣。

We would like to offer our services as an importer of your products.
✎ 我們願意提供您進口產品的服務。

We would like to offer to be your agent.
✎ 我們願意提供您代理商的服務。

We would like to know if you have considered expanding the market in Southeast Asia.
✎ 冒昧詢問貴公司是否有意願擴展東南亞市場？

We would like to recommend our company as the sole agent for your products.
✎ 我們想要推薦敝公司成為您的獨家代理商。

We specialize in kitchen utensils in Northeast Asia markets.
✎ 我們在東北亞市場專營廚房用具。

We have long experience in marketing.
✎ 我們有非常長久的行銷經驗。

We have been importing this kind of products for more than thirty years.
✎ 我們進口此類產品已超過三十年。

We have many offices and show rooms in the major cities in Taiwan.
✎ 我們在台灣主要的城市都設有辦公室及展示間。

The excellent quality and modern design of your products appeal us very much.
✎ 貴公司的產品品質優良且設計新穎，非常吸引我們的注意。

We are well prepared to do business with you if your price and terms are competitive.
✎ 如貴公司的價格及條件具有競爭力，我們就會準備好與您交易。

Part 1
Part 2
Part 3
Part 4
Part 5
Part 6

We are sure we would be of tremendous assistance for your company to expand the market in Taiwan.

🖉 我們相信敝公司能夠大力協助貴公司拓展在台灣的業務。

We will devote full attention to establishing your products in Southeast Asia.

🖉 我們將會全力在東南亞銷售您的產品。

We are confident that we will be able to provide a wide range of customers for your goods.

🖉 相信我們可以提供大量的產品客戶。

We would like to discuss the possibility of establishing an agency agreement with your company.

🖉 我們希望能與貴公司討論合作代理事宜。

Our manager will call you tomorrow to inquire about setting an appointment with you.

🖉 我們的經理明天會致電詢問與您的會面事宜。

進階補充站　Let's learn more!

 實用資訊Focus

代理商vs.經銷商 🔍

　　代理商（agent）與經銷商（distributor；dealer）是商務關係中常見的詞彙，兩者的意義不同，以下分別說明：

1. 代理商（agent）：一般所謂的代理商指的是銷售代理商，指接受國外廠商或供應商的委託，代理供應商向國內進口商推銷商品，從而收取佣金或報酬。因代理商代理的範圍包括整個行銷作業系統，合約可能涵蓋品牌、定價、文宣等內容，所以供應商對代理商有較大的約束力。

2. 經銷商（distributor；dealer）：經銷商會從企業進貨，再轉手賣出，從中賺取利差，指自己花費成本進貨的商號。一般來說，經銷商只負責商品的銷售，所以供應商對其的約束力較小。

Part 1

Part 2

Part 3

Part 4

Part 5

Part 6

•1-07• 接受合作關係

欲接受合作關係時，可在信中先行提出想與對方討論的項目，如貨物裝運、稅金、佣金等內容，讓對方能預先做準備。

Subject Re: Establish Business Relations

Dear Sir:

Thank you for your mail of June 6. We are pleased to know that you find our products satisfactory. We are very interested in your **proposition**[1]. We are also willing to expand our market into Asia.

We would like to **discuss**[2] the possibility of establishing a business relationship with you and look forward to **receiving**[3] your call. We would like to discuss the details, including the shipping **arrangement**[4], the import duties, and commission.

We **attached**[5] our latest catalog and the price list you requested. If the enclosed catalog does not provide you all the information, we would appreciate it if you could call us at 0800-121323.

Thank you again for your interest and **attention**[6].

Faithfully yours,
Stephen

先生您好：

謝謝您六月六日的來信，很高興您對我們的產品感到滿意。我們對您的提案很有興趣，也很有意願擴展亞洲市場。

我們希望能與您討論商務合作的可能性，也希望接到您的來電。我們想要針對貨品的運送、稅金以及佣金等事宜與您討論。

附上您要求的最新目錄以及價目表。如附件未能提供您所需的所有資訊，歡迎您來電：0800-121323。

再次感謝您的關注。

史蒂芬 謹上

核心字彙充電站 *Key Words*

1. proposition 名 提議;建議
2. discuss 動 討論;商談
3. receive 動 收到;接到
4. arrangement 名 安排
5. attach 動 附加;附屬
6. attention 名 注意

替換好用句 *Copy & Paste*

 開頭感謝語

Thank you for your mail of Jun. 6, introducing yourself and expressing your interest in our goods.
🖉 謝謝您六月六日來信介紹貴公司,表達對本公司產品的興趣。

We received your mail dated June 20 and thank you for your brief information.
🖉 我們在六月二十日收到您的來信,謝謝您的簡短介紹。

Thank you for your mail of Aug. 15, proposing to establish a business relationship with us.
🖉 謝謝您八月十五日來信提案欲與本公司建立貿易關係。

We are pleased to know that you feel there is a room for sales expansion in Taiwan.
🖉 我們很開心得知您認為台灣市場仍有擴大業務的空間。

We are very interested in your proposal.
🖉 我們對您的提案很有興趣。

 簡介自己的公司

We are still a young company but are expanding rapidly.
🖉 本公司雖然剛起步,但擴展快速。

We also introduce ourselves so that you can know more about our company and products.
🖉 讓我們也來向您介紹本公司及旗下產品。

We would like to discuss the possibilities of coming to a business

with you.
🖉 我們希望能與您討論商業合作的可能性。

We are thinking if you would like to give us some ideas of the terms on which you are willing to handle our goods.
🖉 我們希望能夠了解貴公司可以給予何種條件來銷售我們的產品。

We are interested in the chance of developing our trade.
🖉 我們對於進一步發展業務的機會很感興趣。

We assure you that you will be satisfied with the excellent qualities of our products.
🖉 我們確信您會對我們高品質的產品感到非常滿意。

We are sure that you will benefit from our service.
🖉 我們確信您會從我們的服務中獲益。

 提供資料或服務

We have pleasure to send you our catalog with full details of our products.
🖉 我們很樂意寄送包含產品所有相關資訊的目錄給您。

Regarding the products you asked for, we will send you our catalog and price list by airmail.
🖉 針對您所詢問的產品,我們會寄給您相關目錄及價目表。

We hope you will find the catalog useful.
🖉 希望目錄對您有幫助。

We will get in touch with you and arrange a meeting.
🖉 我們會與您聯絡,並安排會面。

We hope that our companies will cooperate in the future.
🖉 希望我們將來可以合作。

We look forward to your prompt reply.
🖉 期待您的即時回覆。

Part 1
Part 2
Part 3
Part 4
Part 5
Part 6

·1-08· 成為代理商並提供協議

可於回覆合作信函中條列出期望的合約內容，供對方先行檢閱，以利下一步合約之草擬及正式簽署。

Subject | Conditions of Agreement

Dear Mr. Chang:

We are pleased to act as your sole agent in France. As we have many customers in the major cities in France, we believe they would provide a promising **outlet**[1] for your LCD products.

Before the **contract**[2] is concluded with **signatures**[3], we would like to confirm the following **terms**[4] and **conditions**[5] as the basis for a formal **agreement**[6]:

1. We operate as the sole agent for a period of two years of your goods.
2. We receive a commission of 20% on the list price.
3. All advertisement cost for the first year to be **refunded**[7] by you.
4. All advertisement cost for the second year to be **divided**[8] equally between you and us.

We look forward to your letter confirming these conditions.

Yours faithfully,
Henry

張先生您好：

很開心成為貴公司在法國的總代理商。我們有許多客戶分布在法國的主要城市，相信他們會為您的液晶顯示產品提供銷售點。

在正式簽署合約前，我們希望確認主要的協議內容：

一、 兩年內，我們為貴公司產品的總代理商。
二、 代理佣金為報價之百分之二十。
三、 第一年的廣告費由貴公司負責。
四、 第二年的廣告費由雙方平均分攤。

希望貴公司來信確認以上條件。

亨利 謹上

Send ▶

1. **outlet** 名 銷路;商店
2. **contract** 名 合約
3. **signature** 名 簽名;簽屬
4. **terms** 名 (契約等的)條款
5. **condition** 名 條件
6. **agreement** 名 協議;協定
7. **refund** 動 退還;歸還
8. **divide** 動 分;劃分

替換好用句 *Copy & Paste*

Thank you for the mail proposing us for your representation in Taiwan.
🖋 謝謝您來信提案敝公司成為您在台灣的代理。

Thank you for your mail and the enclosed catalog and financial statement.
🖋 謝謝您來信附上產品目錄以及信用狀況。

We have great interest in your proposal.
🖋 我們對於您的提案非常有興趣。

Your basic terms are agreeable.
🖋 我們樂於接受您提出的條件。

Please let me know when it will be convenient to call you.
🖋 請告知方便打電話聯絡您的時間。

We would like to discuss the trade terms.
🖋 我們希望能夠討論貿易條款。

We would like to visit you for having a personal interview with your sales manager.
🖋 我們希望能夠親自拜訪貴公司的業務經理。

I look forward to meeting you.
🖋 我期待與您會面。

Part 1
Part 2
Part 3
Part 4
Part 5
Part 6

•1-09• 婉拒對方為代理商

在拒絕的信件中，最好能婉轉地給對方可接受的理由，維持有禮的態度，以利日後的合作。

Subject Re: Establish Business Relations

Dear Sirs:

Thank you for your mail of July 16 proposing to establish business relations between our two companies.

Much as we are interested in doing business with you, we regret to inform that we are not in a position to enter into business relations with any companies in your country because we have already had an agency arrangement with Luckwill Trading Co., Ltd. in Japan. According to our arrangement, only through Luckwill Trading Co. can we export our products to Japan.

We regret that we will not be able to help you this time, but look forward to an opportunity to cooperate with you in the future.

Thank you again for your proposal and your understanding of our position will be appreciated.

Faithfully yours,
Paul

Send

敬啟者：

感謝您七月十六日來函，欲和我方建立雙邊商務關係。

儘管我方對於和貴公司建立商貿關係非常有興趣，我們必須遺憾地通知您，由於我方已與日本拉克威爾有限公司簽署代理協議，所以我方無法再與貴國的其他公司建立商務關係。根據協議，我方只得透過拉克威爾公司出口產品至日本。

很抱歉目前無法與貴公司合作，希望將來仍有合作機會。

再次感謝您的提議，若您能體諒我方的立場，將使我方感激不盡。

保羅 敬上

 **替換好用句** *Copy & Paste*

Thank you for your mail regarding representation in your country.
🖉 謝謝您來信詢問關於我方在貴國的代理事宜。

Thank you for your interests in our products.
🖉 謝謝您對我們的產品感興趣。

We appreciate your offer to represent us.
🖉 謝謝您提供成為我們代理商的機會。

We now have a distributor who handles our products in your country.
🖉 我們目前在貴國已有代理商。

We are very satisfied with our present distributor.
🖉 我們很滿意現在的代理商。

We cannot make use of your proposal.
🖉 我們無法執行您的提案。

We have entered into a contract with another company.
🖉 我們已與其他公司簽署合約。

This is not a good time to expand our business.
🖉 目前並不是我們拓展業務的時機。

We regret to tell you that we made our decision before we received your proposal.
🖉 很抱歉，在收到您的提案前，我們已有其他決定。

We have no immediate plan to make any changes.
🖉 我們目前尚無計畫變動。

It's our policy not to have any sole agents in any countries.
🖉 我們原則上不打算在任何國家設立總代理。

We will keep your name in file.
🖉 我們會將貴公司的資料歸檔。

We will get in touch with you at a proper time.
🖉 等時機適當，我們會與您聯絡。

If the position changes in the future, we would be in touch with you again.

Part 1
Part 2
Part 3
Part 4
Part 5
Part 6

✎ 如果未來情況改變，我們會再與您聯絡。

We look forward to the opportunity to discuss this matter with you in the future.
✎ 我們希望未來能夠有機會再與您討論這件提案。

We hope our reply is not disappointing.
✎ 希望我們的答覆沒有令您失望。

Your letter has been filed for future reference.
✎ 我們已將貴公司的信件存檔，以備將來的合作可能。

 進階補充站　Let's learn more!

 文法/句型Focus

✽ 在拒絕時表示遺憾（委婉口氣）

❶ **We'd love to, but...** 我們很樂意，但是…。

❷ **That would be great, but...** 那樣一定很棒，但是…。

❸ **I wish I could..., but...** 我真希望能…，可惜…。

❹ **It's such a pity that...** …實在太可惜了。

✽ 給予明確原因

❶ **The main reason why...is (that)...** …的主要原因是…。

❷ **...for four major reasons.** …有四個主要原因。

❸ **For this reason, ...** 基於這個理由，…。

Unit 2 產品詢問與回覆

Part 1
Part 2
Part 3
Part 4
Part 5
Part 6

•2-01• 索取產品目錄

在索取產品目錄的信件中,首先可簡單說明來信目的,接著有禮貌地表示欲向對方索取商品型錄,並於信末表達感謝,給收件者一個好印象。

Subject	Request for Catalogs

Dear Sir or Madam:

This is Ella Chen from Zara Inc. We are soon opening our new office in Taipei and we will need some extra desks, lights, and chairs. Can you please send us your catalogs with prices, sizes and colors for these items?

Thank you for your assistance.

Yours faithfully,
Ella Chen

敬啟者:

我是薩拉集團的陳艾拉,我們即將於台北成立新公司,需要桌椅和燈具。請您將包含價目、尺寸以及顏色等資訊的目錄寄送給我們。

感謝您的協助。

陳艾拉 謹上

Send ►

 替換好用句 Copy & Paste

表明目的

We have noted your advertisement in China Post, and are interested in your products.
🖉 我們在《中國郵報》看到貴公司的廣告,並對貴公司的產品有興趣。

Now we are desirous of enlarging our trade in the product.

✎ 目前敝公司極欲擴大我方商品的業務範圍。

We are desirous of extending our connections in your country.
✎ 我們擬拓展本公司在貴國的業務。

We are very interested in your smartphones.
✎ 我們對貴公司的智慧型手機非常有興趣。

We're currently looking for a supplier for our company.
✎ 我們目前正在尋找供應商。

Your website offers the information we want.
✎ 貴公司網站所提供的資訊符合我們的需求。

 ## 索取目錄

We request an up-to-date catalog and price list for your products.
✎ 希望貴公司提供最新的型錄及報價單。

I am writing to request some information about the product price.
✎ 我希望能夠得到產品價位的相關資訊。

Could you please send me a copy of your company's product brochure?
✎ 煩請寄送貴公司的產品目錄。

Could you please send me a copy of your latest catalog?
✎ 請將貴公司最新的型錄寄給我。

I would like to be placed on your mailing list and to receive all of your catalogs for the upcoming year.
✎ 希望能夠加入您的郵寄列表,並收到貴公司來年的目錄。

I would like the information to be provided to us as paper copies.
✎ 希望能夠收到紙本資料。

I should be grateful if you would send us your brochure and price list about your products.
✎ 若您能寄產品的目錄及價目表給我,將不勝感激。

Will you please send us a copy of your catalog, with details of prices and items of payment?
✎ 是否能寄一份貴公司的型錄,並附上價格及付款明細?

We should find it most helpful if you could also supply samples of these goods.
✎ 如果貴公司能提供這些商品的樣品，將對敝公司有極大的幫助。

 索取其他資料

We are looking forward to receiving your quotation as soon as possible.
✎ 我們期待能儘快收到貴公司的報價單。

When quoting, please state terms of payment and time of delivery.
✎ 貴公司報價時，請說明付款條件和交貨時間。

I would also like to know the information about the prices of the shipment.
✎ 我也想了解關於貨運價位的資訊。

It would be appreciated if you also provide a comprehensive list of your charges and your contact information.
✎ 若您能提供詳細的收費表以及聯絡方式，將非常感謝。

Please also provide information regarding: related service charges, additional software and hardware, available warranties, and average timeframes for repairs.
✎ 也請提供以下相關資訊：相關服務的收費、額外的軟體及硬體設備、有效的保證書以及平均維修週期。

It will be appreciated if this information is provided for each brand of products, to give us a basis for comparison.
✎ 若能提供所有品牌的相關資訊以供我們進行比較，將非常感激。

I would also like to know if it is possible to make purchases online.
✎ 我也想知道是否可以經由網路訂購。

I would like to receive any special offers or sales notices as well.
✎ 我也希望能夠收到特惠的相關資訊。

Your courtesy will be appreciated, and we earnestly await your prompt reply.
✎ 對於您的協助我們將感激不盡，敝公司將靜待您的即時回覆。

Part 1
Part 2
Part 3
Part 4
Part 5
Part 6

2-02 提供產品目錄

及早回信給欲索取型錄的潛在顧客是很重要的，如果可以趁機告知產品的優勢或優惠更好。把握機會，以免失去合作良機。

Subject | Re: Request for Catalogs

Dear Mr. Yang:

Thank you for your email. I already sent the latest catalog to you this morning. It shows details of the office **equipment**[1] we can **supply**[2].

You can also see all our products on our website: www.firsthousing.com. We also offer a 5% discount if you **purchase**[3] through our website. I am also attaching a copy of our price list.

Please contact me if you have any questions or would like some **advice**[4].

Yours sincerely,
Terry

親愛的楊先生：

謝謝您的來信。我今天早上已將最新的產品目錄寄給您，內含我們可提供辦公室設備的詳細資訊。

您也可以到我們的網站（www.firsthousing.com）瀏覽產品。如果您在網站上消費，我們亦提供九五折優惠。附件為產品的價目表。

如您有任何問題，或需要建議，請與我聯絡。

泰瑞 敬上

Send

核心字彙充電站 *Key Words*

1. equipment 名 設備；配備　　**2. supply** 動 供給；提供
3. purchase 動 買；購買　　**4. advice** 名 建議；忠告

 Copy & Paste

 開頭感謝語

Thank you for your inquiry about our equipment.
🖋 謝謝您來信詢問我們的設備。

Thank you for your email dated March 19.
🖋 謝謝您三月十九日的來信。

Thank you for your letter of May 21 and your interest in our translation service.
🖋 謝謝您五月二十一日來信,詢問敝公司的翻譯服務。

 提供目錄

In response to your mail of May 21, we have enclosed our catalog and price list.
🖋 謹依貴公司五月二十一日的來信,附上目錄以及價目表。

I have enclosed our catalog, listing various types of translation services and their fees.
🖋 謹附上內含各種翻譯服務項目及其收費的目錄。

Enclosed is the catalog you requested.
🖋 附件為您需要的目錄。

A new catalog has been mailed to you.
🖋 新的產品目錄已郵寄給您。

If there is something you would like to order that is not on our catalog, please let us know.
🖋 如果有任何您需要的產品未出現在目錄中,請告知我們。

 強調公司優勢

We are extremely proud of our smartphones and the design of our new tablet PC.
🖋 我們對於敝公司所出產的智慧型手機以及平板電腦的設計深具信心。

Part 1
Part 2
Part 3
Part 4
Part 5
Part 6

The smartphones are selling wonderfully at some branches of your company.
🖊 在貴公司的某些分店，這款智慧型手機的銷售成績極佳。

Our service is recently used by many famous companies.
🖊 已有許多知名公司使用敝公司的服務。

We have translated our catalog into different languages and will send you a copy of English version before the end of June.
🖊 敝公司的產品目錄已翻譯成多國語言，您將會於六月底前收到英語版的目錄。

I am sure you will find our service make the best use of your company.
🖊 我確信敝公司的服務將能帶給貴公司最大的效益。

I would like to give you a brief introduction.
🖊 我想要做個簡短的介紹。

 其他資料和結尾語

Once again, thank you for your interest in the product.
🖊 再一次感謝您對本產品的支持。

Thank you for your interest in our company.
🖊 謝謝您對敝公司的支持。

We will be happy to quote you a special price for it.
🖊 我們會給您特別優惠。

We are making certain that your name is in its proper place on our mailing list, so that future catalogs will reach you promptly.
🖊 我們已將您的郵件資料存檔，將來您會即時收到最新目錄。

You can sign up on our website and receive our PDF catalog by email.
🖊 您可以登錄我們的網站，並接收我們型錄的PDF檔。

A list of suppliers of our products is on page 3.
🖊 第三頁列出了所有供應商的名單。

Your confirmation of the order will receive our immediate attention.
🖊 我們會立即處理您的訂單。

If you have any questions about our products, please let me know at

any time.
📝 如您有任何產品上的疑問，請隨時告知。

I am more than happy to answer your questions.
📝 我很樂意回答您的問題。

We will look forward to answering any questions you have about our products.
📝 我們會回覆您對於產品的任何疑問。

Please contact us if you would like to order any of these items.
📝 如果您想訂購任何相關產品，請聯絡我們。

 Let's learn more!

 單字/片語Focus

🏷 廣告單 🏷

✱**advertise** 為…作廣告	✱**classified ads** 分類廣告
✱**fly sheet** 宣傳單	✱**leaflet** 小傳單
✱**layout** 版面設計	✱**hit** 暢銷產品
✱**slogan** 口號；標語	✱**jingle** （朗朗上口的）廣告詞
✱**coupon** 折扣券	✱**gift certificate** 禮券

🏷 目錄與型錄 🏷

✱**list price** 目錄上的定價	✱**actual price** 實際售價
✱**bargain** 特價商品	✱**on the block** 打折的
✱**price-cutting** 削價競爭的	✱**half-price** 半價的

Part 1
Part 2
Part 3
Part 4
Part 5
Part 6

·2-03· 索取試用樣品

撰寫「索取試用樣品信」時,首先要表明身分及來信目的,接著有禮貌地詢問欲索取的樣品,強調提供樣品會對商務往來更有幫助;最後,若索取之樣品為試用後需要歸還者,請於信末註明將會歸還。

Subject | **Request for Samples**

Dear Jessica:

This is Kevin Zheng from Homey Corp. We are very interested in your goods. We should find it most helpful if you could send us some samples of your new style jeans of women.

We look forward to your prompt reply.

Yours faithfully,
Kevin

潔西卡您好:

我是家美公司的鄭凱文,我們對貴公司的產品非常有興趣。若貴公司願意提供新款女性牛仔褲的樣品,對敝公司將有極大幫助。

期待您的迅速回覆。

凱文 謹上

Send ▶

替換好用句 *Copy & Paste*

Many of my customers are interested in your new swimming suits and have enquired about their quality.
🖉 許多顧客對您的泳裝非常有興趣,想了解其品質。

Before placing an order, may I request some samples of your goods?
🖉 在決定訂單前,我能先向您索取一些樣品嗎?

Before placing a firm order, I should be thankful if you could send us your new selection of children's shoes.
🖉 在決定訂單前,如果貴公司能夠提供最新系列的精選兒童鞋款,我們將非常感謝。

Could you please mail us some free samples?
🖋 煩請寄送一些免費的樣品。

If available, please send us some samples.
🖋 若方便，請寄給我們一些樣品。

We should find it most helpful if you could send us samples of your products.
🖋 如果貴公司願意提供產品的樣品，將對敝公司有極大的幫助。

We would be very grateful if you could send us some of your samples.
🖋 若您可以寄來一些樣品，我們將非常感激。

Any of the items unsold would be returned.
🖋 未售出的產品將會歸還。

 Let's learn more!

 單字/片語Focus

❦ 談論商品 ❦	
✳**brand** 品牌；商標	✳**brand loyalty** 對某品牌的熱中
✳**price tag** 價格標籤	✳**label** 標籤；貼紙
✳**pattern** 圖案；花樣	✳**design** 設計；花樣
✳**feature** 以…為特色	✳**characteristic** 獨特的
✳**uniqueness** 獨一無二	✳**posh** 時尚的
✳**voguish** 時髦的	✳**prevailing** 流行的

Part 1
Part 2
Part 3
Part 4
Part 5
Part 6

· 2-04 · 提供試用樣品

於「提供試用樣品」的信件中,記得告知樣品提供的數量,並強調商品之優點,表明期待與對方合作。信末,建議主動提供聯絡資訊,以方便對方詢問相關問題。

Subject Re: Request for Samples

Dear Kevin:

Thank you very much for your mail dated May 20 about the jeans of women. We are glad to send you five **samples**[1] of our goods you inquired.

We think the styles will be just what you want for the **fashionable**[2] trade, and the quality of our designs should **appeal to**[3] many buyers.

Thank you again for your interest in our goods. We are looking forward to your order soon and please feel free to contact us if you have any **questions**[4].

Sincerely yours,
Jessica

親愛的凱文:

感謝您於五月二十日來信詢問女性牛仔褲的商品,我們很樂意寄五件樣品給您。

相信我們的設計會非常符合您所需的時尚潮流。我方高質感的設計,肯定會吸引許多買家。

再次感謝您對本公司的商品感興趣,我們期待您儘速下單。如果您有任何問題,歡迎您與我聯繫。

潔西卡 敬上

Send ▶

核心字彙充電站 *Key Words*

1. **sample** 名 樣品;試用品
2. **fashionable** 形 流行的;時尚的
3. **appeal to sb.** 片 對某人有吸引力
4. **question** 名 問題;詢問

替換好用句 _Copy & Paste_

Thank you again for your interest in our goods.
🖊 再次感謝您對本公司商品感興趣。

We thank you for your inquiry of April 20.
🖊 謝謝您四月二十日的來信。

We have sent a copy of our catalog together with some samples of jeans.
🖊 我們已經寄出一份型錄，以及相關的牛仔褲樣品。

We are forwarding some samples of various women clothes as you requested.
🖊 根據您的要求，我們已寄出多款女性衣物的樣品。

We are providing four samples of our most popular dresses.
🖊 我們提供您敝公司最受歡迎的四款洋裝。

We are glad to send you samples of our goods you requested.
🖊 我們很樂意將您所要求的樣品寄給您。

I am pleased to send you a full range of samples of our new sneakers.
🖊 很開心能寄給您敝公司最新款式球鞋的全系列樣品。

Please have a look through the samples.
🖊 煩請參考樣品。

I hope you will find our products suitable.
🖊 希望您覺得我方產品符合您的需求。

Please let us know if we can help by providing further information.
🖊 如果需要更多資訊，請讓我們知道。

It will be a pleasure for us to serve you.
🖊 為您服務是我們的榮幸。

Part 1
Part 2
Part 3
Part 4
Part 5
Part 6

•2-05• 詢問產品現貨

若產品的銷售有季節性，可於詢問現貨時告知需要出貨的日期。

Subject	Luxury Bed Sheets

Dear Ms. Tsai:

We would be grateful if you would send us **patterns**[1] and prices for your **luxury**[2] **bed sheets**[3]. Please also inform us whether you could supply these goods from **stock**[4] because we need them before the Christmas season.

Yours sincerely,
Grace

親愛的蔡小姐：

若您能提供我們豪華床罩的樣式和價格，我們將十分感激。也請告知是否有存貨可供應，因為我們必須在聖誕季節開始前取得這些產品。

葛蕾絲 謹上

Send ▶

核心字彙充電站 Key Words

1. pattern 名 花樣；圖案
2. luxury 名 奢華；奢侈
3. bed sheet 名 床單
4. stock 名 存貨；庫存品

替換好用句 Copy & Paste

 了解庫存量與出貨日期

Please inform us what quantities your company can supply from stock.
✎ 請告知貴公司能提供的存貨數量。

I am writing to request about your stock availability.
✎ 我想了解貴公司的庫存量。

Please let us know your earliest date of delivery.
✎ 請告知您最快能出貨的日期。

Please check your inventory to see if you have 100 digital cameras for delivery by March 10.
✎ 請查詢貴公司庫存，以確定是否能在三月十號前寄出一百台數位相機。

Please check your inventory to see if you have 1,000 bed sheets for delivery.
✎ 請確認您的庫存是否能提供一千件床罩。

If possible, we would like to place an order for twenty laser printers.
✎ 如果貴公司有足夠的庫存，我們需要二十台雷射印表機。

If possible, we need ten more for another delivery.
✎ 如果貴公司有足夠的庫存，我們需要再加購十台。

If we place a large order, would you provide us enough products?
✎ 如果訂單量大，貴公司是否能提供足夠的產品量？

Will you please send us the date of delivery and quantities you can supply from stock?
✎ 請告知您現貨能供應的數量以及出貨日期。

 其他問題

What type of model do you have in your stock?
✎ 貴公司的存貨尚有何種型號？

Please also let us know if your company is prepared to grant a ten-percent discount.
✎ 請告知貴公司能否給予九折的優惠。

 準備訂購

If you can supply from stock, we will give you an order by return.
✎ 若貴公司能供貨，我們便會向您訂購。

Upon receipt of your information, we will place an order with you soon.
✎ 一接到您的回覆，我們便會立即向您訂貨。

Part 1
Part 2
Part 3
Part 4
Part 5
Part 6

•2-06• 回覆產品現貨

在「回覆產品現貨」的信件中，要明確告知產品是否有現貨提供，以及貨運時間，並於信中告知客戶提早下訂單可儘快處理出貨，好讓客戶提早下單。

| Subject | Re: Luxury Bed Sheets |

Dear Grace:

Thank you for your email. We would like to inform you that we have 2,000 bed sheets in stock. Those items in stock are **inclusive of[1] tax[2]**. We would be happy to have our stock emailed to you from now on. We **deliver[3]** three times a week. Therefore, since we have your order, we would deliver the items **as early as possible[4]**.

Yours sincerely,
Ivy Tsai

親愛的葛蕾絲：

感謝您的來信。我們想要通知您庫存尚有兩千件床罩。庫存中的項目已含稅。今後本公司很樂意告知您產品的庫存量。每週出貨三次。因此，在確定您的訂單後，我們會儘早出貨。

蔡艾薇 敬上

Send

核心字彙充電站 *Key Words*

1. **inclusive of** 片 包含的；包括的　　2. **tax** 名 稅；稅金
3. **deliver** 動 運送；傳輸　　　　　4. **as early as possible** 片 儘早

替換好用句 *Copy & Paste*

We have checked our supply of the model you requested.
🖋 我們已確認您所需型號的數量。

We have only a limited stock of goods now.

🖋 我們目前的庫存有限。

Our stock is getting low; therefore, we would ask you to place your order as soon as possible.
🖋 由於庫存量減少，我們請求您儘速下單。

As we are going to clear our stock, we are selling our goods at a 15% discount.
🖋 我們即將出清存貨，貨品將以八五折的優惠價出售。

The digital camera is now out of stock.
🖋 數位相機目前已無存貨。

We are now well-stocked with the products you requested.
🖋 您所需要的產品目前備貨充足。

All models can be supplied from stock.
🖋 所有的款式皆有存貨。

All items can be delivered from stock.
🖋 所有的商品皆可出貨。

 進階補充站　*Let's learn more!*

 單字/片語Focus

💊 貯存與庫存量 💊

＊stockroom 貯藏室	**＊stocktaking** 庫存盤點
＊store 貯存；貯藏	**＊warehouse** 倉庫；貨棧
＊total inventory 庫存總量	**＊superfluous** 過剩的
＊excess 過剩的	**＊ample** 充裕的；大量的
＊bulk 大量的；大批的	**＊shortage** 缺少；匱乏

Part 1

Part 2

Part 3

Part 4

Part 5

Part 6

Unit 3 報價與議價

• 3-01 • 詢問產品報價

　　詢價信包括以下內容：一、向廠商說明從何處得知對方的資料；二、自我介紹並說明理由，例如「我們看到貴公司的產品廣告」，或「我們收到客戶對產品的詢問」等。清楚表明詢問項目以及貨品數量，以方便對方回覆報價；三、要求廠商報價和說明付款條件，並要求提供產品其他資訊；四、說明若價格和品質符合需求，將會下單；五、最後註明靜候佳音，表示期待對方的回信。

Subject	Order 20 New Printers

Dear Ms. Lee:

We are interested in ordering twenty new **printers**[1] for our new office in Taichung. Could you please send us an **estimate**[2] and **provide**[3] the details of **specification**[4] sheet?

Yours sincerely,
Anna Wang

Send ▶

李小姐您好：

我們在台中的新公司，想向貴公司訂購二十台新印表機。可否請貴公司寄估價單給我們，並且附上詳細的規格描述？

王安娜 敬上

核心字彙充電站 Key Words

1. **printer** 名 影印機
2. **estimate** 名 估價；估計
3. **provide** 動 提供
4. **specification** 名 明細單；規格

 Copy & Paste

 說明來信理由

We have seen your advertisement in Washington News and are interested in your printers.
🖊 我們在《華盛頓日報》上看到貴公司的廣告,並對您的印表機有興趣。

We saw your men's suits at the Taipei Fashion Show.
🖊 我們在台北時裝展看到貴公司的男性服飾。

We have received an inquiry from one of our trade connections about your products.
🖊 我們接到顧客詢問您的產品。

We have many inquiries about the following goods:
🖊 我們接到許多關於下列產品的詢問:

I would like to make an inquiry about your goods.
🖊 我想詢問貴公司的產品。

We are interested in buying your computer and would like to know the details.
🖊 我們有興趣購買您的產品,並想知道更多細節。

 了解價格資訊

We would like to know the price of your product that your company has provided currently.
🖊 我們想要了解貴公司目前提供的產品價格。

We would like to know the price of your eBooks.
🖊 我們想要了解貴公司電子書的價位。

We are interested in importing Swiss chocolate and would like to receive the latest price list.
🖊 我們對進口瑞士巧克力有興趣,並想收到最新的價目表。

We are interested in importing Italy wine and would like to receive a copy of your export price list and export terms.
🖊 我們對進口義大利酒有興趣,希望能得到貴公司的出口價目表及出口條件。

Please send us full details of your products and state your earliest delivery date, terms of payment, and discounts.
🖊 請一併告知貴公司產品的詳細情形、最快交貨日期、付款條件以及優惠。

Would you send us some samples with quotation?
🖊 麻煩您寄報價單和一些樣品給我們好嗎？

Would you please send us your quotation for summer clothing?
🖊 煩請您將夏季服飾的報價單寄到敝公司好嗎？

 ## 向對方要求折扣

We may place an order with you if your prices are competitive.
🖊 如價格有競爭力，我們也許會向貴公司訂購。

Would you please let us know on what term you can give us some discount?
🖊 煩請告知折扣的相關條件好嗎？

We would like to confirm your best business terms regarding discount.
🖊 我們想進一步確認貴公司最佳的折扣條件。

We would like to know your best business terms and discount.
🖊 請將您最佳的折扣條件告訴我們。

Please send us your best quotations for these products.
🖊 請告知這些產品的最優惠價格。

We would ask you to make effort to quote at a competitive rate.
🖊 請您儘量降低報價。

How much do you allow for a large order?
🖊 如訂單量大，貴公司可以給予多少折扣呢？

If we place a large order, will you give us some discount?
🖊 如訂單量大，貴公司可否給予折扣？

If there are any special offers or opportunities to obtain the above items at reduced prices, please inform us.
🖊 如果上述產品有機會降價，煩請告知。

Part 1

Part 2

Part 3

Part 4

Part 5

Part 6

•3-02• 回覆產品報價

此封範例為非正式報價，因此只在郵件中附上產品型錄以及價目表。如有價格變動不另行通知時，記得要在信中註明，提前告知客戶。

Subject Re: Order 20 New Printers

Dear Ms. Wang:

Thank you for your inquiry about our new printers. We are pleased to attach our latest catalog and the price list.

Yours sincerely,
Amy

王小姐您好：

感謝您對本公司印表機的詢價，附件為最新的目錄和價目表。

哎咪 謹上

Send

替換好用句 Copy & Paste

開頭的禮貌語

We are greatly glad to provide you with the information you requested.
✎ 我們很開心能提供您所需的資訊。

Thank you for your enquiry of April 6 for further information of our machines.
✎ 謝謝您於四月六日來信詢問問我們機器的進一步資訊。

Thank you for selecting our company to supply your office equipment.
✎ 感謝您選擇敝公司提供您辦公室設備。

We appreciate your interest in our products.
✎ 謝謝您對我們的產品感興趣。

 **回覆報價**

Enclosed is a copy of the price list and estimated costs.
附件為價目表及估價單。

Enclosed is our price quotation.
附件為價目表。

Please see the attached file for photos and price quotation for our products.
請參照附件的產品圖片及報價單。

With reference to your enquiry, we are pleased to enclose our price list and terms of payment for your consideration.
回覆您的詢問，在此附上我們的價目表和付款條件，供您參考。

I am also including a specification sheet about the laser printer. I hope it would answer your questions.
同時附上雷射印表機的規格表，希望能夠解答你的問題。

With thanks, we enclosed an illustrated catalog of our products and details of our terms and conditions of sale.
感謝您的來信，在此附上含產品圖的目錄及相關條約。

We are pleased to quote as follows:
我們的報價如下：

The prices quoted are valid until December 31.
報價金額的期限為十二月三十一日。

The price includes delivery fee.
報價包含運費。

The price does not include delivery and insurance costs.
報價不含運費以及保險費用。

 提供折扣

We give discount of 10% on the order over 100 printers.
若訂購一百台以上的印表機，我們將提供九折優惠。

As you are a valued customer, we will reduce prices by 5%.
由於您是我們的重要客戶，所以我們將給予九五折的優惠。

All prices are subject without notice.
🖉 所有的價格更動不另行告知。

In reply to your enquiry of A700 eBook, we have pleasure in making the following offer to you, which is binding until January 11, 2016.
🖉 有關您所詢問的A700號電子書，我們提供以下特別優惠給您，期限至二〇一六年的一月十一日為止。

This offer will be withdrawn if not accepted within five days.
🖉 特別優惠將保留五天。

We are prepared to offer special terms to customers who place their orders exceeding US$1,000 before the end of this month.
🖉 針對本月底前消費額超過一千美元的顧客，我們將提供特別的優惠服務。

To meet your demand, we will offer a special discount of 10% off the list price for any order you place within seven days of the date hereof.
🖉 為達到您的需求，即日起七天內，我們提供九折的優惠價格。

The offer is subject to our final confirmation.
🖉 報價以本公司的最後確認為主。

 其他表示

We are confident that our goods are both excellent in quality and reasonable in price.
🖉 對於敝公司產品的品質及合理的價位，我們深具信心。

As for the samples, we have sent them to you separately by airmail.
🖉 我們已另外郵寄樣本給您。

As the stocks are low, we hope you would send us your orders as early as possible.
🖉 由於庫存量不多，希望您能儘早下訂單。

If you need any further information about our products, please do not hesitate to let us know.
🖉 針對我方產品，若您需要進一步的資訊，請不吝告知。

We are confident that our goods meet your requirements.
🖉 我們有信心我方的產品能符合您的需求。

We hope you are satisfied with our quotation.
🖉 希望您對我方的報價感到滿意。

Part 1
Part 2
Part 3
Part 4
Part 5
Part 6

·3-03· 正式報價

報價信通常分成三段。第一段感謝對方來信，並簡單複述對方的詢價；第二段提出報價並說明優惠；第三段提醒對方儘速處理訂單，以免錯失優惠。報價時，須清楚寫明商品名稱、數量、價格、折扣、運送時間、付款方式以及報價有效期限等訊息。

| Subject | About The Quotation |

Dear Mr. Wang:

Thank you for your inquiry of May 30, **herewith**[1] we quote our best prices as shown below:

100 *Item No.203 ....US$ 20
100 *Item No.204 ....US$ 22
100 *Item No.206 ....US$ 26

Minimum[2]: 100 sets

We can give a 5% **discount**[3] on all orders of $500 or more, and the prices are **valid**[4] until August 31, 2016.

We look forward to your **comments**[5] or your first order confirmation soon.

Sincerely yours,
Kelly

王先生您好：

謝謝您五月三十日來信詢價，以下為我們的報價：

品項203*100份 20美元
品項204*100份 22美元
品項206*100份 26美元

最小訂購量為一百份。

訂購價格超過五百美元時，我們給予九五折的優惠；報價有效期限為二〇一六年八月三十一日。

希望能儘速收到您的建議或首次訂購。

凱莉 敬上

Send

Subject: Quotation From ABC Company

Dear Mr. Wang:

Thank you for your email of June 21 expressing your interest in our goods. We are pleased to offer you our best **quotation**[6] as follows:

```
100 *Item No.303 .....US$20 ........US$2,000
100 *Item No.304 .....US$22 ........US$2,200
100 *Item No.306 .....US$26 ........US$2,600
```

$6800	
5% Discount	$340
Net price	$6,460
Freight[7] (Keelung to Paris)	$200
Insurance	$120
Total	$6,780

Shipment[8]: Within two weeks after receiving the order.

For acceptance within twenty days.

We hope to receive your order soon.

Sincerely yours,
Kelly

王先生您好：

謝謝您六月二十一日來信表示對我們的產品有興趣，以下為我們的最佳報價：

品項303*100份（單價20美元）2,000美元
品項304*100份（單價22美元）2,200美元
品項306*100份（單價26美元）2,600美元

共6,800美元
5%折扣　　340美元

淨價　　　6,460美元
運費（基隆到巴黎）200美元
保險費　　120美元

總計　　　6,780美元

貨運：收到訂單後的二週內送達。

報價有效期為二十天。

盼能儘早接到您的訂單。

凱莉 敬上

Send

Part 1
Part 2
Part 3
Part 4
Part 5
Part 6

1. herewith 副（書）隨函
2. minimum 名 最小量
3. discount 名 折扣
4. valid 形 有效的
5. comment 名 意見
6. quotation 名 報價單
7. freight 名 貨運
8. shipment 名 裝運

 替換好用句 Copy & Paste

提供報價的說法

The prices you requested are as follows:
您所需要的報價如下：

We are pleased to quote as follows:
我們很開心能提供以下報價：

Please kindly refer to our quotation as following:
請參看以下報價：

Attached is our best quotation for your reference.
附件為我們最優惠的報價。

The quotation and packing details of the items we discussed are below:
關於我們討論過的產品項目，其報價以及包裝細項如下：

Please refer to our price list and you will find our best prices.
請查照我們提供的最優惠報價。

說明報價的內容與異動

The prices quoted in the attached price list are on CIF terms, which means they include postage and insurance.
附件之報價單為包括運費、保險費在內之到岸價格。

The prices below include packing and delivery.
下面的報價包含包裝以及貨運的費用。

Shipment and insurance costs are to be paid by the buyer.
🖊 貨運費用以及保險費用由買方支付。

We may raise our prices because of the increasing cost of the raw materials.
🖊 由於原物料價格上漲，我方的產品價格也有可能跟著調漲。

As our supplier has raised his price, our prices will go up next week.
🖊 本公司的供應商已調漲價格，因此，從下週開始，我們的價格也會隨之調漲。

Our price will decrease as we need to turn over the remainder of the stock.
🖊 由於我們準備出清存貨，因此報價將會調降。

We offer a 3% cash discount.
🖊 我們提供百分之三的現金折扣。

Orders over $2,000 are subject to negotiation.
🖊 若訂購價超過兩千美元，則可議價。

Please note that we have quoted our most favorable price and are unable to entertain any counter offer.
🖊 此報價已為最優惠的價格，恕難還價。

Prices are subject to change without notice.
🖊 價格變動不另行告知。

The prices quoted here are subject to change.
🖊 報價有可能會調整。

The quotation does not represent a final order.
🖊 此報價並非最終報價。

We can grant you a 15% discount on repeat orders.
🖊 後續訂單可享八五折優惠。

 相關事項提醒

For the first-time buyers, we require payment in advance.
🖊 我們希望初次訂購者能預付貨款。

We accept the bank transfers, checks, credit cards or money orders.
🖊 我們接受銀行轉帳、支票、信用卡或匯票。

If you intend to place a large order, please call our sales manager at 0800-112233.

🖊 若您的訂購量龐大，請來電聯絡我們的業務經理：0800-112233。

If you can pay the invoice within ten working days, we would honor your request of quicker delivery.

🖊 如果您可於十個工作天內付款，我們會替您快速出貨。

Orders will be packed and shipped two weeks after we receive your orders.

🖊 貨品將於下訂後的兩週內包裝並寄出。

We need to know if you want our products immediately since there are other customers who are interested in them.

🖊 我們必須確認您是否立即需要此項產品，因為有其他客戶對此產品也有興趣。

We are confident that the offers are competitive with those of other manufacturers.

🖊 相信我方的報價與其他廠商相比非常有競爭力。

We look forward to your initial order.

🖊 我們期待您的初次訂購。

We look forward to receiving a trial order from your company.

🖊 我們期待接到貴公司的試用訂單。

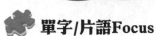

❦ 報價用語 ❦

✻quote sb. 向某人報價	**✻unit price** 單價
✻selling price 售價	**✻retail price** 零售價
✻the price inclusive of tax 含稅的價格	
✻the price exclusive of tax 不含稅的價格	

Part 1

Part 2

Part 3

Part 4

Part 5

Part 6

3-04 詢問服務項目報價

詢價時，基本上直接表示詢價內容即可，但在商務往來上，務必拿捏好語氣，保持禮貌，才能增進彼此的商務關係。

Subject	Translation Services

Dear Sir or Madam:

This is David Lynch from New Year Press Inc. We have seen your advertisement in your catalog No.99 and would be grateful if you could send us the details of your translation services.

Thank you for your prompt response to this enquiry.

Yours sincerely,
David Lynch

敬啟者：

我是新年出版的大衛‧林區。我們在第九十九期的目錄上看到您所刊登的廣告，若您能提供翻譯服務的詳細資訊，我們將十分感激。

非常感謝您能即時回覆詢問。

大衛‧林區 謹上

Send ▶

 Copy & Paste

 從何處得知對方資料

We have seen your advertisement on the newspaper.
🖊 我們在報紙上看到您的廣告。

We were referred by one of our clients.
🖊 我們是由其中一名客戶介紹的。

Your company was recommended by Leader Consulting Company.
🖊 貴公司是由領導諮詢公司所推薦。

 **表明需求**

We would like to request for more information about your service.
🖊 我們想了解您更多的服務資訊。

We are interested in placing advertisement on the newspaper.
🖊 我們想要在報紙上刊登廣告。

We are interested in placing advertisements on the buses.
🖊 我們想要在公車上設置廣告。

We would like to buy some advertising place on different business websites.
🖊 我們想要在各類企業的網站上購買廣告位置。

We intend to purchase advertisement in some business magazines.
🖊 我們想要在商務雜誌上刊登廣告。

We are very interested in your service for cleaning the windows of our office building.
🖊 我們對於您清洗大樓櫥窗的服務感興趣。

Is your company with the capability of translating Japanese into English?
🖊 不知貴公司可否有將日文翻譯成英文的能力？

We are recently developing our website and are planning to translate the website into four languages apart from Chinese.
🖊 近期內，敝公司有意將正在更新的網頁翻譯成中文以外的四種語言。

 請對方給予資訊

Would you be kind to send us an estimate for the above translation project?
🖊 可以請您寄給我們上述翻譯計畫的預估價格嗎？

Please send us your advertising rate card.
🖊 請回覆告知您的廣告刊登價格表。

Please write or call me to provide further information.
🖊 請以電話聯絡、或是寫信給我，以提供更多資訊。

I would be grateful if you could send us your brochure and price list about your translation services.
如果您能寄送貴公司翻譯服務的內容以及價目表，我會非常感謝。

Part 1

Part 2

Part 3

Part 4

Part 5

Part 6

・3-05・ 回覆服務項目報價

回覆報價內容時，要再次強調公司優勢，以及可以提供對方的服務內容，並在信中感謝對方選擇自己公司的服務。

Subject Re: Translation Services & Fees

Dear David:

Thank you for your mail of Sep. 22 enquiring about our **translation**[1] services.

BILINGUA Translation Services offer a full **range**[2] of translation services to help you in the development of sales **literature**[3] and websites. I have pleasure in enclosing our latest **brochures**[4] and price list in which you can see that our prices are highly competitive.

I look forward to calling you in a few days.

Yours sincerely,
Wendy

大衛您好：

謝謝您九月二十二號詢問翻譯服務的來信。

雙語翻譯服務公司提供多樣化翻譯服務，以幫助您拓展您的業務銷售及網頁內容。附上最新的服務資訊及價目表，您可參考本公司的價目，並發現其非常具有競爭性。

期待能於近日與您聯絡。

溫蒂 敬上

Send ▶

核心字彙充電站 *Key Words*

1. **translation** 名 翻譯
2. **range** 名 範圍；區域
3. **literature** 名 文獻
4. **brochure** 名 小冊子

We appreciate your inquiry of August 15 about our service.

🖋 感謝您於八月十五日來信詢問我們的服務。

We appreciate the opportunity to bid on your contract to clean the windows of your office building.

🖋 關於清洗大樓玻璃的招標，我們感謝您提供我們投標的機會。

We would like to ask you three questions as follows:

🖋 我們想請您回覆下列三點問題：

Your answers will help us provide the accurate bid.

🖋 您的答覆可以幫助我們做精確投標。

We will need more specifications about the work before I can give you a firm offer.

🖋 在此需要您提供更詳細的資訊，以便給予您精確的報價。

We are glad to enclose a copy of our brochure in which you will find various translating services.

🖋 我們很樂意提供一份資料給您，其中包含各種翻譯服務。

Thank you for selecting our company to place your advertisement in the magazines.

🖋 感謝您選擇本公司替貴公司刊登雜誌廣告。

We are pleased that you select our company to print your catalogs.

🖋 感謝您選擇本公司替您印刷目錄。

We offer a free consultation for the first-time clients.

🖋 我們提供新客戶一次免費的諮詢服務。

We appreciate the chance of working with you.

🖋 我們很感激能有與您合作的機會。

We look forward to receiving your reply soon.

🖋 我們期待能很快收到您的回覆。

If you have further questions about our products, please let me know.

🖋 若您對我方的產品有其他問題，請讓我知道。

針對報價進行議價

訂貨前的議價，可表示現今市場環境競爭激烈而請求對方降價；也可提出若本次訂購順利，後續將有長期配合的可能，如此較具有說服力。

Subject Re: About The Quotation

Dear Kelly:

Thank you for your quotation of January 12, 2015.

According to[1] our **initial**[2] **research**[3], the **leather**[4] shoes are very **popular**[5] in Europe. However, we need the most competitive price. If you would lower your price to $5 per item, we would like to place an order with you for 2,000 pairs of leather shoes. All the other terms are **acceptable**[6].

I hope to receive your confirmation soon.

Best regards,
John Wang

凱莉您好：

謝謝您於二〇一五年一月十二日的報價。

根據我們的初步調查，皮鞋在歐洲非常受歡迎。但是，我們仍然需要具競爭力的價格。如果您的產品單價願意降五元，我們願意訂購兩千雙皮鞋。其他條件都沒有問題。

盼能儘早接到您的確認。

王約翰 敬上

Send

核心字彙充電站 *Key Words*

1. according to 片 根據
2. initial 形 開始的；最初的
3. research 名 研究；調查
4. leather 形 皮革的
5. popular 形 受人歡迎的
6. acceptable 形 可接受的

Part 1
Part 2
Part 3
Part 4
Part 5
Part 6

替換好用句 Copy & Paste

點出報價這個主題

We have discussed your offer carefully.
✐ 我們仔細討論過您的報價。

Your quotation has been reviewed.
✐ 我們已檢閱您的報價。

We have studied your offer in detail.
✐ 我方已詳細檢閱您的報價。

與其他公司相比

We have received quotations from other companies.
✐ 我方也從其他公司取得報價。

There are also other companies which are available at very lower prices.
✐ 其他公司也提供非常低的報價。

The quotations we received from other companies are much lower.
✐ 我們從別家公司接到的報價要低得多了。

Because of the current exchange rate, many other manufacturers would offer us lower prices.
✐ 根據目前匯率，許多其他製造商願意提供我們較低的報價。

Your prices are higher than other dealers.
✐ 您的價格高於其他業者。

These prices are not competitive enough in the market here.
✐ 目前的報價在這個市場上沒有足夠競爭力。

表示己方的難處

We find the price is higher than our expectation.
✐ 您的價格已經超出我們的預期。

Our customers are not satisfied with the price.
🖊 我們的客戶對此價格不滿意。

The value of Euro is increasing.
🖊 歐元價格上漲。

Our profit would be very little.
🖊 我們的利潤很少。

We have to compete with other manufacturers.
🖊 我們必須與其他製造商競爭。

The prices you offered would be difficult for us to promote the products in the market.
🖊 您提供的報價使得我方難以在市場上促銷產品。

Please understand the high prices will make our customers to seek other suppliers.
🖊 請您體諒，太高的價位會使我方的客戶尋求其他供應商。

The price of the raw materials is on decline at the moment.
🖊 原料目前正在降價。

 明確表示無法接受報價

We feel your quotation is unreasonable.
🖊 我們覺得您的價格不合理。

We feel the prices are not competitive at this time.
🖊 我們覺得此價格不具競爭力。

We won't accept the prices you offered us.
🖊 我們無法接受您的報價。

We are not able to conclude the contract because the prices are too high.
🖊 我們無法下訂單簽約，因為這個價格過於昂貴。

If your prices are still the same, we may have to purchase the products from China.
🖊 如果您的報價維持不變，我們可能會向中國訂貨。

If you cannot give us better prices, we would give up.
🖊 如果您無法提供優惠價格，我方將會放棄。

Part 1
Part 2
Part 3
Part 4
Part 5
Part 6

We could go as high as $12 for the unit price.
✏ 我們單價最多只能接受十二美元。

 委婉要求對方重新考慮報價

Could you do a better price for us?
✏ 可以算我們便宜一點嗎？

We would like to ask you to reconsider the price.
✏ 我們希望您重新考慮報價。

We would like to ask you to offer us a 15% discount of the list price.
✏ 我們希望您能降價百分之十五。

Would it be possible to lower your price?
✏ 不知貴公司是否能降低價格？

We would like to ask you to reduce the prices quoted by 5%.
✏ 我們希望您能降價百分之五。

Your understanding by giving us more discount will be greatly appreciated.
✏ 您若能體諒並提供更多的優惠，我們會非常感激。

We hope you could give us a 15% discount of the price list.
✏ 希望您願意提供百分之十五的折扣。

 提出有利的條件

If the price per item is reduced by $5, we will place an order soon.
✏ 如果每項產品可以降價五元，我們會儘速下訂單。

If we place a large order, we hope that you would consider reducing the price.
✏ 如果我們下大量訂單，希望貴公司考慮降價。

We would increase the volume of our order if you increase your discount form 5% to 10%.
✏ 如果貴公司將百分之五的折扣提升至百分之十，我們會增加訂單量。

If we place orders with you on a regular basis, would you please to grant us a 20% discount of the list price?

🖋 如果我方定期下單，您是否可以提供百分之二十的折扣呢？

If you can make the prices a little easier, we shall probably be able to place an order.
🖋 如果您能再降一點價格，我們也許會下訂單。

Would you reduce the price if we place a larger order?
🖋 如果我們大量訂購，可以算便宜一點嗎？

Would there be a discount if we pay in cash?
🖋 如果我們付現，會有折扣嗎？

We will place a trial order with you if the prices are competitive.
🖋 如果價格具競爭性，我們將會下試驗性訂單。

We will place our order as soon as we receive your reply regarding the discount.
🖋 得到您對價位的確認後，我們將會儘速下訂單。

 有接受報價的前提

We will accept your offer if you can ship the goods within one week after receiving the order.
🖋 如果您可以在接到訂單後一週內出貨，我們可以接受您的報價。

We would accept your offer if you will let us pay in installments.
🖋 如果能分期付款，我們可以接受您的報價。

We will be able to accept the price you offered if it includes delivery and insurance costs.
🖋 如果您的報價含運費以及保險費用，我們將會接受您的報價。

We will accept your quotation if the delivery could be done by the end of September.
🖋 如果能在九月底前出貨，我們願意接受您的報價。

We would accept your offer if you could provide some samples of your latest products.
🖋 若您能提供一些新產品的樣品，我方願意接受您的報價。

If you can guarantee that the quality of these items is good, we will accept your offer.
🖋 若您能擔保產品的品質優良，我們願意接受報價。

Part 1

Part 2

Part 3

Part 4

Part 5

Part 6

· 3-07 · 回覆議價

回覆潛在買家之議價時，可強調產品本身的優越性，或是由於原料上或匯差上的因素而無法接受殺價；或者，亦可給予有條件的議價，如大量訂購則可提供折扣。

Subject **Re-quote Products**

Dear Mr. Batson:

We have received your email with attention. We are very sorry that you could not find our offer **attractive**[1] to you. Although our products are **slightly**[2] more **expensive**[3] than other **similar**[4] goods, our quality is far more excellent.

However, **bearing in mind**[5] the special character of your trade, we will **grant**[6] you a special discount of 5% on the first order for $2,000.

We look forward to your reply.

Best regards,
Vera

貝特森先生您好：

我們已收到您的回信，非常遺憾您不滿意報價。雖然我們產品的價格較其他相似的產品高，但品質非常優良。

然而，考量到您的商業特性。若您的首批訂單達兩千元，我們便會給予九五折的優惠。

期待您的回覆。

薇拉 敬上

Send

核心字彙充電站 Key Words

1. **attractive** 形 有吸引力的
2. **slightly** 副 稍微地
3. **expensive** 形 昂貴的
4. **similar** 形 相似的；類似的
5. **bear in mind** 片 記住
6. **grant** 動 同意；授予

開頭表示

Thank you for your reply.
🖋 感謝您的回覆。

We are sorry to hear that you are not satisfied with the quotation.
🖋 我們對於您不滿意報價深感遺憾。

I am sorry that the terms we offered did not meet your requirements.
🖋 很遺憾我們的報價無法符合您的需求。

Thank you for your mail containing your counter offer.
🖋 謝謝您來信議價。

We have received your mail regarding price reduction.
🖋 我們已收到您要求降價的回信。

接受議價

We have considered our future business relationship; therefore, we agree to your request.
🖋 為了未來的合作關係,我們同意您的要求。

Regarding your request for a reduction in price of 3%, we agree to this in order to help you extend the sales.
🖋 我們同意降價百分之三以提升您的銷售量。

We accept the terms you specified for this order.
🖋 我們接受您的議價。

We would like to reduce the price by $2 per item.
🖋 我們願意針對每項產品調降兩元。

In order to meet your request, we would offer you a special discount of 10%.
🖋 為了符合您的要求,我們願意提供您百分之十的折扣。

Part 1
Part 2
Part 3
Part 4
Part 5
Part 6

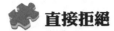 **直接拒絕**

We cannot agree to your counter offer.
🖉 我方無法接受您的議價。

We are afraid that we can not make a better offer to comply with your request.
🖉 我方恐怕無法根據您的要求再提供更好的價位。

Your counter offer is too low for a small amount of order.
🖉 就您的訂購量而言,您的議價過低。

 委婉拒絕

Unfortunately, we cannot give you the discount you requested.
🖉 很遺憾,我們無法提供您所要求的折扣。

Unfortunately, we are unable to supply you with the items at the price you asked.
🖉 很遺憾,我方無法針對您要求的產品降價。

We have difficulties to make any further reductions.
🖉 進一步降價對我方來說有困難。

 表示已給予折扣

We can understand your situation.
🖉 我們能了解您的狀況。

We have quoted you with our best prices.
🖉 我們已給您最好的報價。

We are sure the terms of our offer are very competitive.
🖉 我方確信報價條件非常有競爭力。

We have done our best to make our prices as low as possible.
🖉 我方已盡力壓低價格。

The price we offer in our last mail is the best price we can give.
🖉 我們已在上封郵件中提供最好的價格。

We hope you could understand that the discount is the maximum we

can offer.
🖉 希望您能了解我們已經提供您最大的折扣。

We have already reduced the prices down by 5%.
🖉 我們已經價降百分之五。

 說明難以降價的原因

Our NT dollar has appreciated.
🖉 台幣升值了。

Our NT dollar has depreciated.
🖉 台幣貶值了。

The prices of raw materials have increased.
🖉 原物料價格上漲了。

Considering the high production cost, we do not feel our price is too excessive.
🖉 由於製造成本昂貴，我方不認為價格過高。

The cost of the goods is increasing because the raw materials have been going up.
🖉 由於原物料價格上漲，因此產品成本增加了。

Our margin of profit is getting smaller.
🖉 我方的利潤空間越來越小。

Our profit margin won't allow us any concession.
🖉 因為利潤太少，我方無法讓步。

The quality of our products is far superior to other similar articles.
🖉 我們的產品品質遠優於其他類似產品。

 提出替代方案

I would like to offer a few alternatives.
🖉 我願意提供其他的替代方案。

If you increase your order volume, we would be happy to allow you the 10% discount.
🖉 如果您增加訂購量，我們願意提供九折優惠。

Part 1
Part 2
Part 3
Part 4
Part 5
Part 6

We hope you increase your order to 2,000 pieces, which is our minimum production number.
✎ 我們希望您能增加訂購量至我們最小的生產額：即兩千份。

We can only offer 3% price reduction instead of 6% you requested.
✎ 我們只能提供百分之三的折扣，而非您要求的百分之六。

 結尾可用

We are confident you will be satisfied not only with the quality of the goods, but also with our post-sale service.
✎ 我們相信您會對於本公司產品的品質以及售後服務感到滿意。

We hope you can reconsider our offer.
✎ 希望您能重新考慮。

We look forward to your favorable reply.
✎ 我們期待您的回覆。

We look forward to your order by return.
✎ 我們期待您的訂購。

We hope you would like to place an order regarding this revised offer.
✎ 我們期待您針對修改後的報價來信訂購。

 Let's learn more!

 文法/句型Focus

＊幣值升貶的說法

❶ **a 2 percent upward revaluation of its currency** 其貨幣升值2%

❷ **to devalue its currency by 3 percent** 其貨幣貶值3%

❸ **to adopt market-based exchange rates** 採用市場匯率

❹ **to intervene in currency market** 干預貨幣市場

Part 1

Part 2

Part 3

Part 4

Part 5

Part 6

Unit 4 訂購及回覆

4-01 訂購貨品

條列式的訂貨信件，讓繁忙的收件者一眼就能清楚了解訂貨內容。記得，在訂貨信件中清楚說明項目、金額、數量以及其他條件，以方便對方處理訂單。

Subject | **Purchase Order**

Dear Sirs:

With your **reference**[1] to your quotation of July 7, we would like to place a firm order for:

(1) 250 pairs of men's **leather shoes**[2] Reference: 22245; size: 11 @$10 (inclusive of tax)
(2) 150 pairs of women's leather shoes Reference: 23115; size: 6 @$12 (inclusive of tax)

Total inclusive of tax: $ 4,300
Invoices[3]: 3 copies
We will pay cash on delivery.
Please deliver within three weeks to our office in Taipei and confirm this order by **return**[4].

Yours sincerely,
Fiona

敬啟者：

根據您七月七日的報價，我們希望正式訂購：

(1) 250雙男用皮鞋
型號：22245；尺寸：11；每雙10元美金（含稅）
(2) 150雙女用皮鞋
型號：23115；尺寸：6；每雙12元美金（含稅）

總價：四千三百元（含稅）
請附上三份發票，貨到付款。

請於三週內寄送至我們位於台北的辦公室，並請回覆以確認訂購。

費歐娜 謹上

Send ►

1. reference 名 提及；涉及　　2. leather shoes 片 皮鞋
3. invoice 名 發票；發貨單　　4. return 名 回答

替換好用句 *Copy & Paste*

接受報價與其他

We can accept your offer on these goods.
✐ 我們同意您的報價。

We agree to your terms of payment and shipment.
✐ 我們同意您提出的付款以及送貨方式。

Thank you for your quotation of May 21 on your leather shoes.
✐ 謝謝您於五月二十一日寄來的皮鞋報價單。

Having looked over your samples, we found that the quality of your goods meets our requirements.
✐ 看過貴公司的樣品後，我們認為您的產品品質符合我們的需求。

We are disappointed at the low discount; however, we will still place a trial order.
✐ 我們對於折扣不多感到失望，但仍會下試用訂單。

We have decided to accept the 15% discount you offered and terms of payments.
✐ 我們決定接受您所提供的八五折優惠以及付款條件。

All the terms you offered in your mail are agreeable to us.
✐ 我方同意您提供的所有條件。

We understand the price quoted is CIF Taipei.
✐ 我們了解您的價格為送達台北港口的到岸價。

訂購商品

Thank you for your catalog concerning the leather shoes; we are attaching our order No.123.

✏ 謝謝您寄來的皮鞋目錄，在此附上我們編號123號的訂購單。

Please supply the following goods:
✏ 請提供以下商品：

We are pleased to place a formal order for these goods.
✏ 我們正式向貴公司訂購此批貨物。

We would like you to send us the quantities of your goods as follows:
✏ 請貴公司寄送以下數量的產品：

We have studied your catalog and confirmed our order for the item No.101.
✏ 我們已研究過您的目錄，並確認訂購編號101號的產品。

We would like to order the following items:
✏ 我們欲訂購以下商品：

 指定送達時間

Please confirm that you can supply this quantity by the end of July.
✏ 請您確認七月底前可以提供此數量貨品。

Please do your best to meet the delivery time on Sep. 22.
✏ 請您務必在九月二十二日前送貨。

Please dispatch all items no later than August 19, 2016.
✏ 請在二〇一六年八月十九日前寄送貨物。

This order is subject to your guarantee of delivery within two weeks.
✏ 這份訂單的條件為保證二週內交貨。

Please inform us if the expedited shipping will not be possible.
✏ 如果商品無法迅速送達，請通知我們。

 特別要求

Please issue us a P/I (proforma invoice) for the goods.
✏ 請提供預付發票。

Please send the invoice to the address below:
✏ 請將發票寄送到以下地址：

Part 1

Part 2

Part 3

Part 4

Part 5

Part 6

Please send us the original and five copies of the invoice.
🖊 請寄送發票正本以及五份副本。

Please attach the invoice, packing list and a B/L to the goods if you send them by air.
🖊 若使用空運，請將發票、裝箱單以及提貨單一併附在產品中。

Please send us by registered mail with the invoice and packing list.
🖊 請將發票以及裝箱單以掛號寄出。

Do you dispatch your goods overseas?
🖊 您的貨品有寄送海外嗎？

Every item should be packed in an individual cardboard box.
🖊 每樣貨品應使用紙盒包裝。

We would like to request a further order by air as soon as possible.
🖊 我們想要再次下訂單，並希望能及早空運。

Your mail, dated on May 11, convinced me to place a trial order.
🖊 您於五月十一日的來信讓我決定下試用訂單。

If this order turns out satisfactory, we would like to place a large order in the future.
🖊 若此次交易令人滿意，我們會在近日內下大筆訂單。

If any items are out of stock, please provide another quotation for a substitute.
🖊 若有商品缺貨，請提供替代品的報價單。

If you don't have them in stock, please do not send substitutes to replace them.
🖊 若物品缺貨，請勿寄送替代產品。

If you don't have these items in inventory, please replace them with another model of similar quality.
🖊 若您的產品缺貨，請提供品質相仿的其他產品。

Please confirm that the quality of the goods is the same as that of the samples we received.
🖊 請確認訂購貨物的品質與樣品一致。

These goods are urgently required; we hope you can arrange an immediate delivery from stock.
🖊 我們極需此批貨品，希望您能立即出貨。

We would like to ask you to ship the goods by FedEx.

✎ 我們希望您能以聯邦快遞寄出貨品。

Please ship the items as soon as possible via UPS expedited shipping.
✎ 請使用優比速快遞儘速寄出產品。

We will cover the costs for the urgent delivery.
✎ 我們會付急件的運費。

 付款方式

Would you please let us know the shipping costs?
✎ 能否告知運費是多少呢？

Please inform us of the payment method by return.
✎ 回函請告知付款方式。

Can we pay in NT dollars?
✎ 能否使用台幣付款？

Please inform me if you cannot accept orders on a COD basis.
✎ 若無法採用貨到付款的方式交易，請通知我。

The payment would be made in cash in ten business days.
✎ 十個工作天後，本公司會付現。

The payment would be paid quarterly.
✎ 付款為按季結算。

Payment will be paid by banker's draft tomorrow.
✎ 明日將由銀行匯票支付款項。

 請對方回函確認

We would be grateful if you could confirm the order by return.
✎ 如您能回函確認訂單，我們會感激不盡。

We would like to ask you to send your order confirmation by return.
✎ 請您回覆確認訂購。

Please confirm this order by email or fax.
✎ 請經由電子信件或傳真確認此訂單。

Part 1
Part 2
Part 3
Part 4
Part 5
Part 6

·4-02· 接受訂貨

接受訂貨時，須小心確認所有交易內容。國際貿易實務中，賣方會開出預付發票（Proforma Invoice）註明產品明細、交貨期限、付款條件、價格、數量等細節，並請客戶簽名確認。

Subject Thank You for Your Order No.245

Dear Fiona:

I am writing to confirm your order via email on July 20 for the following items:

(1) 250 pairs of men's leather shoes
Reference: 22245 size: 11 @$10
(inclusive of tax)
(2) 150 pairs of women's leather shoes
Reference: 23115 size: 6 @$12
(inclusive of tax)

As all the items are in stock, we would deliver them by UPS after receiving the funds.

We hope you will find our goods satisfactory. Once again, thank you for doing business with us and we hope to receive further orders from you.

Sincerely yours,
Tony

費歐娜您好：

此函為確認您七月二十號的訂單，如下：

(1) 250雙男用皮鞋
型號：２２２４５；尺寸：11；每雙10元美金（含稅）
(2) 150雙女用皮鞋
型號：23115；尺寸：6；每雙12元美金（含稅）

產品皆有存貨，一收到貨款即以優必速快遞寄出。

希望您滿意我們的產品。再次感謝您的訂購，希望能夠與您再次合作。

東尼 謹上

Send ▶

 Copy & Paste

訂單往來的開頭

We appreciated that you have been placing large orders with us recently.
🖊 感謝您近日大量訂購產品。

Thank you for your purchase order No.123.
🖊 感謝您來信訂購,訂單號碼123號。

We are pleased to acknowledge your order for the items below:
🖊 我們已確認您的訂單,訂購內容如下:

Attached you will find your purchase information.
🖊 附件為您的訂購資料。

We ensure that your order will have our careful attention.
🖊 我們保證會細心處理您的訂單。

We would fulfill your order by this Friday.
🖊 本週五前我們會處理好您的訂單。

Your order is already being carried out.
🖊 您的訂單已處理完畢。

告知寄送貨品時間

Once we receive the payment, the goods will be dispatched immediately.
🖊 收到您的貨款後,產品會馬上寄出。

Your order for these items will be dispatched as soon as you fill out the credit card information on our website.
🖊 您在網頁上填寫信用卡資料後,產品便會寄出。

Delivery will be made immediately on receipt of your check.
🖊 收到您的支票後,產品會馬上寄出。

All the items are in stock and can be dispatched to you by the end of September.

✎ 所有產品皆有存貨，並可於九月底前寄出。

The delivery will be made within twenty days after receiving your order.
✎ 收到訂單後的二十天內會寄出貨品。

As soon as we receive your L/C, we will ship the goods immediately.
✎ 一收到您的信用狀，我們就會馬上寄出貨品。

We would prepare materials and schedule your order earlier.
✎ 我們將及早安排產品和運送時程。

We are now making arrangement for shipment.
✎ 我們目前正在安排貨運。

We can guarantee that you will receive the goods before July 13.
✎ 我們可以保證您於七月十三日前收到貨品。

As soon as the order is ready, we will deliver them via FedEx.
✎ 貨品確認後，便會由聯邦快遞寄出。

As you requested, we will inform you of the date of delivery immediately upon completing shipment.
✎ 根據您的要求，貨品寄出後我們會告知您送貨日期。

 ## 回應特別要求

The goods will be packed according to your instructions.
✎ 我們會根據您的要求包裝。

As requested, your invoice and packing list will be sent by registered mail.
✎ 根據您的要求，發票和裝箱單將以掛號寄出。

We have sent you some sales promotional literatures by airmail.
✎ 我們已將銷售文宣寄送給您。

 ## 要求對方配合的事項

Please open an L/C as soon as possible.
✎ 請及早開出信用狀。

When you have the L/C, you can fax us first.
🖋 當您收到信用狀後，您可以先傳真一份給我們。

Please confirm it by signing the P/I return.
🖋 請簽妥預付發票後寄回，以確認訂購。

 ## 付款相關規定

Attached are our payment forms, we would ask you to complete the forms and send them back.
🖋 附件為付款表格，請填妥後寄回。

You could contact us for other payment options.
🖋 您可以詢問其他付款方式。

We would like to extend your payment deadline until the last day of June.
🖋 我們願意延長付款期限至六月三十日。

 ## 感謝與其他確認

We hope our goods will meet your expectations.
🖋 希望您滿意我們的產品。

We are sure that you will be extremely satisfied with our products.
🖋 我們相信您會對我們的產品非常滿意。

We hope your first order with us will lead to further business.
🖋 希望首次交易能夠帶來更多合作商機。

Thank you again for giving us the chance to serve you.
🖋 再次感謝您給予我們服務機會。

If you have any question about the products, please contact me.
🖋 若您對產品還有任何疑問，請與我聯絡。

Don't hesitate to let us know if you have any questions.
如有任何疑問，請隨時告知。

Part 1
Part 2
Part 3
Part 4
Part 5
Part 6

進階補充站　Let's learn more!

單字/片語Focus

❧ 處理訂單 ❧

lead time 前置期	**queue time** 排隊時間
backlog 存貨;備用品	**backorder** 延遲交貨
freight 貨運	**transport** 運送;運輸
B/L = bill of lading 託運單	

實用資訊Focus

何謂訂單處理? 🔍

　　訂單處理(Order Processing)指的是「由訂單管理部門處理客戶的需求」,這是物流活動的關鍵之一。是從客戶下訂單開始到客戶收到貨物為止,這一過程中所有單據的處理活動。

訂單的估價與報價 🔍

訂單的估價,必須遵守企業的相關規定,基本上有幾個關鍵必須注意:

1. 產品名稱、數量及金額。
2. 具體的付款條件:付款日期、付款地點、付款方式等。
3. 從接到訂單到交貨之間的期限(特殊情況可另外附註)。
4. 交貨地點、運送方式等相關交貨條件。
5. 售後服務條款等。

·4-03· 拒絕訂單

在「拒絕接受買方訂購」的信件中，必須禮貌並誠懇地表達無法接受訂單的原因，並提供其它可行的替代方案，以製造下次的合作機會。謹記，切勿輕易喪失與客戶洽談未來合作的任何可能。

Subject | **Declining Order**

Dear Mr. Huang:

Thank you very much for your order No.123 of May 2. **Unfortunately**[1], we are very sorry that we will not be able to fill your order due to the **shortage**[2] of the supplies of leather materials. Therefore, the leather shoes are **out of stock**[3] now.

However, we can order the materials from **abroad**[4], but there will be a **delay**[5] of up to five weeks for **production**[6] cycle. We would appreciate if you agree to this.

I am looking forward to hearing from you.

Yours truly,
Nancy

親愛的黃先生：

謝謝您於五月二日寄來的123號訂單。很遺憾地，由於皮革原料短缺，因此皮鞋製品目前缺貨。無法處理您的訂單，我們感到非常抱歉。

然而，我們可以從國外訂購原料，但是製造流程會延遲五個禮拜；如果您能接受，我們將會非常感激。

期待您的回信。

南希 敬上

Send

核心字彙充電站 Key Words

1. **unfortunately** 副 不幸地
2. **shortage** 名 缺少；不足
3. **out of stock** 片 無庫存
4. **abroad** 名 異國；海外
5. **delay** 名 延遲；耽擱
6. **production** 名 生產

Part 1
Part 2
Part 3
Part 4
Part 5
Part 6

 Copy & Paste

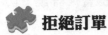 **拒絕訂單**

We are sorry that we must turn down your order.
✒ 我們很遺憾必須拒絕您的訂單。

We are really sorry for the declination of your order.
✒ 有關拒絕訂單一事，我們深感抱歉。

We regret to inform you that we cannot accept such a small order quantity.
✒ 很遺憾，我們無法接受小額訂單。

According to the terms of payment, we regret we cannot accept the D/P terms.
✒ 根據付款條件，我們無法接受付款交單。

We are sorry we cannot grant you a draft at 60 days under D/A.
✒ 很抱歉我們無法接受六十天承兌交單之匯票。

We are unable to comply with your request because of insufficient time.
✒ 由於時間不足，我們無法處理您的訂單。

We are sorry to inform you that the items mentioned in this order are out of stock currently.
✒ 我們很遺憾告知：您要的貨品目前缺貨。

There is no inventory in our warehouse now.
✒ 目前倉庫無存貨。

The items in your order have been discontinued.
✒ 您所需的貨品已經斷貨了。

Production of that special model has been discontinued.
✒ 該項特殊產品已經停止生產了。

Our company has ceased production of this model last year.
✒ 我們已在去年暫停生產此商品。

We no longer manufacture this product over the past two years.
✒ 我們已經停止生產此商品二年了。

Our production lines have been fully booked now.
🖊 我們的生產線目前已滿單。

The schedule is all booked in September.
🖊 截至九月底已滿單。

If the revised quotation is unacceptable, we have no choice but to place the order on hold.
🖊 若您仍無法接受修正過後的報價，我們只好暫時擱置此訂單。

We only accept the order on a cash basis.
🖊 我們只接受現金付款訂單。

Regretfully, we have to decline your order as our factory is closing for two months.
🖊 很遺憾地，因為工廠休息二個月，我們必須婉拒您的訂單。

In this case, it would be better for us to decline your order.
🖊 在此狀況下，我們必須婉拒您的訂單。

Under the circumstances, we are sorry that we have to turn down your order.
🖊 在此狀況下，我們必須婉拒您的訂單。

 通知延遲交貨

The delivery date requested by you does not give us sufficient time to prepare the goods.
🖊 因為時間不夠充足，所以我們無法在您要求的貨運時間前出貨。

Due to the shipment problem, there will be a delivery delay of up to eight weeks.
🖊 由於貨運問題，將會有八週的延遲。

Due to the cut in supplies from China, there will be a delay in receiving goods.
🖊 由於中國方面供應短缺，您的貨品將會延遲出貨。

The minimum period required for preparation is six to eight weeks.
🖊 準備時間最少需要六至八週。

The minimum period for production of these items is at least four weeks.
🖊 製造這些商品的時間至少要四週。

Part 1

Part 2

Part 3

Part 4

Part 5

Part 6

We hope you would give us more time to prepare the goods and shipment.
🖊 我們希望您能多給我們一些時間準備貨品以及貨運。

 提供其他方案

We can supply you with other similar products from the stock.
🖊 我們可以提供您類似產品。

We put forward our new model 1236 for your consideration, which is a good replacement.
🖊 請考慮以我們型號1236號的新產品做為替代。

Its function and specifications are greatly improved.
🖊 其功能以及規格皆經過改良。

The suggested item sells well in the market.
🖊 我們建議的這個商品在市場上的銷售良好。

We recommended other models with the similar function and quality.
🖊 我方建議其他有類似功能及品質的產品。

If the suggested model meets your requirement, please inform us soon.
🖊 如建議的產品符合您的需求，請儘速告知我方。

We are confident the new model will give you complete satisfaction.
🖊 我們有信心您會滿意新的產品。

 致歉

If you would like to cancel this order, it would be understandable.
🖊 若您決定取消訂單，我們能夠諒解。

Again, we hope you could receive our sincere apology.
🖊 再次祈求您接受我們的致歉。

We hope you will understand our difficulties and situation.
🖊 希望您能了解我們的困難和處境。

Please inform us your decision as soon as possible.
🖊 請儘早通知我們您的決定。

We hope there will be other opportunities to do business with you.
✎ 我們希望仍有其他與您合作的機會。

We hope we can serve you in the future.
✎ 我們希望未來能替您服務。

 Let's learn more!

單字/片語Focus

🎀 存量與訂購 🎀	
✱**irrevocable** 不可撤回的	✱**insufficient** 不充足的
✱**warehouse** 倉庫；貨棧	✱**cease** 終止；停止
✱**apologize** 道歉；認錯	✱**comply with** 遵守；依從
✱**agree to** 同意；接受	✱**turn down** 拒絕
✱**respite** 暫緩；使暫息	✱**belated** 誤期的
✱**total inventory** 庫存總量	✱**volume** （交易）量
✱**quantity on hand** 目前實際存貨量	
✱**quantity on order** 可訂貨生產存貨量	

實用資訊Focus

何謂D/A？ 🔍

　　D/A = Documents against Acceptance 承兌交單，為國際貿易付款方式之一。出口商在貨物運出後，開具一遠期匯票，連同貨運單據委託銀行辦理託收，指示銀行在匯票上承兌後，即可領單提貨，待匯票到期日始付清貨款。

Part 1
Part 2
Part 3
Part 4
Part 5
Part 6

4-04 取消訂單

　　造成取消訂單的原因很多，如果是因為對方的疏失，可展現強硬的態度；如果是本身的決定，則簡短有力說明取消訂單的理由，但結尾仍須謙虛有禮請求對方諒解，以維持雙方愉快的合作關係。

Subject	Cancellation of Order

Dear Mr. Wu:

We have placed our order for 500 **electronic**[1] **calculators**[2]. However, we have to cancel this order due to customer **cancellation**[3].

We hope you will agree to this cancellation and we thank you **in advance**[4].

We are truly sorry for the inconvenience.

Yours truly,
Betty

吳先生您好：

我們有一份五百台電子計算機的訂單，然而，因客戶取消訂購，所以我們也必須取消訂單。

我們希望您能同意取消，並在此感謝您。

造成不便，我們深感抱歉。

貝蒂 謹上

Send

核心字彙充電站 *Key Words*

1. **electronic** 形 電子的
2. **calculator** 名 計算機
3. **cancellation** 名 取消
4. **in advance** 片 預先

 取消訂單

Due to financial reasons, we have to cancel our order.
因為財務上的考量，我們必須取消訂單。

Due to customer cancellation, we are forced to cancel this order.
由於客戶取消訂購，所以我們被迫取消訂單。

We have stressed the importance of shipping our order by the end of May.
我們已強調貨運必須在五月底前送達的重要性。

We have to cancel this order since we have not received the goods.
因尚未收到任何貨品，我們必須取消訂單。

According to your delay in shipment, we decided to cancel the order.
因貨運延遲，我們決定取消訂單。

Due to the inferior quality of your products, we regret that we have to cancel our order.
由於產品品質不佳，我們很遺憾地必須取消訂單。

Please cancel the order as our customer cannot accept the late shipping date.
由於我們的客戶無法接受延遲送貨，所以我們必須取消訂單。

 致歉的說法

We are very sorry for the inconvenience.
很抱歉造成不便。

We hope you will accept our sincere apologies.
希望您接受我們誠摯的道歉。

We are terribly sorry for cancelling our order.
要向您取消訂單，我們真心感到抱歉。

We apologize for any inconvenience this may have caused you, and we hope there will be other chances to do business with you.
若造成不便，敬請見諒，也希望日後能有機會與您合作。

寫「催促買方訂貨」的信件時，要記得給予催促的原因，例如價格即將調整、或是存貨即將售罄，以增加買家想要儘速下訂單的動機。

Subject Re: Item No.6668

Dear Mr. Freeman:

Please **refer to**[1] our email dated August 23 and our quotation for item No.6668. We would like to know if you have any **conclusion**[2] now. Would you please confirm the order as early as possible?

Due to the **rising**[3] cost of raw materials, the price of our products will go up soon. However, we will **maintain**[4] our offer until the end of September.

Please kindly understand and take this opportunity by confirming return soon.

Truly yours,
Rita

弗利曼先生您好：

請詳見八月二十三日信件中，我們針對編號6668號貨品的報價。我們想要了解您是否有了結論。可否請您儘速確認訂單呢？

由於原物料上漲，所以我們的產品也即將漲價。然而，我們會維持此報價到九月底。

感謝您的諒解，並請儘早確認。

芮塔 敬上

Send

核心字彙充電站 *Key Words*

1. **refer to** 片 參考
2. **conclusion** 名 結論；決定
3. **rising** 形 上升的；升起的
4. **maintain** 動 維持；保持

 Copy & Paste

因故而請對方及早下單

Due to the rush of orders, we would like to ask you to confirm your order.
✎ 由於訂單量激增，我們想要請您確認訂單。

As we have got many orders this month, it would be better for you to place an order as early as possible.
✎ 由於本月的訂單量很大，所以我們希望您能及早下訂單。

As you know, the price of raw materials has been rising these two years.
✎ 如同您也了解的，這兩年原物料價格持續上漲。

We will raise our prices when the present stocks are exhausted.
✎ 此批庫存售罄後，我們將會漲價。

As soon as we run out our stocks, the price will be revised.
✎ 庫存售罄後，價格將會調整。

As the demand will be very heavy before Christmas, we would like to ask you to place your order as early as possible.
✎ 由於聖誕節前夕的產品需求量很大，我們希望您能早日下訂單。

If you wish to ensure delivery before Chinese New Year, please place an order soon.
✎ 若您希望在農曆年前收到貨，請及早下訂單。

When our current stock is exhausted, we would not manufacture the same model in the future.
✎ 目前庫存售完後，我們將不再生產這批型號的產品。

These products are very popular in Taiwan; therefore, we have received a very large order.
✎ 這些產品在台灣非常受歡迎，因此我們收到大量訂單。

We would suggest you give us your order by this weekend since our schedule is very tight.
✎ 由於我們的生產線非常忙碌，希望您能在本週末前下訂單。

As our schedule is booked up until September, please confirm your

order soon.
🖉 生產線目前已滿單至九月底，請您儘速確認訂單。

 強調已方產品的優勢

Our products are superior to many similar goods on the market.
🖉 和市場上許多相似的產品相比，我方產品優良許多。

Our terms and prices are very competitive.
🖉 我方的條件及價位都非常有競爭力。

With fine quality and attractive design, our goods have been selling extremely well.
🖉 我方產品因其優良的品質及良好的設計，在市場上的反應極佳。

Our schedule is very full; therefore, we advise you to place an order soon.
🖉 我們的生產線非常忙碌，建議您及早下訂單。

We urgently need to know the quantity of your order so that we can reserve a space for you.
🖉 我們急需您的訂單數量，以便為您安排生產線。

We would like to serve a space for you.
🖉 我們可以為您安排生產線。

We would like to put your order into our production line this month.
🖉 我們想要將您的訂購商品排在這個月的生產線上。

We are sure it will benefit your sales if you place your order regularly.
🖉 如果您定期下訂單，我方產品肯定能為您帶來利潤。

We would advise your order without loss of time.
🖉 我們建議您把握時機下單。

We hope you will let us have your order before we raise the price.
🖉 希望您在我們漲價前下單。

We would be delighted if you place an order with us.
🖉 若您能與我方合作，我們將會非常高興。

Unit 5 付款與催款

·5-01· 準備付款

　　準備付款時，需再次確認付款的內容，如金額、期限、付款方式、對方的銀行帳號等，以確保付款順利。

Subject | Payment Notice (Order No.991AL110)

Dear Mr. Liu:

We are looking forward to **receiving**[1] the invoice for May. Could you please send that to us first? When the **due date**[2] is done, we will **transfer**[3] the **funds**[4] to you.

Best regards,
Danny

劉先生您好：

我們在等五月份的帳單，可以請您先寄給我們嗎？付款日到時，我們會轉帳給您。

丹尼 謹上

Send ▶

 Key Words

1. **receive** 動 收到；接到
2. **due date** 片 期限；到期日
3. **transfer** 動 轉讓；轉帳
4. **funds** 名 現款；資金

 替換好用句 Copy & Paste

🧩 帳單明細

Please mail us an itemized pay statement.
✎ 請寄發票明細給我們。

Our records show that we have not received payment for the May

invoice.

✎ 根據我們的紀錄，我們仍未收到五月份的現款。

Thank you for mailing the invoice for May.

✎ 謝謝您寄來五月份的帳單。

We have smudged the invoice. Would you please send us a new one?

✎ 我們弄髒了帳單，請您再寄一份好嗎？

Please email our invoices every month.

✎ 請每月以電子郵件寄送帳單。

Would you please forward us our invoice as a PDF file?

✎ 可否請您將帳單以PDF檔寄給我們？

 ## 支付款項的問題

We wonder if you omitted the 5% discount that we agreed on April 5.

✎ 我們在想，您是否遺漏了四月五號所協議的百分之五折扣呢？

Please quote the price in Euro.

✎ 請以歐元報價。

Do you accept US dollars?

✎ 您接受美金嗎？

We would like to pay in cash.

✎ 我們想要以現金支付。

We would like to pay by check.

✎ 我們想要以支票支付。

Do you accept credit cards?

✎ 您接受信用卡嗎？

Do you accept credit cards issued by an overseas bank?

✎ 您接受海外銀行發行的信用卡嗎？

We would like to pay by international money orders.

✎ 我們想要以國際匯票支付。

We will make payment by postal order.

✎ 我們會以郵政匯票支付。

We would like to pay initially of $1,000, and the remainder in 3 installments.

🖊 我們會先支付一千元，餘額分三期付款。

We will send a bank check to you for the purchase.

🖊 我們會寄給您銀行支票以支付款項。

Please fax us the name of the remitting bank and the remittance number.

🖊 請傳真告知匯款銀行以及帳號。

Please inform us of your bank's name and your account number.

🖊 請告知您的銀行名稱和帳號。

 進階補充站 Let's learn more!

 實用資訊Focus

國際電匯所需資料 🔍

1. 申請人（Applicant）：中文及英文

2. 申請人證號（I/D）：身份證號碼

3. 申請人出生日期（Date of Birth）

4. 住址（Address）：中文地址

5. 電話（Tel/No.）

6. 受款地區國別（Country）

7. 受款人資料（Beneficiary Information）：包含帳號、戶名、住址、電話、E-mail。

8. 受款銀行（Beneficiary Bank）：包含銀行名稱（Bank）、分行別（Branch）、銀行代號（SWIFT Code）、銀行城市及國家（Country and City）、匯款銀行費用（Charges）、匯款明細（Details of Payment）。

·5-02· 付款通知

在「付款通知」信件中，記得告知正確的訂單號碼以及金額，以免付款時發生錯誤。

Subject | **Payment Notice (Invoice No.22256)**

Dear Mr. Liu:

I write to inform you that we have transferred US$6,000 as payment for your invoice No.22256. Please kindly check.

Furthermore[1], we are pleased with the way you **executed**[2] our order. The order arrived **on time**[3] and could be put on sale without delay.

We thank you for your **prompt**[4] attention on this matter.

Best regards,
Danny

劉先生您好：

我們已將帳單編號22256的六千美金轉到您的戶頭，請查收。

此外，我們對於您處理訂單的過程很滿意。貨品準時送達，讓我們得以準時將商品上架。

謝謝您對訂單即時的處理。

丹尼 敬上

Send

核心字彙充電站 *Key Words*

1. furthermore 副 此外
2. execute 動 執行；實行
3. on time 片 準時
4. prompt 形 迅速的；即時的

 Copy & Paste

Part 1
Part 2
Part 3
Part 4
Part 5
Part 6

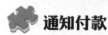 通知付款

The bank has credited your account with the amount of the check.
🖉 銀行已把支票上的金額轉入您的帳戶。

Referring to your payment request on May 20, 2016, an application of our bank for remittance was made today.
🖉 根據您二〇一六年五月二十日要求之付款事宜，我們已向我方銀行申請匯款。

We have made the remittance today to your account with The Taipei Branch of The China Trust Bank.
🖉 我們今天已經透過中國信託的台北分行匯款給您。

The remittance number is No.55362.
🖉 匯款號碼為55362號。

The amount of $2,000 US dollars will be transferred to your bank account.
🖉 兩千元美金將會轉進您的戶頭。

We have remitted $1,500 to your bank account.
🖉 我們已匯一千五百元至您的銀行帳戶。

We have made the first payment on time.
🖉 我們已準時付清第一筆款項。

We will prepare the second payment soon.
🖉 我們近日會準備第二筆款項。

I will send the check for $1,500, which is the final payment.
🖉 我會寄出一千五百元的支票，支付最後的款項。

We included the details of the name of the remitting bank and the remittance number.
🖉 我們會附上匯款銀行的名稱以及匯款號碼等細節。

We have pleasure in sending the postal order for $5,000.
🖉 我們很樂意寄出五千元的郵政匯票。

The postal check can be cashed at any post office.
🖉 這張郵政支票可在任何一間郵局兌現。

We have sent you a bank draft for $2,000 in settlement of invoice No.6553.
🖊 我們已經寄給您一張面額兩千元的銀行匯票，用以支付編號6553號的發票。

 **相關提醒**

Please confirm if you have received the check.
🖊 請確認您是否有收到支票。

Please contact us if you do not receive any advices on our remittance from your bank.
🖊 如您尚未從您的銀行收到匯款通知，請與我們聯絡。

We look forward to your confirmation of receipt of the payment.
🖊 我們希望收到您確認已收款的訊息。

We also faxed a copy of remittance slip to you.
🖊 我們同時傳真了一份匯款通知單的副本給您。

When you receive the remittance, please inform us.
🖊 當您收到匯款單時，請通知我們。

 表達謝意

The entire shipment arrived in good condition.
🖊 貨物安全抵達。

The shipment arrived safely on May 21.
🖊 貨物在五月二十一日安全抵達。

Thank you for your prompt handling of our order.
🖊 謝謝您迅速處理訂單。

We appreciate the work efficiency of your company.
🖊 我們感激貴公司的工作效率。

We hope to do business with you again very soon.
🖊 希望近日能再與您交易。

Part 1
Part 2
Part 3
Part 4
Part 5
Part 6

·5-03· 收到款項

賣方在收到款項後，同樣必須回覆有關訂單以及收到的款項內容，與買方核對是否無誤；另外，告知買方貨品的最新處理狀況，能讓買方更清楚作業流程並更信賴賣方。

Subject **Payment Confirmation (Order No.22235)**

Dear Mr. Liu:

The bank has informed us this afternoon that we received $5,000 regarding your order No.22235. Thank you very much for the payment.

The products you ordered will be shipped from Keelung Port tomorrow. I will keep you up to date on this information.

As always, thank you for doing business with us.

Best regards,
Danny

劉先生您好：

銀行通知我們，今天下午已收到您訂單號22235的匯款。謝謝您的付款。

您訂購的貨品將安排明天從基隆港出貨，我會持續通知您有關貨運的消息。

感謝您的合作。

丹尼 敬上

Send ▸

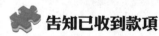 *Copy & Paste*

告知已收到款項

Thank you for sending your remittance for invoice No.567.
🖉 謝謝您寄來發票567號的匯款。

We have received your remittance of 5,000 US dollars.
🖉 我們已經收到您五千美元的匯款。

Thank you for your mail this morning, advising us of your remittance.
✏ 謝謝您今早通知我方你已匯款的消息。

We hereby confirm the receipt of $5,000 in our account this morning.
✏ 我們今早確認已經收到五千元款項。

Your payment has been received.
✏ 已收到您的款項。

This mail is the confirmation of receipt of all fees.
✏ 此郵件是要確認已收到所有費用。

Please be informed that full payment has been received.
✏ 茲告知已收到所有款項。

All fees have now been paid in full.
✏ 所有款項均已結清。

Thank you for your prompt settlement of invoice No.252.
✏ 謝謝您盡速支付252號發票的款項。

 寄送發票相關

Please advise us which bank you remitted the money.
✏ 請告知我方您的匯款銀行。

We will address all invoices to your accountant in the future.
✏ 我們之後會將發票寄給您的會計。

A receipt will be sent to you.
✏ 發票會寄送給您。

 禮貌結尾

We are sure you will be satisfied with our goods.
✏ 我們保證您會滿意我們的產品。

Thank you for your continued business.
✏ 謝謝您的持續惠顧。

We look forward to serving you again.
✏ 希望能夠再為您服務。

We hope to receive another order from you again in the very near future.

✎ 希望近日可以再收到您的訂單。

We look forward to the opportunity to do business with you again soon.

✎ 希望近日能夠再與您合作。

 *Let's learn more!*

 單字/片語Focus

❧ 折扣種類 ❧	
✱**on sale** 拍賣	✱**discount** 折扣
✱**coupon** 折價券	✱**open box sale** 開箱折扣
✱**rebate** 回扣	✱**member rate** 會員價

 實用資訊Focus

何謂第三方支付？ 🔍

　　第三方支付（third-party payment）指的是介於買賣雙方中間的獨立平台，提供代收／代付的服務。當買方以第三方支付服務消費，此平台就會代收款項，並通知賣家出貨；買方收到商品後，再由第三方支付業者撥款給賣家。這種貨到撥款的交易方式有擔保的作用，可以防堵詐騙情形、減少消費糾紛，主要存在於網路交易。

何謂open box sale？ 🔍

　　美國常見的折扣種類之一，常用於電器用品上。某樣商品被消費者退貨，但原包裝箱已被開封，此時就可能已open box sale的方式做促銷。這類商品並非瑕疵品，且該有的零件、手冊、保固都很完整。

291

5-04 請求延遲付款

　　「請求延遲付款」的信件內容，可強調本身的困難，以及所遭遇的突發狀況，請對方體諒，表示並非刻意欠款，態度誠懇地請求對方延長付款期限、或要求協助。

Subject Extension of Payment (Invoice No.223)

Dear Mr. Nagakawa:

Referring to your invoice No.223 dated April 30, which is due for payment on May 20, we have to inform you that it is not possible for us to pay you the **sum**[1] of $10,000 **at the moment**[2].

Due to the **economic**[3] **slack**[4], the customers who usually buy our goods have been very **hesitant**[5] in their purchase.

Despite[6] our **desperate**[7] efforts in **collection**[8], money is coming slowly. Therefore, we would ask you for a two-month **extension**[9] of payment.

We do hope you will agree to the extension of the **deadline**[10] and look forward to your confirmation.

Best regards,
Minnie

中川先生您好：

關於您四月三十日的發票223號，付款日期為五月二十日，我們必須通知您，本公司目前無法支付這一萬元的款項。

由於經濟蕭條，我們的常客最近在購買產品時變得很猶豫。

雖然本公司極力籌措，但進帳速度仍緩慢。因此，希望您能同意延後二個月付款。

希望您能同意此提議，並盼望得到您的確認。

米妮 敬上

Send

核心字彙充電站 *Key Words*

1. sum 名 總數；總和；總計	2. at the moment 片 目前
3. economic 形 經濟上的	4. slack 名 蕭條（期）
5. hesitant 形 猶豫不決的	6. despite 介 不管；儘管
7. desperate 形 絕望的	8. collection 名 收帳
9. extension 名 延長；延期	10. deadline 名 截止期限

替換好用句 *Copy & Paste*

 延遲繳款的請求

According to the contract, we must settle the account by November 11.

🖊 根據合約，我們必須在十一月十一日前付款。

We would like to ask you to reschedule the payment deadline on December 31.

🖊 我們希望您能重新安排付款日期至十二月三十一日。

We would appreciate it if you could give us another fortnight to settle the account.

🖊 如果貴公司能夠再寬限二週，我方將感激不盡。

It would be much appreciated if you could wait for our payment for another ten days.

🖊 如果您能夠多寬限十天的付款期限，我們會不勝感激。

Please extend one more week for the payment.

🖊 請再給予一週付款寬限期。

Would it be possible if we settle this account on July 20?

🖊 可否於七月二十日付款呢？

Would it be possible for us to make a late payment for the previous invoice and the present one?

🖊 上個月和這個月的帳款是否能延遲支付呢？

Could you allow us to pay you $1,500 by this week, and the remainder to be paid next week?

Part 1
Part 2
Part 3
Part 4
Part 5
Part 6

✏ 您能否同意我們本週先付一千五百元，下週再付餘款？

Please accept our request for an extension of the deadline for payment.
✏ 請接受我們延長付款期限的請求。

We would like to ask you to let us pay your invoice in three installments.
✏ 希望您能同意我們分三期付款。

We will send you one third of the payment, namely $3,000.
✏ 我們會寄出三分之一的款項：三千元。

We will send another third on June 20 and the balance on July 10.
✏ 我們將在六月二十日寄出另外三分之一，並在七月十日寄出餘款。

Would you please allow us to postpone the settlement of the account?
✏ 能請您同意我們延後付款嗎？

We will try to clear the balance within the next three weeks.
✏ 我們會盡力在三週內付清餘款。

The balance will be paid by June 20.
✏ 餘款會在六月二十日付清。

 致歉與承諾

Please accept our regrets on paying late.
✏ 請原諒本公司延遲付款。

We are sorry for not meeting our financial obligations with you.
✏ 很抱歉沒有及時付款給您。

We sincerely apologize for any inconvenience caused by the delay.
✏ 我們對於延遲付款造成的不便感到抱歉。

We are very sorry for the tardiness in the payment of your invoice dated May 1, 2016.
✏ 很抱歉，尚未支付您二〇一六年五月一日的帳款。

We are sorry for taking so much time to pay your invoice.
✏ 我們很抱歉這麼慢才付款。

We will definitely settle the account on time in the future.
✏ 今後我們一定會準時繳款。

解釋延期的原因

We would like to explain our awful situation.
🖉 我們需要解釋我們目前的慘況。

A sudden fire occurred at our factory which caused us great losses.
🖉 一場意外的工廠大火讓我們損失慘重。

Despite our best efforts in collecting money, the money is coming slowly.
🖉 即使我們盡力籌款，但是進帳速度仍緩慢。

Due to devaluation of dollars, there is a setback in business.
🖉 美元的貶值導致我們生意衰退。

Recently, there have been sharp declines in sales in our markets.
🖉 近來，我們市場的生意驟降。

Due to the dock strike, we cannot ship the goods to our customers.
🖉 由於碼頭罷工，因此我們無法出貨給客戶。

Our customers have not paid us yet.
🖉 我們的客戶尚未付款。

Due to the flood in our factory, we are still waiting for the compensation from the insurance company.
🖉 我們工廠受洪水波及，目前仍在等待保險理賠。

A large number of our products were destroyed.
🖉 我們有大量貨品遭毀損。

We hope you could bear with us until the matter is resolved.
🖉 希望您能寬容我們的情況，直到事情解決。

As you are aware, we have always settled our accounts promptly.
🖉 如您所知，我們一直都準時付款。

We are sorry that we are forced to make this request.
🖉 我們很抱歉，迫不得已提出此要求。

We hope you can understand our present situation.
🖉 希望您能體諒我們的現況。

We look forward to receiving your favorable reply.
🖉 我方希望可以得到您的善意回應。

Part 1
Part 2
Part 3
Part 4
Part 5
Part 6

•5-05• 接受延遲付款

如果對方不幸發生意外時，當下釋出善意，答應延遲付款對未來雙方關係會很有助益。此外，也必須衡量公司自身的狀況，判斷是否答應對方延遲付款的條件。

Subject	Re: Extension of Payment (Order No.991)

Dear Mr. Hu:

Thank you for writing to us **frankly**[1] about your **inability**[2] to **settle**[3] your account. We can understand the unfortunate **earthquake**[4] happened in your country is an **exception**[5]. We **are willing to**[6] grant you the extension you asked for.

Best regards,
Alex

胡先生您好：

謝謝您來信，據實以告有關您無法付清款項的事。我們能理解貴國發生地震是不幸的意外。我們會接受您的延期要求。

艾力克斯 謹上

Send

核心字彙充電站 *Key Words*

1. **frankly** 副 率直地；坦白地
2. **inability** 名 無能；不能
3. **settle** 動 支付；結算
4. **earthquake** 名 地震
5. **exception** 名 例外
6. **be willing to** 片 願意的；樂意的

替換好用句 *Copy & Paste*

 已看到請求

Thank you for your mail explaining the reason why you cannot settle the account on time.
🖋 謝謝您來信解釋不能準時繳款的原因。

Thank you for your mail concerning the outstanding balance on your account.

✎ 謝謝您來信提及未付餘額的相關事項。

We have received your mail requesting the postponement in payment.

✎ 我們已收到您要求延後付款的郵件。

We are obliged to hear from you regarding your overdue payment.

✎ 我們感激您提供有關過期帳款的消息。

 ## 同意延遲繳款

We can fully understand your economic conditions.

✎ 我們完全可以理解您的財務狀況。

We are aware of your financial difficulties.

✎ 我們了解您所面臨的經濟困難。

We can accept your explanation of your market situation.

✎ 我們可以接受您市場狀況不佳的解釋。

Thanks to the regularity of your payments; therefore, we reply favorably to your request.

✎ 感謝貴公司以往總是準時付款,因此我們願意答應您的要求。

Thanks to our good business relations, we would agree to your proposal to postpone the payment.

✎ 由於我們以往良好的合作關係,我們答應您延遲付款。

As we have done business with each other for a long time, we will defer payment for another five working days.

✎ 由於我們已經來往合作好一段時間,我們同意寬限您五個工作天。

As you are a valued customer, we would like to extend your credit period by another week.

✎ 由於您是我們寶貴的客戶,因此我們樂意將信用期限延長一週。

We can sympathize with certain situations that may lead to late payment.

✎ 我們能夠體諒某些導致延遲付款的狀況。

We sympathize with the earthquake happened in your country, and are willing to allow you to extend the payment for another six weeks.

✎ 我們同情貴國地震後的處境,所以同意您延後六週付款。

Part 1

Part 2

Part 3

Part 4

Part 5

Part 6

同意延期並表達難處

We allow you to extend your payment, but we insist on payment by the end of July.
🖉 我們同意您延期付款，但堅持必須在七月底前繳清。

We agree to the extension, but only until December 15.
🖉 我們同意延期，但只到十二月十五日。

We suggest that you make a part payment of $1,500 now, and pay the balance by the end of August.
🖉 我們建議您先付一千五百美元，再於八月底前付清餘額。

We found it difficult to agree to your proposal, though.
🖉 雖然我們覺得很難同意您的提議。

However, we have reluctantly decided to agree to your request.
🖉 但是，我們還是很勉強地答應您的請求。

Accordingly, please settle the account no later than December 31.
🖉 因此，請勿超過十二月三十一日付款。

It will cause us some financial embarrassment if you delay the remittance again.
🖉 如果您再次延遲，將會導致我們財務上的困難。

 寬慰對方

We sincerely hope that your financial problem will be solved soon.
🖉 我們誠摯地希望您的財務問題能儘快解決。

We hope that your problem is transient and you will find a rapid solution.
🖉 我們希望您的困難只是暫時的，盼您可以儘快找到解決方法。

With enough time, we believe you will adjust the account totally.
🖉 我們相信您能在足夠的時間內付清款項。

Part 1

Part 2

Part 3

Part 4

Part 5

Part 6

5-06 拒絕延遲付款

在「拒絕延遲付款」的信函中，要明確告知自己公司也有困難，因此無法答應對方的延遲付款要求，但可建議替代方案，以讓對方有所選擇。

Subject Re: Extension of Payment (Order No.991)

Dear Mr. Lu:

Regarding your **proposal**[1] in last mail for extending the payment deadline, we really **sympathize**[2] with your **situation**[3] for the losses and **inconvenience**[4] caused by the **flood**[5] which **occurred**[6] in your country.

However, please understand that we have our financial difficulties as well. Therefore, we are willing to accept a **partial**[7] payment of 50% of the amount by May 20, with the remaining 50% being paid by June 20. We think that this alternate plan may be a good **solution**[8].

I hope this plan meets with your approval. If you have any questions, please feel free to contact me.

Best regards,
Kevin

盧先生您好：

您上次來信提及延後付款期限，我們非常同情貴國遭遇洪水災害導致您的損失和不便。

但是，請您了解我們本身也有財務吃緊的狀況。因此，我們可以接受在五月二十日前，您先付一半的費用，在於六月二十日前付清剩下的款項。我們覺得此替代方案會是很好的解決方式。

希望您能同意。如有任何問題，請隨時聯絡我。

凱文 謹上

Send

核心字彙充電站 *Key Words*

1. **proposal** 名 提出；提議　　2. **sympathize** 動 同情；憐憫

3. **situation** 名 處境；境遇　　4. **inconvenience** 名 不便

5. **flood** 名 洪水；水災　　　6. **occur** 動 發生
7. **partial** 形 部分的；局部的　　8. **solution** 名 解決（辦法）

替換好用句　Copy & Paste

說明難處及原因

We have considered the proposal you mentioned in your mail.
🖋 我們考慮過您的來信建議。

We can certainly understand your difficulty.
🖋 我們完全可以了解您的困境。

However, we need to pay our suppliers as well.
🖋 然而，我方也需要付款給供應商。

We of course understand your difficulties, but we have ours, too.
🖋 我們當然了解您的困境，但我方也有困難。

As our margin of profit is very little, we cannot agree to the extension of the payment.
🖋 由於我們的利潤很少，我方無法同意延後付款。

The offer we gave you is on a small profit basis.
🖋 我方給您的報價很低，因此賺取的利潤很少。

You have delayed your payment frequently.
🖋 您時常延遲付款。

We regret that it's hard for us to accept your proposal.
🖋 很抱歉，我方難以接受您的提案。

拒絕的說法

Therefore, we still need to ask you to settle the account at once.
🖋 因此，還是要請您立即付款。

Otherwise, we are compelled to take the legal actions.
🖋 否則，我們就必須採取法律行動。

We must insist on payment within ten days.
🖊 我方必須要求您十天內付款。

We must ask you to arrange the payment immediately.
🖊 我方必須要求您立即付款。

If the payment is not made in accordance with the contract, I am afraid we would cancel the order.
🖊 如果貨款沒有根據合約付清，我方恐怕要取消訂單。

If you failed in clearing the account on time, we will claim damages for your failure to honor the contract.
🖊 如果您無法準時付清款項，我方會因您無法履行合約要求索賠。

We urge that you clear the balance without delay.
🖊 希望您能準時清償餘款。

An early remittance will be highly appreciated.
🖊 敬請提早匯款。

Your failure to pay on time has caused a great inconvenience.
🖊 您的逾時付款造成我方極大的不便。

 Let's learn more!

 文法/句型Focus

✱ 針對某件事（提及主題）

❶ **As you requested, ...** 如您所要求的，…。

❷ **Regarding + (NOUN PHRASE), ...** 關於…（接名詞片語）

❸ **As you mentioned in your email, ...** 如同您信中所提到的

❹ **Further to this question, ...** 針對此問題的進一步討論

❺ **Regarding your enquiry about...** 關於你對…的要求。（接名詞片語）

❻ **In answer to your question about...**
回答您關於…的問題（接名詞片語）

5-07 第一次催款信

第一次催款時，因為尚未掌握情況，所以宜用「提醒」取代「催繳」。態度須有禮並簡單表明催款原因，切勿過於責難以免破壞往後的合作關係。

Subject **Payment Reminder (Order No.991AL110)**

Dear Mr. Chen:

We would like to remind you that our April **statement**[1] **amounting to**[2] $5,000 is **overdue**[3]. We would be **grateful**[4] if you could send us your check as soon as possible.

Best Regards,
Terry

陳先生您好：

我們想要提醒您四月份結算金額為五千元，付款期已過。若您能儘快將支票寄出，我們將感激不盡。

泰瑞 謹上

Send ▶

核心字彙充電站 *Key Words*

1. statement 名 結單
2. amount to 片 總計；等同
3. overdue 形 過期的
4. grateful 形 感謝的

替換好用句 *Copy & Paste*

通知款項逾期

This is a reminder that charges for your order will be due on June 15, 2016.

🖉 提醒您：訂單款項將於二〇一六年六月十五日到期。

This is to inform you that payment on the invoice No.525-1 is now more than sixty days overdue.

🖉 通知您：發票525-1號的貨款已逾期六十天。

Please kindly note that our statement of account dated May 1 is still waiting for settlement.
🖊 謹此通知您五月一日帳款仍未付清。

We expect payment two weeks ago, but we still have not received your check.
🖊 我方原本預期兩週前收到結款，但現在仍未收到您的支票。

Up to this date, it appears that we haven't received your remittance.
🖊 我方到現在仍未收到您的匯款。

As your payment is considerably overdue, we must ask you to remit the sum immediately.
🖊 您的貨款已經逾期很久了，我方希望您立即付款。

We have to remind you that the payment for your last order is due three weeks from the date of invoice.
🖊 我們必須提醒您：您的貨款已經延遲三週了。

I am writing this mail to remind you that we have not received your payment for the products which were delivered to you last week.
🖊 此信是想通知您：貨品在上週已經寄給您，但我方尚未收到您的貨款。

This mail is to remind you that your remittance for last order has not been made yet.
🖊 我們想通知您：上次的貨款尚未付清。

According to the contract, you have to settle the account within twenty days after you received the shipment.
🖊 根據合約，您必須在收到貨物後的二十天內付款。

Our records show that your account has not been paid yet.
🖊 我們的紀錄顯示：您的貨款尚未結清。

 欲了解情況

Since we have always received your payment on time, we are puzzled to have had neither remittance nor reply from you.
🖊 以往我方都準時收到您的款項，但是這次卻沒有收到您的款項或是回應。

As you are usually very prompt in settling your account, we would like to know why we have not received the payment.
🖊 由於您一向不拖欠付款，我方想要了解為何仍未收到款項。

Part 1
Part 2
Part 3
Part 4
Part 5
Part 6

We are very concerned as you have always been prompt in making your payments.
✎ 由於您總是準時付款，因此我方十分關切您的狀況。

We wonder why the account was still not paid.
✎ 帳款仍未付清這件事讓我們感到疑惑。

 表示體諒

I am sure the seasonal rush might keep you busy and the invoice might have been overlooked.
✎ 相信最近您因業務繁忙而忽略了帳單。

Perhaps you are unaware that invoice No.552 is still outstanding.
✎ 也許您不曉得552號帳單尚未付款。

We understand that our invoice may not have reached you.
✎ 我們了解也許您尚未收到發票。

It is maybe an oversight.
✎ 也許這只是個疏失。

We understand that delays can happen for a variety of reasons.
✎ 我們了解可能因為各種原因造成延遲付款。

We understand payments could be overlooked sometimes.
✎ 我們可以理解有時候會漏看帳單。

We wonder if you have overlooked the invoice No.6553 for $5,000 which was due two weeks ago.
✎ 不知您是否漏看了發票6553號，金額五千元，繳款期限為兩週前。

 重傳帳單給對方

We would like to take this opportunity to send a second copy of the invoice.
✎ 我們會再寄一份發票給您。

Just in case you have misplaced your copy of invoice, we will send it to you again.
✎ 若您找不到那份帳單也無妨，我們會再寄一份給您。

I have faxed again the copy of our invoice No.223 to you this morning.
今早我已再次傳真發票223號的副本給您了。

In case you may not receive the statement of account, I have attached the file showing a balance owing $1,500.
或許您尚未收到我們的對帳單，我再一次附上檔案，欠款餘額為一千五百元。

 ## 要求盡速結清

We ask you to settle the account immediately.
我方希望貴公司立即付款。

According to the terms of the seasonal account agreed upon, we would like to receive settlement by 15th April.
根據雙方同意的每季合約條款，我方希望能在四月十五日前收到款項。

Please make an immediate payment to our bank account.
請儘速匯款至我方銀行帳戶。

Please submit payment through your usual account.
請用您慣用的帳戶匯款給我們。

You can transfer the funds to the Bank of Taiwan.
您可以匯款到台灣銀行。

You can pay by company check.
您可以用公司支票付款。

You could transfer the payment to our bank account.
您可以匯款到我們的銀行帳戶。

We hope to hear from you soon with a remittance.
我們希望儘快收到您的已匯款通知。

We look forward to receiving your remittance within five days.
我們希望在五天內收到您的匯款。

We believe you will send the remittance soon.
我們相信您會儘快匯款。

Please do it without any delay.
請勿有任何延遲。

With invoice No.2456, please make full payment as soon as possible.
參照2456號發票，請儘速付清款項。

Part 1
Part 2
Part 3
Part 4
Part 5
Part 6

Please make remittance within the period agreed.
🖊 請在規定時間內付款。

All orders will be shipped upon receiving the remittance.
🖊 確認匯款後，產品隨即寄出。

 澄清各項疑問

We would like to know when you will settle the balance of $5,000.
🖊 我方想要知道您何時可以付清五千美元的餘款。

Please make sure if you can meet the deadline, and if you cannot, please contact us.
🖊 請確認您是否能準時付款，如果不行，請告知我方。

If there are other reasons we should know, please inform us.
🖊 如果有其他原因，請通知我們。

As always, please contact me if you have any concerns.
🖊 一如往常，若有任何問題，請隨時與我聯絡。

If you have any queries unresolved regarding the invoice, please let us know.
🖊 如果您對帳單有任何疑問，請讓我們知道。

 進階補充站 Let's learn more!

 實用資訊Focus

面對欠款（Overdue Payments）🔍

　　在商務交易的過程中，難免會遇到沒有準時繳納的款項，這個時候，就必須以催款信提醒對方。不過，催款當然還是能避則避，因此，在合作時，可注意以下的情況：

1. 在報價時，除了商品價格之外，若延遲繳款有酌收的費用，請與對方說清楚。
2. 確定付款條件清楚，若是初次合作的客戶，可將付款時間縮短一些。
3. 調查對方的信用程度（credit checks）。
4. 確保給對方的發票準時寄送，並追蹤發票是否已順利寄達。

Part 1

Part 2

Part 3

Part 4

Part 5

Part 6

• 5-08 • 第二次催款信

當提醒已經發給對方，卻依然沒有回應時，就必須再次催促對方付款。在第二次的催款信中，語氣可以稍微強烈些，並可於信末加上「如果您已經付款，請忽略此信件」等類的敘述，會比較恰當。

Subject **2nd Payment Reminder (Order No.991AL110)**

Dear Mr. Chen:

Two weeks ago, we have **reminded**[1] you of the outstanding balance of $5,000. **So far**[2], we still have not received your check.

Please let us have your payment as soon as possible and give an **explanation**[3] of why the invoice is still outstanding.

If you have sent the payment, please **ignore**[4] this mail.

Best regards,
Terry

陳先生您好：

二週前我們已經提醒您有關尚未付清的餘額五千元。截至目前，我們尚未收到您的支票。

請儘速付款，並告知延遲的原因。

如果您已經付款，請忽略此信件。

泰瑞 謹上

Send ▶

核心字彙充電站 *Key Words*

1. remind 動 提醒

2. so far 片 到目前為止

3. explanation 名 解釋

4. ignore 動 忽略

替換好用句 Copy & Paste

點出尚未結清的款項

Referring to our mail two weeks ago, in which we drew your attention that our May statement for $2,000 was still overdue.

關於我們兩週前的去函，是想要提醒您五月份的結算單二千元尚未結清。

This is the second mail regarding your account which has not been cleared.

這第二封信是有關您尚未付款的事項。

I am writing to you again to remind you that the balance still outstanding is $3,300.

再次提醒您：帳單仍積欠三千三百元。

In our last mail, we have reminded you about your unpaid account.

我們在上封郵件提及您未繳的款項。

We have written to you on May 1 concerning our April statement which is still outstanding.

我們已於五月一日寫信通知您：四月份的結算金額尚未繳清。

On April 4, we wrote to alert you that we had not received the payment for your order.

我們已於四月四日通知您：本公司尚未收到您訂單的款項。

We are still waiting your payment for order number 5287-1.

我們仍在等候5287-1號訂單的結款。

針對款項溝通

Your previous payment record shows your sincerity to keep your account up-to-date.

您先前的付款紀錄顯示，您總是很有付清帳款的誠意。

We therefore assume something has happened to make it difficult to make your payment.

於是我們猜測可能發生了什麼讓您無法付款的事。

Please let us know what happened and perhaps we can suggest a

solution.
🖉 請知會我們，也許我們能提供解決方法。

We don't know what might be causing the delay in payment.
🖉 我們不清楚導致延遲付款的原因。

If you would like to discuss other payment options, we would be happy to oblige.
🖉 如果您想要討論其他的付款方式，我們很樂意配合。

We would like to provide the best service to our customers under all circumstances.
🖉 我們無論如何都希望能夠提供客戶最好的服務。

If you have any difficulties, please let us know.
🖉 如果您有任何困難，請告知我方。

We have not pressed for the payment as you have a good record.
🖉 由於您的良好紀錄，我們從未催討款項。

Twenty days have passed; we still have not received your reply.
🖉 二十天已過，我們仍未收到您的回覆。

If there is some special reasons for the delay in payment, we would welcome an explanation.
🖉 如果此延遲付款有任何特殊原因，我們很樂意了解。

We hope you will not withhold the settlement any longer.
🖉 希望您不要再延遲付款。

In your reply to my mail, you promised you would clear the account yesterday.
🖉 您在回函中承諾昨日要結清帳款。

Please let us have your payment by April 13.
🖉 請於四月十三日前付款。

Please let us have your check to clear the amount.
🖉 請寄支票來結清帳款。

Part 1
Part 2
Part 3
Part 4
Part 5
Part 6

5-09 第三次催款信

第三封催款信，態度須更為強烈，告知對方經多次催詢仍無回應，甚至可提及將採取法律行動。但還是要提醒對方仍有妥協機會，請對方務必表達誠意。

Subject Notice to Pay (Order No.991AL110)

Dear Mr. Chen:

We have reminded you of the outstanding balance by many mails, but have not received any reply or remittance from you.

If we do not receive your response within the next three days, we will have to hand this matter to our lawyers. We would be very sorry for taking such legal action after a long connection with your company. We sincerely hope this will not become necessary.

Best regards,
Terry

陳先生您好：

我們已多次寫信通知您未付清款項，但仍未收到您任何的回應。

三天內若仍沒接到任何回應，我們會將此事交由律師處理。雙方都已合作好長一段時間，採取法律行動的作法讓我們感到非常遺憾。真心希望不會發生這種事。

泰瑞 謹上

Send

替換好用句 Copy & Paste

對方遲遲不予回應

We have sent you our statement for your May account twice.
🖉 我們已寄給您兩次五月份的結算單。

We are unhappy that we still have had no reply from you.
🖉 您遲遲未回覆的態度讓我們很不高興。

Neither a reply nor the remittance from you is received.
🖉 我方未收到您的回覆或是款項。

We have written you two mails to ask you to clear the balance.
🖉 我們已經寫了兩封信請求您繳清餘款。

We have not received any replies to our previous mails of 1 and 8 May for payment.
🖉 我們在五月一號和八號寄出繳款郵件，但我方仍未收到任何回覆。

You still owed us the sum of 5,000 pounds in payment of the invoice No.55564.
🖉 發票55564號的帳款，您仍然欠我方五千英鎊。

Your balance of $1,550 for order No.22569 is now more than forty-five days overdue.
🖉 您22569號訂單的款項已經逾期四十五天。

You have not responded to our earlier mails about the overdue settlement.
🖉 您仍未回覆我方先前有關逾期帳款的信件。

We have made several attempts to contact you by telephone to remind you of the payment.
🖉 我們已多次去電，試圖提醒您付款事宜。

Please give us an explanation or settle your account ASAP.
🖉 請馬上告知您未付款的原因，或盡速付款。

We trust your credit and reputation are still good.
🖉 我們相信您的信用及聲譽依然良好。

We always esteem you as a reliable customer.
🖉 我們一直認為您是可靠的客戶。

You are not only an important customer, but also a friend of ours.
🖉 您不只是一位重要客戶，更是我方的朋友。

Please don't be silent anymore.
🖉 請勿再沉默。

Please understand it's a serious situation.
🖉 請了解這件事的嚴重性。

Please try your best to settle this matter urgently.
🖉 請您儘速解決問題。

Part 1
Part 2
Part 3
Part 4
Part 5
Part 6

The amount is seriously delinquent.

🖊 這筆款項已經嚴重拖欠。

Our records show you have always delayed the payment during this year.

🖊 我們的紀錄顯示，您今年總是延遲支付貨款。

Attached you will find the original invoice details as well as the previous reminders.

🖊 詳見附件內容，為原發票以及前幾封通知信。

 要求對方回應或解釋

We are disappointed that we have not received any response from you.

🖊 我們很失望尚未接到您的任何回覆。

We hope you would at least explain why the account continues to be unpaid.

🖊 我們希望您至少可以解釋未付款的原因。

Please offer an explanation for the delayed payment.

🖊 請您告知延遲付款的原因。

Unless the explanation is satisfactory, we would not allow the amount to remain unpaid.

🖊 除非有合理解釋，否則我方無法允許帳款賒欠。

We believe that the goods we shipped to you were satisfactory and our records are in order.

🖊 我們相信寄去的貨品令您滿意，而本公司的紀錄也無誤。

If there is any problem with the shipment or the invoice, please contact us as soon as possible.

🖊 如果貨運或發票有任何問題，請儘早通知我方。

If there is not any problem with the goods, you must pay the account in full immediately.

🖊 如果貨品沒有問題，請您立即付清款項。

You are given enough time to clear the balance.

🖊 您已獲得足夠的付款時間。

We insist on payment with the next three days.

🖉 我們堅持此款項必須在三天內結清。

🧩 強硬的口吻與處理

Since you have not paid, we will have to cancel your order.
🖉 由於您未付款，因此我方必須取消訂單。

This is the third and final notice for the payment.
🖉 這是第三封，也是最後一封催款通知。

We will be compelled to take legal actions unless we receive you remittance the next three days.
🖉 如果三天內未收到匯款，我方會採取法律行動。

We are willing to overlook this delinquency if you can settle the account by May 10.
🖉 如果您於五月十日前付款，我方將不予以追究本次逾期。

Please do not delay any longer in contacting us.
🖉 請立即與我方聯絡，勿再拖延。

Please be informed that our legal department intends to file a lawsuit against you to collect payment of invoice No.552.
🖉 此信通知您：我方法務部門將訴諸法律，收取發票552號的款項。

Unless we receive your check for $4,500, your account will be placed in the hands of our attorneys for collection.
🖉 除非我們收到您四千五百元的支票，否則該筆款項將交由我方律師託收。

Your failing payment by December 31 will leave us no choice but to place the matter in other hands.
🖉 如果您沒有在十二月三十一日前付款，我們只好採取其他途徑。

We have no choice but to turn the matter over to our lawyer.
🖉 因為我方沒有其他選擇，所以只好將此事交由律師處理。

We feel that we have shown our patience and treated you with consideration.
🖉 我方認為我們已經很有耐心，也考量過您的立場。

We hesitate to do this currently.
🖉 我們現在猶豫是否要這麼做。

You should know if we take legal actions, it will damage your standing in the community.

Part 1
Part 2
Part 3
Part 4
Part 5
Part 6

✏ 您應該知道，如果我方採取法律行動，會傷害您在本區的聲譽。

We hope you will send us the full settlement by May 20.
✏ 我們希望您能在五月二十日前付清款項。

After the date, we will proceed with the further action I have mentioned.
✏ 過了此日期，我們會採取以上行動。

We will hand this matter to our lawyer.
✏ 我們會交由律師處理此事。

We are prepared to give you a further opportunity.
✏ 我方仍希望再給您一次機會。

Please give the matter your immediate attention.
✏ 請立即關照此事。

The legal action will damage your credit standing.
✏ 法律訴訟必會損害您的信譽。

Please telephone me and make an effort to show that you are willing to meet obligations.
✏ 請致電予我，並請展現最大誠意表示您願意付款。

We sincerely hope we can avoid the unpleasantness of taking legal actions.
✏ 我們衷心希望能夠避免令人不快的法律途徑。

If you still keep silent, the next mail you receive will be from our lawyer.
✏ 要是您仍保持沉默，將會交由我方律師寄下一封通知給您。

We must regrettably inform you that your invoice No.552 has been forwarded to our collection agency.
✏ 我們很遺憾在此通知您：552號發票的請款書已交給我們的債務公司了。

The matter of your overdue account has been turned to a collection agency.
✏ 您逾期繳款一事，已交由我們的收帳公司處理。

We regret to take legal actions to recover payment.
✏ 我們對於接下來要訴諸法律強制償付的行動感到遺憾。

We have to take this case to court.
✏ 我們會訴諸法院。

We hope such unpleasant condition can be avoided.
🖉 我們希望能避免不愉快。

If we take legal actions, you may be liable for the legal expenses.
🖉 如果我們訴諸法律，您可能還必須負擔訴訟費用。

To preserve your credit standing, won't you please settle your payment within the next three days?
🖉 為確保您的信用，可否請您於三天內付清款項？

The decision is yours.
🖉 決定權在您。

We are writing to you in a final effort to ask you to clear your account.
🖉 我們盡了最後的努力要求您付款。

Please help us to avoid other legal actions.
🖉 請勿讓我方採取任何法律行動。

We regret that we will have to inform our attorney if the payment is not made right away.
🖉 如果沒有立即收到款項，我們就必須通知律師。

 進階補充站 Let's learn more!

 單字/片語Focus

💘 法律訴訟管道 💘

✲**owe** 欠債；欠錢	✲**render** 呈報；匯報
✲**delinquent** 到期未付的	✲**delinquency** 違法行為
✲**attorney** 律師；法定代理人	✲**litigation** 訴訟；爭訟
✲**defendant** 被告	✲**summon** 傳喚
✲**arrest** 逮捕	✲**prosecution** 起訴
✲**appeal** 上訴	✲**retrial** 再審
✲**mediation mechanism** 調解程序	

Part 1

Part 2

Part 3

Part 4

Part 5

Part 6

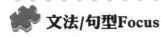 **文法/句型Focus**

✻ 在兩者中選擇

both...and... …和… （兩者皆是）

...as well as... …和… （兩者皆是）

not only...but also... 不僅是…同時也是… (兩者皆包含)

either...or... … 不是…就是… （二者選一）

not...but... 不是…而是… （兩者中的一個）

neither...nor... 既不…也不… （二者皆非）

✻ 訴諸法律

❶ **take legal actions** (**against**+人；**on/over**+事)
They decided to take legal actions against their neighbor.
他們決定對鄰居採取法律途徑。

❷ **sb. file a lawsuit** 提出訴訟
If you still don't pay the bills, we will file a lawsuit.
若你還是不付款，我們就會提出訴訟。

❸ **sth. be brought to a lawsuit** 被提出訴訟
The case will be brought to a lawsuit since neither of them compromised.
因為雙方都不妥協，所以這件案子將被提出訴訟。

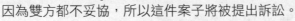

Part 1

Part 2

Part 3

Part 4

Part 5

Part 6

·5-10· 匯款延遲致歉

撰寫道歉信件時態度務必誠懇。另外，直接誠懇的道歉會比絮絮叨叨找一堆理由搪塞來得有效，切勿拐彎抹角。

Subject　Re: Payment Reminder (Order No.991)

Dear Mr. Chang:

We have received your mail informing us that we have not cleared the balance. Upon checking the cause of the delay, we found it had not been paid due to an **oversight**[1] on our part.

We have sent our check for $1,500 this morning. It will reach you within two days. We are very sorry to **keep you waiting**[2]. Please **accept**[3] our sincerest apology for any inconvenience this matter has caused you.

We hope you will **realize**[4] that we have no intention to delay the payment.

Best regards,
Victor

張先生您好：

我們已收到您通知我方未付清帳款的郵件。經過調查後，發現是我方的疏失。

我們已經於今早寄出一千五百元的支票，您會在兩天內收到。很抱歉讓您久等，造成您的不便，請接受我方誠摯的道歉。

希望您能了解我們並沒有故意要延遲付款。

維克多 敬上

Send ▸

Subject　Apologies for Delayed Payment (Order No.991)

Dear Mr. Chen:

Due to the economic **downturn**[5], our sale of the books has **dropped**[6]. We are very

陳先生您好：

由於經濟蕭條，因而造成我方書籍的銷售量驟減。

sorry for the 5-day late payment. However, we still hope you can understand our situation.

We ensure that you will receive the remittance on time in the future. Thanks again for your understanding.

Best regards,
Betty

非常抱歉我們逾期了五天才支付款項。然而，我們仍希望您能了解我方立場。

我們保證您之後都會準時收到款項。再次謝謝您的諒解。

貝蒂 敬上

Send ▶

核心字彙充電站 *Key Words*

1. **oversight** 名 失察；疏忽出錯
2. **keep sb. waiting** 片 讓某人等待
3. **accept** 動 接受；領受
4. **realize** 動 了解；認識到
5. **downturn** 名 衰退；下降
6. **drop** 動 下降；降低

替換好用句 *Copy & Paste*

 致歉與承認疏失

I am replying your mail of May 20 requiring us to settle our payment due on May 1st.
🖋 此函回覆您五月二十日要求我們付清五月一日款項的郵件。

We found that we made an oversight in sending the check to you.
🖋 我方發現在寄送支票上有所疏失。

Let me apologize for not having settling the account first.
🖋 有關尚未付款一事，請先接受我的道歉。

We checked our records immediately after receiving your mail.
🖋 收到您的信件後，我們立即查看了紀錄。

We are sorry we have not yet cleared the statement for $5,000.
很抱歉我們尚未付清五千元的帳款。

The remittance procedures took longer than we expected.
匯款程序的所需時間比我們想像的還要長。

We were surprised to receive your mail in which you mentioned that you had not received our check.
我們很訝異您來信提及未收到支票的事。

Our check was posted to you on November 3.
我們已於十一月三日那天將支票寄給您。

You should be able to confirm the receipt of the money in your account on April 6.
您應該會於四月六日收到帳款。

We will correct the mistake.
我們會馬上更正錯誤。

We are sure the remittance should be arrived tomorrow.
我們保證您明天會收到款項。

I have checked our records and found our oversight.
我已檢查我方紀錄,發現是我們漏看了。

We have asked our accountant to settle the account to you.
我們已請會計師付款給您。

We have asked our accountant for an immediate payment of the amount to you.
我們已要求會計儘速付款給您。

Our overdue payment will be remitted to your account today.
我方逾期未繳的款項將於今天匯入您的戶頭。

We have posted a check for $5,000 by registered mail.
我們已經用掛號寄出五千元的支票。

We will try our best to send you either the whole or part of the amount before June 20.
我們會盡力在六月二十日前寄出部分、或全部貨款。

Part 1

Part 2

Part 3

Part 4

Part 5

Part 6

 **先前已付款**

We are afraid that the check might be astray.
✎ 恐怕支票已經遺失。

We have instructed our bank not to pay on the check.
✎ 我方已指示銀行申請止付。

A replacement check will be sent to you soon.
✎ 我們會儘速寄出另一張支票給您。

Our book shows that we have paid you $2,500 by bank remittance on May 20.
✎ 我方帳目顯示：我們已於五月二十日由銀行匯款兩千五百元給您。

We have instructed our bank to remit the balance some time ago.
✎ 我們先前已指示銀行匯寄餘額的款項。

We will fax you a copy of appliance sheet of remittance.
✎ 我們會傳真銀行提交的匯本申請單影本給您。

We don't understand why you haven't received our remittance until now.
✎ 我方不明白為何您目前仍未收到匯款。

Maybe the bank has not advised you yet.
✎ 也許銀行尚未通知您。

Please check with your bank.
✎ 請向您的銀行確認。

 說明延遲的原因

Please allow me to explain the reason for our overdue payment.
✎ 請讓我簡單說明延遲付款的原因。

Our accountant was sick last week, so that was the reason we were unable to settle the account.
✎ 我們的會計師上週生病，因此無法付款。

As I was sick and absent from the office, it is my failure to leave instructions to pay the account.
✎ 因為我生病請假，未交代要支付這份帳單，這是我的疏失。

One of our customers went bankrupt; therefore, we are facing the financial problem now.
🖊 我們的客戶破產，因此我方目前正遭遇財務困難。

We have experienced a serious of non-payments by our suppliers.
🖊 我方面臨供應商均未付款的嚴重問題。

Would you please give us another week to settle the account?
🖊 可否請您再給我們一週的寬限時間呢？

We would appreciate if you will give us a little more time to settle the account.
🖊 您若能再多給我們一點時間清償款項，我方會感激不已。

 結尾用語

Please be patient to wait until next Monday for the payment.
🖊 請耐心等待於下週一收到款項。

Your patience is highly appreciated.
🖊 感謝您的耐心。

We are deeply sorry for not clearing the account sooner.
🖊 我方對拖延帳款深感抱歉。

Please let us know if there is any problem.
🖊 若有任何問題，請與我方聯絡。

 Let's learn more!

 單字/片語Focus

🎀 常見的郵件種類 🎀	
＊postcard 明信片	**＊printed matter** 印刷品
＊air mail 航空信	**＊ordinary mail** 平信
＊prompt delivery 限時專送	**＊registered letter** 掛號信
＊prompt registered letter 限時掛號信	

Part 1
Part 2
Part 3
Part 4
Part 5
Part 6

Unit 6 出貨、反應瑕疵商品

· 6-01 · 出貨通知

出貨通知上需要告知欲讓收件人得知的訊息，如訂單號碼、貨品名稱、數量、到達時間以及到達港口等。

Subject | **Shipment (Order No.12553)**

Dear Mr. Hu:

We have shipped your order No.12553 this morning. They will arrive at Taipei on the 20th at 5:00 p.m. If you have any questions, please let me know as soon as possible.

Thank you for doing business with our company.

Best regards,
Bella

胡先生您好：

我們已於今早寄出您的12553號訂單商品，該批貨物將於二十號下午五點抵達台
北。若您有任何問題，請儘早告知。

感謝您與本公司交易。

貝拉 敬上

Send ▶

替換好用句 *Copy & Paste*

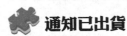 通知已出貨

Please note that your order has been dispatched this morning.
🖉 您的訂單今早已出貨。

Your order No.335 has now been shipped by Evergreen Shipping Co. Ltd. sailing on May 20 from Kaohsiung to Edinburgh.

🖊️ 您的335號訂單已由長榮海運自高雄運至愛丁堡。

This is as a notification of shipment.
🖊️ 此為出貨通知。

The method of shipment was Federal Express.
🖊️ 貨品經由聯邦快遞寄出。

Your shipment's tracking number is N2255410003.
🖊️ 您的貨品追蹤號碼為N2255410003。

We have sent you the shipping documents by air.
🖊️ 我們已經用空運寄出貨運資料。

As you requested, we have shipped your order by air on May 20.
🖊️ 如您要求，我們已於五月二十日用空運寄出您的貨品。

We shipped the following items on November 20, 2016.
🖊️ 我們已於二〇一六年十一月二十日寄出下列物品。

 ## 到貨時間

The estimated arrival time for your order is June 15.
🖊️ 您估計會於六月十五日收到貨品。

Your item will be taken to the port tomorrow afternoon.
🖊️ 您的貨品會在明日下午送至港口。

Delivery of goods will be arrived to the address with five to seven working days.
🖊️ 貨品需要五至七個工作天到達您指定的地點。

Shipping from London to Taiwan takes an average of two weeks.
🖊️ 從倫敦到台灣的運送時間約為兩週。

You will receive your goods by the end of January.
🖊️ 您將於一月底收到貨品。

You will receive your order within three working days.
🖊️ 您會在三個工作天內收到貨品。

We assure you to receive your goods on the expected time.
🖊️ 我們確保您會在預估時間內收到貨品。

Part 1
Part 2
Part 3
Part 4
Part 5
Part 6

 **貨品處理**

As you requested, we have wrapped your fragile items in bubble wrap.
🖊 根據您的指示，您的易碎物品已用氣泡紙包裝。

We have faxed you the relevant shipping information.
🖊 我們已傳真相關運送資訊給您了。

We would appreciate confirmation when the shipment has safely reached port.
🖊 貨品到港後請告知我們。

Please inform us as they are arrived.
🖊 收到貨品後請告知我們。

We believe your consignment will arrive safely.
🖊 我們相信貨品會安全抵達。

 Let's learn more!

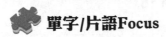 **單字/片語Focus**

✎ 貨運常見單字 ✎	
✱airway bill; AWB 空運提單	✱arrival notice 到貨通知
✱B/L（Bill of Lading） 託運單	✱carrier 海空運業者
✱consignee 收件人	✱L/C（Letter of Credit） 信用狀
✱gross weight 毛重	✱net weight 淨重
✱packing list 包裝明細	✱pre-alert 出貨通知
✱export declaration 出口報單	✱import declaration 進口報單

Part 1
Part 2
Part 3
Part 4
Part 5
Part 6

·6-02· 確認到貨

通知對方到貨狀況，內容可包括訂單號碼、時間日期、產品名稱等資訊，可於「確認到貨」的信件中再次確認。

Subject Re: Shipment (Order No.12553)

Dear Bella:

Your shipment No.12553 has arrived at Taichung Port yesterday. Thank you for the speed with which you delivered our items on time. Those items were **urgently**[1] needed in order to **dispatch**[2] to our **customers**[3] by the end of May.

As agreed, we will settle the bill **immediately**[4] and we look forward to doing further business with you soon.

Best regards,
Howard Hu

貝拉您好：

運送號12553的貨品已於昨日抵達台中港。感謝您的快速寄送，我們非常需要在五月底前寄送此批貨物給客戶。

如之前談好的協議，我們會立即付款，並希望再度與您合作。

胡霍華 敬上

Send

核心字彙充電站 Key Words

1. **urgently** 副 緊急地；急迫地
2. **dispatch** 動 發送；快遞
3. **customer** 名 顧客
4. **immediately** 副 立即；馬上

替換好用句 Copy & Paste

Our order was received on March 2.
🖉 我們已於三月二日收到貨品。

This is to advise you that our order has arrived at Taichung Port this morning.
🖉 謹告知：我方貨品已於今早抵達台中港。

We are pleased to report that our goods have arrived safely at Tokyo Port.
🖉 很開心通知您：我們的貨品已安全抵達東京港。

Thank you for expediting our order.
🖉 謝謝您快速處理我們的訂單。

We were able to meet our production schedule due to the punctual arrival of our order.
🖉 貨物如期抵達，使我們能趕上生產進度。

Those materials are needed urgently to make sure of our production.
🖉 我們極需這些材料，以確保生產線順暢。

Thank you for the shipment.
🖉 謝謝您的出貨。

 進階補充站　Let's learn more!

 單字/片語Focus

💥 運送至碼頭 💥

✱**destination** 目的地	✱**dock** 碼頭
✱**port** 港口	✱**waterway** 水路；航道
✱**barge** 用駁船運載	✱**vessel** 船；艦
✱**on board** 在船上	✱**cargo** 裝載的貨物
✱**load** 裝；裝載	✱**unload** 卸貨
✱**container** 貨櫃	✱**pallet** 貨板
✱**ETA = estimated time of arrival** 預計抵達時間	

Part 1
Part 2
Part 3
Part 4
Part 5
Part 6

·6-03· 延遲出貨抱怨

抱怨出貨延遲時，記得在信中寫明應該收貨的時間，並具體告知對方目前尚未收到貨品，強調希望對方能夠儘速採取行動，並請對方交代延遲的原因。

Subject **Delay in Delivery**

Dear Mr. Hu:

The goods we ordered **were supposed to**[1] arrive on July 10. However, we have not received them as of July 16. Would you kindly explain what is going on?

The **delay**[2] causes us great inconvenience, since we have **promised**[3] our customer early delivery. Please take this as an urgent matter.

We look forward to a **rapid**[4] reply.

Best regards,
Bella

胡先生您好：

我們訂的商品預定七月十日到貨。然而，截至七月十六日，我們仍未收到貨品，您可以解釋原因嗎？

我們已向客戶保證貨物會提前運送，因此，這樣的延遲造成我們極大的不便，請務必緊急處理此事。

期盼您儘速回覆。

貝拉 謹上

Send

核心字彙充電站 *Key Words*

1. be supposed to 片 應該；應當
2. promise 動 承諾；答應
2. delay 名 延遲；延誤
4. rapid 形 快的；迅速的

替換好用句 *Copy & Paste*

The merchandise was supposed to be delivered by the end of April.
✎ 這批貨品應於四月底前寄送。

According to the terms, the items should be delivered no later than September 25.
✎ 根據合約條款，貨品應該在九月二十五日前寄出。

Contrary to your notice, the shipment of our order has not arrived yet.
✎ 儘管收到您的通知，但這些貨品仍尚未送達。

We have not received any notification that you have shipped our order.
✎ 我們尚未收到任何寄出貨品的通知。

Unless the order is arrived within five days, we shall have to cancel the order.
✎ 如貨物五天內未寄達，我們將會取消訂單。

As agreed, the punctual shipment was very important because we need to deliver them to our customers at promised time.
✎ 按雙方同意，準確的送達時間對我們承諾客戶的送貨時間很重要。

As your delivery is very attractive, we made this order with you.
✎ 因貴公司的送貨條件吸引人，我們才予以下單。

We have waited for one month for shipment of these goods.
✎ 我們已等待此批貨物一個月了。

We cannot delay supplying our dealers with these products.
✎ 我們無法延遲對經銷商的出貨。

We must supply those goods to our dealers by this Friday.
✎ 我們必須在週五前出貨給經銷商。

Could you please investigate the reason for delay immediately?
✎ 可否請您立即調查延遲出貨的原因？

As we are running out the raw materials, those items we ordered are urgently needed.
✎ 由於原物料已經耗盡，所以我們極需這批貨物。

If you haven't shipped them yet, we hope you can expedite your shipment by air.
如果貨物尚未寄出，我們希望您以急件空運寄送。

The delay will affect our reputation and sales.
延遲出貨會影響我們的聲譽以及銷售。

It will cause us losing some customers.
延遲出貨會造成我方流失客戶。

As the goods have not been delivered, we must ask you to ship them without any delay.
貨物如尚未寄出，請您盡速寄出，勿再有延遲。

Please do everything possible to ensure a punctual shipment.
請盡力確保準時出貨。

We are awaiting your reply and please specify a new delivery date.
請告知結果，並確定新的寄送時間。

Please inform us by return when you can ship them with certainty.
請回信告知確定的出貨時間。

Please respond this issue as soon as possible.
請儘速回覆此問題。

 Let's learn more!

 文法/句型Focus

✱ 表「拖延」的單字比較

❶ **postpone / put off** 延期到某一特定時間（後者較口語）。

❷ **delay** 多指因外界因素而延遲或耽誤。

❸ **suspend** 暫時中斷，待符合某種條件後繼續（例如：暫時被吊銷駕照）。

❹ **prolong** 把時間延長，超過正常的限度。

有關延遲貨運的問題，應該要一收到對方的通知就立刻調查原因，並在釐清原因後迅速回覆，以表誠意。回信時，詳細說明延遲的原因，誠懇地致歉，並提供解決方式，避免麻煩對方再度來信詢問。

Subject **Apology for Late Delivery**

Dear Bella:

We apologize deeply for the delay in shipment. **Due to**[1] **peak season**[2], it is very difficult for us to **process**[3] your order in time.

However, we have packed your goods and are ready to send them this afternoon. We **assure**[4] that you will receive them this Friday.

We sincerely apologize for the inconvenience. Thank you very much for your consideration.

Best regards,
Howard Hu

貝拉您好：

我們對於延遲出貨深感抱歉。目前正值業務巔峰時期，所以我們很難及時處理您的訂單。

然而，我們已替您包裝好貨品，並準備於今天下午寄出。我們保證您會在本週五收到。

造成不便之處，我們深感抱歉，並感謝您的諒解。

胡霍華 敬上

Send ▶

🔌 核心字彙充電站 *Key Words*

1. due to 片 因為
2. peak season 片 巔峰時期
3. process 動 處理
4. assure 動 擔保；保證

 替換好用句 *Copy & Paste*

表達歉意

We would like to apologize for the delay in shipping your merchandise.
🖊 我方很抱歉延遲運送您的貨品。

We are sorry for this unfortunate delay of shipment.
🖊 我們對於延遲出貨感到抱歉。

We are very sorry for delaying shipping your goods.
🖊 我們很抱歉延遲運送您的貨品。

We appreciate you for bringing this matter to our attention.
🖊 感謝您提醒我方此事。

We will find out the reason and report to you as soon as possible.
🖊 我方會追查原因,並儘速回報您。

說明延遲的原因

Due to the occupied production, it is impossible for us to produce the products in time.
🖊 由於生產線繁忙,我們無法及時生產貨品。

Due to the bad weather, we cannot deliver the items to you.
🖊 由於天候不佳,我們無法寄送物品。

Due to the typhoon warning, we are afraid the shipment will be delayed.
🖊 由於颱風警報,我們恐怕得延遲出貨。

Due to the sudden overwhelming orders, our present inventory has been depleted.
🖊 由於突如其來的大量訂單,現在存貨告罄。

Due to a shortage of raw materials, we cannot fill your order now.
🖊 由於原物料缺乏,我們現在無法處理您的訂單。

Due to a great shortage of shipping space, we are afraid we cannot

Part 1
Part 2
Part 3
Part 4
Part 5
Part 6

ship the goods on time.
🖊 由於貨運空間不足，我們恐怕無法準時出貨。

Due to a sudden blackout, it causes delays on our production.
🖊 由於突然停電，導致生產線停擺。

Due to a serious machine breakdown, the factory is closing currently.
🖊 由於機器故障，工廠目前關閉。

Due to the unexpected fire at our plant, our materials have been destroyed.
🖊 由於工廠發生火災，我們的原料全毀。

Due to high demand of this model, we are out of stock now.
🖊 由於此商品熱銷，目前無庫存。

Due to the strike of the shipping company, the goods are still on board.
🖊 由於船運公司罷工，貨品目前都還在船上。

We found our shipping department made some mistakes and has delayed several shipments, including yours.
🖊 我們發現運送部門出了一些差錯，因此造成您與其他顧客的出貨延遲。

The political situation in the Middle East has forced our suppliers to go out of business.
🖊 由於中東地區的政治因素，使得我方的供應商結束營業。

As the traffic flow is very slow, the driver told us that he cannot make the goods to you on time.
🖊 貨運司機告知：由於交通堵塞，貨品無法準時送達。

 保證與解決問題

We will send your order as soon as possible.
🖊 我們會儘快出貨。

We will ship the products within one week without fail.
🖊 我們保證會在一週內出貨。

We have arranged another shipping company to deliver your order immediately.
🖊 我們已另外安排其他貨運公司，馬上替您送貨。

We are trying to remedy this situation as quickly as possible.
✎ 我們正設法盡速解決此問題。

We will try to make our efforts to deliver the goods by the first direct vessel tomorrow morning.
✎ 我們會盡力將貨品裝運上明天最早的直達船班。

We are sure you will receive the goods tomorrow.
✎ 我們確定您明天會收到產品。

 強調致歉的誠意

Please accept our deepest apology for the inconvenience.
✎ 對此不便，請接受我們最誠摯的道歉。

We hope you will forgive our mistake.
✎ 尚祈原諒我方疏失。

I assure you that our company has a solid record of on-time deliveries.
✎ 我保證本公司一向交貨準時。

We hope the delay doesn't cause you too much inconvenience.
✎ 希望此次延遲沒有造成您太大的困擾。

We assure you that such delay won't happen again.
✎ 我們保證不會再發生這種延遲的狀況。

We look forward to receiving your agreement to this new delivery date.
✎ 我們希望您能同意新的交貨日期。

We look forward to having another opportunity to serve you again.
✎ 我們希望能有再次為您服務的機會。

Your understanding will be highly obliged.
✎ 非常感激您能諒解。

The further confirmation about the shipment will keep you informed.
✎ 我們會隨時告知您貨運的消息。

Part 1
Part 2
Part 3
Part 4
Part 5
Part 6

進階補充站 *Let's learn more!*

文法/句型Focus

＊ 表示原因與理由

❶ **Since /As ..., ...** 因為（某原因），所以…。

❷ **The reason (why)...is that...** …的原因是…。

❸ **Because of / On account of..., ...** 因為（某原因），所以…。

❹ **Due to / Owing to..., ...** 因為（某原因），所以…。
（to在此為介系詞）

 實用資訊Focus

🔍 賣方延遲交貨

　　在商務交易中，不按其交貨的情況經常發生。當賣方確實有交貨的困難時，應即時通知買方，請求買方同意延長交貨期。一般而言，遇到延遲交貨的情況，買方有兩種處理方式：

1. 當賣方的延遲交貨符合根本違反合約的情況時，買方得以撤銷合約。若賣方尚未交貨，買方可先提供對方一段合理的延遲時間，並聲明若賣方不在這段時間內交貨，買方將撤銷訂單。

2. 當延遲交貨的情況發生時，除了其他補償之外，買方還可以請求賠償。

　　上述兩種的方式，有其根本上的不同，撤銷合約／訂單只有在賣方根本違約的情況，才能行使；請求損害賠償則沒有這種限制。

Part 1
Part 2
Part 3
Part 4
Part 5
Part 6

• 6-05 • 抱怨瑕疵商品

在「抱怨商品內容」的信件中，清楚說明商品損壞的內容，或是拍照夾帶於電子郵件中讓對方看清楚。抱怨的態度要誠懇而堅定，並於信中告知希望得到的補償方式。

Subject **Damaged Goods (Order No.1553)**

Dear Mr. Tang:

We have received our order this morning. However, when we open the cases, there are several glasses broken even they are **wrapped**[1] **properly**[2] in **the bubble wrap**[3]. I believe that I am **entitled**[4] to a **replacement**[5].

Please let me know your solution on this **issue**[6].

Thank you for your prompt reply.

Best regards,
Mark Tsai

親愛的唐先生：

我們已於今早收到貨品。然而，當我們打開箱子時，發現有些玻璃杯儘管有用氣泡紙包起來，卻依然破碎了。我相信我有要求更換的權利。

請告知您的處理方式。

感謝您的立即回覆。

蔡馬克 謹上

Send

核心字彙充電站 *Key Words*

1. **wrap [+up/in]** 動 包；裹
2. **properly** 副 恰當地
3. **the bubble wrap** 片 氣泡紙
4. **entitle** 動 給…權力（或資格）
5. **replacement** 名 代替；取代
6. **issue** 名 問題；爭議

替換好用句 *Copy & Paste*

 抱怨商品損壞

Some goods are damaged due to improper packing.
🖊 有些貨品因為包裝不當而損壞。

- -

As you can see the attached photos, some goods are badly damaged when arrival.
🖊 如附件照片所示，部份商品到貨時已經損壞。

- -

Upon examination, we have found that some of the machines are severely damaged.
🖊 經檢查，我們發現有些機器受到嚴重損傷。

- -

It seems that the goods arrived in damaged condition.
🖊 有些商品似乎抵達時就損壞了。

- -

The container seemed to be stuck by a heavy object.
🖊 該箱貨物似乎曾遭重物撞擊。

- -

We found that about 20% of the package is broken.
🖊 我們發現近百分之二十的貨品包裝破損。

- -

When the cases were opened, some of the goods were soaked by rain.
🖊 開箱時，有些物品已被雨水浸濕。

- -

As the problem was due to your carelessness, we are not prepared to pay the freight charge.
🖊 由於是貴公司的疏失，因此我方不準備承擔運費。

- -

We will return the damaged goods and hope you would replace them immediately.
🖊 我方會將毀損的商品退回，並希望貴公司能儘速替換新品。

- -

We expect you to take these damaged goods back and replace them immediately.
🖊 我們希望您能取回毀損的貨品，並儘速置換。

- -

I would like to know if you will replace them or just refund the money to us.
🖊 我方想知道貴公司準備換貨還是退款。

- -

We would be grateful if you could replace the damaged goods within three days.

✎ 如果您能於三天內替換，我們將感激不盡。

Please send us the replaced items by air cargo as soon as possible.

✎ 請用空運迅速寄送替換品。

Please send us the new products as soon as possible.

✎ 請儘速寄來新產品換貨。

Please send the shortage without fail within one week.

✎ 請於一週內將不足的產品寄達。

 ## 抱怨商品數量、項目錯誤

Thank you for your promptness in shipping the goods we ordered.

✎ 謝謝您迅速寄來我們訂購的產品。

Please be informed that the quantity of the shipped goods do not correspond to the invoice.

✎ 貴公司寄來的貨品數量與出貨單不符。

The delivered goods are missing by fifty pieces.

✎ 貨品數量少了五十件。

The colors of the goods are dissimilar to your original sample.

✎ 產品的顏色與樣品不同。

The size of the women's shoes we received is not what we ordered.

✎ 女鞋尺寸與我們訂購的不符。

Upon opening the container yesterday, we found there were three cartons of products we didn't order.

✎ 開箱後，我們發現有三盒不在訂單內的貨品。

We found you sent us desk lamp No.225 instead of what we ordered: No.223.

✎ 我們發現你們寄送成225號桌燈，而非我們要的223型號。

Under the circumstance, we are forced to place orders from other suppliers immediately.

✎ 在此狀況下，我們只好馬上向其他供應商下單。

We are returning these items by parcel post for immediate

replacement.

🖋 我們將以包裹退還這些產品，並請您寄替換品給我們。

These extra goods will be held in our warehouse until you come to collect them.

🖋 多出來的貨品會保管在我們的倉庫裡，直到您的人員前來領回。

We would like to ask you to replace these items in correct size.

🖋 我們希望您能夠把這些商品換成正確尺寸。

 ## 抱怨品質不良

Our customers are very disappointed with their purchase.

🖋 我方客戶對於購買的產品很失望。

We have currently received many complaints from customers about your products.

🖋 我們最近收到很多客戶抱怨貴公司的產品。

Upon unpacking the cartons, we found the quality is far inferior to the approval sample.

🖋 打開包裝箱後，我方發現商品的品質遠低於樣品。

The products you shipped are much more inferior in quality to what we have expected.

🖋 您寄來的產品與我們預期的品質差距甚大。

The quality of the products is too inferior to meet the requirement for our consumers.

🖋 產品的品質太差，無法滿足消費者的需求。

Those products you sold us have caused numerous complaints.

🖋 您出售給我方的產品，已經引起許多抱怨。

Due to the dissatisfaction of our customers, we have to refund the purchase price on many of the products.

🖋 因為許多客戶的抱怨，我方必須把錢退還給他們。

We are writing to you that we are not satisfied with your goods.

🖋 此函是為了通知您：我方不滿意貴公司的商品。

You should control the quality of your products.

🖋 貴公司應該要管控品質。

Regarding your inferior quality of your goods, we claim a compensation of US$1,000.

🖊 針對貴公司的產品品質低劣，我們求償一千美元。

We are writing to complain about the quality of the goods supplied by you.

🖊 此函是要申訴您所提供的產品品質。

 ## 表明嚴重性

These damaged goods are unsalable.

🖊 這些損壞的貨品無法出售。

These goods are unusable.

🖊 這些產品無法使用。

Please check your factory for the cause.

🖊 請檢驗工廠以查明原因。

The damaged goods appear to have been mainly caused by the faulty packing.

🖊 很顯然，包裝出問題是造成損壞的主因。

We have requested you to pack the items individually.

🖊 我們已要求您個別包裝貨品。

Due to this situation, we have lost some of our best customers.

🖊 由於此狀況，我們已損失部分重要客戶。

We hope you could compensate us for the loss.

🖊 希望貴公司能夠賠償我方的損失。

I am afraid I will have to ask for a refund for this order.

🖊 我方恐怕將要求退款。

A reasonable compensation cannot be avoided.

🖊 我方必須向您要求合理的賠償。

We need to reduce our selling price by 10% for those damaged goods.

🖊 我們必須以九折賣出這些損壞貨品。

Please make us an allowance of 15% on the invoice cost.

🖊 請給予我們發票金額百分之十五的折扣。

Part 1
Part 2
Part 3
Part 4
Part 5
Part 6

Your defective goods will affect our promotion next week.
✎ 您的瑕疵商品會影響我們下週的促銷活動。

We are grateful if you would propose a settlement to solve the problem.
✎ 我方希望貴公司能夠解決問題。

We would be pleased if you will look into the matter immediately, and let us know the reason for the damage.
✎ 希望您能立即調查此事,並告知原因。

 提醒對方

Please make sure that you use cushions around the products.
✎ 請在產品周圍加上襯墊。

Please pay more attention to our instructions in the future.
✎ 請貴公司今後更加注意我方的指示。

The surveyors of our insurance company will investigate the extent of the damage.
✎ 保險公司的調查員會來調查損傷程度。

We will forward our report and the claim.
✎ 我們會提供調查表以及索賠內容。

The surveyor's report is attached herewith.
✎ 附上調查報告。

I would appreciate it if you can send a technician to fix the machine.
✎ 希望您能派一名維修人員來維修機器。

We hope you could take precautions to prevent a repetition of the damage.
✎ 我們希望您可以預防並避免重蹈覆轍。

We hope you will bear this in mind in handling our future shipment.
✎ 我們希望您能在未來處理貨品時謹記在心。

We hope you will be careful of packing for our next order.
✎ 希望您下次包裝時能小心。

Part 1
Part 2
Part 3
Part 4
Part 5
Part 6

·6-06· 針對抱怨致歉

回覆抱怨時，應該提供解決方式或替代方案，最好先不要做任何辯解，讓收信者感受到願意解決問題的誠意才是最重要的。

Subject Re: Damaged Goods (Order No.1553)

Dear Mr. Tsai:

Thank you for your letter regarding the **damaged**[1] goods arrived yesterday. We were very surprised to hear that some of the goods were damaged.

Replacement for those damaged goods has been dispatched to you this morning. Thank you for putting the damaged ones to one side for us. We will send our shipping driver to **bring them back**[2] next Monday.

We are now seeking the advice of a packing **consultant**[3] in order to **improve**[4] our **methods**[5] of **handling**[6]. We hope the steps we are taking will make sure the safe arrival of all your orders in the future.

Best regards,
Paul Tang

蔡先生您好：

謝謝您來函指出有關昨日寄達的貨品損壞，我們很訝異某些貨品損壞了。

今早，我們已寄出替換的物品。謝謝您暫時替我們保管損壞的物品。我們的貨運司機將於下週一去取回商品。

我們目前正在尋求包裝專家的建議，希望可加以改善我們的處理方式。希望我們採取的措施，能夠確保您未來的商品安全抵達。

唐保羅 敬上

Send

核心字彙充電站 Key Words

1. **damage** 動 損害；毀壞
2. **bring sth. back** 片 帶回；取回
3. **consultant** 名 顧問
4. **improve** 動 改善
5. **method** 名 方法；辦法
6. **handle** 動 處理；操作

替換好用句 _Copy & Paste_

 針對商品損壞致歉

We apologize for the damaged goods that you received this morning.
🖉 對於您收到損壞的商品，我們感到很抱歉。

Please accept our deepest apology for the unsatisfactory delivery this morning.
🖉 有關今早讓您不滿意的貨品，請接受我們誠摯的道歉。

We do apologize for damaging the products during the transportation.
🖉 我們對於運送途中損傷貨品感到抱歉。

We are very sorry that you have lost customers.
🖉 很抱歉您失去了客戶。

We apologize for the defective products.
🖉 對於本公司的瑕疵商品，我們感到很抱歉。

We will replace the merchandise free of charge.
🖉 我們會免費置換商品。

Please let us know when you want your alternative items to be delivered.
🖉 請告知您希望替代貨品送出的時間。

We accept full responsibility for the damaged vases.
🖉 本公司願意付起有關花瓶損壞的責任。

We are thoroughly investigating the matter and will contact you as we have some answers.
🖉 我們目前正在調查此事，一有結果便會與您聯絡。

We have checked with the Dispatch Section and they told us that the merchandise left here in perfect condition.
🖉 我們已與配送部門確認，物品送出時完好無缺。

We will send our technician to repair the machine.
🖉 我們會派維修人員去維修機器。

We have contacted with the shipping company, and asked them to explain how the goods were damaged.

✏ 我們已聯絡貨運公司，並請他們解釋損壞的原因。

We will ask the shipping company to arrange compensation.
✏ 我們會與貨運公司交涉賠償事宜。

The flood has caused our warehouse soak in the water.
✏ 洪水導致倉庫泡水。

It will not be necessary for you to return the damaged products.
✏ 損壞貨品毋需退回。

Those damaged goods may be destroyed.
✏ 這些損壞的貨品可被銷毀。

We would like to ask you to send those defective goods to us by airmail at our expense.
✏ 我方希望您能寄回該批瑕疵品，運費由我方支付。

We do not think we should be responsible for the claim.
✏ 我方不認為應該要承擔此次索賠。

We have passed your claim to the insurance company.
✏ 我們已將您的要求告知保險公司。

You should file your claim for the damage with the shipping company.
✏ 貴方應向貨運公司提出損壞賠償。

Your cooperation and patience in this matter are greatly appreciated.
✏ 謝謝您對此事的寬容與合作。

 針對數量、項目錯誤致歉

Thank you for bringing the error to our attention.
✏ 謝謝您告知我們這個問題。

We thank you for your mail in which you claimed the wrong size of the shoes.
✏ 感謝貴公司來函申訴鞋品尺寸不合。

Please accept our sincere apology for delivering ten instead of fifteen laser printers to you.
✏ 關於本公司應該寄送十五台、卻寄成十台雷射印表機這件事，我們深感抱歉。

We are sorry to find that the goods were sent to the wrong address

by our driver.

🖊 很抱歉，我們的貨運司機送錯地址了。

The mistake was caused by the oversight of our production department.

🖊 這是本公司生產部門的疏忽。

The women's dresses we have sent to you were the wrong size, and we are very sorry about that.

🖊 我們非常抱歉寄送錯誤尺寸的女性洋裝。

We are sorry for the short delivery of the items.

🖊 我們為商品短缺致歉。

This mistake occurred due to the staff shortage during the busy season.

🖊 因為正逢旺季、又遇上人手不足的狀況，而造成這個錯誤。

According to your order, the quantity should be twenty-five boxes of papers, not twenty.

🖊 根據您的訂單，您的數量應為二十五箱紙，而非二十箱。

We have just checked your order and realized we have sent you extra five boxes of toys.

🖊 我們檢查過您的訂單，發現多寄了五箱玩具給您。

We apologize for our mistake and sent the correct items to you this morning.

🖊 我們很抱歉，於是今早已經將正確商品寄給您。

Would you accept that we resupply the remaining items in the next shipment?

🖊 不知您可否接受下次出貨時補足其他貨品？

Tomorrow morning, we will send you the correct products at our expense.

🖊 我們明早會寄出正確的產品給您，運費將由我方負擔。

Your account will be credited with the invoiced value.

🖊 寄錯的產品款項將被刪除。

We hope to provide you with our usual quality service in the future.

🖊 本公司希望今後能再次提供您高品質的服務。

We are prepared to accept any claim.

🖊 我們準備接受貴公司求償。

We appreciate your business and value our relationship.
✎ 我們重視您的惠顧以及我們的良好關係。

 針對品質不良致歉

Thank you for your mail dated May 20, pointing out the faults in our goods supplied to you.
✎ 謝謝您五月二十日來信，告知我方提供給您的產品有瑕疵。

This problem has caused us a good deal of concern.
✎ 本事件已引起我方的注意。

We regret your dissatisfaction with our products.
✎ 我們很遺憾您不滿意我方的商品。

We are sorry our products do not live up to your expectations.
✎ 很抱歉，產品沒有達到您的要求。

Please send us the unsold goods.
✎ 請寄回未售出的產品。

The cost of postage will be reimbursed at our expense.
✎ 郵資將由我方承擔。

The faults have been traced back to one of the machines.
✎ 產生瑕疵的原因，是有一台機器出了問題。

We have passed the defective goods to our engineers for inspection.
✎ 我方已將有瑕疵的產品轉交給工程師檢查。

We will send the brand-new products right away.
✎ 我們會立刻寄出全新的產品。

We are confident that the replacement will make you satisfactory.
✎ 我們相信更換的產品會讓您滿意。

We will do our best to improve our quality of service.
✎ 我們會盡力提高服務品質。

 給予保證

We will certainly exchange the goods.

✏️ 我們一定會更換商品。

We assure you that we are taking steps to ensure this kind of mistake will not happen again.
✏️ 我們保證此狀況不會再發生。

We would like to offer you a 20% discount on your next order.
✏️ 我們願意在下一筆訂單給予您八折的優惠。

We will deliver replacement this afternoon at 3 p.m.
✏️ 我們將於今天下午三點寄出替代品。

I have spoken to the shipping department and hope they will not make this kind of problem again.
✏️ 我已與運送部門談過，希望他們不要再犯同樣的錯誤。

We will take necessary steps to correct our mistake.
✏️ 我們會採取必要步驟來更正錯誤。

We will take this problem seriously.
✏️ 我們會嚴肅處理此問題。

We will do our best to make sure it will not happen again.
✏️ 我們保證不會再發生同樣的事情。

 **進階補充站** Let's learn more!

 單字/片語Focus

💊 做決定和下決心 💊	
*hope to 希望	*wish to 但願
*decide to 決定	*would like to 想要
*offer to 提議	*agree to 同意
*promise to 承諾	*determine to 下決心
*attempt to 嘗試	*endeavor to 努力

Part 6

工作職場篇 ～提升表現這樣貼

Unit ❶ 公司內部通知

Unit ❷ 公司對外的通知函

Unit ❸ 祝賀函與邀請函

動 動詞　名 名詞
副 副詞　形 形容詞
介 介系詞　片 片語

Point

除了交易信函之外，還有一種工作時經常會用到的 E-mail，以「人」為主體，像是通知員工消息，或者給同事的祝賀函或邀請函，這些 E-mail 的寫法也都能左右他人對你的印象呢。

Unit 1 公司內部通知

·1-01· 會議通知

「會議通知」的撰寫重點在提及正確的開會時間以及開會地點,並提醒收信者務必準時出席。

Subject | Sales Meeting on May 5

Dear Managers:

Please be **informed**[1] that a manager's meeting for the sales **strategy**[2] will be held at 9:00 a.m. on Friday, May 5, in our Meeting Room 2.

Please **make sure of**[3] your **presence**[4].

Best regards,
Kevin

諸位經理:

謹通知,公司將在五月五日(週五)早上九點鐘,於第二會議室針對銷售策略舉行主管會議。

請務必出席會議。

凱文 謹上

Send ▶

核心字彙充電站 *Key Words*

1. **inform** 動 通知;告知
2. **strategy** 名 策略;對策
3. **make sure of** 片 確保
4. **presence** 名 出席;在場

替換好用句 *Copy & Paste*

 提及時間和地點

There will be a meeting about sales promotion at the head office next

month.
✐ 總公司預計於下個月召開會議，討論促進銷售量的議題。

The next Monthly Management Meeting will be held at 10:00 a.m. on Friday.
✐ 下個月的主管會議將於週五早上十點舉行。

A manager's meeting will be held at 4 p.m. next Monday, July 27, in the meeting room.
✐ 經理級會議將於下週一，七月二十七日下午四點鐘，於會議室舉行。

There would be a meeting to discuss the marketing issues at 6 p.m. on Tuesday, May 29 at Trump Tower.
✐ 五月二十九日，週二下午六點，在川普大樓將有一場討論行銷議題的會議。

Our training on the new computer software will be given on Friday, May 5.
✐ 新電腦軟體的訓練課程定於五月五日星期五。

The monthly meeting has been postponed to May 31.
✐ 本月例行會議延後至五月三十一日。

Please mark your calendar accordingly.
✐ 請依此註明您的行程。

The meeting will be held in our Meeting Room No.1 at the office.
✐ 會議將於公司的第一會議室舉行。

The meeting will be held in the Conference Room No.5 at the head office.
✐ 將於總公司的第五會議室舉行一場會議。

 ## 說明開會目的

The purpose of the meeting is to discuss the design of our new products.
✐ 會議目的為討論新產品設計。

Our primary focus of the meeting will be the products promotion into the China market.
✐ 會議主要目的是針對中國市場促銷。

We would like to invite you to attend a meeting to learn how to use the Apple software.

Part 1

Part 2

Part 3

Part 4

Part 5

Part 6

🖊 我們想要邀請您來參加一場會議，學習如何使用蘋果軟體。

There will be a top sales' meeting about sales promotions at the head office next week.
🖊 下星期在總公司將會舉行頂尖銷售員會議，教您成為推銷達人。

The purpose of the conference is to discuss the international marketing strategy in Europe.
🖊 會議的目的是要討論歐洲國際市場的策略。

The conference will discuss our new office in Shanghai, China.
🖊 會議將討論我們在中國上海成立新辦公室的計畫。

We need to have a meeting to consider the withdrawal from the Europe market.
🖊 我們有必要針對退出歐洲市場一事開會討論。

 ## 其他事項提醒

Please do some homework by reading the following reports in advance.
🖊 請預先閱讀以下的報告。

Please come and prepare with questions and suggestions.
🖊 出席時請準備好提問與建議。

The following is the tentative agenda.
🖊 以下為初步開會議程。

Following is the agenda for the meeting:
🖊 以下為當日開會的議程：

If you have other topics you'd like to add, please let me know.
🖊 若想增加其他議題，請告知我。

If there are any issues you would like to be placed on the agenda, please let me know via email by Wednesday.
🖊 如有任何其他想討論的議題，請於週三前寄電子郵件給我。

As the details are attached, please thoroughly read through in advance.
🖊 附上相關訊息，請詳讀。

Be sure that you are ready with questions and comments.

✍ 請您準備好問題與建議。

要求對方出席

Your presence is requested.
✍ 請您務必出席。

It is imperative that you attend the meeting.
✍ 請您務必出席會議。

All of you are required to be present at the meeting.
✍ 您們各位都必須出席本次會議。

Your attendance at the meeting this Thursday is important to us.
✍ 我們慎重地邀請您參與本週四的會議。

Please send someone on your behalf if you are unable to attend the conference.
✍ 如無法出席，請派代理人與會。

If you are unable to attend, please let me know who will be attending for your department.
✍ 如果您無法參加，請告知貴部門的出席者名單。

Please make sure that you are present.
✍ 請確認您能出席。

Please contact us if you cannot attend the meeting.
✍ 若您無法參加會議，請與我們聯絡。

 進階補充站 *Let's learn more!*

文法/句型Focus

✱ 表達意見

❶ **I'm positive that...** 我很確定⋯。

❷ **I (really) feel that...** 我（真的）覺得⋯。

3 In my opinion... 在我看來，…。

4 The way I see things... 我個人的觀點是…。

5 If you ask me, I tend to think that... 如果你問我的話，我會覺得…。

✱ 詢問他人意見

1 Are you positive that...? 你確定…？

2 Do you (really) think that...? 你真的認為…？

3 How do you feel about...? 你覺得…怎麼樣？

4 (name), can we get your input?
（人名），我們可以聽聽你的想法嗎？

 實用資訊Focus

開會注意事項🔍

1. 搞清楚開會目的

2. 召開會議前的準備工作：確定時間、預定好開會的場地、以及通知大家開
會。（建議事先用電話和與會人員敲定時間，再發出會議通知提醒，並留下
紀錄。）

3. 掌握會議進行：針對開會目的，確保有做出決議。

4. 即時發出會議紀錄：最好是開完會的當天就用E-mail發出會議紀錄，最晚不要
超過第二天下班，原則上以「條列式」提點即可。信末可另外註明Please feel
free to let me know if there is anything missing or any incorrect information.
Thank you.（若有任何遺漏或不正確的內容，請讓我知道，謝謝您。）

Part 1

Part 2

Part 3

Part 4

Part 5

Part 6

1-02 開會時間更改

遇到「更改開會時間」的情況時，請確定E-mail中提及更改過後的正確時間，並提醒收件者注意此更改。

Subject Monthly Management Meeting for May

Dear Managers:

The **Monthly¹ Management²** Meeting, **previously³** scheduled for this Friday, has been **rescheduled⁴** for next Monday, May 10, the same time, in the same meeting room.

Best regards,
Kevin

經理諸君：

每月召開的主管會議時間已從本週五更改為下週一，五月十日，時間與地點不變。

凱文 謹上

Send

核心字彙充電站 *Key Words*

1. monthly 形 每月一次的
2. management 名 管理
3. previously 副 事先；以前
4. reschedule 動 重新安排⋯的時間

替換好用句 *Copy & Paste*

I'm afraid I have to request to reschedule our meeting of June 15.
🖉 我恐怕必須更改六月十五日的會議時間。

Unfortunately, I will have to travel to Boston that week.
🖉 很不巧，我那週將到波士頓出差。

May I suggest June 19 at 3:00 p.m.?
🖉 可以將會議更改到六月十九日下午三點鐘嗎？

I'm sorry for any inconveniences this may cause you.

✎ 造成您的不便，敬請見諒。

I await your confirmation.
✎ 我等待您的確認。

 **進階補充站** Let's learn more!

 單字/片語Focus

❧ 會議室裡的物件 ❧

✱**conference** 正式會議	✱**meeting room** 會議室
✱**projector** 投影機	✱**screen** 投影布幕
✱**whiteboard** 白板	✱**marker** 白板筆
✱**chairperson** 主席	✱**chart(s)** 圖表
✱**participant** 與會者	✱**minutes** 會議記錄
✱**agenda** 議程	✱**report** 報告書
✱**microphone** 麥克風	✱**jot down** 快速作筆記

❧ 公司部門 ❧

✱**Head Office** 總公司	✱**Branch Office** 分公司
✱**Business Office** 營業部	✱**Personnel Dept.** 人事部
✱**HR Dept.** 人資部	✱**Marketing Dept.** 行銷部
✱**Sales Dept.** 銷售部	✱**Public Relations** 公關
✱**Advertising Dept.** 廣告部	✱**Planning Dept.** 企劃部
✱**R&D Dept.** 研發部	✱**Secretarial Pool** 秘書室
✱**Service Dept.** 客服部	✱**Purchase & Order Dept.** 採購部

Part 1
Part 2
Part 3
Part 4
Part 5
Part 6

·1-03· 請假及職務代理人通知

「休假通知」信件，是在休假前寫信告知相關同仁休假的期間，以及重新開始上班的時間，讓對方得以做出相應的安排。若有需要，還必須告知休假期間的職務代理人，以方便彼此作業。

Subject Notice of Absence

Dear **Colleagues**[1]:

I will be staying in Korea from next Monday to Friday for five days and back to work on May 5.

Sorry for the inconvenience, and please reschedule your events **accordingly**[2].

Best,
Sales Manager

Send ▶

親愛的同仁：

我下週一到週五要待在韓國五天，五月五日才會回來上班。

很抱歉造成困擾，並煩請重新規劃您的行程。

銷售經理 上

Subject Notice of Absence

Dear Colleagues:

Please be informed that I will be **out of office**[3] from Wednesday through Friday, May 5-7 due to **the business trip**[4] to Japan. In my **absence**[5], Mr. Thomas Chang will be managing Marketing Department. He can be reached at thomaschang@gmail.com, or telephone: 0922-222-333.

During my trip, I will be connecting to the

親愛的同仁：

謹此通知，從週三到週五，五月五日到七日，我會到日本出差。出差期間，由湯馬士先生代理我的行銷部門管理職務。您可以寄電郵至：thomaschang@gmail.com，或打電話至：0922-222-333聯絡他。

Internet in the hotel in order to **catch up with**[6] your program progress.

Please feel free to contact me by email if you need my assistance urgently.

Thank you very much!

Marketing Manager

出差期間，我將會在旅館使用網路，以便確認你們的工作進度。

如果您迫切需要幫忙，請與我用電子郵件連絡。

非常謝謝您！

行銷經理 上

Send ▶

核心字彙充電站 Key Words

1. **colleague** 名 同事
2. **accordingly** 副 照著；相應地
3. **out of office** 片 不在公司
4. **a business trip** 片 商務旅行
5. **absence** 名 不在；缺席
6. **catch up with** 片 趕上

替換好用句 Copy & Paste

 代表公司發信通知

We are informing you that ABC Company will close for the Chinese New Year's holidays from Jan. 29 to Feb. 5 and reopen on Monday, Feb. 6.
✎ 謹此通知，ABC公司於一月二十九日至二月五日的農曆新年期間休假，二月六日重新開始上班。

Our store will close during the Easter holidays and reopen on Wednesday, May 20.
✎ 我們的店於復活節假期的期間停止營業，並於五月二十日（星期三）重新營業。

The store will close on Monday night due to the annual dinner party.
✎ 星期一晚上為年終晚宴，因此停止營業。

The shop will close on Wednesdays and Sundays.
✐ 本店週三及週日公休。

The store will close on every Thursday night and Saturday all day from now on.
✐ 即日起，本店將於每週四晚間及週六全天公休。

For your information, our company just confirmed with us that Feb. 28 and Apr. 4 (both are Mondays) are official days off.
✐ 在此通知您，二月二十八日與四月四日（皆為週一），已確認為本公司的公休日。

It is our pleasure to announce that from this year, we will have a Labor Day off on May 1st.
✐ 很榮幸宣佈，今年起五一勞動節放假。

Please enjoy your Chinese New Year holiday.
✐ 請享受您的農曆年假。

Wish all of you have a wonderful holiday.
✐ 祝福您們全體假期愉快。

Have a great new week and Happy Holidays by then!
✐ 祝你有個美好的一週，並祝佳節愉快！

 ## 個人身分發信

This is to inform that I will be out of office from May 1st to 5th.
✐ 謹此通知，我將於五月一日至五日出差。

I will be out of office on a business trip to Hong Kong from May 1st to 5th.
✐ 我五月一日至五日在香港出差。

For urgent issues, please contact Mary at 07-2172-3563.
✐ 若有緊急事故，請聯絡瑪莉，電話為：07-2172-3563。

Email me at brown.chen@yahoo.com.
✐ 請電郵給我至：brown.chen@yahoo.com。

You can telephone him on 9242-3173 ext. 123 during the business time.
✐ 您可以在上班時間打電話到：9242-3173，轉分機123與他聯絡。

You can fax him on 8808-7707.
✐ 您可以傳真至8808-7707給他。

Part 1
Part 2
Part 3
Part 4
Part 5
Part 6

If you want to discuss the project, my msn account is jim@yahoo. com.tw.

🖊 如果您想要討論企劃，可以加我的MSN帳號：jim@yahoo.com.tw。

Please email me first to tell me that you want to contact me via MSN.

🖊 在加我的MSN之前，麻煩請寫電子郵件告知我。

 進階補充站　Let's learn more!

 單字/片語Focus

❤ 休假的類型 ❤	
✱**unpaid leave** 無薪假	✱**annual leave** 年假
✱**sick leave** 病假	✱**personal leave** 事假
✱**maternity leave** 產假	✱**paternity leave** 陪產假

 實用資訊Focus

🔍 辨別「放假」類單字

　　英文單字中的holiday、vacation、break、leave、days off都有「放假」之意，但對老外來說，各自隱含不同的意思，千萬要分辨清楚。

1. holiday通常指「國定假日」或「宗教節慶」，為大多數人會放假的日子。例如：Dragon Boat Festival（端午節）。

2. vacation泛指任何假期，時間較長。常見的例子如：學生的summer / winter vacation（暑假／寒假）。

3. break則指短暫的休息。例如：球賽的中場休息時間、課堂間的下課時間、會議間的短暫休息（a 10-minute break 十分鐘的休息時間）。

4. leave表示休假與請假，用於「員工因某種因素而獲准的假期」。例如：sick leave（病假）、annual leave（年假）、maternity leave（產假）。

5. days off指不用上班或上學的日子。例如：be off today（今天休假）、have two days off a week（週休二日）。

Part 1

Part 2

Part 3

Part 4

Part 5

Part 6

1-04 歡迎新進員工

　　「歡迎新進員工」的信件中，重點在讓同事知悉新成員的資訊，讓之後的共事更加順利，因此請記得給予新進員工之相關資訊，如姓名以及職稱等，讓收信者有個心理準備。

Subject **Welcome Our New Colleague**

Dear Tina:

We have added a new face to our HR department this week. Please note Mr. Brown has been **promoted**[1] to the HR manager. He will work with you and your **co-workers**[2] in your department.

We hope the **upcoming**[3] meeting will give you a chance to meet our newest **personnel**[4].

Sincerely yours,
Robert

蒂娜您好：

本週人資部門增加一位新面孔。請注意：布朗先生被晉升為人資部的主管。他將會與您的部門及員工工作。

希望能在最近的會議上介紹新進人員給您認識。

羅伯特 謹上

Send ►

核心字彙充電站 Key Words

1. **promote** 動 升遷；升職
2. **co-worker** 名 同事
3. **upcoming** 形 即將來臨的
4. **personnel** 名 人事部門

替換好用句 Copy & Paste

We are glad to announce the hiring of Bella Chou.
✎ 我們很高興宣布聘請周貝拉。

I am glad to announce that Tasha will be appointed as our sales manager.

🖉 我很開心宣布：泰莎被任命為業務經理。

We decided to add a new face to the team.

🖉 我們決定為團隊增加新面孔。

We are very happy to announce, effective from today, the appointment of Tasha Brown as the sales manager to our company.

🖉 我們非常高興地宣布：即日起，本公司業務經理將由泰莎・布朗女士擔任。

Tina has many years of experience in the marketing area.

🖉 蒂娜有許多年的行銷經驗。

We believe her experience will bring invaluable asset to our company.

🖉 我們相信她的經驗將帶給公司無價的資產。

Please join us in welcoming Ms. Brown to our company!

🖉 請大家一起歡迎布朗女士！

進階補充站　Let's learn more!

單字/片語Focus

🎀 向新進人員介紹 🎀

＊policy 政策	＊posting 職位
＊promotion 升職	＊demotion 降職
＊long-term trend 長期趨勢	＊labor-hour 工時
＊internship 實習	＊corporate culture 企業文化
＊job description 工作說明	＊job specification 工作規範

Part 1

Part 2

Part 3

Part 4

Part 5

Part 6

1-05 職務升遷通知

在「職務升遷通知」中，首先可恭賀對方獲得升職，並說明升遷的原因，希望未來對方能夠繼續努力。

Subject | Notice of The Promotion

Dear Eric:

It is our **pleasure**[1] to inform you that you have been promoted to the **challenging**[2] and **demanding**[3] **position**[4] of our Factory Chief.

You have **achieved**[5] this promotion within a **span**[6] of one year with all your hard work and **dedication**[7] towards your work. We expect the same **behavior**[8] from you in the future even though you got a promotion. Your new **salary**[9] structure and details about **compensation**[10] will be **mentioned**[11] in the official promotional letter which will be given to you very soon.

If you find any **queries**[12] or difficulties related to this matter, you can contact the human resource department.

Once again, many congratulations to you and all the best for the future growth.

Sincerely yours,
Sally

艾力克您好：

很開心通知您被晉升為富有挑戰性的工廠廠長一職。

因為您這一年努力的工作、賣命的付出，才有今天的升遷。即使升遷了，還是期待您未來也能如此努力。調整後的薪資及相關津貼細項，將於近日即將寄給您的正式升遷信件中列出。

如果您有任何問題以及困難，可與人力資源部門聯絡。

再次恭喜您，希望您的未來一片光明。

莎莉 敬上

Send

核心字彙充電站 Key Words

1. **pleasure** 名 愉快；高興
2. **challenging** 形 具挑戰性的
3. **demanding** 形 高要求的
4. **position** 名 職位；職務
5. **achieve** 動 完成；實現
6. **span** 名 一段時間
7. **dedication** 名 奉獻
8. **behavior** 名 行為；舉止
9. **salary** 名 薪資；薪水
10. **compensation** 名 補償金；津貼
11. **mention** 動 提到；說起
12. **query** 名 疑問；詢問

替換好用句 Copy & Paste

This promotion is in recognition of the fine work you have done for the company.

🖊 因為您過去在公司的表現良好，所以在此提升您的職位。

We are sure that you will meet the new responsibilities of being the Factory Chief.

🖊 我們相信您會負起廠長應有的責任。

We are extremely pleased to inform you that the President has considered you suitable for the post.

🖊 我們非常開心地通知你，總裁認為您適合這個職位。

You have therefore been promoted to Product Manager with effect from September 1st, 2017.

🖊 你被升為產品經理，從二〇一七年九月一日開始任職。

You are requested to hand over charge of Sales Representative to Mr. Chen taking over latest by August 31.

🖊 八月三十一日前，您必須將業務專員的職務移交給陳先生。

Congratulations on your achievement and we wish you all the very best in the coming years.

🖊 恭賀您的成就，我們期待您未來的表現。

進階補充站  Let's learn more!

單字/片語Focus

❦ 工作職稱（依職位高低排列）❦

✽CEO 總裁；執行長	✽President 總裁
✽Vice President 副總裁	✽Director of Board 董事
✽Supervisor 監事	✽General Manager, G.M. 總經理
✽Chief Financial Officer, CFO 財務長	
✽Consultant 顧問	✽Special Assistant 特別助理
✽Factory Chief 廠長	✽Factory Sub-Chief 副廠長
✽Director 協理；處長	✽Manager 經理
✽Assistant Manager 副理	✽Junior Manager 襄理
✽Section Manager 課長	✽Supervisor 主任

❦ 工作性質與範圍 ❦

✽accounting 會計	✽administrative 行政
✽auditorial 稽核	✽customer service 客服
✽financial 財務	✽general affairs 總務
✽hardware 硬體	✽software 軟體
✽legal 法務	✽maintenance 維修
✽network 網管	✽patent 專利
✽quality control 品管	✽procurement 採購
✽human resources 人力資源	✽marketing 行銷
✽marcom = marketing communication 行銷企劃	

Part 1

Part 2

Part 3

Part 4

Part 5

Part 6

363

·1-06· 工作改進通知

　　「工作改進通知」分為兩類，第一種為「尚不嚴重的提醒」，第二種則是「不改善不行的嚴重警告」。無論是哪一種，都必須明確地點出要對方改善的內容，若是嚴重警告，可於信末補上將給予最後的改善期限。

Subject **Performance Improvement**

Dear Peter:

We are pleased to have you in our department. Confirming the **annual**[1] **feedback**[2] from your director, we expect that you shall **improve**[3] your **performance**[4] in the near future by:

1. **Attending**[5] the meeting on time.
2. Finishing the report before the due date.
3. Cooperating with other colleagues.

We believe that you will be the excellent employee very soon.

Yours sincerely,
Henry

親愛的彼得：

對於你身為我們部門的一份子，我們感到榮幸。從你主管口中得知你這一年的工作情況，我們希望你能在近期內改善工作表現，如下：

一、請準時參加會議。
二、在期限內完成報告。
三、請與同仁互相配合。

我們相信，您很快就會成為一位表現良好的員工。

亨利 敬上

Send ▶

Subject **Performance Improvement**

Dear Anna:

You received a **warning**[6] from our company few months ago asking you to improve

親愛的安娜：

幾個月前你有接獲公司的警告，要求注意你的工作

your performance. Recently, however, there have been **incidents**[7] that **indicate**[8] your work performance has not improved. We have found that you still do not follow certain **regulations**[9].

When I was reviewing the orders you processed, I discovered that quite a lot of orders were not signed by your supervisor. This shows that you did not follow the **standard**[10] procedure.

The company will now give you a final trial period of one month. You must immediately improve your performance. If your problems continue to persist, we will take further actions.

Sincerely yours,
General Manager

表現。但是,近日你的工作表現仍然沒有改善,我們發現你依舊沒有遵守應遵循的作業程序。

當我檢視你處理的訂單時,發現很多訂單缺少你主管的簽名,顯示你沒有依照標準程序處理。

公司現在給你最後一個月的檢驗期,你必須立即改善你的工作情況。如果一個月後,問題持續存在,那我們將會有進一步的處置。

總經理 上

Send

核心字彙充電站 *Key Words*

1. **annual** 形 一年一次的
2. **feedback** 名 反饋
3. **improve** 動 改善;改進
4. **performance** 名 工作表現
5. **attend** 動 參與;參加
6. **warning** 名 警告
7. **incident** 名 事件;插曲
8. **indicate** 動 指示;指出
9. **regulation** 名 規章;規定
10. **standard** 形 標準的

Part 1
Part 2
Part 3
Part 4
Part 5
Part 6

替換好用句 — Copy & Paste

We would like to tell you about certain unsatisfactory aspects of your performance in our company.
🖊 我們想要與你討論，關於你在本公司一些不良的工作表現。

We expect that in the future, you shall improve your performance by:
🖊 我們期待您在將來改變您的工作方式，如下：

Call the manager if you want to ask for sick leaves.
🖊 如果要請病假，要打電話通知經理。

Follow the regulations concluded by the meeting.
🖊 遵守會議時所做的規定。

Clear your cubicle every week.
🖊 每週要清理自己的工作隔間。

Finishing your work on time.
🖊 準時完成工作。

Arriving the office on time.
🖊 準時上班。

We have confidence the problem will not be repeated.
🖊 我們有信心，這些問題不會重覆發生。

進階補充站 — Let's learn more!

 實用資訊Focus

有效的績效評估 🔍

　　事實上，績效評估一般包含兩個重要目的：

1. 評估（evaluation）：簡單來說，就是檢討員工過去的表現，做出具體的評價，決定是否應給予適當的獎勵與報酬，例如調薪或是升遷等。

2. 指導（coaching）：第二階段的評估，必須針對員工未來的發展，提供必要的協助與諮詢。例如：員工是否有專長尚未獲得完全的發揮？

Part 1

Part 2

Part 3

Part 4

Part 5

Part 6

•1-07• 辭職通知

準備辭職之際，禮貌上要寄出通知，以便讓收信者理解往後配合的對象有異動。記得要在信中註明正式離職的日期，並感謝收信者於在職期間的照顧與配合。

Subject | **Resignation**

Dear Mr. Chen:

I would like to inform you that I am **resigning**[1] from my position as Marketing Manager for Far East Company, **effective**[2] May 1.

Thank you for the support and the opportunities that you have **provided**[3] me during the last three years. I have enjoyed my **tenure**[4] with the company.

If I can be of any **assistance**[5] during this **transition**[6], please let me know. I would be glad to help.

Kind regards,
Winnie

陳先生您好：

謹此通知您，我將於五月一日卸下在遠東公司的行銷經理職務。

謝謝您這三年來給予我的支持以及機會，我在公司這段期間很開心。

在此過渡時期若有需要幫忙請告知，我很樂意提供協助。

溫妮 敬上

Send ▸

核心字彙充電站 *Key Words*

1. **resign** 動 辭職；放棄
2. **effective** 形 生效的
3. **provide** 動 提供
4. **tenure** 名 任期
5. **assistance** 名 協助；幫助
6. **transition** 名 過渡期

替換好用句 Copy & Paste

 告知離職

Please accept this message as notification that I am leaving my position with Philips Company, effective September 15.
🖊 謹此通知您：我將於九月十五日離開飛利浦公司。

I am writing to notify you that I am resigning from my position as HR Manager with Guilin Company.
🖊 此函通知您：我即將卸下人力資源部門主管一職，離開吉琳公司。

I am writing to inform you of my decision to resign from Sheraton Inc. effective March 1.
🖊 在此通知您：我決定於三月一日起離開薛若頓公司。

The purpose of this letter is to announce my resignation from UMC Company, effective two weeks from this date.
🖊 此函目的為通知您：我即將在二週後離開UMC公司。

I'd like to let you know that I am leaving my position at the company.
🖊 在此告知您：我即將離職。

My last day of employment will be May 30.
🖊 我最後一天的上班日為五月三十日。

 感謝對方

I feel that I have learned a lot, and grown professionally during my time in your employ.
🖊 在您的帶領下，我學到很多，專業能力也成長許多。

Thank you for your understanding of my decision to leave the company and all your support over the years.
🖊 謝謝您諒解我離開公司的決定，也謝謝您這些年的支持。

I appreciate the opportunities I have been given at CTC, and your professional guidance.
🖊 很感謝CTC公司給我的機會，以及您給予的專業培訓。

I have enjoyed my tenure at BBC and I appreciate having had the

opportunity to work with you.

✎ 在BBC工作的這段時間我很開心，也感謝有與您共事的機會。

Thank you for the support and encouragement you have provided me during my time at the company.

✎ 謝謝您在我任職期間給予的支持與鼓勵。

I've enjoyed working with you and being a member of your team.

✎ 很開心與您共事，也很高興能成為您團隊中的一份子。

I have enjoyed my tenure with the company.

✎ 我很享受過去在公司的工作。

I learned so much from my experience working at your firm, but felt it was time to move on to another position.

✎ 我在貴公司學習到許多，但仍覺得是該往前的時候了。

Thank you for the professional and personal development you have assisted me over the last three years.

✎ 謝謝您過去三年來在專業上及個人養成上給予我的協助。

I know the professional skills I have developed while working at your company will be extremely useful for my future career.

✎ 在貴公司學到的專業技術，對我未來的職涯必定非常有用。

Even though, I will miss all my colleagues and clients.

✎ 即使如此，我將會想念我的同事及客戶。

I have greatly enjoyed working with you for the past three years.

✎ 過去三年來很高興與您共事。

On my part, this was not an easy decision to make.

✎ 對我而言，這不是個容易的決定。

The past ten years have been very rewarding.

✎ 過去十年所體驗到的事很珍貴。

This opportunity gives me the chance to grow professionally.

✎ 這個機會給我一個在專業上進一步成長的契機。

I consider just about everyone I have met here to be friends of mine, and I will miss you all.

✎ 這裡的每個人都是我的朋友，我會想念大家。

I feel it is time to move onto new opportunities and challenges.

✎ 我覺得該是把握新機會和挑戰的時候了。

Part 1

Part 2

Part 3

Part 4

Part 5

Part 6

 **提及離職原由**

My illness will require extended treatment and recovery.
🖉 我的疾病需要長期的治療以及休養。

I plan to return to school to pursue my interest in Computer Science.
🖉 我計畫重返學校攻讀我喜歡的電腦科學。

I have accepted a position as Magazine Editor at a growing publisher in Taipei.
🖉 我已經接受台北一家成長中出版社所提供的職位，擔任雜誌編輯。

 信末的祝福與結尾

I wish you all the best for your continued success.
🖉 希望您一切順利並成功。

I wish you and the company success in the future.
🖉 希望您與公司未來皆成功。

I am looking forward to my new position and the challenges that await me.
🖉 我很期待新的工作以及等待著我的挑戰。

Please keep in touch.
🖉 請保持聯絡。

I can be reached at mary.chen@hotmail.com or via cellphone 0927-282-331.
🖉 可以寫信至：mary.chen@hotmail.com給我，或是致電：0927-282-331。

Please feel free to contact me with any questions about the projects I have been working on.
🖉 若我著手進行的企劃有問題，歡迎隨時與我聯繫。

I wish you and the company all the best.
🖉 祝福您以及公司。

Again, thank you so much for an excellent five years with Philips company.
🖉 再次，感謝過去五年在菲利浦公司的共事時光。

進階補充站 Let's learn more!

實用資訊Focus

人事交接信 🔍

寫人事交接信給客戶時，原則上會有下面幾項內容：

1. 感謝對方的關照。
2. 未來動向：告訴對方將要離職，可提及離職的時間及簡述原因。
3. 工作交接：若有接任工作的人，請向客戶提及和介紹，以利他們日後的業務往來。
4. 道別問候：可表達日後希望能與對方維持聯繫。

　　除了上述這種「提及自己離職的同時，向客戶介紹繼任的同事」以外，人事交接信還包含另外一種型態 — 自己是新窗口，寫信向客戶自我介紹。無論內容為何，兩種類型的開頭都要先感謝對方的生意往來。

離職的禮節 🔍

　　一般而言，離職並非只有遞出辭呈、離開公司這樣簡要的過程，在處理離職的過程中，最好能維持禮儀，留下好印象的同時，對自己未來的職涯也會有一定的幫助，以下為一些提醒事項：

1. 準備離職前務必先向主管口頭報告與溝通，主管應允後才正式提出辭呈。
2. 辭呈核准前，千萬別在公司喧嚷，以免讓別人留下不良印象。
3. 絕對不可以在辭呈核准前向客戶表達離職意願，影響公司營運。
4. 無論離職原因為何，對於工作要心存感謝，千萬不可在離職前後故意抱怨公司的種種或煽動同事。
5. 不管與主管相處得是否愉快，都要表達自己對他的敬重，對於主管的教導表示感謝。
6. 在尋求新工作時，不可故意洩漏公司機密。
7. 離職後，無須與舊公司斷得一乾二淨，偶爾也可以回公司關懷主管及同事。

1-08 退休通知

在「退休通知」的信件中，可回顧過往的職涯，感謝曾經共事的同事，並可於信末表示希望與同事保持聯絡。

Subject **Notice of Retirement**

Dear All:

The time has come for me to leave Philips Inc. I will be leaving the company at the end of June after the thirty happy years.

I would like to sincerely thank you all for the **enjoyable**[1] working **relationship**[2] and wish you all the best for the future.

Thank you kindly for the **retirement**[3] party and the gifts. I shall certainly think of you all every time I play golf!

Keep in touch.

Kind regards,
Joseph

親愛的各位：

是時候要離開飛利浦公司了——一個我待了三十個快樂年頭，即將於六月底離開的公司。

很開心也很感謝能與你們愉快的共事，祝福你們未來一切順利。

謝謝你們幫我舉辦的派對還有禮物，我會在每次打高爾夫時想到你們！

記得保持聯絡。

喬瑟夫 謹上

Send ▶

Subject **Notice of Retirement**

Dear All:

I would like to inform you that I will be retiring from my position with HTC Inc. as of the end of June.

親愛的各位：

謹此通知：我將於六月底退休，離開宏達電子公司。

I would like to take the opportunity of thanking you for the professional working relationship we have enjoyed over the last five years.

I am looking forward to my retirement but will **sorely**[4] miss working with you all. If I can be of any assistance during the next few weeks, please don't hesitate to contact me.

Sincerely yours,
Terry

藉此機會感謝過去五年與您們專業上的合作。

我很期待退休生活，也肯定會很想念你們。若是接下來幾週有需要我幫忙的地方，請不要客氣，儘管與我聯絡。

泰瑞 敬上

Send ▸

 Key Words

1. **enjoyable** 形 快樂的；有樂趣的 2. **relationship** 名 關係
3. **retirement** 名 退休；退役 4. **sorely** 副 很；非常

 Copy & Paste

 告知退休與感謝

I am writing to thank you and all the staff at ABC Inc. for the party you held in my honor last week, and also for the beautiful watch you presented me as a leaving gift.

✎ 這封信是要感謝ABC公司的各位同仁幫我舉辦退休派對，也謝謝您們為我準備的漂亮手錶退休禮。

As I said in my speech, I've really enjoyed my fifteen years with the company.

✎ 如同我所說，這十五年在公司我真的過得很開心。

It has been a fantastic place to work and I enjoyed being part of such

Part 1
Part 2
Part 3
Part 4
Part 5
Part 6

a dedicated team.
這裡有很棒的工作環境，我很開心和這麼努力的團隊一起工作。

I certainly won't miss getting up so early in the morning, but I will miss being part of the team.
我不會懷念早起上班的生活，但我肯定會懷念與團隊一起工作的日子。

I look forward to seeing you all again sometime in the near future, perhaps for a round of golf or a wee drink.
希望在未來有空可以和大家見面，不論是打高爾夫或是喝杯小酒。

Thanks again for the most enjoyable evening.
再次感謝你們帶給我這麼快樂的夜晚。

I have decided to take my retirement because I am not growing any younger.
由於年事已高，因此做出退休的決定。

I want to enjoy the very last moment of my life with my family and grandchildren.
我希望能夠在晚年享受天倫之樂。

 ## 較為正式的表達

I wanted to thank you for giving me the opportunity and privilege to work in your company.
感謝您給我機會在貴公司工作。

I would like to inform you that I am about to retire from my position as a sales manager from the company, effective Jan 25, 2016.
在此通知您：我將於二〇一六年一月二十五日正式離職，自業務經理的職務退休。

I appreciate the things that the company has done for me, and I wanted you to know that I will treasure them for the rest of my days.
感謝公司為我做的一切，我會在往後的日子裡好好珍惜這些回憶。

Even though I am looking forward to my retirement, I will certainly miss my work, our clients and my colleagues.
雖然我期待退休生活，但我也會想念我的工作、客戶以及同事。

The company helped me so much in developing my professional and personal growth.
公司培養我的專業，也讓我個人成長許多。

Truly, I have enjoyed working in your company, and I appreciate your sincerity to help me during my tenure.

我真的很享受在貴公司的工作，也很感謝在職期間，您給我的幫助。

If I can be of any assistance, never hesitate to call me over the phone.

如果需要幫忙，請隨時與我電話聯繫。

If I can be of any assistance, feel free to contact me with my number or email.

如果需要幫忙，請隨時打電話或是以電郵聯絡我。

 ## 以第三者的角度通知

It is a pity that we have to tell you that, owing to the ill health, Mr. Tsai, our Vice President, will be retiring from active business on June 30.

本公司副總裁蔡先生，由於健康因素，將於六月三十日退休，特此告知，至感遺憾。

His place as Director will be taken by me.

他的處長一職將由我代替。

It is with feelings of sadness and emptiness that I am announcing the retirement of one of the foundations of our company, Mr. Thomas, our department manager.

在此感傷的宣布：公司的創辦人之一，同時也是我們部門的經理湯馬士先生即將退休。

Mr. Lee has been with the company for more than thirty years.

李先生已在公司服務超過三十年了。

During his tenure, the company experienced phenomenal growth.

在職期間，他見證了公司驚人的成長。

The people who have been under his supervision all reported his good nature and great skills in handling them.

在他管理下的同事們都讚賞他的能力以及處事態度。

Without him, there would have been many problems with some of our staff.

沒有他的話，同事間或許會有些問題。

Let us all wish him the best of luck on his retirement.

讓我們祝福他的退休生活順利。

Part 1
Part 2
Part 3
Part 4
Part 5
Part 6

進階補充站 Let's learn more!

單字/片語Focus

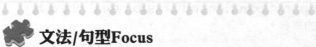

💝 離職與退休 💝

✱poach 挖角	**✱be laid off** 被資遣
✱announce 宣布；公告	**✱completion** 完成
✱process 過程；進程	**✱successor** 繼任者
✱career change 轉換跑道	**✱leave from one's job** 辭職
✱take early retirement 提早退休	
✱hand in one's resignation 遞出辭呈	

💝 年度相關的獎勵 💝

✱get a raise 加薪	**✱promotion** 升遷
✱year-end party 尾牙	**✱annual outing** 年度旅遊
✱year-end bonus 年終獎金	

文法/句型Focus

✱ inform vs. remind

兩者在文法上有相似的用法，但inform意指「通知」，例如退休的消息就可以用inform通知大家；remind則為「提醒」，以下介紹這兩個單字的三種結構：

❶ **inform / remind sb. of sth.** 通知／提醒某人某事

❷ **inform / remind sb. to + V** 通知／提醒某人做某事

❸ **inform /remind sb. (that) S + V** 通知／提醒某人（某事件）

Part 1
Part 2
Part 3
Part 4
Part 5
Part 6

·1-09· 回覆退休通知

祝福他人退休時，記得對於退休者在職期間的工作表現給予讚揚，並祝福未來退休生涯順利。

Subject Re: Notice of Retirement

Dear Joseph: Congratulations on your retirement! Thirty years have passed and now it's time for you to enjoy the next chapter in your life. We would like to thank for your continuous hard work over the years, your loyalty to the company and the professional working relationship we have had. You will be sorely missed and we wish you a happy and healthy retirement. Sincerely yours, Henry	親愛的喬瑟夫： 恭喜您退休！ 三十年已過，該是時候向您人生的下一章節邁進了。我們感謝這些年您不間斷的努力，也感謝您對公司的忠誠，以及在公事上所呈現的專業。 我們會想念您，也祝福您的退休生活快樂、健康。 亨利 敬上

Send

 替換好用句 *Copy & Paste*

I am hereby confirming your notification of your retirement and relieving you from Qisda Inc., effective June 20, 2016.
🖉 在此通知：您在啟思達公司的退休核准，並將於二〇一六年六月二十日生效。

I hope you have had a great tenure with our firm.
🖉 希望您在本公司任職愉快。

Thomas, you have been with us for thirty years.
🖉 湯馬士，您已經與我們一同工作三十年了。

After thirty years of service here at HannStar Inc. as Vice President, it is hard to believe that you have reached retirement.
在翰星公司擔任三十年的副總裁一職，很難相信您已經要退休了。

We have been informed of your retirement and would like to congratulate you on your long career.
得知您即將退休，我們想要恭喜您在工作上畫下圓滿的句點。

You will get all your funds and dues cleared from Account Department a day before your official farewell.
在歡送會前一天，您會從會計部收到您的款項。

I appreciate your valuable contribution towards Cathy Inc. from the core of my heart.
我由衷感激您對凱西企業的奉獻。

I have always noticed your dedication, punctuality and sincerity towards work.
我總是注意到您對工作的認真、準確度以及努力。

You have always shown such competence and efficiency.
您總是那麼盡職且有效率。

We shall miss your visit to our company.
我們會想念您的來訪。

I am writing to you this letter because I wanted to thank you personally for your valuable contributions to our department.
我寫此信感謝您過去對本部門的貢獻。

Ever since you worked at our office, the company has grown so much in terms of size and profitability.
自從您在本公司服務，公司不論在規模還是利潤的層面上都成長許多。

Because of you, the company has become one of the best in the business.
因為您的關係，公司成為同業間的佼佼者。

It is hard for us to let go of an employee like you.
真的很不願意讓您離開。

Again, I wanted to say thank you for your great efforts for making the company on top.
再次感謝您的努力，帶領公司達到高峰。

During your tenure here at Toyota Inc., you have given generously of

your talents and strengths.
✎ 您在豐田公司工作期間，慷慨貢獻了您的天分與能力。

We are grateful for all your dedications and are left with no words for appreciation.
✎ 我們很感激您的付出，一切盡在不言中。

We hope you have enjoyed being here.
✎ 我們希望您很享受在這裡的日子。

It is tough for me to see you going today, but congratulations on your retirement.
✎ 對我來說，看您離開很不好受，但還是要恭喜您退休。

If I can be of assistance, just give me a call or simply drop by at my office.
✎ 如果需要幫忙，請來電聯絡、或隨時來辦公室找我。

I wish you all the best for your retirement.
✎ 祝福您的退休生活順利。

 Let's learn more!

 單字/片語Focus

❧ 各種情緒 ❧

✱**embarrassment** 困窘	✱**sulk** 生氣；慍怒
✱**anger** 生氣；怒氣	✱**anxiety** 憂慮；焦慮
✱**depression** 沮喪	✱**anticipation** 期待
✱**despair** 絕望	✱**fear** 害怕；恐懼
✱**rage**（一陣）狂怒，盛怒	✱**excitement** 興奮
✱**worry** 擔心；煩惱	✱**surprise** 驚奇；驚喜
✱**annoyance** 惱火	✱**indifference** 無所謂；冷漠
✱**stress** 壓力；緊張	✱**pain** 痛苦；疼痛
✱**sadness** 悲傷	✱**helplessness** 無助

·1-10· 裁員通知

通知裁員時必須交代以下資訊：一、裁員職務；二、生效時間；三、暫時性或是永久性；四、解釋原因；以及五、後續聯絡人資料。

Subject Realigning Resources and Reducing Costs

Dear Mary:

We had been hoping that during this difficult **period**[1] of **reorganization**[2], we could keep all of our **employees**[3] with the company. Unfortunately, this is not the case.

It is with regret, therefore, that we must inform you that we will be unable to **utilize**[4] your services after June 30. We have been pleased with the qualities you have exhibited during your tenure of employment with us, and will be sorry to lose you as an employee of the company.

Please accept our best wishes for your future.

Very truly yours,
Fred

親愛的瑪莉：

在本公司重組時期，我們希望能維持本公司目前的員工人數；但不幸的是，事實並非如此。

很抱歉，我們必須通知您：六月三十日後我們無法繼續讓您服務。我們很滿意您在本公司的服務品質，很抱歉必須讓您離開公司。

祝您有個美好的未來。

弗瑞德 敬上

Send ▶

核心字彙充電站 *Key Words*

1. period 名 時期；期間 　　**2. reorganization** 名 改組；改編
3. employee 名 員工 　　**4. utilize** 動 利用

 替換好用句 Copy & Paste

Due to the loss in business, we regret to inform you that we are laying off some of our employees for the winter and spring.
🖊 由於經營上的虧損，我們很遺憾地通知您：本公司必須在冬天和春天解雇員工。

Due to the change of company's policy and direction this year, we are sorry your working ability does not meet our requirements any more.
🖊 因為今年公司的政策方向改變，很抱歉，您的工作能力將不再符合本公司的需求。

As you have been informed, the company is reducing its workforce due to the need of reducing the operating costs.
🖊 如您所知，由於公司必須減少開銷，目前正在進行人力縮編。

As you may know, recent changes in the economy have forced us to make some difficult decisions here at TCT Company.
🖊 如您所知，因為經濟上的波動，導致TCT公司必須做出困難的決定。

I regret to tell you that our services will have to be terminated.
🖊 很遺憾地告訴您，公司即將停止營運。

I am afraid that I have brought you bad news.
🖊 我恐怕要告訴您壞消息。

In order for the company to succeed in the future, we must streamline our organization today.
🖊 為了日後的成功，我們必須簡化公司組織。

Therefore, it is with regret that we are eliminating your position and terminating your employment, effective June 30.
🖊 因此，很遺憾要通知您：我們必須終止您的職務，六月三十日生效。

The decision to eliminate jobs is a very difficult one.
🖊 裁員是一項非常困難的決策。

We regret having to take this action.
🖊 我們很遺憾必須採取此行動。

Our sales have dropped forty percent in the last six months.
🖊 我方過去六個月的銷售量已降低了百分之四十。

You are entitled to two week's severance pay, which will be paid in full on your next paycheck.

Part 1
Part 2
Part 3
Part 4
Part 5
Part 6

✏️ 您可以在下次的薪水中多領到兩週的資遣費。

Thank you for your hard work and dedication to Beiersdorf Company.
✏️ 謝謝您努力為拜爾斯道夫公司工作。

On your last day of work, June 30, please be sure to return your keys and any other items belonging to the company.
✏️ 在您最後的工作日，也就是六月三十號那天，請歸還公司鑰匙和物品。

Please arrange for the return of any company property in your possession.
✏️ 請安排歸還您使用的公司物品。

We will provide severance pay in the amount of $20,000.
✏️ 我們會提供兩萬元的資遣費。

You will receive your severance pay and final paycheck on July 5.
✏️ 您將於七月五日收到資遣費和最後一份薪資。

We have been pleased with the work that you've accomplished during your employment here.
✏️ 我們很高興您在本公司努力完成工作。

A packet with information regarding this layoff will be provided to you.
✏️ 有關此次的裁員資訊，會在之後寄給您。

Thank you for your contributions to the company.
✏️ 謝謝您對公司的貢獻。

You will get all legal welfare in accordance with Labor Law.
✏️ 您會得到勞基法裡所規定的合理福利。

Please accept our best wishes for your future!
✏️ 請接受我們對您未來最衷心的祝福！

We wish you all the best in your new endeavors.
✏️ 祝福您在新的工作崗位上順利。

Should you have any other questions regarding this information, please feel free to contact me at 2428-3631.
✏️ 如果您還有任何問題，請與我聯絡，電話為：2428-3631。

Should you have any questions, please contact Paul Lai: 04-2227-3358.
✏️ 如有任何疑問請與賴保羅聯絡，電話是：04-2227-3358。

 Let's learn more!

文法/句型Focus

✳ 委婉表達「解雇」的說法

❶ **We no longer require your services.** 我們不再需要您的貢獻。

❷ **Your employment will be terminated.** 您的受雇合約將被終止。

❸ **We are sorry that we have to let you go.** 對於要讓您離開公司的事，我們深感遺憾。

❹ **We are going to cut down on staff number due to the financial crisis.**
因為金融危機，所以我們將裁減員工人數。

 實用資訊Focus

表示「解雇」的單字 🔍

lay off、fire和dismiss這幾個英文單字都能用來表示「解雇」與「辭退」，但其中所隱含的意義並不相同，以下分別敘述：

1. lay off所表示的「裁減員工」，原因通常來自於公司業績不佳或市場不景氣，導致公司無法負荷成本，因而被迫採取的策略，多半基於商業考量，而非針對個人的懲罰性決策。

2. fire和dismiss皆為「針對個人行為的撤職」，通常是因為員工犯錯或道德操守出問題，因而採取的懲罰性決策。相比之下，dismiss的語氣較為和緩。

Part 1
Part 2
Part 3
Part 4
Part 5
Part 6

Unit 2 公司對外的通知函

·2-01· 公司開張

Subject New Company Accouchement

Dear Sirs:

We should like to bring your notice the fact that we have **established**[1] ourselves as a trading firm under the following name and address:

A&P Trading Co., Ltd.
No. 111, Tien Yu Street,
Taipei City, R.O.C.

We have been the Taiwan representatives for Tokyo Trading Co., Ltd. for more than ten years. Therefore, we can say that we have considerable trading experience in both Taiwan and Japan markets. We can offer you an unusually large variety of first-class Taiwan **computer**[2] **accessories**[3] at **competitive**[4] prices.

Any information that you may require, we would be glad to forward to you.

Yours faithfully,
Fiona

Send ▶

敬啟者：

在此通知：我們已成立一家貿易公司，名稱與地址如下：

A&P 貿易股份有限公司
台北市天玉街111號

我們擔任日本貿易公司的台灣地區代表超過十年，可以說有非常多的台日貿易經驗。我們能提供第一流並有競爭價格的電腦周邊商品。

如果需要任何資訊，我們樂意隨時奉上。

費歐娜 敬上

Part 1

Part 2

Part 3

Part 4

Part 5

Part 6

 核心字彙充電站 *Key Words*

1. **establish** 動 建立；創立
2. **computer** 名 電腦
3. **accessory** 名 配件；附件
4. **competitive** 形 有競爭力的

替換好用句 *Copy & Paste*

宣布開店

It is our pleasure to announce that we have started a new company in Tainan.
🖊 很開心通知您：我們在台南開設了一家新公司。

I have the honor to inform you that we have just established a new company.
🖊 很榮幸通知您：我們開設了一家新公司。

We have worked for many years to provide the best products and services in insurance and financing solutions.
🖊 我們有多年的經驗，將提供您保險財務方面的產品及服務。

The first 100 customers will become our VIPs.
🖊 前一百名客戶將成為我們的重要客戶。

I am very pleased to announce the opening of my footwear shop.
🖊 很高興宣布我的鞋店開幕了。

We are pleased to inform you that on account of a rapid increase in the volume of our products, we decided to open another new company.
🖊 由於產量遽增，我們決定另外開設一家新公司。

I am pleased to inform you that I shall commence the business of metal products from this day.
🖊 很高興通知您：今後我將會經營金屬製品。

給予保證

We have worked for many years to provide the best products and services in insurance and financing solutions.

我們有多年的經驗，將提供您保險和財務方面的優良產品及服務。

The first 100 customers will become our VIPs.
前一百名客戶將成為我們的重要客戶。

We would be delighted if you would take full advantage of our services and favorable shopping environment.
請善加利用我們的服務和良好的購物環境。

Under the circumstances, we are sure that we will make you the fullest satisfaction.
在此情況下，我們確定您會十分滿意。

 Let's learn more!

 文法/句型Focus

✱ 各種公司型態

➊ Corporation, Corp. 股份有限公司，公司的資本被劃分為股份，股東持有股份，間接持有公司，並享受權利、負擔義務。公司為獨立的法人，股東與公司為分開的個體。

➋ Incorporation, Inc. 與**Corporation**的意思相近，但更為廣義，不限於營利性質的公司。

➌ Limited Liability Company, LLC 有限責任公司，這種型態在美國很常見。當公司被求償時，股東（**Member**）的責任是有限的。**LLC**通常為小型企業，甚至一人公司也有可能。

➍ Private Limited Company, Ltd. / Co. Ltd. 股東僅就其股份為限，對公司負責，與**Corporation**不同的是，它屬於封閉式的公司，不對外公開募股。

Part 1

Part 2

Part 3

Part 4

Part 5

Part 6

2-02 成立分公司

在「通知成立分公司」的信件中，除了提及成立時間，亦可提及成立分公司之原因，如：因應市場需求、加快訂單處理速度及出貨速度等。信末可提供公司網址，讓收信者直接點選連結以尋求更多資訊；或提供電子郵件信箱，供收信者回覆。

Subject | **Opening of New Branch in Paris**

Dear Mr. Huang:

We take pleasure in announcing the opening of our new **branch**[1] in Paris! The new office will open on June 30 and our branch in London will close as of May 20.

You are **cordially**[2] **invited**[3] to our opening **ceremony**[4] on June 30.

For more information, please send email to admin@paris.com.

Best regards,
Benny

黃先生您好：

我們很高興在此告知您：我們在巴黎的分公司即將開幕！新辦公室將於六月三十日開幕，屆時倫敦分公司將會在五月二十日結束營業。

我們誠心地邀請您參加六月三十日的開幕典禮。

欲知更多資訊，請來信：admin@paris.com。

班尼 敬上

Send ►

 核心字彙充電站 *Key Words*

1. branch 名 分公司；分行
2. cordially 副 熱誠地；誠摯地
3. invite 動 邀請；招待
4. ceremony 名 儀式；典禮

 替換好用句 *Copy & Paste*

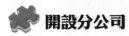 開設分公司

This is to inform you that we have opened a new branch in Edinburgh.
🖉 此函通知：我們即將在愛丁堡成立分公司。

I am writing to inform you that our new office in Tokyo is ready to begin our operations.
🖉 在此通知您：我們的東京分公司已準備好開始營運了。

We are glad to announce the opening of a new office in Taipei.
🖉 很開心通知您：我們的台北分公司即將開幕。

We are glad to announce that a new branch of our company in New York has been opened.
🖉 很開心通知您：我們的紐約分公司已經開幕了。

Next month, we shall be opening a Taichung branch.
🖉 我們下個月會在台中開設分公司。

We wish to inform you that we have opened a new office in Paris.
🖉 我們希望能夠通知您：我們在巴黎成立了新的辦公室。

Thank you for your business and support of our goods for such a long time.
🖉 謝謝您長久以來的合作與支持。

Due to the popularity of our goods, we will be opening a new branch office in Tainan.
🖉 由於產品大受歡迎，我們即將在台南開設分公司。

As the demand of our trade in Taiwan is increasing, we will open a new branch in Kaohsiung next month.
🖉 由於在台灣的產品需求量增加，我們下個月將在高雄開設分公司。

Due to a constantly expanding demand for our products, we decided to supply our Taiwan customers with a new branch in Taichung.
🖉 由於持續成長的銷售量，我們已決定為台灣客戶成立新的台中分公司。

Due to the rapid demand from our customers, we are going to open another branch.
🖉 由於客戶的需求量增加，我們將再開設分公司。

We are very honored by your attendance to our opening ceremony.

✎ 我們非常榮幸您蒞臨我們的開幕典禮。

We will be pleased to have you come to our opening ceremony this Friday night.

✎ 若您能蒞臨我們於本週五晚上舉辦的開幕典禮，我們會非常高興。

We would be pleased if you could attend our opening ceremony in Taipei.

✎ 如果您能參加在台北的開幕典禮，我們會非常開心。

We hope the new branch will be most helpful to our clients in Southern Taiwan.

✎ 希望新成立的分公司對我們南台灣的客戶能有所助益。

 ## 保證與聯繫方式

We would be able to process your orders more efficiently.

✎ 我們處理訂單的效率將會變得更高。

We would deliver the goods much quicker.

✎ 我們寄送貨品的時間會縮短。

Our esteemed colleague, Ms. Eva Hung, will be the manager of our new branch.

✎ 我們尊敬的同仁，洪伊娃小姐將任新設分公司的經理。

The new branch manager has ten-year experience in the market.

✎ 新設分公司的經理擁有十年相關經驗。

Please feel free to contact our new branch manager.

✎ 歡迎與我們新上任的分公司經理連絡。

The new branch is located at the following address:

✎ 新設分公司的地址如下：

Our telephone and fax number are as follows:

✎ 我們的電話與傳真號碼如下：

You can contact me at rubylin@mail.net if you have any questions about our goods.

✎ 如果您對我們的產品有任何問題，歡迎來信至rubylin@mail.net。

Part 1
Part 2
Part 3
Part 4
Part 5
Part 6

•2-03• 公司合併

公司合併信件的內容，除了合併的事實之外，更重要的是給予收信者明確的資訊，包含合併生效日、合併後是否更改聯絡方式、以及合併對於公司的助益等等。

Subject | **Notice of Merger**

Dear Customers:

We would like to announce the **merger**[1] of our company with NYSE Co., effective May 1, 2017.

The new company will be called Samsung Co. It will be at our **present**[2] address. All telephone and fax number will be the same.

This merger represents a pooling of the **expertise**[3] of two major cellphone firms, in an effort to **develop**[4] and produce a **superior**[5] line of cellphones. It will also allow us to shorten our delivery time as we will have a much larger distribution **network**[6].

We hope the new company will provide you with better service and quality products.

Best regards,
Daniel

Send

親愛的客戶您好：

在此通知：我們將與NYSE公司合併，於二〇一七年五月一日生效。

新公司名稱為三星公司，會在我們的原址，所有的聯絡電話和傳真號碼都不會變更。

二家擁有專業手機技術公司的合併，主要用意為製作出更優越的產品；此外，配送網路的擴大，也將縮短我們的貨運時間。

希望新的公司能提供您更高品質的服務與產品。

丹尼爾 敬上

Part 1
Part 2
Part 3
Part 4
Part 5
Part 6

核心字彙充電站 *Key Words*

1. **merger** 名（公司等的）合併
2. **present** 形 目前的
3. **expertise** 名 專門技術
4. **develop** 動 發展；使發達
5. **superior** 形 上級的；較高的
6. **network** 名 網狀系統

替換好用句 *Copy & Paste*

 通知合併公司事宜

NYSE Company and 3M Company are pleased to announce a merger, which will take effect next month.
🖉 NYSE和3M公司很高興宣布合併，於下個月生效。

AmBev Company is proud to announce that we have merged with Amoco Company to form AmBeo Company.
🖉 我們很驕傲地宣布：我們安倍夫公司即將和艾摩可公司，合併成為「安貝爾公司」。

From May 1, FOX Company will merge with our company to form Intercomm Company.
🖉 五月一日起，福斯公司會與我們公司合併成立「音德康公司」。

The new company will be known as Bosch Company with headquarters at NO. 123, Tien-Yu St., Taipei City.
🖉 合併後的公司名稱為博世公司，總公司設在台北市天玉街123號。

The new firm, DKNY Company's headquarters will be located at No.14, Tien-Yu St., Taipei City.
🖉 新的DKNY總公司將位於台北市天玉街14號。

 維繫與客戶的合作關係

In light of this move, customers should now look more favorably on the new company's larger scale.
🖉 按此變動，希望客戶能夠樂觀地看待規模變得更大的公司。

This friendly merger will double the size of our staff and enable us to consolidate some of our back office functions.
🖉 友好的合併會使本公司的員工人數加倍，並讓本公司的效更加穩固。

As a result of this merger, we are able to offer you a large range of business machines and electrical equipment.
🖊 公司合併後，將可提供您更大量的事務機器以及電子設備。

Please give us an opportunity of supplying you with our extended range of products.
🖊 請給予我們為您提供多元化產品的機會。

Our company name, contact information and commitment to quality will remain the same.
🖊 公司的名稱、聯絡方式和產品品質，保證會一樣。

 ## 提供聯繫方式

Stockholders with questions or who need assistance about the status of their shares may call 02-2272-3533.
🖊 股東如有疑問或需協助，請來電撥打：02-2272-3533。

If you have any questions on this change in Audi Company, please do not hesitate to call our toll-free number.
🖊 如果您對此合併有任何問題，請撥打我們的免付費專線。

Any of our customer service representatives will be happy to address the concerns you might have.
🖊 我們的客服人員將很樂意回答您的問題。

 Let's learn more!

 ## 單字/片語Focus

🐛 企業組織與改變 🐛	
✱**incorporate** 把…合併	✱**mandate** 委任
✱**corporate merger** 公司合併	✱**sister corporation** 關係企業
✱**parent corporation** 母公司	✱**subsidiary corporation** 子公司
✱**corporate reorganization** 公司重整	

Part 1

Part 2

Part 3

Part 4

Part 5

Part 6

2-04 公司搬遷

在通知公司搬遷的信件中，必須確切告知搬遷後的地點以及聯絡方式，才能讓業務上的合作關係得以順利繼續。

Subject Notice of Change of Address

Dear Customers:

This is to inform you that our office is moving to a new location as of May 31, 2016. Our new office address and telephone number are as follows:

Address: No.369, Chung Shan Road, Taichung
Telephone number: 04-2233-2233

You can also find directions to our office on our website: www.sunnyside.com.tw

Best regards,
Lucy

親愛的客戶您好：

此函通知您：本公司將於二〇一六年五月三十一日遷往新的地點，地址與電話如下：

地址：台中市中山路369號
電話：04-2233-2233

可於本公司網站取得資訊：www.sunnyside.com.tw 位置地點

露西 敬上

Send ▶

 Copy & Paste

 告知公司搬遷和地點

We are pleased to announce that our office is moving to a new location.
🖊 本公司很高興宣布：正式搬遷至新辦公室。

Please allow me to inform you that we have moved to the Chung-Shin Building in Shi-Lin.

✎ 在此通知您：本公司已搬遷至士林的中興大樓。

Our warehouse will also be at our new location, making it easier to process your orders.
✎ 我們的工廠也將搬遷至新址，以便更容易處理您的訂單。

We are glad to inform you that we have moved to much larger and more convenient premises at:
✎ 在此通知您：我們即將搬遷到以下的地址，新地點較大，也更方便：

We have decided that a larger office is necessary to cope with the increasing demand of our products.
✎ 因應產品日漸增多的需求量，我們決定擴大辦公處。

We will relocate to a newer and larger place on May 1.
✎ 五月一日起，我們會搬遷至更新、更大的地點。

From May 10, our company will move to a new location.
✎ 五月十日起，我們將搬至新地點。

The new address, phone number, and fax number are as follows:
✎ 以下為新的地址、電話以及傳真號碼：

Please address all correspondence to our new office as of May 31.
✎ 五月三十一日後，請將信件寄到本公司的新地址。

Both the new telephone and fax number will be in operation from May 1.
✎ 新的電話和傳真，會於五月一日開始運作。

Please send all correspondence to us at:
✎ 請將信件寄到以下住址：

We are going to move to our new residence next Monday and will send you our new address.
✎ 我們預計下週一搬遷，稍後將通知您新的地址。

The new premises include a buyer's lounge.
✎ 新公司有一間客戶休息室。

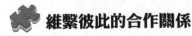 **維繫彼此的合作關係**

We look forward to having you as a guest in our new office.
✎ 我們期待您來訪參觀新辦公室。

Please feel free to call on at any time.
🖊 歡迎隨時來訪。

We would be happy to have you visit us if you are in our area.
🖊 如果您到附近，歡迎蒞臨指教。

We would be pleased if you take the time to drop by our new office when you are in our area.
🖊 如果您來這附近，歡迎來參觀我們的新辦公室。

We are celebrating our move to Taipei with a reception at the new office, from 7 to 10 p.m. on Friday, May 11.
🖊 我們將於五月十一日，星期五晚上七點到十點，於台北辦公室舉辦喬遷晚會。

Please let me know if you could attend the party, I may send you an invitation.
🖊 如果您能來參加，請讓我知道，我將會寄發邀請函給您。

We look forward to continuing to provide you with quality service.
🖊 期盼今後仍能繼續提供您高品質的服務。

 *Let's learn more!*

 單字/片語Focus

❧ 企業經營 ❧

✱**initiate** 開始	✱**assessment** 評估；評量
✱**compete** 競爭	✱**confront** 面臨；遭遇
✱**relocate** 搬遷	✱**reputation** 聲望；名聲
✱**resource** 資源	✱**eliminate** 撤除；淘汰
✱**statement** 聲明	✱**streamline** 效率化
✱**inefficient** 效率差的	✱**yield** 收益；生產量

❧ 企業發展 ❧

✱**sponsor** 贊助；予以補助	✱**patronize** 資助；光顧
✱**coterie** 圈內人；夥伴	✱**principal** 資本

Part 1
Part 2
Part 3
Part 4
Part 5
Part 6

✳property 財產;資產	✳ownership 所有權
✳private assets 私有資產	✳intangible assets 無形資產

 文法/句型Focus

✳ 通知客戶

❶ I am writing to inform you... 我寫信是為了通知您…。

❷ Please note that... 請注意,…。

❸ We would like to inform you that... 我們想要通知您…。

❹ I am delighted to tell you that... 我很高興通知您…。

❺ We hereby inform you that... 我們在此通知您…。

❻ Notice is hereby given that... …,特以此函告知。

❼ We are glad to announce that... 我們很高興宣布…。

✳ 提供幫助

❶ We would be happy to... 我們很樂意…。

❷ Please feel free to contact me if you need help.
若您需要幫助,請與我聯繫。

**❸ Please let me know if there's anything we can do
to help.**
若有我們能幫忙的地方,請讓我知道。

·2-05· 公司歇業

在商業合作上，若遇到公司歇業的情況，禮貌上最好通知有往來的客戶。一般來說，歇業通知函的內容須註明：一、日期；二、理由；三、業務承接；四、感謝對方的長期配合。

Subject | **Discontinuation of Business**

Dear Customers:

We would like to inform you that our company will **discontinue**[1] **business**[2] operations as of January 20, 2016.

Because of the high interest rates, we are **no longer**[3] able to provide the service that our customers **deserve**[4]. We have made arrangement for all of our business **transactions**[5] to be handled by Fuji Company. They will be contacting you in the near future to **discuss**[6] the future relationship with you.

We would like to thank you for your support and tell you how much we have enjoyed having you as our customer. We hope this does not cause your company any serious inconvenience.

Yours very truly,
Paul

親愛的客戶您好：

在此通知您：本公司將於二〇一六年一月二十日結束營業。

由於利率偏高，本公司無法再提供客戶應得的服務。我們已將後續業務交由富士公司處理，他們將於近日與您聯絡，並討論後續的商務關係。

本公司很感謝您過去的支持，也很開心為您服務。希望這件事不會帶給貴公司太大的不便。

保羅 敬上

Part 1
Part 2
Part 3
Part 4
Part 5
Part 6

 核心字彙充電站 *Key Words*

1. **discontinue** 動 停止；中斷
2. **business** 名 生意；公司
3. **no longer** 片 不再
4. **deserve** 動 應得；該得
5. **transaction** 名 交易；業務
6. **discuss** 動 討論

 替換好用句 *Copy & Paste*

永久停業的通知

Our business will be discontinued after the end of August 1.
🖉 我們將於八月一日結束營業。

We would like to inform you that FOX Computers will be closing on May 30, 2016.
🖉 在此通知：福斯電腦公司將在二〇一六年五月三十日結束營業。

We wish to inform you that we will discontinue all business operations from May 1.
🖉 此函通知：本公司即將在五月一日起，結束營業。

This letter is notification that due to unavoidable financial difficulties, Sunshine Computers is regrettably closing for business on May 20.
🖉 在此通知：陽光電腦因為經濟困難，將於五月二十日停止營業。

Due to circumstances beyond our control, we decided not to continue with the business of Tour Company.
🖉 基於各種因素，我們決定中止和旅遊公司的業務。

Our company will not place any additional orders to your company.
🖉 我們將不會再接受貴公司任何的訂單。

We will not be placing any additional orders with your company.
🖉 我們將不會再向貴公司下訂單。

暫停歇業的通知

This is to inform you that we are going to suspend business for some time.

✒ 謹以此信通知：本公司將暫停營業一段時間。

Pleased be informed that our company will be closed temporarily from May 1st to 20th due to renovations to the interior of the building.
✒ 在此通知：本公司因內部整修、重新裝潢，將於五月一日到二十日暫停營業。

We are informing you that Honda Company will close for the New Year's holidays from December 25 to January 4, and will reopen on Monday, January 5.
✒ 我們要通知您：本田公司即將在十二月二十五日到一月四日新年假期期間休業，並於一月五日（星期一）重新開始營業。

The restaurant will close during the holiday and reopen on Thursday, 28 February.
✒ 本餐廳將於假期期間暫停營業，並於二月二十八日（星期四）重新開張。

Our firm has made our decision to upgrade service equipment from today.
✒ 本公司決定進行服務設施的升級作業。

Our company will be on holiday from May 1 to 5.
✒ 本公司五月一日到五日，將暫停營業。

We will reopen on May 21.
✒ 我們將於五月二十一日重新營業。

 出現財務困難

My company is now in the process of bankruptcy.
✒ 本公司目前面臨破產危機。

Over the next two weeks, we are reviewing our accounting records and paying any outstanding invoices.
✒ 接下來的二週，我們會開始處理帳務並付清款項。

If we have outstanding balance from your company, we will contact you to confirm our current obligation to your company so that we can settle the accounts.
✒ 如果我方還有欠款，我們會聯絡您，並在了解款項後付清。

Over the next sixty days, we are reviewing our accounting records and paying any outstanding invoices.
✒ 接下來的六十天，我們會處理未付清的帳款。

Part 1

Part 2

Part 3

Part 4

Part 5

Part 6

停業的後續處理

Arrangement has been made to ensure the smooth continuation of business operations.

🖊 有關後續的業務，我們已做好妥善的安排。

Next Monday, we are holding a closing out sale.

🖊 下週一，我們會舉辦清倉拍賣會。

Stock on hand will be cleared regardless of cost.

🖊 庫存將不惜成本賣出。

Prices will be marked down by as much as on half.

🖊 所有商品皆以半價銷售。

As the sale is likely to be well attended, we hope you make a point of visiting the store as early as possible during the opening days.

🖊 此次特賣可能會吸引很多人，希望您在清倉前儘早前來。

 信末結尾

Please don't hesitate to call if there is anything I can do for you before May 20.

🖊 如有任何疑問，請於五月二十日前來電。

We hope we will have the pleasure of doing business with you again in the future.

🖊 我們希望未來還有機會為各位服務。

We are deeply sorry for any inconvenience it may cause.

🖊 對於造成的不便，我們深表歉意。

Your continued support is highly appreciated.

🖊 感謝您長年以來的支持。

We really appreciate your support over these years.

🖊 感謝您這幾年來對我們的支持。

We hope this won't cause you too much inconvenience.

🖊 希望這不會帶給您太大的不便。

Unit 3 祝賀函與邀請函

Part 1
Part 2
Part 3
Part 4
Part 5
Part 6

·3-01· 祝賀公司成立

Subject **Congratulations on Opening A New Company**

Dear Mr. Thomas:

I am pleased to know that your company will be open next week. Please accept my **warmest**[1] congratulations and best wishes.

With your excellent **leadership**[2] and unusual abilities, I am sure the new company will have a **brilliant**[3] future and **booming**[4] business.

Best regards,
Victor

湯瑪士先生您好：

很高興知道您的公司將於下週開幕，請接受我誠摯的恭賀與祝福。

在您優越的領導下，我相信貴公司未來前途光明，並且生意興隆。

維克多 敬上

Send

核心字彙充電站 Key Words

1. **warm** 形 衷心的；熱情的
2. **leadership** 名 領導
3. **brilliant** 形 傑出的；優秀的
4. **booming** 形 大受歡迎的

替換好用句 Copy & Paste

 表示祝賀

I am very happy to know that you have opened a company.

401

✏ 很高興得知您創辦了公司。

We are delighted to know that your new company is starting business today.
✏ 我們很高興得知貴公司今日開始營業。

I'd like to add my congratulations to the many you must be receiving.
✏ 我也在此加入向您祝賀的行列。

With your excellent background and achievement, I am sure that the new company will be prosperous day by day.
✏ 以您傑出的背景及成就，一定會使您的公司欣欣向榮。

 ## 給予祝福

Best wishes for setting a new record!
✏ 預祝創造佳績！

Good luck in all that you will achieve in the future.
✏ 祝您未來一切順利。

I congratulate on your new business.
✏ 恭祝您鴻圖大展。

I wish you every success in the future.
✏ 祝福您未來成功。

I wish you gain the greatest possible success in the future.
✏ 希望您未來工作能夠獲得佳績。

As your company continues to grow and prosper, let me know if I can assist you.
✏ 在貴公司成長與發展的階段，如有可以效勞之處，煩請告知。

You can look forward to our active support in the years ahead.
✏ 對於貴公司今後的發展，本公司願盡力支持。

We wish you every success and happiness in your important position.
✏ 希望您在要職上順利成功。

Part 1

Part 2

Part 3

Part 4

Part 5

Part 6

·3-02· 祝賀佳節愉快

　　每一種節日都有其需要慶祝的背景意義及祝賀話語。基本上不外乎是幾個重要的節日：台灣有農曆新年、中秋節、端午節（很少在寫賀卡）；美國則是聖誕節、感恩節。其他節日則視個人狀況而定，例如情人節，近來也愈來愈趨向盛大慶祝此一節日。

　　一般說來，祝賀信的內容越來越生動活潑，也更具創意。發信者可依據與對方的交情，決定信件內容走向。不過大體說來，只要記得在這些重要節日給予祝福，都會讓人感到非常窩心。

Subject | **Happy New Year!**

Dear Friend:

It's been an **eventful**[1] year.

2015 was simply **incredible**[2] and **memorable**[3] for all of us, all that craziness **amidst**[4] the hard work. Still, we pulled off an amazing job together.

I wish your New Year countdown to 2016 be filled with kisses, **festive**[5] noise and drunken toasts! Wherever you are, have fun!

Also, I wish you all and your families good health, love and happiness in 2016!

Cheers,
Linda

Send ▸

親愛的朋友：

今年真是個多事之年。

二〇一五年很特別，也充滿了許多回憶。工作上有苦有樂，儘管如此，我們的合作還是非常成功。

希望您二〇一六年的跨年倒數充滿香吻、歡樂的喧鬧聲以及愉快的敬酒！不論您在哪，希望您開心！

另外，也祝福您的家人在二〇一六年身體健康、快樂！

琳達 上

Subject Happy New Year!

To All Friends from Apple Company:	給所有蘋果公司的朋友：
Thanks for the great **memories**[6] in 2015!	感謝二○一五年的美好回憶！
Here's wishing you a blessed and a holy Christmas! And Happy Holidays and Happy 2016!	祝福您聖誕佳節以及新年愉快！
Take care and keep in touch!	保重，隨時保持聯絡！
Best, Helen	海倫 敬上

Send ▸

Subject Valentine's Greetings!

Dear All:	親愛的各位：
As the world **celebrates**[7] this day of hearts, take a moment and give a kiss, even a hug to everyone special in your life.	當全世界都在慶祝這個愛的節日時，記得給身邊那位特別的人一個香吻及擁抱。
I hope you could blow a kiss my way. =)	也希望您給我一個飛吻(笑)。
Happy **Valentine's**[8] Day!	情人節快樂！
Best, Judy	茱蒂 敬上

Send ▸

Part 1

Part 2

Part 3

Part 4

Part 5

Part 6

Subject **Merry Christmas!**

Dear Customers:

The holiday season is a wonderful time for us to remember the friends and customers who help our business and make our jobs a pleasure all year long. Our business would not be possible without your continued support.

So we'd like to take this moment to say thank you and send our best wishes to you and your families. May your new year be filled with all the success and happiness!

Happy Holidays!
Nancy

親愛的客戶您好：

這個節日讓我們想到長年支持我們的朋友及客戶。沒有您的支持就不會有現在的我們。

我們希望趁此機會向您致謝，並向您及家人獻上我們最深的祝福。希望您來年事事成功、快樂。

祝 佳節愉快！

南西 敬上

Send

Subject **Merry Christmas!**

Dear Mr. Washington:

As the holiday season **approaches**[9], we'd like to take this opportunity to thank you for your continued business. It is business **associates**[10] like you who make our jobs a pleasure and keep our business successful.

May your holiday season and the New Year be filled with a lot of joy, happiness and success. We look forward to working with you in the coming year and hope our

華盛頓先生您好：

佳節將近，希望趁此機會向您對我們的支持致上感謝。因為有您的支持，才能讓我們的工作愉快且順利。

祝您新年愉快，盼望來年我們合作愉快，也希望我們的合作關係長久。

business relationship continues for many years to come.

Happy Holidays!
Mark

祝 佳節愉快！

馬克 敬上

Send

 核心字彙充電站 *Key Words*

1. **eventful** 形 變故多的	2. **incredible** 形 難以置信的
3. **memorable** 形 難忘的	4. **amidst** 介 在…之中
5. **festive** 形 歡樂的；歡鬧的	6. **memory** 名 回憶
7. **celebrate** 動 慶祝	8. **valentine** 名 情人
9. **approach** 動 接近	10. **associate** 名 夥伴；合夥人

 替換好用句 *Copy & Paste*

Best wishes for the New Year!
🖋 新年愉快！

May peace and happiness be yours in the New Year!
🖋 希望您在新的一年中平安快樂！

The happiest New Year to you and your family.
🖋 祝您和家人新年愉快。

May the New Year find you in the enjoyment of health and happiness!
🖋 希望您新年愉快平安！

As the Christmas season approaches, may you and your family all of the joy and happiness that you deserve!
🖋 聖誕節將近，希望您和家人得到應有的喜悅和祝福！

Best wishes for a merry Christmas!
🖋 聖誕節愉快！

Wish all the blessings of a beautiful Christmas season.
🖉 願您擁有聖誕節的祝福。

Best wishes for Christmas and the Chinese New Year!
🖉 恭賀聖誕節以及新年快樂！

We wish you and your staff a Merry Christmas and a Happy New Year.
🖉 謹祝福您與員工聖誕暨新年快樂。

Best wishes for Christmas and the New Year!
🖉 祝聖誕暨新年快樂。

We are very pleased to send you and your colleagues our very best wishes.
🖉 向您和您的同事致上最美好的祝福。

We hope that this New Year will see the growth of your firm and the achievement of your projects.
🖉 祝貴公司來年業務蒸蒸日上，祝您事業有成。

May the next year bring you and your family health, happiness, peace and prosperity!
🖉 希望您與家人明年健康愉快，平安興盛。

May it see your hopes fulfilled!
🖉 祝您實現願望！

May it be rich in the successful accomplishment of your highest aims!
🖉 祝您達成目標！

May fortune smile upon you and favor you with many blessings.
🖉 希望幸運降臨且祝福您。

We wish you a Happy New Year, a year big with achievement, a year mellow with happiness and contentment.
🖉 希望您來年有成就且快樂滿足。

May the coming year bring you happiness in fullest measure.
🖉 希望您未來的一年歡樂滿溢。

May the New Year bring you health, happiness and all other good things!
🖉 希望您來年健康快樂，事事順心！

May the New Year be a good year to you - full of health and happiness!
🖉 祝您來年健康快樂！

Part 1
Part 2
Part 3
Part 4
Part 5
Part 6

May each of the three hundred and sixty-five days of the New Year be the happy one for you!
🖋 希望您未來三百六十五天都能快樂地度過。

Happy Holidays!
🖋 佳節愉快！

Warm greetings and best wishes for happiness in the coming year.
🖋 衷心祝您來年快樂。

Allow me to congratulate your family on this special day.
🖋 謹向您的家人在這特別的日子裡表示祝賀。

 進階補充站 *Let's learn more!*

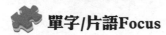 單字/片語Focus

🎋 常見的中外節日 🎋

✱**New Year's Day** 元旦	✱**New Year's Eve** 除夕
✱**Chinese New Year** 春節	✱**Valentine's Day** 情人節
✱**White Day** 白色情人節	✱**Lantern Festival** 元宵節
✱**Arbor Day** 植樹節	✱**Children's Day** 兒童節
✱**April Fool's Day** 愚人節	✱**Qingming Festival** 清明節
✱**Labor Day** 勞動節	✱**Teachers' Day** 教師節
✱**Mother's Day** 母親節	✱**Father's Day** 父親節
✱**Easter** 復活節	✱**Halloween** 萬聖節
✱**Thanksgiving Day** 感恩節	✱**Christmas** 聖誕節
✱**Dragon Boat Festival** 端午節	✱**Mid-Autumn Festival** 中秋節
✱**Hungry Ghost Festival** 中元節	
✱**Chinese Valentine's Day** 七夕情人節	
✱**International Women's Day** 國際婦女節	

Part 1

Part 2

Part 3

Part 4

Part 5

Part 6

❧ 與春節相關 ❧

*incense 香	*firecracker 鞭炮
*red envelope 紅包	*red couplets 春聯
*the lion dance 舞獅	*the dragon dance 舞龍
*around the fireplace 圍爐	
*bring in the new year 守歲	
*make a New Year's visit 拜年	
*sweet glutinous rice pudding 年糕	
*eight treasure rice-pudding 八寶飯	

❧ 與聖誕節相關 ❧

*Christmas tree 聖誕樹	*Christmas carol 聖誕頌歌
*Christmas stocking 聖誕襪	*Christmas meal 聖誕大餐
*poinsettia 聖誕紅	*Boxing day 聖誕節隔天的特賣日
*reindeer 麋鹿	*Santa Claus 聖誕老人
*Jesus Christ 耶穌基督	*Christmas wreath 聖誕花環
*mistletoe 槲寄生	*sleigh 雪橇
*candy cane 拐杖形糖果	*gingerbread 薑餅
*snowman 雪人	*stable 馬廄

 實用資訊Focus

萬聖節的Trick or Treat 🔍

　　據說起源於愛爾蘭。古時的愛爾蘭異教徒相信鬼魂會在萬聖節前夕群聚於住家附近，並接受款待。因此，村民們就自己扮成鬼魂或精靈，在村外遊走，藉此引導鬼魂離開。於此同時，村民們也會注意在屋前放置一些食品，他們相信這樣可以餵食鬼魂，讓他們不至於傷害人類，這一習俗延續下來，就演變成現在孩子們的Trick or Treat了。

·3-03· 祝賀升遷／任職

Subject **Congratulations on The Promotion**

Dear Charlotte:

Congratulations on your new position as Marketing Manager! I was not surprised by the news since you have always showed your enthusiasm when you work in the past years. As people say, "Hard work pays off."

I would like to express my hearty congratulations on this good news. We are sure that your will make great success in your position.

Best regards,
Billy

親愛的夏綠蒂：

恭喜您當上行銷部的主管！聽到這個消息我一點也不驚訝，因為過去幾年，您總是懷抱熱忱努力工作著。俗話說得好：「有努力便有回報。」

在此獻上我誠心的祝賀，我們相信您會在這個職位發光發亮。

比利 敬上

Send ▶

 Copy & Paste

 恭喜得到升遷

Please accept our congratulations on being named manager of the Marketing Department.
🖋 恭喜您當上行銷部主管。

I have just learned that you have been appointed as the chairman for the Asia area.
🖋 我剛得知您被任命為亞洲地區的總裁。

Congratulations on your promotion!
🖋 恭喜您升遷！

I am so happy to learn of your promotion.
🖊 很高興得知您升遷的消息。

May we congratulate you on your promotion to Marketing Manager!
🖊 恭喜您當上行銷部經理！

I am very delighted to hear that you have been appointed as General Manager.
🖊 很高興您被指派為總經理。

It was a great pleasure to hear of your appointment as President.
🖊 很開心得知您被指派為董事長。

The news of your promotion came as no surprise to us in view of your brilliant work and achievements.
🖊 因為您的傑出成就，沒人對您的晉升感到訝異。

We'd like to send you our warmest congratulations on the occasion of your new appointment as Vice President.
🖊 我們誠摯恭賀您就任副董事長。

Please allow us to extend our warmest congratulations on your promotion.
🖊 請讓我們由衷地祝賀您升遷。

I am so happy to hear about your promotion.
🖊 我很開心聽到您升遷的消息。

All the employees want to congratulate you on your promotion.
🖊 全體同仁恭賀您榮升。

As your co-worker, I am proud of your hard-working attitude and promotion.
🖊 身為同事，我以您的工作態度以及升遷為榮。

The news that your husband was promoted to the chief of Marketing Department of Qisda Company has made me truly happy for you.
🖊 聽聞您的先生晉升為綺思達公司的行銷主管，我由衷地替您感到開心。

Please accept our congratulations.
🖊 請接受我們的祝賀。

Please accept my sincerest congratulations.
🖊 請接受我最誠心的祝賀。

Please accept my best wishes for every success in your new position.

Part 1

Part 2

Part 3

Part 4

Part 5

Part 6

✏ 請接受我衷心的祝福，希望您在新職務上能夠成功。

Congratulations on your recent promotion to Executive.
✏ 恭喜您晉升為執行長。

It's our sincerest wish that under your enlightened leadership, your company would continue to prosper.
✏ 祝福貴公司在您的開明領導下，業務蒸蒸日上。

Congratulations, my dear friend.
✏ 真是恭喜您了。

 恭喜就職

I am very happy to hear that you have secured a job in Apple as a software engineer.
✏ 我很開心您得到蘋果電腦軟體工程師的工作。

I was thrilled to hear about your new job with the Yankee Company.
✏ 我很開心聽到您在洋基公司找到新工作。

Best luck in your new job.
✏ 祝福您在新工作上表現出色。

Congratulations with your new job.
✏ 恭喜您找到新工作。

I know it's been a long search to find the right position, but it seems like this is going to be a good match for your skills and experience.
✏ 我知道您已求職許久，這份工作看起來很符合您的能力以及經驗。

Please convey to him my heartiest congratulations.
✏ 請轉達我對他真誠的祝賀。

It's a great achievement to get a job in such a huge multinational company.
✏ 能夠在如此大型的跨國企業工作，真是莫大的成就。

You will feel the presence of very intelligent and professional people in the office.
✏ 您會在辦公室遇到許多聰明的專業人士。

Now you must work hard to stay among them and learn a lot of things from them.

✎ 現在，您必須在他們之間認真學習許多事。

I know our colleagues will enjoy working with you.
✎ 我相信同事會很開心與您工作。

 對工作態度予以肯定

You really deserve it!
✎ 這是您應得的！

You have worked so hard these years.
✎ 您過去幾年如此認真工作。

I know how hard you have worked to earn the recognition you presently enjoy at Chi Mei Company.
✎ 我知道您是多麼辛苦的工作，才能贏得在奇美公司的地位。

I feel that your company is very wise in having made their choice.
✎ 我認為貴公司做的抉擇很明智。

Working with you in the past five years has shown me how capable and enthusiastic you are.
✎ 在過去五年與您共事的經驗中，一直覺得您才能出眾，對工作也懷有熱忱。

Looking back on your activities, we all know that your experiences are the qualities which are needed for this position.
✎ 回顧您以往的工作態度，您的經驗是這個職位所必備的特質。

We all know you have worked so hard for the company.
✎ 我們都知道您為公司努力工作。

Your enterprise and your cooperative attitude are certain the qualities that support you in the new position.
✎ 您的熱忱和協調能力都將是支持您任居此職位的特質。

Having worked with you so long, I can confidently say that you are the right person in the right position.
✎ 與您共事這麼久，我敢說您是此職位的最佳人選。

We feel the appointment is timely as well as it is well deserved.
✎ 我們覺得這項指派來得正是時候，也恰如其分。

Your success is certainly the fruit of your tireless effort.
✎ 您的成功是您不屈不撓努力的結果。

Part 1

Part 2

Part 3

Part 4

Part 5

Part 6

 **表達期許與鼓勵**

I expect this advanced position will challenge and teach you even more about the strategies in marketing.
🖋 我期待這個高階職位將更有挑戰性，並能讓你學到更多行銷策略。

I am sure your professional experience has prepared you to meet such challenge.
🖋 相信您的專業已經讓您準備好接受挑戰了。

We are sure that you will achieve great things for the organization through this opportunity.
🖋 我們相信您會以此契機，為公司創造更多成就。

I wish you every success in managing the affairs of the organization.
🖋 祝福您在管理公司事務上能夠成功。

You will definitely make greater success in the near future.
🖋 您必定會在不久的將來獲得更大的成功。

I am confident that you are more than equal to the difficult task that awaits you.
🖋 我相信以您的能力，要處理難題綽綽有餘。

 歡迎對方加入團隊

Welcome to our office.
🖋 歡迎來到我們辦公室。

Welcome to our company.
🖋 歡迎來到我們公司。

We are so happy to have a new colleague.
🖋 我們很開心有新同事加加入。

We are most fortunate to have you.
🖋 很榮幸有您的加入。

Great to hear that you will join our team.
🖋 很開心有您的加入。

We look forward to your continued success.
🖋 我們期盼您越來越成功。

3-04 開幕邀請

其實邀請信函（invitation）上最重要的資訊，當屬主題（theme）、日期（date）、時間（time）和地點（place），以及希望對方回覆的方式。邀請函的重點在簡潔明確，所以只要確定這幾項重點，就足以寫出一封清楚的邀請E-mail了。

Subject | **Grand Opening Invitation**

Dear Sirs:

Our new branch office in Taipei is opening on Friday, May 10, 2016.

We will have an office party on Friday night. You and your staff are cordially invited to attend our Grand Opening Party. It will be an informal affair with cocktails and snacks.

Please come and join us! We are looking forward to seeing you at the party!

Sincerely yours,
Alex

諸君：

我們新的台北分公司即將在二〇一六年，五月十日星期五開幕。

當晚會舉辦派對，敬邀您與您的員工前來參加開幕派對。此為非正式派對，我們將提供雞尾酒與點心。

請前來與我們同樂！希望能在派對上見到您！

愛力克斯 敬上

Send

替換好用句　Copy & Paste

We are going to have an opening ceremony at our Taipei office.
✐ 我們將會在台北分公司舉辦開幕典禮。

We would like to invite you and your wife to be present at the celebration.

Part 1

Part 2

Part 3

Part 4

Part 5

Part 6

415

✐ 我們希望能邀請您與尊夫人參加慶祝活動。

We are inviting all firms that have contributed to our success.
✐ 我們邀請所有對我們的成功有貢獻的工作夥伴。

We request the pleasure of your presence at the opening ceremony of the company on Monday.
✐ 我們希望能有這個榮幸，邀請您前來參加星期一的開幕典禮。

Attached is the map to our new office which is located only ten minutes on foot from MRT Shilin Station on the Tamsui line.
✐ 附件為辦公室地圖，新辦公室為在淡水線士林站步行十分鐘的地點。

A luncheon will be arranged at the Hilton Hotel, followed by the opening ceremony and a tour of the new factory.
✐ 午宴將會在希爾頓飯店舉行，隨後將是開幕典禮和參觀新工廠的行程。

There will be a banquet in the evening.
✐ 晚間將有一場酒宴。

All arrangements for your stay overnight on that day will be made by us at our expense.
✐ 我方將支付您當天晚上的住宿費用。

We hope you can make an effort to attend our ceremony.
✐ 希望您能盡量出席。

Your presence is requested.
✐ 敬邀您的光臨。

I do hope that you will be able to spare the time to share this occasion with us.
✐ 希望您能撥冗參加我們的聚會。

We kindly request your presence.
✐ 我們敬邀您的光臨。

Please join us if you have time. We will be pleased to see you at the party.
✐ 若您有時間，請務必出席，我們會很高興有您參與派對。

We will be expecting your presence.
✐ 我們會期待您的出席。

 **進階補充站** *Let's learn more!*

 文法/句型Focus

✳ 提出邀請

❶ **(Company) cordially invites you to...** （公司名）誠摯地邀請您…。

❷ **We are pleased to invite you to attend...** 我們很榮幸邀請您來參加。

❸ **We would be pleased if you could...** 如果您能…，我們會很開心。

❹ **We have pleasure in inviting you to...** 我們很榮幸邀請您…。

❺ **You are cordially invited to...** 誠摯地邀請您…。

❻ **Would you like to join us...?** 您是否願意和我一起…？

❼ **I would like to invite you to...** 我想邀請您…。

❽ **On behalf of... , I would like to invite you to...** 我僅代表…邀請您…。

❾ **We would be delighted if you could come.** 如果您能來，我們會很開心。

✳ 期待對方答應邀請

❶ **We look forward to your participation at...** 我們期待您參與…。

❷ **We hope you will be able to join us.** 我們期望您能加入我們的活動。

❸ **We hope you can make it.** 我們期望您能夠參與。

✳ 詢問對方口味偏好

❶ **Do you like...?** 您喜歡…嗎？

❷ **Is there any kind of food you don't like?** 您有不喜歡的食物嗎？

❸ **Please let me know if you have any dietary restrictions.**
若您有任何飲食方面的限制，請告知我。

參加公司宴會

邀請他人參加公司宴會時，請務必於信中詳細說明地點與時間，並於文末再度誠摯地邀請對方參加。

Subject 20th Anniversary Invitation

Dear Mr. Black:

To celebrate the 20th **anniversary**[1] of Tokyo Motors Taipei Branch, we are planning **a dinner party**[2] at the Grand Hotel in Taipei from 6:00 to 10:00 p.m. on Saturday, May 20, 2016.

You are cordially invited to the party so that we can express our **sincere**[3] appreciation to you for the **generous**[4] support you have **extended to**[5] us for a long time. For your information, the party will be attended by many top executives of leading Taiwanese and Japanese auto manufacturers.

We believe this will be the excellent opportunity for us to **get acquainted with**[6] each other. We hope that you will be able to join us in this opportunity to meet the **senior**[7] **directors**[8] of our company.

We look forward to seeing you on Saturday, May 20, 2016.

R.S.V.P. by e-mail at admin@tokyomotor. com.tw

With warmest regards,
Clair

布雷克先生您好：

為慶祝東京車業台北分公司二十週年紀念，我們將在二〇一六年五月二十日星期六，六點到十點在台北圓山大飯店舉辦慶祝酒會。

為了感激您長久的合作與支持，我們誠摯地邀請您前來參加宴會。此外，還有許多台日車產業界的高級主管也會來參與。

我們相信這是認識彼此的最佳機會，希望您能趁此機會前來認識我們的高階主管。

盼於五月二十日見到您。

敬請回覆至以下信箱：
admin@tokyomotor.
com.tw。

克蕾兒 敬上

Send ►

Part 1

Part 2

Part 3

Part 4

Part 5

Part 6

 核心字彙充電站 *Key Words*

1. **anniversary** 名 週年紀念
2. **a dinner party** 片 晚宴
3. **sincere** 形 衷心的；真誠的
4. **generous** 形 慷慨的；大方的
5. **extend to** 片 給予；提供
6. **get acquainted with** 片 與…相識
7. **senior** 形 高階的
8. **director** 名 主管；主任；處長

 替換好用句 *Copy & Paste*

通知公司舉辦宴會

The President of the Tokyo Motor Company requests the pleasure of your company at a banquet to be held at the Far East Hotel.
✎ 東京車業總裁邀請貴公司參加在遠東飯店的晚宴。

The pleasure of your company is cordially requested at Tokyo Motor Anniversary Celebration.
✎ 誠摯地邀請貴公司出席東京車業周年紀念慶祝會。

You are invited to our 30th Anniversary Party.
✎ 請您參加本公司的三十週年慶派對。

I would like to invite you to our formal dance party.
✎ 我希望能夠邀請您來參加正式舞會。

On May 20, we are giving a luncheon for Mr. Jonathan.
✎ 五月二十日，我們將為強納森先生舉辦一場午餐宴會。

Cambridge Health Food Institute cordially invites you to attend our 20th Anniversary Party.
✎ 誠摯邀請您參加劍橋健康食品協會成立二十周年的紀念派對。

You are cordially invited to be our guest at the ceremony.
✎ 我們誠摯地邀請您出席典禮。

We request the pleasure of your company for cocktails.
✎ 我們邀請貴公司出席雞尾酒會。

The annual dinner is an occasion for us to thank our friends and supporters.

✎ 為了感謝我們的友人以及支持者，我們將舉辦年度晚宴。

Therefore, I write to invite you to attend our 2016 Annual Dinner on Friday, May 18, 2016 at the Ballroom of the Kodak Hotel.
✎ 因此，我想邀請您參加在柯達飯店舉辦的二〇一六年度晚會，時間為五月十八日。

Please stop by for a wine and cheese on Saturday, May 2nd, and help us celebrate the launch of our new products.
✎ 請於五月二日，星期六前來參加一場乳酪與酒的派對，幫我們慶祝新產品上市。

We would like to request the pleasure of your company at our Year End Party.
✎ 我們想請貴公司光臨我們的年終尾牙。

The Board of Directors of Foxconn Electronics Inc. cordially invites you to join its 15th Annual Customer Appreciation Banquet.
✎ 鴻海精密企業董事會誠摯地邀請您參加第十五屆年度酬賓宴會。

Our reception starts at 6:30 p.m. and dinner is to commence at 7:30 p.m.
✎ 宴會於六點半開始入場，七點半開始用晚餐。

The party will be held at the Royal Hotel in Tainan.
✎ 派對將在台南的皇家飯店舉辦。

Refreshments will be served from 2.30 p.m. to 5.00 p.m.
✎ 茶點的供應時間為下午兩點半到五點。

 ## 請對方回覆

Would you please respond to this invitation by June 10?
✎ 請您於六月十日前回覆好嗎？

Would you please tell us if you could attend the party?
✎ 請告知您是否能參加好嗎？

We would like to finalize our arrangement by June 20, so please respond to this invitation by this Friday.
✎ 我們希望在六月二十日前安排內容，所以，請您於週五前回覆。

Please email me by the end of March, letting us know if you can attend.
✎ 請於三月底前告知您是否能出席。

I will call you on Thursday morning to make sure your decision.
🖉 我會於週四上午致電，與您確認決定。

 信末強調邀請

We do hope that you will be able to join us in this occasion.
🖉 希望您能前來參與盛會。

Please come to help us celebrate this occasion.
🖉 請前來與我們一同慶祝。

Please come and celebrate with us!
🖉 請前來與我們同樂！

We request the honor of your company!
🖉 敬請光臨！

I do hope you can join us for an evening of fun.
🖉 真心希望您能夠與我們同歡。

Hope you will have a great time at this party.
🖉 盼您在這場派對中玩得愉快。

 Let's learn more!

 單字/片語Focus

❦ 舉辦宴會 ❦	
✱**invitation** 邀請函	✱**mingle** 交際
✱**host** 主辦人	✱**catering** 外燴餐點
✱**guest** 賓客	✱**decoration** 佈置
✱**refreshments** 飲料和點心	✱**dance floor** 舞池
✱**dress code** 服裝規定	

Part 1
Part 2
Part 3
Part 4
Part 5
Part 6

Subject | Guest Speaker Invitation

Dear Dr. Liao:

All our staff of the RIDATA Company have long admired your excellent **research**[1] **activities**[2] and would enjoy learning more about your work.

Therefore, we are willing to ask you to be our **guest speaker**[3] at a **seminar**[4] to be held at the Hilton Hotel, Taipei, on May 23 at 10 a.m.

We would be very pleased if you could give a talk of about fifty minutes. After the talk, a 20-minute question and answer period would be ideal. About fifty people are **expected**[5] to attend the seminar. Most of them are our top **representatives**[6] in our company.

All the traveling **expenses**[7] are made by us. We would pay you a fee for $10,000NTD. We would appreciate having your reply by April 30, so that we can arrange the **agenda**[8].

We do hope you will be able to present on this occasion.

Yours faithfully,
Owen

廖博士您好：

RIDATA公司的所有員工長久以來一直欣賞您傑出的研究活動，並樂於向您學習。

因此，我們有意邀請您於五月二十三日早上十點，在希爾頓飯店發表演講。

屆時希望您提供五十分鐘左右的演講。演講後，二十分鐘的問答時間為最理想的安排。大約有五十人會參加這場研討會，大多是我們頂尖的公司代表。

我們會負擔所有的差旅費用。除了三天在台中的住宿費，我們會另外支付您一萬元新台幣。希望您四月三十日前給予我們回覆，以便我們安排行程。

我們企盼您能參加此次聚會。

歐文 敬上

Send

Part 1

Part 2

Part 3

Part 4

Part 5

Part 6

核心字彙充電站 Key Words

1. **research** 名 研究;調查
2. **activity** 名 活動
3. **guest speaker** 名 特邀講者
4. **seminar** 名 專題演討會
5. **expect** 動 期望;預期
6. **representative** 名 代表
7. **expense** 名 花費;支出
8. **agenda** 名 議程

替換好用句 Copy & Paste

邀請前來演講

Our company would like to invite you to speak at our annual seminar.
🖉 本公司希望能夠邀請您在年度研討會中演講。

The English Department of Kyoto University would like to extend to you an invitation to be our guest speaker at the annual conference.
🖉 京都大學英文系所特邀您出席學術年會,並擔任演講者。

As you know, our department is interested in the 20th century English literature.
🖉 如您所知,本系所對於二十世紀的英國文學很有興趣。

Since you are very familiar with the field, we know your views will be extremely interesting to us.
🖉 因為您很熟悉此領域,所以您的見解肯定會很吸引我們。

We hope you will be able to attend this conference and give us the benefit of your experience.
🖉 我們希望您能蒞臨此次會議,並分享您的寶貴經驗。

I would be grateful if you could give a presentation on the topic of solar energy and solar panel.
🖉 如果您能對太陽能以及太陽能板發表演講,我會非常感激。

Your participation will have great significance to our seminar.
🖉 您的出席將為我們這次的研討會帶來重要意義。

It would give us great pleasure if you could come to Taichung to give a talk to our English teachers.
🖉 如果您能蒞臨台中為英語教師發表演講,我們將感到非常榮幸。

提供細節資訊

The number of expected participants will be 1,000.
參加者預計有一千人。

The participants will consist of nurses, doctors and the general public.
參加的人包含護士，醫師以及一般群眾。

The seminar runs for two hours, and we would be glad if you could give a one-hour lecture.
研討會總共兩小時，我們希望您能提供一小時的講座。

You will receive further details later, but we would appreciate your acceptance soon, so we may complete our agenda.
隨後您會收到相關細節，但希望您儘快給予答覆，以便我們安排行程。

表達邀請的誠意

We can offer you a fee of $5,000NTD plus transportation and accommodation.
我們可以支付您新台幣五千元費用，及交通和住宿費用。

We ask you to receive our sincere thanks for your pleasant acceptance.
如您願意接受，我們會非常感謝。

Although we realize you are busy, we hope you can find time to accept the invitation.
我們知道您很忙碌，但仍希望您能撥冗參加。

If you are not convenient at that scheduled time, we can reschedule it for an earlier or later slot.
如果這個時間您不方便，我們可以重新安排提前或延後時間。

If you are unable to come, please let us know.
若您不克前來，請讓我們知道。

Your presence will be appreciated.
若您能撥冗參加，將感激不盡。

Part 1

Part 2

Part 3

Part 4

Part 5

Part 6

3-07 參展邀請

　　邀請收信者參加活動時，除了詳細列出展覽訊息，如果需要入場券，記得提醒索取方式、或是附於信中附件。

| Subject | Private Preview Showing- Summer Fashion Collection |

Private¹ Preview² Showing - Summer Collection³ 2017 - Ticket No.23557.

Dear Mrs. Lee:

As one of our longtime valued customers, we would like to invite you to our special Private Preview Showing of our Summer Fashion Collection for 2017.

The show will take place at our downtown store at 123 Beverly St, Los Angeles, Monday evening, May 20, 2017 from 3:00 p.m. to 5:00 p.m. Limited free parking will be available in our parking **garages⁴** on the Beverly Street side of the store.

For **entry⁵** into the show, you will be required to produce this **original⁶ invitation⁷** with your ticket number printed on it. Therefore, please print this email as your invitation ticket.

In order that we may plan for snacks and **refreshments⁸ appropriately⁹**, if you plan to attend, please call Mary at 514-982-7593 and advise her by May 1.

Please note: If Mary doesn't hear from you by Friday, May 2, we will **assume¹⁰** that

非正式的預先展示秀，二〇一七年夏季時裝展。入場號碼23557號。

親愛的李女士：

由於您是我們重要的客戶，因此我們敬邀您參加我們的二〇一七年的私人夏季時裝展。

時裝秀地點在我們城中店，位於洛杉磯比佛利街123號，時間為二〇一七年五月二十日，星期一下午三點至五點。比佛利街上的停車場車位有限。

進入會場需要提供此封含有入場號碼的信函，因此請您列印此郵件以便入場。

為確認需要準備的茶點數量，請於五月一日前撥514-982-7593，來電告知瑪莉是否參加。

you are not attending the show and we will issue your ticket number to someone else.

Everyone here at The Fashion House looks forward to meeting you and sharing our Summer Collection with you at our Preview Private Showing.

Sincerely yours,
Judy

注意：如果瑪莉沒有在五月二日前收到您的回覆，我們馬上會將您的入場號提供給他人，並視您不克前來。

時尚屋的全體同仁期待您參與本次的夏季服裝預展。

茱蒂 敬上

Send ▶

Subject: 10th Annual Trade Show Invitation

Dear Mr. Thomas:

The 10th Annual Trade Show, **featuring**[11] the most **advanced**[12] 3C products, will be held in Taipei next month as follows. You are cordially invited to attend this most exciting event of this year.

Dates: September 1st to 5th, 2017.
Time: 9:00 a.m. to 5:00 p.m.
Place: Taipei World Trade Center Exhibition A

We will **exhibit**[13] our latest products. Our staff will be on hand to provide you with all the information you need and answer any questions you may have. Free drinks and snacks will also be provided. You are welcome to bring along your friend.

湯瑪士先生您好：

第十屆年度商品展示秀將於下個月在台北展出，此次展出為最先進的3C產品，誠摯地邀請您參加今年最令人興奮的盛會。

日期：二〇一七年九月一日至五日
時間：早上九點至下午五點
地點：台北世貿A展場

我們會展出最新商品，現場將有專人為您提供資訊，並為您解答疑惑。備有免費茶點，歡迎攜伴參

For more details, please see our **homepage**[14]: http://www.e-book.com.tw/tradshow. We look forward to seeing you at the show.

Best regards,
Nick

加。

展示會的詳細介紹可以參考本公司首頁：http://www.e-book.com.tw/tradshow，期待在展示會上看見您。

尼克 敬上

Send

Part 1
Part 2
Part 3
Part 4
Part 5
Part 6

 核心字彙充電站 *Key Words*

1. **private** 形 非公開的
2. **preview** 名 預展
3. **collection** 名 特定季節的時裝
4. **garage** 名 車庫
5. **entry** 名 進入；入場
6. **original** 形 原始的
7. **invitation** 名 邀請函
8. **refreshment** 名 茶點（常複數）
9. **appropriately** 副 適當地
10. **assume** 動 假定為
11. **feature** 動 以…為特色
12. **advanced** 形 高級的
13. **exhibit** 動 展示；陳列
14. **homepage** 名 首頁

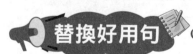 替換好用句 *Copy & Paste*

邀請對方參展

You are invited to a special show of our new e-Books.
✎ 請來參加我們的新電子書展示會。

The International Book Show will take place from July 7 to 10 in Taipei.
✎ 國際書展將在七月七日至十日於台北舉行。

You are invited to a special show of our new line of the new software.
✎ 誠摯地邀請您參加敝公司新軟體商品的特別發表會。

The World Trade Fair falls on June 20 at the World Trade Center in Taipei.
✎ 世界貿易展覽會預計將於六月二十日在台北世界貿易中心舉行。

We would like to invite you to attend the exhibition, which our company will be participating.
✎ 我們想邀請您參加敝公司的展示會。

BCN Inc. invites you to an exclusive showing of its latest CD-ROM products.
✎ BCN公司邀請您參加我們最新的光碟機展示會。

We are giving a luncheon at Grand Hyatt Hotel at 10 a.m. on Tuesday to introduce our newest products.
✎ 我們即將於星期二上午十點在君悅飯店舉辦午茶會，同時介紹最新產品。

The presentation will take place at the Evergreen Hotel at 3 p.m. on May 21.
✎ 說明會在長榮酒店舉辦，時間為五月二十一日下午三點。

 展覽的目的

We hope that this exhibition will enable us to establish long term business with our prospective clients.
✎ 希望此次參展，可與潛在顧客建立長期的商務關係。

To seek out Taiwanese distributors, we attend this exhibition.
✎ 我們參展是為了尋求台灣的批發商。

 提供資訊

There are expected to be more than 100,000 visitors to attend the exhibition.
✎ 預估會有超過十萬人次前來參加展示會。

There are more than 500 exhibitors in attendance from around the world.
✎ 有超過五百家從世界各地前來的廠商參加展示會。

We are planning to exhibit our new software for designing.
🖉 我們預計展示新的設計軟體。

Of course, we will have our full line of other products on display, too.
🖉 當然，我們也會展示其他的產品。

You would benefit from a visit to see our best line of products.
🖉 您看了我們的產品後，將受益匪淺。

Our staff will be there to assist you with any inquiries during exhibition.
🖉 我們的員工會在現場為您解答問題。

During the show, we will offer a special 10% discount on all of our products.
🖉 在展出期間，我們提供全產品九折的優惠。

A special discount is only available once a year during the show period.
🖉 特殊折扣只有在每年展覽期間才有。

For more information, please contact us by email, or call 02-2222-3333.
🖉 如需更多資訊，請以電子郵件或電洽：02-2222-3333聯絡。

For more details and an official invitation card, please see the attached files.
🖉 請參看，附件為詳細資訊，以及正式邀請函。

 *Let's learn more!*

 單字/片語Focus

💖 展覽相關用字 💖

✱**exhibition** 展覽	✱**exposition** 博覽會；展覽會
✱**visit** 參觀；訪問	✱**ticket booth** 售票口
✱**crowd** 人群；人潮	✱**collector** 收藏家

Part 1
Part 2
Part 3
Part 4
Part 5
Part 6

·3-08· 接受邀請

接受邀請時，並不需要太冗長的回信，簡單表明樂意參加即可。

Subject Re: 20th anniversary Invitation

Dear Sir:

President and Directors of Imperial Motors thank you for your kind invitation to the anniversary dinner party held at the Grand Hotel. They are pleased to attend.

Yours faithfully,
Rose

先生您好：

帝國車業的總裁以及主管們，感謝您誠心邀約在圓山大飯店舉辦的周年慶祝晚宴，他們樂於參加。

蘿絲 敬上

Send

 Copy & Paste

 感謝對方的邀請

Thank you very much for your kind invitation to the formal party on May 20.

✎ 非常感謝您邀請我們參加五月二十日的派對。

I thank you for your kind invitation on the occasion of your opening ceremony.

✎ 謝謝您邀請我參加您的開幕典禮。

Thank you for inviting me to the dinner party.

✎ 謝謝您邀請我參加晚宴。

Thank you very much for your invitation.

✎ 謝謝您的邀請。

I accept the kind invitation for your anniversary dinner party with pleasure.

✎ 謝謝您誠心地邀請我參加周年晚宴。

Thank you for remembering us.
✎ 謝謝您記得我們。

I would like to express my gratitude.
✎ 在此表達本人的謝意。

We are pleased to receive your invitation and will participate in the seminar.
✎ 我們很開心接到本此研討會的邀請函，並將出席。

It is really kind of you to include me in your event.
✎ 感謝您邀請我參加盛會。

 表達願意參加

We look forward to your opening ceremony.
✎ 我們很期待您的開幕典禮。

We are pleased to accept and will travel by flight arriving Taipei at 5 p.m.
✎ 我們很開心受邀，當天會搭乘飛機於五點抵達台北。

I am happy to attend your forum.
✎ 我很開心能參加論壇。

It would be an honor to attend your opening party.
✎ 能夠參加您的開幕典禮是我的榮幸。

We would be glad to join your opening celebration.
✎ 我們很開心能夠參加您的開幕慶祝會。

I am happy to attend the party.
✎ 我很樂意參加派對。

It is my pleasure to join you at the party.
✎ 能夠參與您的派對是我的榮幸。

I am delighted to attend the party.
✎ 我很開心能參加聚會。

Many thanks for your kind invitation to the Grand Opening Ceremony.
✎ 非常感謝您邀請參加開幕典禮。

I shall be very happy to come, and I look forward with pleasure to

Part 1

Part 2

Part 3

Part 4

Part 5

Part 6

meeting you.
🖊 我很樂意參加，並且期待與您會面。

I will be there by seven.
🖊 我七點會抵達。

I will be happy to be at your party at 7:00 p.m. on Saturday, May 11.
🖊 我很開心能夠參加您五月十一日，星期六晚上七點的派對。

I am very happy to attend your annual party.
🖊 我很開心參加您的年度派對。

It is our honor to participate in this wonderful occasion.
🖊 能出席這樣美好的場合，我感到很榮幸。

 祝福對方公司發展

Congratulations on your success in opening a new office!
🖊 恭喜你成立新辦公室！

I understand how hard you have worked to reach this milestone.
🖊 我非常理解您如何努力才達到今日的成功。

We wish you every success for the future.
🖊 盼您未來事業蒸蒸日上。

We are looking this opportunity to wish your organization continued success.
🖊 利用此機會，我們希望貴公司的經營成功。

Please accept my hearty congratulations.
🖊 請接受我衷心的祝賀

We wish you every success in your business.
🖊 祝福您事業成功。

Part 1

Part 2

Part 3

Part 4

Part 5

Part 6

·3-09· 拒絕邀請

拒絕邀請時，記得口氣婉轉並提供合理的理由，文末可以再次感謝及祝賀。

| Subject | Re: 20th Anniversary1 Invitation2 |

Dear Sir:

Mr. Liu, President of Imperial Motors, thanks you very much for the invitation to a dinner party at the Grand Hotel.

He would be delighted to accept your invitation. However, he has already made arrangements to attend another important meeting in Milan in June. The meeting cannot be cancelled. Unfortunately, Mr. Liu will not be able to attend your dinner party.

Mr. Liu wishes to extend his cordial greetings to your President, Mr. Chang.

Yours faithfully,
Linda

先生您好：

帝國車業總裁，劉先生感謝您邀請參加在圓山大飯店的晚宴。

他很希望能夠參與，然而，他六月已安排了在米蘭的會議行程，此會議無法取消。因此很不巧，劉先生無法參加晚宴。

劉先生希望能給與貴公司總裁，張先生誠心的祝福。

琳達 敬上

Send ▶

 替換好用句 *Copy & Paste*

婉拒和提供理由

I am really happy to receive your invitation to the annual dinner.
✎ 我很開心收到您年度餐會的邀請。

I would be obliged to accept. Unfortunately, I cannot attend the party

owing to a prior appointment.

✎ 我很樂意參加，但很可惜，因為我先前已有其他邀約而無法參加。

I am sorry I am unable to join the forum in Taipei.

✎ 很抱歉，我無法參加這場在台北舉辦的研討會。

I am terribly sorry that I will be unable to make appearance at your dinner party.

✎ 非常抱歉，我無法參加您的晚宴。

Unfortunately, I have to miss the party because of a prior appointment.

✎ 很不巧，因為我已先有其他安排，因此無法出席派對。

Unfortunately, the timing does not allow me to attend.

✎ 很不巧，由於時間不允許，恕我無法出席。

On behalf of me, Mr. Wu, the manager of Sales Dept. of our company, will attend the party.

✎ 我們的業務部經理，吳先生會代表我參加派對。

I would like to attend, but I am afraid I will have to let you down.

✎ 我很想參加，但很抱歉要讓您失望了。

I have already made arrangements to attend another meeting which cannot be cancelled.

✎ 我原先已預定要參加一項無法取消的會議。

We are sorry to inform you that we have to decline your invitation due to a prior engagement.

✎ 由於事先有約，所以無法應邀，非常抱歉。

We would love to go, but we are afraid we couldn't make it.

✎ 雖然我們想參加，但我們恐怕無法前往。

I would be out of town on business on that day.

✎ 我那天必須出差，所以不會在城裡。

Owing to a previous engagement, we are unable to accept.

✎ 由於已有其他約會，我們無法答應。

I am scheduled to be in Europe in late June.

✎ 六月底我人在歐洲。

We have to decline your invitation owing to a prior engagement.

✎ 由於事先有約，我不得不婉拒您的邀約。

Regretfully, I won't be able to join you at that time.
🖊 很抱歉，當天我無法參加。

I regret that I am unable to accept because I have a prior engagement.
🖊 很抱歉，我無法參加，因為事先已有其他的約會。

I do hope you will understand the reasons preventing my attendance.
🖊 希望您能諒解我無法參加的理由。

We regret that we are unable to accept the kind invitation of the party.
🖊 很抱歉，我們無法參與這場派對。

I greatly regret that I am unable to join you next Friday.
🖊 無法參與您下週五的約會，我深感抱歉。

I am really sorry that I couldn't make it.
🖊 很抱歉，我無法參與。

 ## 感謝語和其他

Please accept my thanks again for inviting me.
🖊 再度感謝您的邀約。

Thank you again for including me.
🖊 再次感謝您邀請我。

I hope your party will be a great success.
🖊 希望您的派對圓滿成功。

I hope you understand.
🖊 盼您諒解。

We look forward to another opportunity like this.
🖊 期待有下一次的機會。

Wish you have a great time.
🖊 希望您玩得開心。

Part 1
Part 2
Part 3
Part 4
Part 5
Part 6

進階補充站　*Let's learn more!*

 文法/句型Focus

＊ 婉拒邀約

① **I am afraid that I will not be able to...** 我恐怕無法…。

② **I will be unable to... due to...** 因為……，所以我無法……

③ **I will be unable to... owing to...** 因為……，所以我無法……

④ **I cannot make it... because...** 因為……，所以我無法……

⑤ **I am sorry to tell you that I will not be available to...**
很抱歉要告知您屆時我無法…。

⑥ **Unfortunately, I will not be able to join you because...**
遺憾的是，因為…，所以我不克參加。

⑦ **I am sorry, but I cannot attend (event) because...**
很抱歉，因為…，所以我無法參加（某活動）。

⑧ **I would be obliged to..., but unfortunately...**
我很樂意…，但很可惜…

實用資訊Focus

婉拒信函的寫用 🔍

　　收到邀請函後，若不克參加，除了婉拒的口吻要拿捏得當之外，也必須注意回函的內容，一般而言，婉拒信函會包含以下三部分：

1. 感謝對方的邀請：對於收到邀請，必須於信函開頭表達感謝之意。
2. 委婉拒絕邀約：請注意此處的用字遣詞，須明確拒絕，但口吻婉轉。
3. 提供原因：最好提供自己無法出席的原因，避免產生誤會。

•3-10• 感謝款待

拜訪過客戶後，可寫信給提供招待的人以表示禮貌。信件內容無須太過冗長，但仍需正式。

Subject | **Thank You for the Hospitality**

Dear Ms. Chen:

Thank you very much for the outstanding help that I received during my visit in Taiwan. I greatly appreciate the generosity that was extended to me by everyone. Please convey my thanks to all the members in your office.

Sincerely,
Willy

陳小姐您好：

前陣子拜訪台灣，謝謝您的特別幫忙，也特別感謝大家對我的親切款待。請代我向貴公司所有職員致謝。

威利 敬上

Send

替換好用句 *Copy & Paste*

感謝對方的招待

I wish to express my appreciation for the hospitality extended to me while I was in San Francisco last week.
上週在舊金山受到您的款待，在此致上感謝。

Thank you very much for showing me your factory and for the warm hospitality extended to me while I was in Taichung last week.
上週在台中受到您的熱情款待，謝謝您帶我參觀工廠。

You will accept my warmest thanks for the hospitality extended to me during my stay.
致上最誠摯的感謝，謝謝您在我停留期間的熱情款待。

I would like to thank you again for the opportunity you gave me to

Part 1
Part 2
Part 3
Part 4
Part 5
Part 6

visit your office.
🖉 再次感謝您給我參觀您辦公室的機會。

I am pleased to have the chance to hear something about the latest products in your factory.
🖉 我很開心有機會了解您工廠的新產品。

On behalf of our entire delegation and myself, I thank you for your warm welcome.
🖉 謹代表本團體與我個人，感謝您的熱情款待。

I would like to thank you for your excellent hospitality during my stay in London.
🖉 謝謝您在我停留倫敦期間的熱情款待。

Thank you so much for the nice dinner and magnificent hospitality.
🖉 謝謝您的晚餐與熱情款待。

I surely will not forget the personal contacts I had during my stay here and kindness shown by yourself and your staff.
🖉 我不會忘記在短暫的停留時間，您與您的同仁對我的熱情款待。

Thank you for such a detailed presentation on your products.
🖉 謝謝您詳細的產品介紹。

I appreciated your kindness very much in showing me around your new office.
🖉 謝謝您帶我參觀新的辦公室。

Thank you for explaining to me the unique features of your company's products.
🖉 謝謝您向我解說貴公司產品的獨特之處。

Please convey my appreciation to your wife.
🖉 請替我向尊夫人致謝。

My visit to America turned out to be very successful.
🖉 此次美國之行非常成功。

I would like to thank you most sincerely for the efforts you put into organizing the meeting for me.
🖉 感謝您的大力相助，替我安排此次會議。

Thank you so much for your assistance.
🖉 謝謝您的幫忙。

明確點出受益之處

Your presentation was not only very well organized, but it was also extremely interesting.
🖉 您的解說條理分明，且十分富有趣味。

It was a stimulating experience for me.
🖉 對我來說，這是個令人興奮的經驗。

The new methods will certainly be useful in my work in Taiwan.
🖉 新的方法對我在台灣的工作很有助益。

I was able to learn a lot from my visit to your factory.
🖉 我從參觀您的工廠中學到許多事。

 訂下邀約

I look forward to thanking you personally when you come to Taiwan.
🖉 希望您來台灣時，我能當面謝謝您。

Please do visit us when it is convenient for you.
🖉 要是您方便，一定要來讓我們招待。

I really hope that you will have a chance to visit us in Taiwan.
🖉 希望您有機會來台灣拜訪我們。

I hope I will have the opportunity reciprocating your kindness in the near future.
🖉 希望未來有能夠回報您的機會。

I hope that I can be able to receive a visit from you someday.
🖉 希望有一天您也能來訪。

Please come visit us if you have a chance to do so.
🖉 若有機會，請務必來拜訪我們。

Please let me know if you come to Taiwan. We will be thrilled to meet you.
🖉 若您來台灣，請讓我知道，我們會很高興見到您。

I will be pleased if I could show you around next time.
🖉 若下次有機會帶您到各處看看，我會很高興。

Part 1

Part 2

Part 3

Part 4

Part 5

Part 6

NOTE

NOTE

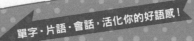

國家圖書館出版品預行編目資料

隨手貼+替換句：100%英文E-mail萬用貼大全 / 張翔
編著. --初版. --新北市：華文網, 2015.07
　　面；　公分. -- (Excellent ; 77)
ISBN 978-986-271-610-6(平裝)

1.英語　　2.電子郵件　　3.應用文

805.179　　　　　　　　　　　　　104008114

100% 隨手貼＋替換句
英文E-mail
萬用貼大全

知識工場・Excellent 77

隨手貼+替換句
100%英文E-mail萬用貼大全

出 版 者／全球華文聯合出版平台・知識工場
作 者／張翔　　　　　　　　印 行 者／知識工場
出版總監／王寶玲　　　　　　英文編輯／何牧蓉
總 編 輯／歐綾纖　　　　　　美術設計／蔡億盈

郵撥帳號／50017206 采舍國際有限公司（郵撥購買，請另付一成郵資）
台灣出版中心／新北市中和區中山路2段366巷10號10樓
電話／（02）2248-7896
傳真／（02）2248-7758
ISBN-13／978-986-271-610-6
出版日期／2019年最新版

全球華文市場總代理／采舍國際
地址／新北市中和區中山路2段366巷10號3樓
電話／（02）8245-8786
傳真／（02）8245-8718

港澳地區總經銷／和平圖書
地址／香港柴灣嘉業街12號百樂門大廈17樓
電話／（852）2804-6687
傳真／（852）2804-6409

全系列書系特約展示
新絲路網路書店
地址／新北市中和區中山路2段366巷10號10樓
電話／（02）8245-9896
傳真／（02）8245-8819
網址／www.silkbook.com

本書為名師張翔等及出版社編輯小組精心編著覆核，如仍有疏漏，請各位先進不吝指正。來函請寄
mujung@mail.book4u.com.tw，若經查證無誤，我們將有精美小禮物贈送！

知識工場
Knowledge is everything !